MAR 2 2

GEMINI

Paul D. Klarc

PAGE PUBLISHING, INC.
Conneaut Lake, PA

First originally published by Page Publishing 2021

ISBN 978-1-64701-542-8 (hc)
ISBN 978-1-64701-541-1 (digital)

Printed in the United States of America

CHAPTER 1

I'M DRIVING INSIDE another dark night with no reflections of distant sunlight from the nonpresent moon to guide my way. The rain falls heavily on my windshield as I drive south on Interstate 75 heading towards Arcadia, Florida. The rain is only calm for now as the storm of Hurricane Abby is still far from land directly southwest of Florida and heading toward Naples, Florida. The storm is far away from where I need to be but close enough to Florida to have me worried. Bad weather and Florida go hand in hand like sandlots and trailer parks. The highway is clear because no one is heading south into the storm. Almost all the cars are safely going north toward Tampa. I'm not visiting any big city around here. My navigation points south on I-75 to Port Charlotte and then directs me to Arcadia, Florida.

Arcadia is a little hillbilly town about an hour south of Tampa in the middle part of the desolate state. If you have never been to Florida outside the main areas of Miami, Orlando, Tampa, or Tallahassee, you aren't missing anything. All the small-town and two-lane roads here look the same—empty fields, cows, a few straight trees with no leaves, and lots of palmetto bushes with a few palm trees here and there for character.

I've been driving for twelve-long hours along the rural nothingness of countryside that Interstate 75 flows through. I left Durham,

North Carolina, and my dorm at Duke University at six in the morning. I'm a college freshman earning a degree in Advertising. It's been a long drive, and the drops of rain have been shielding my view since the Florida-Georgia line. I'm growing accustomed to the rubber squeak of the wiper blades on my windshield of my Camaro. I enjoy the view of rain and dull green palmetto bushes for miles at a time. At least the ride is smooth since I have a new Camaro, and the playlist on my iPhone has been going nonstop since I left the university.

Arcadia is a town with only one high school, a Walmart, and one post office. They recently built a Chili's and upgraded their Home Depot. Besides a McDonald's and a Pizza Hut, that's the whole entire town. When my twin brother and I moved to Arcadia, Florida, from Boston, Massachusetts, it was culture shock. I hated living there and didn't stay long. My brief stay of a few months was four long years ago. Now I'm going back to find out how my past is haunting my future. I left my college in Durham, North Carolina, because of the three dead girls and the unanswered questions of why. Arcadia, Florida, is where my mom lives and where my past ended years ago. I haven't seen her in almost four years because I left home on bad terms when I was only a high school freshman. Things were so bad between us that I ran away and never looked back. I wasn't a totally bad child back then. I was just confused with no guidance and nowhere to turn. The amusing part about my journey is my mother doesn't even know I'm coming to see her. Once the police found a third dead girl, I knew I needed help. I realized Friday that I had to go back to the place I once ran from and look for answers to questions that I can't find at Duke University. I'm returning to my once forgotten home of Arcadia because aspects of my life in North Carolina are reflecting the horror story of a life I once had there just four years ago.

My freshman year in Arcadia was bad and full of emptiness because of my parents' divorce. My mom moved away from Boston, the city I loved, and moved here. My mom then sued for custody, and my twin brother and I were on our way to Florida right after Christmas. As I said, I didn't stay long because my brother committed suicide, and I took off. I thought it was never to be seen again, but here I am.

4

Between my parents' divorce that year, us being shipped to Nowhere, Florida, and then my brother killing himself, I couldn't take it anymore. I ran away. The pressure was too much, and I hated my mom. My dad didn't want us anymore while my brother and I were stuck in the middle of a parental showdown. With my brother dead and my family out of the picture, I was free to do whatever I wanted. I found a new high school in Florida that summer. I ended up at Oviedo High School right outside Orlando. With a lot of luck and a little bite of faith, Mr. Beacon took my weary teenage self in and claimed me as his own.

I was lost, and every day in high school at Oviedo, I would wonder what was going to happen to me. Was anyone looking for me? Would I be found? Could I get caught as a runaway? And what would become of my future? That's when I became a loner and had very few friends during my first two years at Oviedo High School. My Oviedo years were my sophomore through senior years. Mr. Beacon was my parent for now, and he always stressed good grades and hard work. I'm glad he took me in, but the depression of being an unwanted teen was tough. My twin brother's suicide weighing on me was even tougher. Loneliness and isolation made me one of the best basketball players at my new high school, in the shadow of UCF. It was a long road from Boston to Oviedo via Arcadia, but after a while, I made the best of it.

I was a good basketball player when I was a freshman in Boston, but I was not great. I did get better and better every year, and then I learned how to dunk. I worked hard during my high school years to develop my basketball skills in the streets, high schools, and college courts of Orlando. It paid off; we won the state basketball championship of Florida during my senior year. That was just a few months ago, and there I was holding the trophy with my teammates under the basketball net. I never thought about my photo being in the paper as being detrimental to my health, until now.

My mother saw my picture in the paper for winning the state championship. I was front and center with the rest of my team. Oviedo High School won state, and that's how she found me. After four years of nothingness, of being missing in action, I got a card at school from my forgotten mother.

When I left Arcadia and nobody came looking for me, I thought I would never hear from her or my dad again. The mother I left cold, never looking back or reflecting upon, is alive again and sending me a card. I decided to call her, and we talked briefly. After our conversation ended, I never wondered or even cared what happened to her. My mother and I are strangers to each other, and we still keep our distance. She didn't come to my graduation this past June, and she still never calls me. I don't call her either. Oh well, life goes on.

Since my high school graduation in June, I have been living in Durham, North Carolina, attending Duke University. I bought this Camaro with my own money that I saved. I worked two jobs all summer long during my sophomore and junior year, waiting tables and mowing lawns summer after summer, year after year. I worked hard for what little I have. Nothing was ever given to me. In that same fashion, almost everything is being taken from me. Now I have to fight to keep what little life I have left in me. Again, I'm here because of the questions surrounding my past and future. My past leads to a dead twin brother and a forgotten mom and dad. My future at Duke leads to the three dead girls in the last two months.

It is just after dusk, and the pouring rain continues. I see the green sign that reads "Port Charlotte Next Three Exits" among the country remains of a lost civilization. As I drive, I pass the fields of gray sand and trees that dominate the outskirts of the small towns. The last of the three exits is Port Charlotte, Arcadia, Kings Highway. This is where I get off I-75, and from here the GPS gives me turn by turn through the emptiness.

This reminds me of when I deserted Arcadia. I left on this same road. I took Interstate 75 north to Tampa and ended up going east toward Lakeland and then Orlando on Interstate 4. For now, I'm back, and so is the horror in my life that all started in Arcadia. As I reminisce, I tell myself, as I take the off-ramp to Kings Highway, that I am not a fourteen-year-old kid anymore. I can't run from what is haunting me. Whatever happened in Arcadia ages ago was not my fault, and whatever is happening to me now isn't either. I'm here to find the answers that condemn my future.

The stories of murder and mayhem in North Carolina all point toward me, although there is no solid connection that links these crimes to me. I've always had a rock-solid alibi to prove my innocence, but no one believes me. These crimes are not victimless. Three college girls are dead. The only reason I'm not in jail right now is because the university doesn't want the heat and bad press. The sad thing about all this is that I am being set up for these murders, and I think I know by whom. This thing happening to me by this person, whom I think is responsible for all this mayhem, is dead. I know he's dead. I was there, and it all happened here in Arcadia.

I'm Ray Beacon. I once had a twin named Rodney Beacon. The day that divided Rodney and I was one of the saddest days in my already tragic life. My twin brother, who was once my best friend, is gone. Because of my brother, I left Arcadia and haven't returned until now. I am here to get answers to solve the puzzle of who has done this and who is doing this to me. I am here to find Rodney, my twin brother, and make sure he stays dead.

A voice awakes me from my trance. "State road 72 ahead. Turn right," says my GPS. I have my iPhone volume on low so I can concentrate. The rain is still falling down, and the day is gray and dark at only 6:00 p.m. In minutes, I am driving through the little sleepy town, past Peace River, past the middle school, and toward Desoto High School, and then I turn right onto Cypress Street. I notice a police car has been following me since I crossed over Highway 17. The Desoto County Deputy Sheriff follows me all the way to my mother's house. I pull into the driveway, and the sheriff's car passes me by. It must be the North Carolina plates on a jet-black Camaro with tinted windows that look suspicious.

I know where my mom lives only because she has not moved since I left. I remember seeing the house as it was when it was on fire. This house shivers within the hellacious fires of my subconscious. I pull into the driveway, and it is daylight, four years ago, all over again in my head. I am fourteen, and I see the horrible memory of what my life once was. It's a miserable depression I must shake from my mind. Arcadia and this house are a dreadful dream that will burn into my future.

I stop the car in the driveway. Everything around me is gray, from the sky to the houses and street. I hear the pings of large raindrops fall on the carefully structured body of my black Camaro. I look at the stucco house and try not to see the past. The gloomy sky gives the house a macabre presence. I pull the key out of the ignition and look at my keys. I fumble for the one that opens the front door of my mom's house. Yes, I kept the key, but I have not used it. What will the inside of the house look like? What awaits me on the other side of the front door? I would have used my cell phone to call her, but I never saved the number.

A million questions and answers all flash through my mind. There are no lights on in the house and no car in the driveway. I am alone here as I feel my heartbeat quicken with anticipation. I feel as if I am at my first basketball game and I keep saying, "Try harder, go faster, and score more. You can do it, Ray! You are a winner!"

I shake the anxiety away and step out of my car. It is a short walk in the rain to the doorway. The house is a typical one-story with a doorway on the left, big living room window in the middle, and bedroom window on the far right. The carport is on the extreme left, and the wooden door at the end of the carport leads to the laundry room. The house is exactly the same as I had remembered but not how I left it. I ran away from home for many reasons, but the last straw in that once horrifying haystack, the one that pushed me over the edge, was Rodney. That same day I emptied my bank account, all $1,200, and left town. No kisses, no hugs, just goodbye. I just walked away from the misery in my life and never looked back, until now. And now it just may be too late.

I hide in the doorway of the house away from the billowing rain. The house looks as if nothing has changed even though so much has. Mom still lives on the corner, and the lot across the street is still empty with perfectly mowed grass. In four years, nothing has changed in this little town. Nothing except for me, and I'm not willing to change things back. I push forward through the memories of old and put the key in the door and it unlocks. I push the door open and take my first step into the haunting house. While clicking on the light, I see that the entire decor of the house is more traditional in furnishings with lots of throw pillows for decoration. The furniture in the room is average with a brown sofa and love seat with a brown, high-back leather chair off to the side. All the colors are dark brown in contrast to the light-brown wood floors and off-white walls. The old wooden stand has only a big HDTV, DVD player, and a small stereo. The walls are empty with the exception of one picture of a New England countryside hanging above the couch. I see three different New England lighthouses on the top of the entertainment stand, but there are no pictures of my brother and me in sight. I just think to myself, *How sad.* Despite all that has happened, I keep a picture of the old Beacon family in my wallet. I guess, like my mom, we are both hiding from our past.

"Any one home?" I call out as I stand by the door. "Mom?" I ask as my voice echoes through the house. I click on more lights and walk slowly through the house. I head toward the right side of the house, down the hallway, to the two bedrooms and the bathroom. One bedroom of which belonged to Rodney and me.

I knock on the door to my mom's bedroom and wait for an answer. "Mom?"

I open the door and see an empty bed surrounded by an oak dresser with a large mirror on it. An armoire and another chest of drawers are on the other side of the bed. The oak bedframe with a blue comforter and matching blue pillows is typical of Mom. Pictures of countrysides and landscapes hang on the wall.

It seems as if no one is home. I walk to see what has become of the bedroom in which all the nightmares began and ended. Curiously, I push open the door and click on the light. My old room is now an office with a long desk. A twenty-seven-inch monitor sits on top of the desk with the computer idling on the floor. Bookcases line each side of the room, and there is a filing cabinet with an inkjet printer and scanner sitting on top of it.

The décor of the room is bare, with nothing on the walls, brown curtains, and a fake palm tree in front of the window. Inside the closet are stacks of boxes shielded by a thin layer of dust. The office is typical of my mother—nothing lively and no memories of her past.

Since there is no time like the present, I decide to find out what happened the week my brother died and the week after that. Since my mother works for Desoto County, she has a link directly to the town's archives. The *Desoto County Times* is the local paper of Arcadia and the journal I'm looking for. I walk over to the desk and get comfortable in the black leather chair. I surf the Internet to find the paper and dig for the dates I need. The paper is weekly and about half as thick as your Sunday paper. I'm just looking for a certain two-week period, and then I'll be on my way. There are four entries for March of that year. Rodney died the second week of March, three months before our birthday. June 2 was our day of introduction into the world. We are Geminis. What a sarcastic world it is. "Every bright light is sure to fade, every life destined for tragedy." Well, I don't believe that bullshit at all, and I am not going to let anyone blow out my candles for me.

The local *Times* list several headlines for local tragedies during that week. The coroner and his son both died the same week as my brother. Who would have performed the autopsies then? The headline reads, "Local Coroner Dies." The article describes the tragic car accident killing him and his son. There is little insight into their deaths. "Dentist Office Vandalized" is the next headline. An excerpt on the front page tells a summary of us. I print out the front page with the rest of the local news.

I flip to the week after and see that I'm front-page news. It reads, "Two missing." There are two black-and-white pictures, one of Maria Lennon and another of Rodney and I. The article makes it sound like I kidnapped this girl or we ran away together. I do not even know her, but she does look familiar. With a flick and a click of the mouse, I print out this front page also. Maybe I will find some insight in it later.

"What are you doing, son?" a tall, muscular, dark-skinned Desoto County sheriff says to me as he enters the room. This guy is big and dark in a tan Boy Scout uniform with a badge and huge silver gun leading the way.

"Put your hands where I can see them. I mean it!" he orders me in a demanding but frightened tone.

I'm sitting at the desk, looking at him as if he's crazy.

"This is my mom's house. I'm Ray Beacon, Kim Beacon's son," I say from my seat as he approaches me with his gun drawn and outstretched toward me.

A second Deputy Sheriff, younger white kid, hides behind the door with his handcuffs already out.

"What the hell is going on?" I say as I look at the two officers. I slowly put my hands up and slide backward away from the desk.

With guns drawn, both officers are as nervous as caffeine-filled dragonflies with an unexpected tension oozing out of their pores.

"Don't do anything, kid!" the first officer demands as he walks toward me, slowly and cautiously. "You don't do anything stupid!"

"Don't shoot me either!" I rapidly reply back to the officer as I sit in the chair with my hands raised. "You guys are famous for shooting unarmed kids!"

"You're breaking the law, kid! Just don't make any sudden moves!" the other officer says as he steps into the room as second deputy now with his gun drawn on me.

I'm thinking to myself, *I know this a small town, so I must be big news here, but for what reason? I didn't do anything yet.*

I'm in front of the two officers as I get up from my chair and step away from the desk. Together the three of us form a triangle in the small room. I'm looking at the two of them with my hands in the air, and I'm moving slowly as the room is in complete silence. One policeman moves to the far side of the room. I'm up against the wall with my hands in the air, looking at the two of them. The second officer pounces on me and cuffs me while the first officer is aiming his revolver right at my head.

"What am I being cuffed for?" I yell as we struggle, and the officer takes me to the floor of the office.

The officer then pulls me up from the floor by my shirt and begins dragging me into the living room.

"What the Hell is going on?" I yell again.

The officer throws me face first into the couch like a rag doll. I bounce off the couch and fall to the floor. I jump up and surprise the two officers with my sudden burst of energy. I can see it in their faces that they are scared. Nobody is telling me what's going on! I'm confused as my mind races with answers to the questions I haven't just asked. I know I need to calm down before I get shot. I'm six feet two inches tall but only weigh a hundred and ninety pounds. I'm tough compared to other eighteen-year-old kids but no match for a deputy in his thirties.

"Sit down!" the dark-skinned officer says as he checks his gun back into its holster.

"Don't you have a football game or rodeo to go to or something?" I say sarcastically with a smile on my face. "Is this small-town justice beating up on kids? Take these cuffs off and we'll see how tough you are!" I say this as I rise up and stand in front of the officer.

"The boy's a comedian," the Deputy snickers.

Being sarcastic and humiliating others mentally is how I have fun and let out aggression. I've just driven for over twelve hours. I'm agitated and a bit tired, and this is what comes to mind.

Bam! The officer punches me right in the stomach as hard as he can. Awe! My God! The pain! It feels like he hit my spine via my stomach. Awe! The pain is sharp and long, moving slowly, burning through my abdomen. I try to shake off the pain. I fall into the couch with my hands still cuffed behind me. I'm not going to let them get me down. I sit straight up and try to pretend the pain is gone.

"How do you?" I ask. And *pow*! A fist to the sternum. The same officer punches me again. My breath is now rushing out of my lungs. Everything is turning white. I'm sure my face is bright red from the strained blood vessels. This cop is very strong. This pain is like fire burning in my lungs. I can hardly breathe!

"Had enough?" the officer says to me as I am hunching over the couch, my hands still in cuffs behind my back.

I gasp for breath for almost a full minute as the bright red color leaves my face. I start to laugh painfully as I remember another joke.

"What do you call..." That is all I could get out before being hit with a billy club across my head.

"Raymond! Raymond, wake up!"

I wake up to smelling salts, and for about ten seconds everything is blurry. I realize I was just knocked out cold by the officer.

"Wake up, Raymond!"

Five people surround me now. There are three uniformed deputies in front of me—one guy, tall in a long coat, and an officer holding a towel to my head.

I come to and find blood on the Duke sweatshirt I'm wearing. The dumbass that hit me split my head open. I am wide awake now, adrenaline flowing wildly through my veins, and I am raging with anger.

"What the hell did that asshole hit me for?" I scream out as rage of adrenaline surges through my mind and body. "Why am I cuffed? This is my house! What the Hell is going on?" I scream out in my loudest voice, jumping around on the couch and trying to get loose from the handcuffs.

One officer says to the guy in the suit, "He was resisting arrest."

"You're a liar!" I yell out in a rage. "Why would I resist arrest in my own house? Asshole!"

"Shut up, kid," the man in the suit says to me. "I'm Franklin, Chief of Police."

Having had to deal with this kind of bullshit from cops for the past few weeks, one can understand why I'm being uncooperative. I am more frustrated than anything since I am getting my ass kicked in my mom's house. My own characteristics won't let me behave. I'm hyper, high strung, and pissed off!

"Am I being charged?" I yell out. "If so, why am I not downtown or in jail? These cops are dirty. And why did that cop hit me?" I yell in frustration. "I'm going to sue your ass for busting my head open. Uncuff me now, asshole, and tell me what is going on before I break these cuffs off and kick your ass!" I yell out in a rage from the couch as the officers just stand around me in the living room.

No one is listening to me. This is how it started in North Carolina. From experience, I know it gets worse from here. For the past few weeks, things have progressively gotten worse.

CHAPTER 2

THE LAST FEW weeks all roll into another long day. I'm back where I was just a week ago—the dreaded prison cell. The room I'm confined to is a cold and damp holding cell with only one small window in the door. Yep, the police handcuffed me, put me in the car, and then threw me in a jail cell. I was not processed, fingerprinted, and I didn't get my phone call. I'm still in Arcadia, the little Mayberry town full of cows and cowboys. I'm the only person in the cell, probably the only person on the cellblock. The hurricane that approaches is now turning inland and is close by. Hurricane Abby should be hitting Fort Myers, which is about fifty miles southwest of us, soon. My watch says it's still September 1, almost 7:00 pm., and I should be in Durham, North Carolina, partying with my friends at the university. Instead, I'm spending my Sunday night in jail. What the Hell is happening to me? My life is falling apart. I came to Arcadia to find out about my past. Instead, I ended up getting harassed, got a small skull fracture, and the deputy took my Duke sweatshirt.

Arcadia has always been bad news for me. This desolate town of rednecks in old pickup trucks is where I ended up after my parents' divorce. My mother left Boston to live in the countryside of America, leaving the fast-paced life and snow of Boston far behind. My life turned into a disaster after the divorce. I was sent to live with my dreaded mother in Hillbilly, Florida. On the ride from the airport, I remember we actually passed a farm tractor driving on the road. We actually saw a Jeep driving down the road with a paper sign in the back window that read "US Mail." There are plenty of red barns on the way to Mom's house from the airport. That first hot ride in the car from the airport was dreadful. I expected some kind of city. But not here in Florida. There aren't any suburbs, just counties. All that's here is rolling flatlands, barbed wire fences, and cattle. I could only think, *What am I getting myself into?*

All the guys here talk with funny Southern drawls, chew tobacco, and wear cowboy boots. All the buildings in the center of town are old, single-story, gray brick buildings with porches. What do they do around here for fun? Spit watermelon seeds? And of course, Arcadia is home of the rodeo.

I grew up in Boston, Massachusetts. My life then was great. A city with bright lights, subways, high-rises, huge megamalls. It's a place with a great history—the Revolution, Paul Revere, Salem witches, and Nathaniel Hawthorne. Boston has millions of people with different cultures, and the city was my home. Nothing could compare to the city of Boston: four seasons, the harbor, and the greatest people in one of the biggest cities on the East Coast. Then on the most fragile year of my young adolescent life, my mom moved to a sand-infested cow field of a town in the middle of nowhere, surrounded by nothing. It's not even near a beach in Florida.

Once I was forced to live in Arcadia, I turned into a demonic child. Resentful and very unhappy, I turned on my mother and blamed her for taking my life in Boston away from me. It was a life filled with sports, friends, and good times. I turned into a troubled youth, yelling at my mother all the time, usually calling her a good-for-nothing bitch. I never came home before it was dark. People made fun of my Boston accent, which led to fights at school all the time. I was hated, I hated my life, and I hated the slow-paced life of imitation cowboys that ran Arcadia like the Crips and Bloods of Los Angeles. I think back to those rocky days, and I was only fourteen years old.

When I lived in Boston, I was having the time of my life. My dad let us do whatever we wanted as long as we earned good grades. I was always an honor student, always on the all-star team, had a girlfriend that adored me, had tons of friends, and I had a paper route for extra money. I went from being a prince in Heaven to an outcast living in the dungeons of Hell.

Now I'm in jail in the town that once tried to take my soul. On top of all that, a hurricane is steadily approaching Arcadia, and it is pouring down rain. The winds are blowing at about fifty miles an hour, howling through the edges of humanity. It is pitch-black in here, and I have been in this cell for about an hour. I can feel the wind hitting my cell walls. With all this heavy rain, I figure things can't get much worse. Or can they?

I don't even know why I am here. I'm waiting for my mother, who I have not seen in years, to come bail me out. I don't even know if anyone is going to bail me out. I haven't made any phone calls yet, and I left my phone in my Camaro. I don't even have my mom's number. She wasn't even home. Therefore the police have to track her down. In the meantime, here I am in jail. I wonder if this will affect my scholarship, which is already in jeopardy. I'm in enough trouble as it is with the university.

As for my scholarship and college, I'm a very talented basketball player, and Duke gave me a scholarship to play for the Blue Devils. Then they red-shirted me. I guess I have to tell my coach I was arrested again, but I do not think anyone will press charges. I hope to get out early tomorrow. Since Monday is Labor Day, I won't have to be back in Durham until Monday night for classes Tuesday morning. I still have so much to do and a lot to find out before I go back to class on Tuesday.

I sit in this cell and think about my mother. My mother and I still have only talked once in the last four years. At the time of my departure from Arcadia, I was a troubled teen full of angst. My twin brother just died. We had a horrible fight, she hit me, and I yelled at her. She hit me again and I walked away. My mother was very selfish and couldn't handle two boys on her own away from my dad. Plus, she believed in child abuse as a form of discipline. The only reason

I was in Arcadia was so my mother could sue for child support. She couldn't make it on her own, and she needed the extra money. Child support for two kids was $500 a month for each child, and in a one-horse town like Arcadia, that's a lot of dinero. Especially since her mortgage on a two-bedroom house with no garage was pretty cheap. The child support went toward her new car, mortgage, new clothes, and many weekend getaways. Not to us. Rodney and I never saw a dime of the money. My mom had a greedy soul, leaving us to live like neglected dogs. That's why I went wild as a youth, with no direction or support from my own mom.

I boldly remember the year before the divorce. It was nasty. My parents fought all the time at all hours of the day and night. My dad would come home either very early and take us out or come home very late when my mother was already asleep. Then he just quit coming home altogether. Divorce papers were served, and my mother agreed to take the money and run. Then she sued for custody, and we were on our way to Florida. Mom got her money, her new car, and more expensive furniture for the two-bedroom house on the corner. All I could remember thinking was, *This is the beginning of the end.*

Everything was going great for my mother, until Rodney died. That was the second turning point in my life. That was when life went from bad to worse. My mother was no longer going to receive her precious child support. It was cut in half. The day Rodney died, a policeman talked with me for a long time. I told him Rodney was the lucky one since his pain was now gone. He didn't have to suffer in this cruel world anymore. I said that he committed suicide. That made things worse for me. The policeman talked to my mom the day of the fire. He was going to file a report with the state, claiming dear old Mom was the demon's seed. That was going to lead to more questions and family counseling. I told the policeman everything as the smoke glowed from the flames of our burned house. I told him about the child abuse, the money problems, of my mother's bad habit of never coming home days at a time, and her sex fest on the first date with any guy. I was just making a bad situation worse. HRS and the police were now thinking Rodney took his own life. HRS was going to stick me in a foster home or a halfway house. Now I had no brother, no life, and my father didn't want to take me back either. I was devastated by circumstance, and now I was going to a foster home. The fire wasn't even out. The police were talking to Mom, and HRS had her surrounded.

That's when my mother threw a hissy fit in front of the police. She went from tears about her son, Rodney, being dead to a rage about me telling the family secrets. She blamed me for the fire. She kept yelling, and then she slapped me. Then she slapped me again. That was the last straw. I was so mad then and enraged that I could have killed her right then and there. Instead I waited and planned my escape.

As for Rodney and me, we were not really close as most twin brothers are. I miss him. I cried for days after his death, and I'm sure my mother just went on with her life like she just lost her cat instead of acting like a woman who just lost her son. I found out that nothing ever happened to dear sweet Mom for abusing her children mentally and physically. A few days later, Rodney's death was ruled a suicide. What was left of Rodney was cremated. No real funeral, just ashes to ashes, dust to dust. Sad! I can't even visit my brother's grave. My mother proved every day how much she did not care about us. I told you, she was a bitch. Her kids were just excuses for child support, cheap rent, and a car payment. I guess it is true—nice guys finish last, dead last.

I'm here in the town I hate, and of course I'm in trouble again due to no fault of my own. The only things that have changed is I'm older, have a car, and I have my name and the number forty-four tattooed in a basketball on my chest over my heart. Thank God I have basketball to keep me focused. The number 44 was my high school basketball number and my college jersey number at Duke. I look at that tattoo every day and remind myself how lucky I am and that basketball saved my life.

I can hear the thunder and lightning inside my holding cell. This prison cell I'm in is archaic. It's about ten feet wide by ten feet long, made of huge gray cement blocks, no windows except for the one in the door, and a small toilet and sink in the corner. Because of the huge storm outside, the cell is damp and dark. The hallway is dimly lit with soft white lamps surrounded by little metal cages. The cell door is solid metal, about three inches thick. The small window in the door is two inches thick and hardly lets any light shine in. I hear an echo in the hallway. I hear a door open and then slammed shut in the distance. I am sitting on the floor with my back to the wall, facing the door. I can barely hear the footsteps coming down the hallway. Then I hear my name bellowing through the hallway.

"Raymond Douglas Beacon, wake up! There is someone here to see you!"

A fat face of a huge man appears in the little window of the door. His embroidered name tag reads "Covey." He punches the door once to get my attention. A loud thud rummages through the cell. My gaze is on the door long before Covey appears.

"Get up, boy!" Covey and his thunderous voice yells into the window.

He opens the door, and it squeaks loudly while it opens. The huge security guard in which Covey is, is shielding most of the light by blocking the doorway. I walk up to him as he pulls out a pair of handcuffs and slams them around my wrists. He then pulls on the little chain and locks the cuffs tight around my wrists.

"Is my mom here?" I calmly ask Covey.

He pushes me up against the prison wall and shuts the holding cell door. Covey is a big man, about six feet six inches tall, and about three hundred pounds with little black dots for eyes. He is not a fat man either; he is a hulk of a man in a dark-blue Desoto County guardsman uniform.

"What did you do before this, hunt elephants?" I say in my most sincere voice with the slightest sense of humor.

Covey just looks at me through the corner of his eye and pulls on my wrists, leading me down the hallway to the other door that leads to the offices and waiting room.

"Taking me to the gas chamber or the showers? I don't kiss on the first date," I say to break the tension in the air.

He pulls on the chains of the cuffs so hard that it pulls me in front of him. He lets go of the cuffs and pushes me forward ahead of him. Covey is now walking behind me, and he is pushing me along with his billy club, not saying a word. His face is that of a baby with fat cheeks, and he has the body of a man who wrestles rhinos. I do not intend to make him mad. I'm sure he is willing to kill me at the drop of a shoelace. God forbid I sneeze and the echo sounds like a gunshot. He would snap me in half with his huge hands. His hands are so big and muscular, they almost look fake, as if someone covered his hands with clay and molded out muscular fingers.

The walk down the hallway is short. Covey yells out, "One!" once we get to the door at the end of the hallway. The electric lock buzzes, and he pushes the door open. Covey puts his powerful hand on my neck and guides me to the left of the door.

"Holy Shit, Covey. Just use the Force next time!" I yell out as he pushes me forward.

He just looks at me with his beady eyes set way back in his eye sockets.

"Not much of a talker, are you?" I ask as I walk and face forward.

Covey just uses his one hand on my neck to lead me along, and his grip is like a wrench. I walk slowly since Covey is setting the pace. He leads me down the hallway through another door and steers me around a corner to an office.

Dr. Franklin is the name on the door. The nameplate on the desk reads the same name. The door is open, and Covey lets go of my neck and pushes me into the office. I turn around quickly and look straight at him.

"Wait," he says as he blocks the doorway with his massive frame.

He then envelops the doorknob in his huge hand and closes the door.

I remember that Franklin is the name of the detective in the trench coat that had me arrested. I'm really good at remembering things, and I have no problems putting two and two together. When we played Wheel of Fortune or Jeopardy at home, I always won. The straight A's in school helped also. The photographic memory I have is good for putting puzzles together. I see things, and something in my brain just goes into action and the pieces fit together.

I'm still in handcuffs, and I wait by sitting in the expensively soft leather chair behind the desk in the office. I'm a curious kid, therefore I look around. I rub my wrists since they are still hurting from the steel handcuffs. I'm wearing the same Nikes, blue jeans, and a red T-shirt that I was arrested in. I am still wondering, *Where is my Duke sweatshirt?*

Dr. Franklin's office exemplifies a modern doctor's office with college degrees on the wall behind the desk. The plaques and certificates all read Dr. Dawn Franklin. The wide cherrywood desk is clutter-free. The desktop computer is dust-free, and the two walls on either side of me have books piled to the ceiling. There are three wooden bookcases on each side of the room full of volumes of books on behavioral sciences, history, and societies. I gather that Dr. Franklin is a therapist and there is a picture of a guy and a kid on the desk.

What does the doctor want with me, and why is the doctor working this late on a Saturday? I look around and see no clock in the room. I figure being a shrink, she would have the clock behind me above the door. No clock though. Not a very good shrink. If that's true, I can see why she is here in this hole of a town.

Since I'm sitting in the chair in front of the computer, I flick on the computer. The whistling wind outside is getting worse, howling faster and louder. The rain is pounding on the one little window that lets the darkness into the square room. The fragile trees are being thrashed by the approaching storm. I touch a few keys on the keyboard, and the time and date appear on the gray screen: 7:30 p.m. September 1. And all I can do is wait, and wait I did. For what, I didn't know. Suddenly the waiting is over.

"Remember me?" a soft voice calls out like the song of an angel.

I look up from the screen and see a middle-aged woman, not very tall with shoulder-length blond hair, in the doorway. She's an attractive woman about four inches over five feet tall with some curves. She is dressed professionally in a black suit jacket with matching skirt with thin gold rims on her eyeglasses. She doesn't smile as she stands in the doorway, and Covey is towering directly behind her, acting as a bodyguard.

"Well, do you?" she asks again.

"Nope," I say as I get up from the chair.

She is now walking toward me. I can now see that she is wearing a dark-blue skirt and a white button shirt. She is a lovely looking woman for someone around forty. She would look sophisticated if she didn't live in Arcadia. She carries no folders and walks into the room with her black high heels on and eyeglasses that frame her petite face.

"Are you the therapist?" I ask. "Because you don't look like a doctor."

"Are you Raymond Beacon? Because you sure don't look like a murderer."

What? Murderer, I think. I can only smile as I await her next move.

What the Hell have I gotten myself into now?

CHAPTER 3

THE WORD *MURDERER* hits me hard, and the overwhelming feeling of impending doom is overcoming me like a waterfall. The small perfect square of the doctor's office is dim from the storm and silent from the apparent confusion. I do not know what to say. I'm in total shock from that word—*murderer*.

The track lighting from the ceiling in the room makes everything look menacing. Lightning flashes outside, making the room a strobe of light, then nothing. Covey's massive frame, which is still blocking the door, casts a huge shadow over Dr. Franklin. She now stands staring at me from the front of her desk. I'm still bewildered and standing alone behind the desk, comprehending the only word that echoes in my mind: *murderer*.

"That's my chair," she says.

Those words awoke me from my trance. I shake off the onslaught of confusion as if shaking off the cold. The thunder outside is getting louder as the storm approaches, and the room sparkles with quick flashes of lighting. Now I'm totally alert and await the fate that controls my future.

"It is your chair. These are your handcuffs also?" I say as I walk to the opposite side of the desk, away from Dr. Franklin, and then into the chair in front of her desk.

Dr. Franklin never takes her eyes off me the entire time I'm walking around the desk. She throws me the key to the handcuffs after I take my seat. I get the cuffs off in a second and lay the cuffs and key on the desk.

"You look shocked and surprised," she says as she sits and gets comfortable in her extra-large, black, leather chair.

I sit in the little wooden chair like the ones that you find at school or at a dinner table in a mobile home.

"I just want to know why you would call me a murderer," I ask.

She cut me off sharply. The look on her face is telling me something is definitely wrong.

"You honestly don't remember me?" she says sternly from her high-back chair.

"No, I don't. I don't remember you," I tell her again as I lean back into my chair, wondering what kind of trick this woman is trying to play on me.

"Let me take you back," she says as she slides her chair a few inches away from the desk, crossing her legs and placing her hands on her knees as she looks briefly toward Covey.

"About four years ago, my daughter's boyfriend died, and that same day my daughter disappeared. I looked high and low for her for years, always praying she would come back home. My life was already a mess as it was back then. I was a high school teacher with a horrifying marriage. My daughter disappears, and my husband leaves me, all in the same year. My only salvation was to get a Master's Degree, become a psychologist, and work for the police to hunt down my daughter. All this work and learning, hoping to find out what happened to my daughter or her killer. Years of finding the little clues, and the whys of what really happened. Well, now all that hard work has paid off."

I remember the newspaper saying a girl disappeared when my brother died.

"If you graduated in Arcadia, it was a small class," I say softly.

Dr. Franklin looks at me in total frustration as she rolls her eyes at me and continues her story once again.

"I did this only to find that every crime has a key. Find that key, and you will unlock the mystery. My daughter is Maria Lennon, and you're my key," she says forcefully as she leans forward and stares at me from behind the cherrywood desk.

"Why me?" I ask as I lean forward and fold my hands on her desk.

I'm thinking this woman is crazy. I have no clue what the hell she is talking about. "What's this 'death follows me' stuff?" I ask.

"My daughter was the first girl you had sex with, asshole!" Dr. Franklin yells out in an irate voice as she slams her tiny fist down on the desk. "You're the reason she ran away!" she yells at me as she stands up from her chair, her hands firmly grasping the desk. "You ruined my life!" she screams from amid the darkness.

I look behind me to see what Covey is doing. I'm not worrying about any five-foot, four-inch woman in heels. It's big bad Covey—The Punisher—that worries me.

While I glance behind me at Covey, Dr. Franklin leans over her desk and grabs me by my shirt. That's when she starts yelling in my face.

"Are you listening to me?" she screams out, her face only inches from mine.

"What's going on, lady?" I yell out as I keep one eye on her and one eye on Covey.

"You need to calm down! I don't know your daughter!"

"I know everything about you, you little shit!" she yells, still holding on to my shirt.

I think for such a little woman, she's spunky.

"Let go of my shirt, lady! Sit your ass down in that chair and calm down! Is this how you counsel patients? No wonder you live in Arcadia!" I yell out in retaliation.

She screams out, "If you don't shut up, I'm going to kill you myself!" Then she pushes me back as she lets go of my shirt, and she sits back down.

"Look, I just came home to find out about my mother!" I yell out as I stand up. "If I'm not being charged with anything, I will be going!" I say right back at her in a calm voice.

Before I could even turn around, Covey puts his hands on my shoulders and puts me firmly in my chair. Resistance is futile, and I still don't know what's going on. So far, I have a psycho psychiatrist yelling at me, I'm in jail, I still hate this town, and I'm still waiting for my mom. Dr. Franklin is not calming down, Covey is holding me steadily in place, and we've seemed to have lost the doctor's little girl. The storm is thrashing the palm trees outside the prison window, and the dark room filled with books and black shadows is silent with anticipation. Dr. Franklin pushes her hair back and fixes her eyeglass frames before speaking again.

"We are charging you with murder," she blurts outs.

"What?" The words fly out of my mouth as I slam my fist on her table in disbelief. "Who is? This is Bullshit!" I yell out in a rage as the blood rushes to my face, turning my cheeks and forehead red with anger.

"For the murder of Kimberly Beacon, your mother."

"What!" I yell out in dismay.

"Your mother is dead. Murdered!" she says again.

The look Dr. Franklin gave me while saying those words says everything.

"Your mom has been found dead, and here you are. Case closed," Dr. Franklin says.

My mother, Kimberly Beacon, is dead. I could tell this was no joke. I sank down into the chair as my heart fluttered for the mother I hardly knew. I didn't know whether to be grieving or indecisive toward the news of her death. I just sat in the chair in the doctor's office as the storm thrashed away at the palm trees and bushes outside. The darkness and bookcases of grandeur are among the nonliving essences that cloud the room. I am now copping with facts dealt to me.

"The police found her Thursday night. Your mother and her boyfriend were both found dead at his house. And again, here you are. Guilty," she says.

"I pulled out the file yesterday on her and found her two sons—one dead, one missing. The name Ray Beacon matched the name in my daughter's diary. Ray Beacon was the last entry in my daughter's diary, and you were the last person to see my daughter alive. When I heard the call today, North Carolina plates with the name Raymond Beacon come over the police scanner, I knew I found my key. The missing piece. Missing for four years," she says in the dark room with the storm outside.

"I moved to Oviedo," I say from my chair.

Dawn smirks and continues.

"I pulled the file on you years ago, and nothing came up. You disappeared without a trace, and now here you are," she says calmly. "And now it's payback time!" she yells out to me with both hands gripping firmly to her desk as she stands up and leans over toward me.

I only hear the words "your mother is dead, murdered." Then some sadness overcomes my thoughts. She wasn't the best mother, but still she did not deserve to be murdered. We didn't have many memories of good times, but there were some. I am still a child; it's hard to believe the roughest years of my life are now. My mother and brother both died in this town. I can only think about the sadness in such losses. There will be no mom there to see me get married. No mother to see me play basketball in college. My mother never saw my high school graduation either, so being at my college graduation was important to me, to prove I made it on my own. Now she's dead. I never said goodbye. I never wanted her to go on before we made amends. I came here to make those amends.

Time evaporates immediately for me. The storm disappears, and the golden silence fills my head as Covey releases me from his grip. I am now the saddest and loneliest person in modern civilization, destined to be in ruins by the hands of another. Death, death, and still more dead bodies and faces streak through my mind over and over and over again. First my brother, then the three girls in North Carolina, and now my mom. The doctor's office is quiet now, and the reality of life is coming to speed once again. The infinite sadness is back in my life here in Arcadia, and the despair haunts me endlessly while I stay in this town. This town killed my brother, murdered my mom, and now it's trying to destroy me. I came here to get away and find answers, but the questions that lie before me are the killers of my future. If I think long enough, I can figure things out. There is so much I don't know, so many pieces of the puzzle missing, and this woman is my only source of information. If I learned anything, it was that communication is the key. Dr. Franklin is the gatekeeper of my time—the time that stands still in this impossible town named for fiery demons. I sit here thinking rapidly, trying to find my own key to the door that lets me out of this Purgatory.

I'm sure my facial expressions utter pure amazement. I can barely breathe the damp air. I keep thinking of the trail of dead bodies that all lead to me. Dr. Franklin is looking at me, hoping for something, but I don't know what to say. Is this all a bad dream? Is my mother really dead?

"Why would I kill my mother?" I ask.

"I don't know," she replies. "But you fit the profile," she adds. "They say Ted Bundy was a genius, a straight A student just like you. He killed only women also," she says as she sits back in her chair. "You've already been convicted. A sensible woman murderer, and we suddenly find her son that has been missing for years. That's more than a coincidence."

"I was in North Carolina all week, including yesterday morning. I was in Atlanta this morning and here all night. I have gas receipts, phone calls, and a GPS to prove it. I was in class all this week, never missing a day of school. I can prove that too. I didn't kill my mother or brother or your little girl," I say slowly and sadly. I'm speaking in the calmest voice possible and sitting in the wooden chair with my hands clasped together on her desk.

"I want to know what happened to my little girl," she says. "You had sex with her, and she disappeared. My little girl was traumatized because of you. You are a hellion, and trouble follows you everywhere!" she yells out as she blames me for her life passed by.

Dr. Franklin never spoke in a conversational tone, but I can tell she is calming down now. I don't think I have to worry about any more outbursts from her.

"I don't know your little girl, lady. I had sex with one girl in Arcadia, and her name was Lee. She was a tall girl with black hair that looks nothing like you. So if you want truth, go buy a Bible!" I say back at her.

Bang! Covey didn't like my humor and just cracked me upside the back of my head with his fist. The blow forces me forward and almost into Dr. Franklin's desk. That is when Covey grabs me by my shirt and pulls me back to an upright position. I'm dizzy, my head is killing me, and I see double for a brief second because the powerful punch of Covey practically rocks my world. My head clears just in time to see the sadness in Dr. Franklin's eyes.

"Lee was short for Lennon. She grew up a tomboy," she said to me from her leather chair. "She liked climbing trees and playing baseball. Her father gave her the name, and everyone called her Lee. Her features took after her father—the height, brown eyes, and dark hair. You knew her, then you both disappeared."

"I knew Lee," I said to her, trying not to smile.

Lee was my brother's girlfriend at Desoto County High School. She was the girl I was with the day before I left Arcadia.

"After the divorce from Tom, months later, I changed my name back to my maiden name. Thus, Dr. Franklin," she says as she points to the nameplate on the desk.

"You didn't waste any time getting remarried," I say as I pointed to the photograph on the desk. "And that's one hell of a ring on your finger. I'd say you're fully recovered."

"You're a punk, kid. Got an answer for everything. Well, where the hell is my daughter?" she asks as she slams her hand down on the desk and yells at me.

"The older detective at my house is your dad. Is that the same guy in the picture on your desk? So you got this job through daddy," I say.

"You're nothing but trouble. How did you ever get into Duke?" she asks.

"Why do you think I know where she is?" I say back to her.

"You disappeared into thin air!" she yells at me from her chair. Her voices echoes off the cement wall of the room.

"You were dead and gone, and now you're here and alive. You reappear just like that." She snaps her fingers. "An intellectual college boy with a scholarship, new iPhone, new car, and everything. The police didn't even know how to find you. I had the FBI looking for you for a year. Nothing came up. No school records, no social security number, no job history or credit cards, and suddenly here you are right in front of me. Just like that!"

"Just like that," I say as I repeat her words back to her.

"Now you have a license in your real name. Here you are, Raymond Beacon. A car in your name, school records, and a scholarship, even a credit card. But for four years, no one could find you. I want to know where you went and what happened to you!" she yells to me from the darkness of her office as she sits in her chair with the lightning flashing behind her.

The storm outside is still thrashing everything around us. The room is in turmoil from all the flashes of light. My mind wanders through the night but is still alert to her intentions. I still can't believe all this horror is happening to me. I'm still invoking the sadness and can't figure out what this woman wants me to tell her. I can see how the loss of a loved one is devastating. I can relate since my mom is dead. I still can't believe it. The death of your mother isn't something you can hear once and recover from, even if you haven't seen her in four long years.

"We have all night," Dawn says. "Covey works the graveyard shift, and this room is much sturdier than my house. We're going to ride out this storm, and you're going to tell me what happened that May, three and a half short years ago. I already know so much, like you were a punk kid, your mother beat you, and your brother died. Besides that, I know you had sex with my daughter right before you both disappeared!" she lashes out as she leans forward into the light of the room.

I'm getting comfortable in my little wooden chair. We both need to know what is going on. My past brought me here, and her future depends on me. She has no idea about the murders in Durham, but somehow everyone who is dead has a path that leads to me. I need to know about the past to solve the problems of my future. All the answers to any of my questions start here in this town.

"It's a long story. I have to take you way back," I say. "Way back to Boston so you will know everything that happened and why. Then I have to tell you about Durham, North Carolina, in the present tense. I didn't come here by chance. I was led here. It's one hell of a story. Stop me along the way if you get lost. I promise not to leave anything out," I say as I lean forward into the light from my wooden chair.

"We've got all night," she says as she looks deep into my eyes from across the big desk. "And back we go."

CHAPTER 4

"I GREW UP in the suburbs of Boston," I state as I get comfortable in the wooden chair. "I had the best friends in the world, and I played hockey and basketball. Once high school started, I went straight to the varsity hockey team as a freshman. Basketball was my backup sport. I was okay playing ball and started, but I loved hockey. I played shooting guard on the basketball team and goalie for the hockey team. I loved life and enjoyed it to the fullest every day. My dad loved sports and had a great job as a lobbyist for an oil company. Mr. James Beacon worked long hours during the week, but my dad was always home on the weekends. Rodney and I weren't the perfect children, but we weren't too bad. We misbehaved at times, but nothing too terrible.

"My dad and I got along since we had sports while Rodney and Dad had politics. Mom was there for rides to games and all the little things like fieldtrips and family weekends. I know I wasn't ever close to my mom, and I don't think Rodney was either. Rodney and I were identical twins and the only children," I say with a smile.

"A perfect life," she says to me. "Until your parents' divorce. And you came to school here?" she asks.

"Yes. And don't forget my brother killed himself," I added.

"My daughter disappeared also," she adds from the dark side of the desk.

I went on.

"The schools in Boston were completely different from Florida. I was way ahead of everyone in my grade here. I took Spanish classes and Algebra in sixth grade. That's why people from Massachusetts who move to Florida do so much better than the other students. Boston's school system teaches kids as much as possible at such a young age. The schools in Massachusetts truly want the children to learn. When Rodney and I got to school in Florida, we were learning things that were taught to us two years earlier. School actually bored us because it was all review."

"Is that why you hated it here?" Dr. Franklin asks.

"I hated Arcadia because it wasn't Boston. I had no friends, and nobody knew about basketball or hockey. I came to Florida thinking about beaches and tan girls, sunset strips and Disney World. The only problem was that I didn't live on the coast. I lived in Arcadia—a sand-infested rathole full of hicks, gray sand fields, dirt roads, cows, and orange groves. The beach was two hours away, and there are more red barns and horses than people in this town. I didn't fit in," I say as I look right at her. "I'd stay home watching *CSI* and other cop shows. I was doing nothing."

"That was up to you," she adds.

"I didn't fit in. I didn't want to fit in. I didn't want to be here. I was depressed. And for the first time, I hated my life."

"What about your friends in Boston?" she fires back.

"I had the best of friends, and we all loved sports. We all lived on the same street. We were a tightly knit group of kids. We had everything we wanted at our young ages—sports, immaturity, fun, and freedom. We had free reign of the city since the subway took us all over Boston. I had good friends, sports, good grades, money, a loving family, and a girlfriend that loved me."

"Who was your girlfriend in Boston?" the doctor asks.

"Colleen Lyons was my first real girlfriend. I was in eighth grade, and I was as happy as could be. My life didn't change until the summer before high school."

"What happened?" Dr. Franklin asks as she sits with her hands folded on her knee.

The night outside is dark, and the wind is still howling through the trees at sixty miles an hour. The storm is close, and the flashes of lightning more frequent. Covey is only inches behind me with his arms folded across his huge chest. The question Dawn is asking about things I barely remember. What did happen?

"Once school got out, my mother went on a summer vacation without my father. She had friends in Florida and decided to visit them for three weeks. My mom was an administrative assistant for the school board, so taking that much time off over the summer was no problem. I was oblivious to my parents' future and mine. I was always out somewhere or at Colleen's studying. Besides that, I had a paper route that occupied all my mornings before school and three of my nights. Weekends were full of church and city league games. I was almost never home. I saw my family for dinner Monday, Tuesday, Wednesday, and that was about it. My dad worked a lot, so he was rarely home for dinner. I was always with my friends and only saw Dad on weekends or when I was in trouble."

"What about your mother's vacation?" she asks.

"My mother's vacation went from three weeks to almost two months. The divorce papers were filed from Florida. Dad wasn't going to fight it either. He wanted out too. Mom raved about the weather in Florida and talked about how laid back it was there in the Florida. My mother came home right before school started. She packed everything and decided she wasn't going to let her family hold her back from a fresh start of Florida living. Mother wanted to be in Arcadia with her new friends. When the divorce was final later that December, I didn't think I'd see her again. That was just a few months into my freshman year in high school."

"What did you think of your mom leaving?" Dr. Franklin asks.

"I knew my mother wanted out. I knew Dad was going to take care of us and Dad didn't intend to let us go. I knew I wasn't leaving Boston, nor did I want to, so I didn't really care. I did notice my mom and dad fighting in the beginning of my eighth-grade year.

Then Dad spent more and more nights at the office. Then he stopped coming home altogether to avoid the fighting."

"Was this because he had a mistress?" she asks as she peers at me through her glasses, still sitting there calm and content on the other side of her big desk.

"Yeah, Dad was smart, always had a plan B. Plan B for Dad was Betty. Mom didn't take that too well and started to take out her frustrations on Rodney and I. She even slapped me once for coming home too late and accused me of doing drugs. She was stir-crazy by then, and all this happened fast."

"How was high school for you in Boston?" she asks with much curiosity as she leans forward to gain insight.

"The first few months were tough but fine. I was going to a catholic high school in Cambridge. They had the best hockey team in the state and a good basketball team. Since Rodney and I were really smart, the school was ecstatic to have us. Especially since we were children of a lobbyist. That meant big money for the private school. I was good at hockey and basketball and was going straight to varsity. As freshman at a big school, we got hazed by older kids. It was all fine, like an initiation. Just kid's stuff."

"What did your girlfriend think of school?" she asks.

"She went to public school. My girlfriend's parents sent Colleen to Somerville High. So our relationship was limited to phone calls, texts, and weekends. Varsity practice for basketball started with running and workouts right when school started. Therefore, my afternoons were booked up until seven at night. Then it was going home and finishing homework. That's when I decided to give up my paper route. Dad's allowance for Rodney and I was more than enough to get us by. Dad gave us fifty dollars each, every week, just for being good kids."

"Keep telling me about your relationship with Colleen," Dawn interrupts.

"As for Colleen, our relationship suffered and then just faded away. Just like that, she quit texting, didn't call, and I didn't miss talking to her. We were both consumed with our new freshman year lives. We just faded away from texting every day and calling to

35

talking once a week then nothing. Colleen didn't live anywhere near my street or my friends, so we never ran into each other either. We literally faded away into nothing."

"What did Rodney think of all this?" she asks.

"Nothing," I reply. "Rodney and I were friends, but he stayed out of my dating life. He liked Colleen, but the three of us never hung out. I saw Rodney every day, so time with Colleen was mine and her time together. Don't get me wrong, he and I were great friends, but we lived separate lives. We had the good life since we went to the same school and had money."

"Were you and Rodney close?" she asks.

"No, we were not," I say with a smile. "We were twins but so different, and we always had different stuff going on. Again, we were twins but as far apart as two people could be. We even had different friends. Since we had our own money, we always did different things. I went one way and he went another. I think if we were poor, maybe we would have been better brothers."

"Why is that?" she asks from the other side of the desk.

"Since we could always do our own things, we did," I say.

"What's money to kids your age?" she asks.

"Nothing really," I added. "It was the toys we had, Xbox and iPhones, video games, new clothes, and shoes at the mall anytime we wanted. Dad bought us the big things like laptops for school and our iPads. As for spending money, Rodney and I had savings accounts, so anything outside of sports and school, we had to cover ourselves. Money for us wasn't an issue since we always had it and almost never used it. We were kids back then, and money only meant spending money. We never had any problems until my dad got a phone call saying his future ex-wife was trying to empty her kid's savings accounts."

"Really?" Dawn asks with sharp curiosity.

"That was Mom's last day in Boston. Dad literally had enough of her shit and wasn't going to take it anymore. Stealing money from your own kids, now that was low."

"What happened?" Dawn asks as she sits back in her big black chair.

"Dad set up bank accounts for Rodney and me. My dad's name was the only name on the accounts, besides ours. When Mom came home from Florida, she tried emptying the bank accounts thinking Dad wouldn't know. When the bank called Dad to verify the transaction, he told the bank not to give her anything. Mom was irate about leaving the bank empty-handed, and Dad was ready to kill Mom for trying to take our money," I say.

"What happened next?" Dawn asks.

"Dad picked Rodney and me up from school and told us what Mom tried to do. Dad also told us Mom was leaving for Florida that day for good. When Dad drove us home, he told us to wait in the car. He went inside and talked with Mom. Mom's stuff was already packed, and that night she left for Florida."

"How did that make you feel?" she asks.

"Rodney and I were glad to be with Dad since we were closer to him than our mother. The first thing Dad did on the Monday after my mother's departure was go to our school and talk with our teachers. Dad wanted to make sure we were doing all right and making As. Dad also talked with my basketball and hockey coaches to have them push me harder so I could do better. Dad's actions proved that he cared. He wanted to make sure we were doing well despite what we told him. Dad also gave all of our teachers his personal phone number. Therefore, if our grades started slipping, he would know. My father wasn't just a stand-in for a dad. He cared about us. That's why he gave Mom the money to set herself up in Florida. I don't know how much my mom had when she left, but Dad did love her at one time. He just couldn't keep her or him happy. Dad wouldn't let her go out into the world blindly. He took care of her as much as he did Rodney and I."

"Your dad quit paying child support years ago. Was he paying alimony to her?"

"Don't know. Stayed out of it, and when I left here, I was gone for good. The divorce, me leaving Boston, and Rodney's death all happened in a six-month period during my freshman year."

"Did you have a hard time after your mom left?" Dr. Franklin asks. "What happened to your girlfriend, Colleen?" she asks.

"Well, people just grow apart at times. I guess that's what happened to you and Mr. Lennon," I say to Dr. Franklin.

"People grow apart for many reasons. Your dad was cheating on your mom. Your dad was cheating on your mom with a stripper, I remind you. Not the greatest of morals," Dawn says fiercely as she stares at me from among the darkness.

"Are you sure you're a psychiatrist? You're really negative! Where did you get your degree? Whatsamatter U!" I say to her with a smirk.

"Pop." Covey backhands me upside my head again. That hit was gentle but hard enough to give me a headache. Dawn is getting comfortable in her big leather chair behind her large wooden desk. Dr. Franklin is a beautiful woman. Her golden blond hair glows against the black leather behind her. She is now sitting back, with one leg crossed over the other. Her hands are folded on her lap, and she watches me from behind her golden rims.

"If he hits me again, he is going to break my neck, and then I won't be able to tell you anything."

"Quit being a smartass," she says calmly in her sweet voice. "You still haven't told me how you ended up in Florida or what happened between you and my daughter or the girls in North Carolina."

"I guess I haven't," I agree and go back to my story. "Things changed drastically for me about the sixth week of school. Mom had been gone two weeks, and things in school were rolling. Rodney and I had friends and even girlfriends. Not real, true love girlfriends, but we were seeing girls. Then that weekend, Dad told us we were going to spend the weekend together. Great, until he said we were moving Betty in."

"Betty was your father's mistress?" she asks with curiosity.

"My father's mistress. Dad talked to us and told us there was no need for him and Betty to live apart anymore. Rodney met Betty once before and told me that Dad did catch a model on his hook. Dad was forty something, handsome, and distinguished. And this Betty woman was twenty-five. She was a model all right—a nude one. Dad met her while she was dancing at a club. Long black hair that was full and flowed down her back. She was Italian and had a great body with big, round, fake breasts. She was about five ten with dark Italian skin and big brown eyes. She worked out, had long legs, and the pretty face. But Betty was an uneducated stripper that had her hooks in my dad for one reason—money! Moving in with us meant free rent, and she couldn't cook for herself, never mind for all of us. Happy homemaker she wasn't. Good in bed, she had to be because she was an idiot."

"Did she have sex with you?" Dr. Franklin asks with some concern as she listens attentively.

"Hell no!" I reply. "I was a virgin, and she would have killed me. I didn't really like her, and I didn't like the fact that she moved in a few weeks after Mom moved out. Granted we had a huge house, but it just wasn't right."

"What happened next?" the doctor asks.

"Then came November and Dana. She would be my first high school girlfriend. My first high school love, and she was a sophomore cheerleader. Everything was perfect until Mom decided to sue for custody, and Betty agreed that children should be with their mother."

"Was Betty the reason you ended up in Florida?"

"Not really. She was just a helping hand. Dad didn't fight the fact that Mom wanted child support. He told us come Christmas, Rodney and I were going to Florida. He was living with Betty and going to marry her. This meant we were no longer Daddy's number one priority. Betty was."

"How did that make you feel?" the doctor asks.

"I was shocked at first but saw Daddy becoming more and more distant. I just started to hang out with Dana more and spent less time at home," I reply.

"What happened to Dana?" Dr. Franklin says while paying complete attention to detail.

"Nothing really. We stayed together every day. She became my best friend besides Rodney. She went to all my games, and I helped her study. We spent every day together from November 1 until I left on February 28."

"You said my daughter was your first. What happened?"

"Nothing happened sex-wise with Dana. It was puppy love."

I say this while getting comfortable in the wooden chair. I'm stretching out now with my feet crossed and leaning back.

"How come? You said she was your first love."

"She knew I was leaving after New Year's. She was in love once before, when she was a freshman. Some guy that was a senior that dated her for about six months. Once he had sex with her, everything changed in their relationship. After a while, that was all he wanted from her. Then he started to abuse her. They broke up about six months before she met me. She was over him but hesitant to have sex with me. We made a promise that if I came back and we got together, we would make love then, knowing it would be love. I wanted my first to be like that. Love."

"So my daughter was your first love?" Dr. Franklin asks.

I try to hesitate, but the words just came right out.

"No, Colleen was my first true love. Lee was just sex!"

CHAPTER 5

THE ROOM SUDDENLY seems darker, and I expect Covey's big fist to hit me any second now. Talking to Dr. Franklin, or Dawn, is getting harder, especially when it comes to telling the truth. I figure any second now, I'll be going back to my cell by the force of Covey. For such a little woman, she worries me because she holds my fate. She is as much a part of my future as I am her past. She could press false charges against me and ruin my chances of playing ball at Duke. I might never leave this town for that fact, or I could just disappear like before. I realize that in small towns, anything could happen. I would just be another unsolved mystery, and no one would care or lose any sleep over me.

"Just sex, huh?" she says to me as she comes out of her trance of astonishment. Meanwhile, the thunder and lightning decorate the dark room from the window behind her.

I didn't reply. I just look at her and await her reaction.

"Just sex," she says again into the darkness.

"There is a lot you still don't know. Rodney was dating her. She probably just got us confused or dated Rod but was in love with me," I say in my defense.

"No," she replies as she shakes her head so slightly. "There is no confusion," she says as she reaches in her desk drawer and pulls out a Marlboro Lights. "I read an insert in her diary. It was short and sweet. The very last thing she ever wrote in her little book said, 'I made a terrible mistake today. I had sex with Raymond Beacon, and this will change everything, forever.' That's what it said," she tells me as she lights her cigarette and then pauses for my reaction. "Her last entry was written the day before the fire."

I knew exactly what fire she was talking about.

"It didn't change anything," I say as I keep my gaze on her in the darkness.

"That was the last diary entry on the night before she disappeared. The next day, your brother died. And the day after, my life changed forever. Suddenly you two were both gone. This changes everything for you and me," she says as she exhales a thin line of smoke into the air of her office.

"I called Duke today and talked to your coaches. I found out a lot, especially about your last three dead girlfriends. But no Maria Lennon there. I called Oviedo, and you didn't show up in Orlando with a girlfriend four years ago either. I spent an hour crying, wondering where my daughter was."

I am very surprised Dr. Franklin didn't talk more about my troubles at Duke and the three girls. The words *my last three girlfriends* just roll off her tongue like water off a duck's back.

"I'm not the reason Lee disappeared," I say to her.

"You were there, and then you disappeared. And she's gone, and I need to know why. I already know about you and Rodney. I told you, I did my homework, and I really did," she says to me in frustration.

I can tell she's getting upset. I think tears are swelling in her soft blue eyes.

"Four years ago, I went to Cambridge and visited your high school to talk to your teachers and some of your friends. I walked Newbury Street and talked to the kids that lived there. You and your brother were like *The Tale of Two Cites*. The same kids on the outside, but very different on the inside." She snickers from behind her desk. "You and your brother were twins, but those were the only similarities. People who hung out with you didn't know or like your brother,

42

and his friends didn't like you. He kept his head in the books because he was the shy one. You were always in the spotlight—played sports, did school plays, went everywhere, did everything. When you played in hockey and basketball games, you would yell out, 'It's on!' like some hero's call," she says to me in an agitated and frustrated voice as she points her cigarette at me.

"You didn't find anything about me. We were all kids. That was four years ago."

"He was the stable one. You were the time bomb. Then you exploded," she says forcefully as she stares at me from across her desk while rolling her lit cigarette between her fingers.

I'm appalled and confused all at once. She did nothing during this investigation. She's convicting me of a crime I haven't committed. Her sentences are hitting me like stupid kid's disses. Does this lady realize I was fourteen when all this happened?

"I'm the victim. I was following my parents' orders when I came to Arcadia. I was sent here! Remember? I was just doing my job as a kid, having fun and following orders that were dictated to me. I was only a child when all this happened," I say to her.

"You were the bad seed. No one here liked you," she says to me in a mean voice.

"Look, Doc!" I say loudly as I sit in my chair. "Enough is enough with this good kid, bad kid routine. Even though your daughter is gone, I'm the victim. Your daughter is missing, and I had nothing to do with it. The fact is, my brother is dead, and I had to leave town to save my life. Remember all the movies you've seen. The good guy always lives and lives on. I am here because I am the good guy, and I am here so I can live on," I say calmly, looking right at her from my little wooden chair.

"The guilty always return to the scene of the crime," she replies nonchalantly.

I'm now on the edge of the chair, talking right at the doctor. She's making me crazy with her insults and lies. She's considerably defensive and always looking for the easy way out of every situation.

"I'm the victim," I say outlandishly in defense. "My dad turned his back on us because his new girlfriend didn't like kids. When I talked to my dad to take me back after the fire, he didn't want me. He said I had to work things out with my mom. My own dad cast me away. So if anyone got screwed in life, it was me!" I yell out as I point at myself. "Now my mom's been murdered, my brother is still dead, my father still doesn't talk to me, and I'm in jail all because your daughter ran away from home four years ago. I don't know where she is!" I scream out as I flail my hands in the air in total frustration.

"You're the bad son!" she yells out to me as she points at me again with her lit cigarette in her hand. "You had an arrest record in high school."

"No, I didn't!"

"Yes, you did!" she yells out! "That man that supposedly beat you, you broke into his house and beat him with a wooden bat. You broke his ribs and his fingers. Do you remember that? You almost killed him, you maniac!" she yells to me as she leans forward on her desk.

"He beat up my mom and the charges were dropped!" I yell out in anger as I slam my hand down on the desk. "I came home and there was coffee all over the wall. He smashed my mom's coffee cup on her head and then slapped her around!" I yell out and relive the situation as I stand in front of her desk. "I'm the one who called 911. They played the tape to the judge. Go listen to it. That asshole admitted to beating up my mom, and this shit town of Arcadia and the police did nothing to him. You call that justice? He didn't spend one night in jail. He said it was her fault!" I yell out with Covey just inches behind me.

"You were a maniac! You broke into his house and dialed 911. Then you put the phone down, picked up the bat, and almost killed him. You said he had to pay for his sins. You made sure of that!"

"That guy was an asshole wife beater. The 911 call was made from his phone. I'm sure there were a lot of people looking to beat the shit out of him. They never caught the guy that beat him up, and I was never convicted. Lack of evidence!" I say.

I'm calm, but the adrenaline rushes through my body as I relive the disaster in my mind. I'm shaking in my chair. This lady is pushing the wrong buttons. She knows more than she is telling, and it is making me mad. On the other hand, Covey is still inches behind me, and even though I'm raising my voice, I'm not leaving my chair.

"You stole a car in Arcadia. You were suspended from school, broke a wooden bat over someone's head, and then disappeared! You even hit your own mother!"

Bam! Covey hit me so hard, my head hit her desk.

"What the Hell was that for?" I scream out, jumping out of my seat and staring Covey down.

"You hit your own mother! Now sit down," he says with a growl. "You have no other choice." He points toward the chair.

Well, I do have this wooden chair in front of me, even though that was the worst of all my options. I sit down by choice, not because I have to.

"You were definitely the bad kid," Dr. Franklin says from behind her desk her legs are crossed, and her right hand drifts into the air as she holds her cigarette.

This situation is lose-lose for me. She is in complete control of how long I stay in jail. Just goes to show you that one person doesn't have control of their own life. Control is an illusion that happens to be a part of everyone's life. "Here today, gone tomorrow" definitely has a new meaning in my mind right now. Now my mind is racing at a million miles an hour. Life taught me that there are always three ways out—your way, their way, and the right way. Now it's time to find the right way. It is time for me to stop this blame game and bust the wounds wide open. It is time to talk about Lee and the fire. It's time to relive my fears. Time to find out exactly what happened the day I left my life as the Beacon's son far behind.

"You won't get away this time," she says to me and into the night air.

"I don't know what you want from me," I say as I get comfy and straighten up in the chair. "All I have is the truth. I don't know where your daughter is."

All the doctor's anger and emotions seem to disappear and reappear. She becomes quiet and excited all at once. I'm quiet as I try to think of exactly what to say. This story is going to hurt, but it's the truth. Exactly how I remember it. I know what I'm about to say, and

I feel the words ready to flow out of my mouth like a stream of air. The guilt of what happened never haunted me because I can wash it away like the dirt of life. I do remember everything vividly.

"I remember you daughter. Lee or Maria or whatever her name is," I say.

Those words just came out like the darkness around us. The silence is deafening and heavy with consequence. I see the doctor's face freeze with curiosity and fear all at once. Dr. Franklin's blond hair and glossy pink lips are highlighting the features of her face. Her expression is something I will remember forever, as if I just kissed her goodbye. I see her, and I also feel the pain of what the future holds for her in my words. I look her in the eyes out of respect. I don't focus on the light of her cigarette as I talk, even though it is the brightest light in the room.

"It was no secret that I was having problems at home," I say to her. "Everything was upside down for me. No friends, no sports, no Boston, no more money. I hated Arcadia, the heat, the humidity, and my mom. I was almost suspended for fighting, and I did take my friend for a joy ride in his dad's Corvette. I was very bitter on the inside. I hated my own peers and vented by fighting back. We all know that."

"What caused all this?" she asks me from the other side of the desk. She then takes a long drag from her Marlboro Lights.

"I don't know. Boredom, maybe?" I answer. "See, we didn't have to start school until the end of January because that's when the next semester began. Rodney and I had a free three-week vacation from January 4 until the end of the month. You know what we did? Nothing!" I say as I shift nervously in my little wooden chair. "My mom didn't take us anywhere. Therefore, we caused trouble for fun. We let horses loose into fields from their barns. We tried to ride cows. We would put cow shit on people's cars just for fun. Well, people started remembering us, and once school started, we got picked on. We were those damn Yankees from Boston—everyone's enemy. The people that lived around us were few and far between. We played the same jokes on the same people over and over. We got a bad reputation and got into several fights. I was miserable, and Rodney was taking life in stride. He met a girl named Lee about a week or so into the new semester."

"That was my daughter, Maria?" Dawn's sad voice asks.

"Yeah, Lee. She was head over heels for Rodney just after a few weeks. She would be his first love. In the meantime, I am beating up mom's boyfriend for hitting her. I hated school because it was all review, and I couldn't stand being here anymore. I hated Arcadia and was frustrated with life," I say to Dawn. "At this time, Rodney and I were distant because we had a few differences of opinion on things. So we weren't talking very much. I usual skipped class to play basketball, and basketball was my only salvation. I remember just getting up in the middle of class, turning in my work, and telling the teacher I had to go see the Dean of Students. My teachers were always more than happy to let me go. So there I was, walking the halls of Desoto County High School. I had already gone to my gym class, and my phys. ed. shirt was sweaty and dirty. Therefore, I went to Rodney's locker, opened it, and there was a clean T-shirt. I took off my shirt and put his on."

Dawn is hanging on every word I say. She is trying to visualize the conversation as if looking at a play and trying to memorize it. I see her across from me on the other side of the table, and as I talk, the guilt sets in because of what I did. This is the only way out though. The past is the past, and hopefully my history will solve my future problems. The truth will set me free. Maybe? I look right at her and continue my story.

"Lee saw me in Rodney's shirt at his locker and assumed I was him. She gave me a big kiss with that wonderful look in her eyes of pure untapped love. Like the love I had for Colleen in Boston."

"'What are you doing?' Lee asked, and my mind just started clicking with ideas. This was my chance to catch a falling star."

"How was my daughter a falling star?" she asks.

I'm in amazement that she is paying that close of attention to the details of the story. I'm glad to see Dr. Franklin is not just here going along for the ride. Dawn actually cares about what happened to her daughter as she analyzes every word I say.

"Lee wasn't the star that was falling. I was. I just wanted to have something, anything special or different, and that moment was my chance," I reply.

"A chance you gladly took?" she asks.

"I wasn't afraid to take a chance. When she kissed me, it was Colleen and Dana all over again. I needed that kiss, and I just felt something. So I looked her right in the eyes and kissed her. She was surprised and shocked at the aggressiveness as we kissed for a while. I looked into to her eyes again, holding her in my arms, and asked her if she loved me."

"What did she say?" Dawn asks as her smoke trails evaporate into the air.

I look around the dark room as I sit up in my wooden chair. The storm outside is violent, and I am hoping that it is not a prelude of what is going to happen to me.

"She said to me she loves me more than anything in the world. I told her to prove it to me. I asked her to skip the rest of her classes and come home with me. We could make love for the first time. I told her I loved her and kissed her again. Then I took a chance. I grabbed her hand, and she followed me like a puppy dog right out the doors of the school. We walked off campus, down the street, and toward my house. We talked very little, and we ran the last fifty yards to my mother's house, laughing. We ran to the front door and kissed in the foyer for what seemed like an eternity. She told me she has never been so happy and excited in her life. We would be each other's first. For her, that was special. For me, it was pure lust for a forbidden woman igniting my veins with the fuel of ecstasy."

The look of total disappointment came from Dawn as I look to her. She is hurt from my story already, and I haven't got to the good part yet. How do you tell a mom that her daughter was a one-night stand, especially since that girl is now dead?

"So my daughter was your plaything. Great!" she says as she puts her cigarette out.

I could tell she is empty on the inside and this insight isn't the story she was looking for.

"I need to go on. I can't stop here," I say as I sit up in my chair.

"By all means, go on," she says as pathetically as she fights back the emotions hidden by the darkness of the room.

"Once we got to my mom's house, everything happened so fast. Before I knew it, we were kissing and naked. I was so scared, and she trembled the entire time. The sexual act seemed to last an eternity. I could tell it hurt her, but we were both so excited. I just happened to look over at the door. In the crack of the bedroom door, there it was." I shake my head in my own disbelief.

"There what was?" Dawn asks.

"A single blue eyeball staring at us through the crack between the open door and the doorframe. Suddenly, I realized school was out and that was Rodney looking at his own girlfriend and me having sex."

"What! What happened next?" she asks me from her big leather chair with the storm echoing behind her.

"We kept going, and Rodney just kept watching. I wasn't worried at all. I rolled her over so she could be on top and in control. Her back was toward the door. I could see his eye getting wilder as he got more angered while peering through the little crack in the door. That's when I rolled her over and pinned her back against the bed. When I looked back over at the door, it was closed all the way. The single eyeball peering at me was gone."

Dawn says nothing as Covey stands behind me as a powerful presence in the darkness. I could tell this was a nightmare everyone wants to know about but everyone should forget. The powerful illusion of being omnipotent could be dangerous, and it is in this instance. Once you know someone's fears and release those nightmares, there's no turning back.

CHAPTER 6

I AM GUESSING that it is two in the morning by now. I have been sitting in this little wooden chair for hours. I'm not comfortable being in this room anymore. I know Dr. Franklin hates me and the world outside is in just as much turmoil as my own mind and situation. The room is half aglow from the light, and the darkness battles the slight luminescence for control of the cement block room. I am here not by choice but by force. I came here to confront my fears of the hideaway town controlled by those selected few demons that haunt my past.

"So is that it?" the somehow hollow but beautiful woman asks. "What happened to my daughter? What happened to Rodney? There is so much you're leaving out," she says forcefully from the other side of the bulky desk.

I hesitate, noticing her sadness and anger addressing me all at once. I have to remember that she is the key that links our past to my future. I'm in the Desoto County Jail, and she is my only way out. The story of my adventures will only get worse for her before it gets better for all of us. To me, life isn't a journey about what it does to you. My voyage is about where I end up. Just like the hurricane among us, there will be an end to the storm and the dawn of a new day. I need to hang in there until the dawn comes and my new day begins. I must not get swept away from the swirling circumstances around me.

"I never saw Lee after that day," I say to the crying mother across from me. "My brother didn't come home that night, and I didn't question where he was either. I woke up the next day and asked my mom where he was, and she gave me some lame answer that I don't recall. I remember Lee didn't come to school the next day either. I didn't think twice about not seeing either of them. Then suddenly, it was ten a.m., and students saw clouds of smoke floating by the school windows. Everyone started saying there was a fire nearby. The intercom came on seconds later, and the principal announced there was a house on fire. The fire department had already been called, and there was no need to worry."

"Your house?" Covey asks from behind me, standing tall in the darkness.

I'm in shock since those are the first words he speaks to me without brute force behind them.

"Yeah, my house," I reply. "At first I wasn't concerned, but I got up anyway in the middle of class and walked outside. The teacher didn't restrict me to stay in class, and nobody came outside with me since I had no friends. You could see my house from the school since I lived about three hundred yards away. As I walked down the hallway and approached the doors, I saw students and teachers pointing toward the fire. I was near the doors when a student ran up to me and asked if that was my house. I reached the entrance and suddenly my life changed. Suddenly there was a sense of urgency to live life. There it was. My house was a big red blaze that could be seen clearly from the school. One-third of the house was engulfed in flames— huge billowing flames that reached twenty feet into the air. I could hear the fire trucks but couldn't see them. I ran toward my house, sprinting all the way. All I kept thinking was, Is there anyone in the house? Is there anything I need to get out? Why is the house on fire in the first place? As I ran home, I watched the flames roll higher and higher into the air. Dark clouds of ash arose from the flames, turning the blue sky black. Only one side of the house was on fire. I kept thinking, What is going on? Where is my family? Why my house?

Why me? And as I ran toward the house, I knew it was arson by the sheer intensity of the blaze."

"That must have been the oddest thing to see. Only a third of the house engulfed in flames," she says to me in a calm voice.

"I reached the lawn just as the fire trucks pulled up to the house. I ran right past them as firemen jumped out of their trucks and headed for the door. There was no doubt in my mind that I was going to break the door down. I crashed through the door full speed and ended up on the living room floor, almost unconscious. I tried to get up, and that was when a fireman grabbed me and pulled me out of the house. I wanted them to let me go. I felt like I needed to be inside, saving something or someone."

"Didn't you realize there was nothing you could do?" Dawn asks me as she sits once again with her one leg crossed over the other and her hands folded, listening to my story.

"I needed to know if anyone was in the house. I don't know why, but it was important to get inside the house. There was nothing I could do, but I needed to be there inside the house. I knew something was wrong. I knew something was out of place. I needed to be inside the house," I say to her.

"Sounds strange," she replies as she looks at me.

"I know," I reply. "I remember the house was filled with smoke, and I couldn't see a thing. I remember asking questions like 'Where are my mom and brother?' The Fire Chief kept telling me, 'Everything's okay. Your mom is on her way here.' I thought my brother was all right because we were twins, and if anything would happen to him, I would know. At that time, I knew something wasn't right, but no sad feelings of loss were inside me. I felt nothing!"

"Strange," she says from her spot behind the desk.

I think back to that day—a day I have forgotten about for many years. None of my current friends even know of my brother, the fire, or my real family. The secrets I have hidden have stayed locked tight in my mind and heart for so many years that I have almost forgotten about them. Now I must set those burdens of my heart free, and I feel the relief as I talk about my past.

"It took the firemen about an hour to put out the blaze. The walls of half the house were gone, and half the roof caved in because of the missing support. The only things left standing were the front wall, the carport, the kitchen, and the far wall of the living room."

"Arson?" she asks.

"The fire was weird. The heat alone from the fire was immense. The firemen had to move everyone across the street, and we could still feel the heat from the billowing rolls of flames. Something was definitely wrong with that fire, and the police knew it. So the police and firemen searched for something, anything, among the black ashes and smoldering remains. They looked for anything that would tell them it was arson that started the fire. Suddenly, one of the firemen started waving other firefighters over to where he was standing. They found a body."

"What a shame," she adds.

"That was when the feeling of unparalleled loss consumed my body. I started to cry instantly. A fireman, with his thick gloves on, pulled away the debris and found a body. Several other firemen and police officers rushed to his aid. I looked on through the tears in my eyes. I was sitting down on the grass in the neighbor's yard across the street. The police had me surrounded, and I wasn't going anywhere. It was about eleven a.m., and the sun didn't shine any of the destruction away. The smoldering ashes and smoke surrounded the house, causing a fog in the area. Every image was still distorted. The firemen rummaged through the debris and found bones that were burned to the skeleton and then crushed by the fallen roof. The mysterious fire went from arson to homicide. The homicide of my brother, Rodney Beacon. My brother was dead!" I say as I cross my hands on my knees and hold my head down as I think about that day.

"How devastating!" the doctor says as she slowly shakes her head in disbelief. "What a horrible way to die. Did they ever find out how it started or who started the fire?"

I lean forward and look up at Dawn as I address her. "The fire was set by a combination of gasoline and other flammable liquids. The fire started in my room and consumed the area in seconds because of the number of flammables used."

"Someone burned your brother to death?" Dawn questioned.

"I thought the fire was Rodney's suicide, but I don't know now," I say. "I kept up with the news for a little while after I disappeared. Everyone thought Rodney killed himself because of the abuse my mother dished out. No coroner was needed since the body was burnt to the bone. The body was mangled and burnt to a crisp then crushed by the roof that caved in on him. The body parts that were left had to be taken out in pieces. My mom then had him cremated since he was turned to dust by the fire anyway."

"I remember the day your brother died. I remember the fire," the doctor says to me with sympathy.

I lean back in my chair and get ready to shock her again.

"Nope," I say as I shake my head while looking at her.

"What do you mean, no?" she asks surprisingly as her eyes widen with curiosity.

The track lighting from above is dim; the light barely illuminates the wall. Dawn and I can see each other clearly, but the shadows still have their way of dancing about the room. The lightning from the storm outside uncovers the room like a strobe light in a dark dance club. Dawn sits at her spacious desk like a judge awaiting a verdict, and I sit before her like a criminal confronting a losing battle. Covey stands as a silent observer of the situation and turns on his enforcement charm like a light switch. The storm approaching is nothing like the nightmare about to be unleashed on Dr. Franklin.

"I realize now. That was what happened to your daughter," I say. "Your daughter died in that fire," I say softly from my chair in the dimly lit room.

"You bastard!" she yells out in anger as she gives me an evil cross-eyed look.

"In my defense, I know, what a horrible thing to say, but it is the truth. The tragedies in North Carolina reflect the fact that Rodney still could be alive," I reply as I sit in the chair with my hands folded on my lap.

"What?" Dawn says as she jumps up out of her chair and grips the table. "Are you saying you really believe my daughter died in that fire?" she asks in a highly agitated voice.

"That is exactly what I am saying," I reply through the horror of darkness and fear as I sit back in my wooden chair, ignoring her aggression.

"Why would anyone kill my daughter?" she yells out in anger as she slams her little fist on the table.

"You said you and your husband were fighting back then. How do you know he didn't find the journal also? He might have confronted your daughter and Rodney. Anything could have happened. Anyone could have done this," I explain to her.

Covey's huge hands grasp my shoulders and glues me to my chair. I am not going anywhere because of the force Covey uses to keep me in place. I realize now that Covey and Dr. Dawn Franklin must be having an affair. I say this because Covey is into hurting me for no apparent reason.

"Lee had a boyfriend before my brother. It could have been a jealous ex-boyfriend. Things could have gotten out of hand. I'm telling you, there are so many possibilities you're not looking at. You know how these small towns are. And you work for the police? You should know that for every crime, there is a witness. Someone here in Arcadia is hiding something and trying to cover up the tracks. And why would anyone kill my mother after so many years?"

"You have no clue what you're talking about!" she yells out as her emotions consume her.

"It was your daughter in the fire," I say again. "My brother is alive. This explains the three dead girls."

Dr. Franklin is fuming with anger and sadness. She is out of her chair and walking around the desk toward me. She gets right in front of me and slaps my face as hard as she can. She's upset, but now I can see the tears in her eyes. Her inner pain is much worse than a slap on the face ever will be.

"You're lying! Why would you say such a thing?" she screams out through her tears. "My daughter isn't dead!" she cries out then covers her face with her hands as she cries aloud. Just as I am feeling low enough in this very unstable situation, and now I have to deal with the pain of a mother's emotions. Covey is unfazed by the incident and is still holding me in place. Reality is escaping this woman, and I am thinking that if this woman's daughter is dead, then so is her drive for finding her and fighting crime. Maria Lennon is the reason Dr. Franklin became a law enforcement officer. She has nothing else to fight for because her dreams have become nightmares. There is no longer hope for this woman to find her little girl. There is no reason for her to climb deeper into the world of crime and violence because she will not find what she is looking for. All her dreams of finding her little girl are shattered. Everything that shimmers of gold is sure to someday fade, and that is what just happened. The doctor's hopes and dreams are fading. I just blew out her candle, and I just lost my key.

"I'm very sorry, but it is true. Your daughter and Rodney might as well be dead, but someone from here is trying to kill me. Just as my mom found me, this killer found me. Way back when I left Arcadia, the dentist's office was vandalized. Therefore, there were no dental records to identify the burned body. The coroner died that week also. Therefore, no autopsy was done on the body. It was the perfect crime until I disappeared," I try to explain to Dr. Franklin. "Someone planned that fire and walked away from a murder. Now that someone is after me."

"No such thing!" she cries out from the other side of her desk.

"I read the paper for the week of the fire. The *Desoto County Times*. No coroner, and the dentist's office was vandalized, so that ruined the dental records! All the clues are there, and now that someone is after me. Who else would kill people I know in Durham and kill my mother? When I was in Oviedo, nobody knew where I was. Then suddenly, killings linked to me start happening at Duke. I have to find the answers to my questions. All of them," I say as I lean forward and put my hands onto her knees to comfort her.

"You're a liar!" the sobbing doctor screams out at me as she slaps my hands away.

She then grabs my shirt and pulls on it, trying to yank me back and forth unsuccessfully. "You're a liar!" She sobs. "A liar!"

Covey is still unfazed by the situation and doesn't say or do anything. Dr. Franklin is crying uncontrollably, and I am afraid to put my hands on her because of Covey. I can only think that this is the end for her but only the beginning for me. The beginning of a long and fruitless journey into oblivion because if I find Rodney, Maria Lennon is surely dead. If I don't find Rodney, I'll be defending myself in murder trials for the rest of my natural life. And if Rodney is dead, Maria Lennon or someone from here is trying to kill me. I need to search out my fears and confront my past to defend my future.

I am not a person that runs and hides, even though I've done it before. I have to find the haunting presence that pursues me in North Carolina before it ruins my college career and my life as Raymond Douglas Beacon. The coaches at Duke will only put up with so much before the school gives me the boot. Sooner or later, the reputation of a prestigious university like Duke won't be able to hold back the press. I'll be on the news for murder, and my life will be over. Dawn may have lost her daughter, but I may lose my life. I've fought too hard to maintain myself at peak levels and will not bow to suddenly have it all taken away. I will fight to survive this nightmare, and I won't lose anything. I will only become stronger from the struggle. If I am wrong, then I am dead.

"Dawn," I say softly. "I need to find what I came for. This isn't over for me."

She doesn't look up or even acknowledge me, but she knows there are answers to many questions out there, and neither of us can do anything in the dimly lit office at the Desoto County Jail. I am going to have to go back to North Carolina. There the saga will continue. For now, we must both wait out the storm.

CHAPTER 7

It's Monday morning, September 2, about 6:00 a.m. I'm in my holding cell again, wide awake. The hurricane passed the sleeping town of Arcadia and is now somewhere to the north of Orlando, Florida, dissolving into yet another memory of a storm that once was. Here now is the aftermath of the storm in which you wake up the next day and evaluate the amount of damage done to the surroundings. Hurricane Abby stayed on the coast, but the winds and rain did some damage. Hopefully, you can see the damage, fix everything, and go on your way without it costing you too much time or money. That is how I feel about Dr. Franklin. Last night was a long night of revelation for both of us. To her, I am a murderer, liar, and the long-awaited key to a haunting past or distorted puzzle. To me, she is a lovely looking, insecure psychiatrist working for her dad with a chip on her shoulder. I need her badge to protect myself, and she needs my soul to redeem herself. It seems she and I are both looking for the same thing—that missing piece that haunts my future as well as her past. We are looking for a murderer, the one that can destroy us all.

I hear the electric door buzzer unlock the thick steel door in the distance. Someone is coming down the hallway; hopefully for me. I still think I'm the only person on the cellblock since I haven't heard any noise from the other cells or anyone calling out to me. I can barely hear the little footsteps coming down the concrete hallway toward my cell. I'm still sitting with my back against the far wall, facing the door. I look at the viewing window in the thick steel door and see nothing but the light of a new day. I no longer hear the little footsteps either.

Suddenly, a little face and yellow blond hair appear in the cell door window for a fraction of a second. I hear a woman's voice on the other side of the door. In a flash, the door unlocks and opens.

"Awake?" Dr. Franklin asks me from behind the door as she peeks in on me like a child hiding from the boogieman.

"What are you doing?" I ask her from my position on the floor.

"I'm taking you out to breakfast. It is breakfast time. You are hungry, right?" she asks me as she gets in front of the door and clearly into my view.

All the hallway lights are on and illuminating Dr. Dawn Franklin. Her facial features are clearly visible, and she is more beautiful than I thought. Her flowing blond hair, big blue eyes with little round cheeks, and cute dimples have transformed her into a delightful woman. Her smile is bright, and her lips are red and thin. I can't believe this is the same woman that I talked with last night in her dimly lit office. She has totally transformed herself into a nice subtle human being. Too bad she's so damn short, about forty and crazy!

"Am I hungry?" I ask myself as I get up from my position against the wall and floor. "Matter of fact, I am really hungry." I hear my stomach growl with emptiness.

"Here is your sweatshirt back," she says to me as she hands it to me.

I notice Dawn is in her best outfit. She looks very professional wearing a white buttoned shirt with no sleeves and a black skirt that stops just past her knees. She is wearing black nylons and the same black high heel shoes from last night. She looks like a woman trying to impress a man. And to think, here I am, tall and thin in a T-shirt, blue jeans, and white Nike sneakers. I could pass for her son if it weren't for my black hair.

"I was wondering if I would ever see my Duke sweatshirt again," I say as I unfold it and notice the drops of blood on the shirt are gone. "No evidence of criminal mischief here, I see." I toss the shirt on my shoulder.

"The Chief didn't want you to hang yourself with it. That's why they took it away from you," she says.

"Then why did they wash it?" I ask as we walk.

She ignores the comment and starts to walk down the corridor toward the electric door.

"Am I being charged with anything?" I had to ask as she walks away from me.

"Not yet," she says as she looks back slightly to see where I am. "You will sign out and be free to go. I just want to talk some more before you leave town."

"Great, getting to know me," I whisper under my breath.

"Two!" she yells out once we reach the big blue door at the other end of the hallway.

An electric buzzer sounds, and the door slides open. I am in the lobby of the jail. I hope this isn't a trick! I think I'm really free to go. No charges are being pressed.

"Where is my car, Doc?" I ask as I follow the petite doctor.

"It's out front in the parking lot. I took the liberty of searching it for evidence like drugs and firearms. But smart boys like you don't do stuff like that, do you?" she asks me as she walks forward to the receptionist. "Plus, you get drug tested at Duke, and you've been clean."

She walks me to the booking counter, and I collect the rest of my belongings. I sign for an envelope and quickly reach for my wallet to see if any money is missing. I see I have $300 in cash and my American Express card.

"All there?" she asks me with a smile as she leans against the counter besides me. "Since you're loaded, breakfast is your treat." And then she puts her arm around mine and leads me away from the counter. "Do you remember where the Paradise restaurant is?" she says as she puts her hand on my arm and pulls me toward her as we walk.

60

We then walk out of the Desoto County Jail toward my car, and Dawn is acting like nothing ever happened last night. I am really lost mentally and now more confused than ever. I think she's using reverse psychology. It seems like this woman is suddenly my new best friend. I think she is up to something, but in the meantime, I'm hungry. I just wish I knew what she was up to. I already know she doesn't trust me, so why be so friendly? She is a cop with an ulterior motive, and I am a pretty smart kid waiting for the other shoe to drop. Hopefully, the other shoe won't land on me.

I walk Dr. Franklin outside. My black Camaro convertible is parked in the handicap spot right in front of the jail with my windows and top down. I hop in and notice the keys are in the ignition.

"I can't believe you left my beauty wide open with the keys inside of it. People usually are killed for less, and don't you know there is a rash of car thefts going on right now?"

She stands outside the car, ignoring me. I start the engine and look over and no one is in the passenger seat. I see that I have been talking to the thin country air of Arcadia. I look up outside the window, and Dr. Franklin is just looking at me.

"Is there something wrong?" I say as I lean over as I look at her outside my car.

"Aren't you going to open the door for me?" she asks as she puts her hands on her hips and waits for my reaction.

"Of course, what was I thinking?" I say as I wonder where my manners went.

I reach over and pull on the door handle from inside the car and push the door open. Dawn looks at me with a disgusted smile and finally sits in the passenger seat.

"Thanks," she says as she pulls the door shut.

"Sorry about that," I say as I put the car in reverse and pull out of the parking lot.

I remember the Paradise restaurant is a quaint place on the outside of town only a mile or two from the jail. It's some mom-and-pop that never wanted to leave this town, but they always wanted to own their own Denny's type restaurant.

Dawn says nothing as we drive. I drive a block along the old wooden houses with tin roofs and rust stains on the siding. The empty fields filled with dead bushes beside congregations of barbed wire and fence posts on the street corners remind me of why I hate small towns. There are many old, empty, rundown buildings that stand only one story high, surrounded by nothingness. This side of town has an all-night laundromat surrounded by nothing but empty fields where trailer parks once stood or maybe an old drive-in movie theater.

As I come to the stoplight on Highway 17, we wait in silence. Neither of us have anything to say, and the drive to the diner is only about five minutes. At 6:15 a.m. in Arcadia, the two-lane roads are bare and filled only with the early morning light of the Florida sun.

"You and your brother were identical twins?" she asks.

"Yes, ma'am. My mother couldn't tell us apart most of the time, and our teachers could never tell us apart."

"Oh, really?" Dawn asks.

"Yeah, really. Since we had the same classes in school, he would study for one test. I would study for another, and after the test, we would just switch shirts, retake the same test as the other brother, and do better on it since we knew the answers."

"You never got caught?" she asks.

"Nope, not once. It was awesome since most of our tests were on Fridays. No stress having to study for multiple tests. Just one and done," I say with a smile as I drive.

"How did you disappear?" Dawn finally asks from the passenger side.

"That's a long story," I say as I drive onto Highway 17.

"We have all day," she replies with a fake smile and gleaming eyes.

"No," I say as I shake my head. "You have all day. I have things to do, and I still have to get back to Durham today. I have class on Tuesday and have to drive to Atlanta to pick up my roommate. That's if he is not dead too," I say jokingly as I glance at her with a smile.

"Enjoy your morning at least. Relax, have breakfast, and then start your day. So how did you disappear?" she asks again. "The whole story."

"Well, once my mom freaked out on me in front of the cops, I just started walking. Before I knew it, I was at the school. I went to my locker and got my wallet, and I happened to have my passport there also. I kept my passport for ID since I was too young to have a license. Then I went to Rodney's locker and took some of his stuff. I walked to this guy Jeff's house and told him I needed a ride to Port Charlotte. He drove me as far as the gas station on Kings Highway and I-75. There I met a trucker at the gas station going to Tampa. We drove along I-75, and I told him I was going to visit my brother in college. He dropped me off in Tampa, and I spent the summer wandering along Interstate 4 going from college to college," I say as we drove.

"What did you do for money?" Dawn asks from the passenger seat of my car.

"The morning I left, I went to the bank and emptied my bank account. Then I went to a different bank and emptied Rodney's accounts. I took three hundred dollars in cash each time and got a cashier's check for the rest. After my mom's episode at the house with the fireman, I went to school and got his ID out of his locker to be both him and I. We had a safety deposit box that we both shared. My plan was to take his passport, so now I had two forms of ID and both bank accounts. Once I decided I was going to stay at UCF, I got a new social security card and just cashed checks at different banks when I needed money," I say as we drive to the diner early in the morning.

"That easy, huh?" she asks.

"It was my money. I'm sure my mom did not care, and my dad didn't want me back. Instead I went from Tampa to Lakeland to Orlando to Daytona Beach. And then in August, I went back to Orlando. I mostly stayed at college dorms and some universities while sleeping on pool decks. I met girls here and there, so life wasn't too bad for short periods at a time. When I got bored, I would just pick up and go to the next college. I went to several college orientations that summer, stayed there for a week or two. I met some people, stayed with them for a while. I had money. I just didn't want to spend it. I would take clothes from people's houses or from laundromats. What a life!" I say to her as I drive onward through the sleepy little town of one-story stucco buildings.

"That doesn't explain how no one could find you once school started in Oviedo."

"No, I guess not," I say as I drive toward Paradise restaurant. "My girlfriend in Boston, Colleen, her mother was an administrative assistant for the county school board. So faking my freshman transcripts wasn't hard. I told Colleen my story, and Colleen's mom didn't want to see me be a failure. I told them I had a legal guardian and a new social security number now, and I didn't want my mom to find me. Colleen's mom made me a student from Somerville High School instead of Desoto County High. Everything worked out, and a man named Douglas Beacon became my new dad in Oviedo, Florida. Once everything was done, my transcripts looked as if I was never in Arcadia. I had my birth certificate, a passport, and ID while Doug and Amanda became my parents. Once I got a new social security card and had original high school transcripts from a school I never attended, it was easy," I say to her as I drive onward on Highway 17.

"It was that easy?" Dawn asks from the passenger seat.

"Kinda. I was a kid walking up highways with only a backpack and a basketball. It rains every day during the summer in Florida. I would sit under bridges or in restaurants for hours at a time, so I didn't get wet. Sometimes I would sleep all day because it would rain all night and all day. I had no home, no friends, and no help. I was fourteen. I spent my birthday alone, ridden with grief just a few months after my brother's death."

"You're a Gemini!" Dawn says. "June 2. Split personalities. I read your file, remember?" she asks me from the passenger seat.

"I couldn't turn back," I say to her with a smirk. "I hitchhiked from Tampa to Daytona Beach and then back to Orlando in a few months. It took me from March to August just to find a home. I got lucky to find someone to help me. Someone that would take me in, no questions asked. It was anything but easy," I reply harshly.

I look at her briefly and can tell she doesn't have a clue what I went through, nor does she care. Everyone has a sad story to tell, and this one is mine. Too bad, so sad, move on.

"How did you meet Mr. Beacon?" she asks with a smile.

"I went back to Orlando for college orientation at Central Florida. I was all for a free weekend of dorm parties and food. I would sometimes wonder if homeless people started out like this and just never stopped wandering. Then suddenly, all their money ran out and there were no more dorm parties or college orientations."

"I don't think that is what happens to homeless people," she says unbelievingly.

"Those days were the scariest of all since I didn't know if I would ever find a home. Luckily, I was safe in Orlando. I made some friends and met some people that loved basketball, and they had a car so I could get around. Then one day, my friends and I went to check out basketball courts. Within a mile of the college, there were four sets of basketball courts. The road that connected them all was Rouse Road. On that road was a little gray one-bedroom house that looked condemned. Right across the street was the University High School. I thought, what a perfect place to live. So I broke into the old house and claimed the empty little wooden two-room shack as mine. The house was a dump, but it had some furniture and running water. As long as no one saw me, I could live there with the roaches," I say with a chuckle.

"Did Mr. Beacon live there?" she asks.

I laugh as I shake my head ever so slightly.

"No, no one lived there, but a retired Mr. Clemmons lived next door with his wife and very beautiful daughter," I say with a smile as I remember their daughter, Connie.

"Did you fall in love with the girl next door?" she asks with some concern as she looks at me and awaits my answer.

"Yes, I did!" I say with a huge smile. "Her name was Connie, but her dad was the one who took me in and saved me from an undeserving life."

"How's that?" she asks.

"I would play basketball at the high school for hours every day, and Mr. Clemmons would watch me from his porch. He'd stay on that porch all day. He would just stay out there and read his paper. Then school started and I couldn't play in the schoolyard anymore. I had to play at the park down the road. All of a sudden, there was Mr. Clemmons at the park, looking at me awkwardly. After a day of watching me play basketball for eight hours at a time, he decided to talk to me. He called me over and said, 'Boy, don't you go to school?' I didn't know what to say. I just broke down. I really wanted to go to school. I wanted to be like the other kids. I really missed school. I didn't know what to do or say."

"So how did he help you?" she asks as the wind blows through her blond hair.

I can see the big sign for the Paradise restaurant ahead on the left of the highway. Breakfast sounds really good since I haven't had a real meal all week, and I've been breaking my strict basketball diet by eating Burger King Whoppers for two days. I would forget about all the low points in my life and focus on food for right now. I am a growing boy. I do need nourishment, lots of it, and a steak and eggs breakfast will definitely help right now. Steak is protein, and basketball players need lots of starch and protein.

"Hello? Anyone home?" Dawn asks.

I just smile as I go from my steak breakfast daze back to the reality of Desoto County.

"Well, I told Mr. Clemmons my story. Starting with my abusive mom, my father who turned his back on me, my dead brother, and the last three months wandering along Interstate 4. And all I wanted to do is go to school again, play basketball, go to college and have a shot at being someone. He told me he could help, and he made a call to Douglas Beacon. Mr. B lost his wife and only son a few years earlier in a car accident. Mr. Beacon was driving and was the only one to walk away from the accident alive. As for me, Mr. B, he agreed to take me in, and I enrolled at Oviedo High School. I literally became a new person, and that's how no one ever found me. If his name wasn't Douglas Beacon, and if Colleen's mom didn't love me, this would never have worked. I got lucky, really lucky. Really, really lucky!" I say.

I ended my story as we were pulling into the parking space in front of the big windows of the diner. The place has five pickup trucks in front of it, and there are a few people eating breakfast inside. I look at Dawn and realize that she is contemplating her next move. To her, I could still be a liar and a murderer, so I am sure she will look up everything in her computer when she gets back at the office.

"Do you think your brother could have done the same thing?" she asks as she steps out of the car.

"No, like I said, I got lucky. And anyone could be doing this to me. My picture was in the paper for winning the state championship. I was on ESPN. I was a high-profile player at a low-profile school," I reply. "Jealousy is my worst enemy."

"You're a legend in your own mind," she says to me as we walk toward the front doors of the diner.

I open the door for her like any gentleman should. She smirks as she walks by me and into Paradise.

"You're such a gentleman," she says sarcastically.

"I am," I say as I follow her.

"Then why did you kill those three girls in North Carolina?" she asks. "You're still a murderer to me!" she adds.

CHAPTER 8

THE ASTONISHMENT OF my situation almost chokes me as I walk into the restaurant. Amazement and uncertainty cloud my thoughts as I realize this woman is smarter than I was led to believe. I almost trip as I walk and catch myself with the door to the Paradise. The three dead girls, wow. I was questioned by police in all three cases, but my name was never mentioned as a suspect, and I was never mentioned by the media. I remember her briefly mentioning the three dead girls. I'm guessing a phone call to Durham police is all it takes when you work for the law in Arcadia.

I ignore her comment for a moment as we stand inside the Paradise, waiting to be seated.

"Hi!" an older woman with bleached blond hair says to us happily. "Just two?" she asks with her Florida accent.

Just two, as if we couldn't find anyone else to have breakfast with us at six a.m., I thought.

The hostess is an old woman who sits us at a booth by the window. The Paradise is almost empty, and our waitress is another older woman with a dark tan and gray hair who smiles as she talks and winks at me after we place our order.

As for the diner, the interior is all white with red vinyl seats. The tables have vinyl checkered red-and-white tablecloths. All the walls have large windows that go from the top of the booths to the ceiling. The windows line the restaurant from the door all the way around the entire restaurant until the kitchen. The trim inside the restaurant is an off white, and there are several ceiling fans throughout the dining room. The morning is moving slowly as the place is quiet with few patrons.

"The three dead girls are the reason I am here," I say finally from my spot on the red vinyl seat across the table from Dr. Franklin.

"Really?" she asks. "The deaths of these girls brought you back to Arcadia?"

"Yeah, to find out what really happened. Now things are much clearer, and I have an idea who is doing this to me," I say as we sit across from each other, waiting for our drinks to arrive.

"You know, now that your mom's dead, you're looking guiltier and guiltier by the second. And I don't think anyone will believe your theories," she says to me calmly.

"I know, but I believe in them," I say to her. "Does this conversation about my guilt have anything to do with me saying your daughter died in the fire? I would hate to think that you are doing all this just to be vindictive," I say to her as we wait for our waitress.

"This has nothing to do with that. You were looking guilty since your disappearance four years ago. All this is just more icing on the cake," she says as she tilts her head so slightly and smiles at me. "And isn't it funny that all these deaths are all revolving around you as the main suspect? Just like four years ago. You got to walk away from your problems back then, but you can't now."

I have nothing to say and just listen since an outside perspective is one thing I need right now. She might give me insight to what I'm missing in the grand scheme of things.

"Within four years, seven people have been murdered or gone missing, and every finger points at you. You knew all of them very closely. I am not saying you're guilty. That is not for me to decide. I am saying you look guilty! G-U-I-L-T-Y!" she spells out to me from across the table.

"Seven?" I ask. "I know of the three girls in North Carolina, your daughter, my brother, and my mom. That adds up to six. Who's number seven?"

"You didn't know your father in Boston died also?"

"What?" I ask in almost utter shock. "What?" I ask again.

I'm sure she can tell that her words are a devastating consequence to me. I'm sure the look of blinding terror tells her I didn't know. I haven't thought of Dad in years, never mind talk to him. I never had Facebook or any social media, especially since I didn't want to be found. When I left Arcadia, I left my entire life behind, and now I'm starting over. And now this!

"What is going on? How?" I ask.

"Murder suicide this past Christmas," she says. "Betty tied your father up during a sexual encounter then stabbed him to death. Betty's little girl heard the screams and called the police. By the time police got there, Betty was locked in the bathroom, slicing her wrist with a razor. She was high on ecstasy and cocaine. She just lost it one night."

"A pretty open and shut case," I reply.

"The story was easy to follow. A Christmas party that night, lots of alcohol, Betty on cocaine and ecstasy. There was sexual misconduct, and two murder weapons were found covered in blood—one in the bedroom and one in the bathroom. Betty's daughter is your stepsister. Your dad married Betty," Dawn added. "By the time the police got there, all they saw was the end of the bloody mess."

"I didn't know any of this," I say as I shake my head ever so slightly in disbelief.

"Betty's daughter inherited everything that was left over from the house, life insurance, and 401(k)," Dawn tells me as we wait in the diner.

"Great, another rags to riches story," I reply. "The stripper's daughter gets everything. How ironic!" I shake my head in disbelief.

"If you would have gone to Boston years ago, he might be alive today. You could have saved him from Betty," she comments.

"I did call my dad. I told you that Dad turned his back on me. Mom had custody, so he told me that life in Boston was over. Betty had her hooks in him. If I would have stayed in Boston, my mom would have called the police and got me back. She needed the money for child support. Since Betty was crazy, I might have died four years ago if I would have stayed there," I reply to her statement.

"You never know," Dawns adds.

"Once we left Boston, he didn't return my phone calls. We didn't get any cards in the mail. He never even returned my call when I told him Rodney was dead."

"I can't say I'm shocked to hear this. Out of sight and out of mind," she replies.

"And look how much fun we're having. I wonder if Betty's daughter is capable of all this?"

"I don't think so. She is only seven or eight years old now," Dawn replies. "Everything for her is being held in a trust fund."

My mind is racing, and I wonder who else I know will end up dead. Dawn just stares at me for a moment as if trying to look inside a machine and trying to figure out how it runs. No comments are made for the moment, and we both wonder what the game of cat and mouse will bring us next.

"So that's seven and eight?" I ask.

Dawn waves her finger at me as to say no. I realize our waitress is approaching the table.

Yolanda, our fifty-something-year-old waitress, brings us two glasses of water, an orange juice, and a coffee for Dawn. She smiles and walks away.

I get comfortable on the red vinyl seat and wait for the second coming of questions as I stretch out in the booth.

"My turn," Dawn says. "What happened to the three dead girls?" she asks as she takes a sip of her water.

I can tell she cares about this story the most. These stories are fresh, and the trail of blood leads right to me. As Dawn holds her white mug with both hands to enjoy her coffee, she sits upright to listen attentively.

"No," I say. "What happened to my mom?" I ask. "And where is she now? Then we can talk about the girls in Durham and Duke."

Dawn puts down her glass and hesitates before answering. I can tell she has a bit of trouble telling me about my mom's death.

"Your mom died last Tuesday night. We don't know exactly when she died, but she didn't report to work Wednesday or Thursday. Her or her boyfriend. They were both found dead at her boyfriend's house."

"How did she die?" I had to ask, trying to keep my voice low from the other side of the dining table.

"She was shot repeatedly with a twenty-two-caliber handgun at close range. A burglar maybe, since it was such a small gun. No fingerprints of anyone else found in the house. The police can't really find anything of value taken. The house was a mess, but that could just be how the boyfriend lived. He was shot repeatedly also."

I only raise my eyebrows in disbelief as I realize this person after my life is a psychopath on a killing spree.

"It was late, and the TV was on. Both were shot, and then their mouths were duct taped. They were both shot again after they were restrained. If the gunshots didn't kill them, they bled to death."

"Brutal," I reply as I sip my orange juice.

"We made a positive ID on them Thursday morning. Then, of course, here you are." She raises her hands slightly into the air to show disbelief in my innocence.

"I can't believe my mom and dad were both murdered," I say.

Now that I know all this, I look more and more guilty. I could be convicted right now on probable cause. I have to fight the horrifying memories that consume my thoughts. Neither of my parents were the best, but I still loved them both. The shock of such brutal murders chills my soul. I swallow my juice and take a deep breath to calm the images of my murdered parents.

"I just can't believe after so many years of emptiness, they are both dead."

"What about those girls?" she asks again, more demandingly.

"We should talk about them after we eat. I wouldn't want to ruin your appetite," I say as I look around for my breakfast. "You can wait until we are done eating, can't you?"

After that, our food came right out—two medium T-bone steaks with scrambled eggs, hash browns, and an English muffin. It's as good as it gets here in Arcadia, and I don't have to worry about going to practice afterward. No Coach yelling at us to go faster or do better. No Duke University worries for the time being. I know I should be worried since I have everything to lose if things don't go well here in Arcadia. Matter of fact, I would lose everything, including my own life. That is what scares me the most.

Dawn unfolds her napkin and places it on her lap. She picks up her utensils and slides a small portion of the scrambled eggs onto her fork. She then looks at me before she takes a bite.

"Anything wrong?" I ask as she stares at me from across the checked tablecloth.

"Are you going to say grace? You know, the prayer before a meal?"

"I didn't plan on it," I say. "But for you I will."

I say a short and sweet grace followed by Amen and start eating. Since I'm eating with a lovely lady, I should eat like a gentleman and actually chew my food. I think that will impress her somehow. I guess I'm on my best behavior. I feel like I am anyway. I hope all this isn't some scam and after breakfast I go back to the lockdown in the Desoto County Jail. That kind of worries me since my fate is in her hands until I get out of this town.

Yolanda comes by and takes our plates away after we finish eating. Dawn orders another coffee, and I get another glass of orange juice. The uncomfortable silence of an almost empty restaurant chills my soul. We are entering an uncomfortable subject, one in which I can't avoid. One in which she, Dawn, knows of—the three dead girls of North Carolina.

"The three dead girls, huh," I say to Dawn as I think to how this dilemma of mine recently began.

I notice she is as acute with attention as when I begin to tell the other stories.

"Tell me what happened to each of them and why everyone blames you for their deaths. Tell me what happened up there."

I kick back and immediately feel sick as I think about the dead girls in North Carolina. Memories jumble through my mind as flashes of the people I once knew now cease to exist.

"I got to school in late June right after my birthday and started a workout program since I play college ball. I took two summer classes just to stay ahead. I was getting to know people and took weekends off to see the Raleigh Durham area," I say as Yolanda passes by to check on us.

"Did you meet these girls at the parties?" Dawn asks from her corner of the booth."

"Only one of the girls I met outside of school. The first girl that the police questioned me about was Kate Rush. She was a second-year student at a community college in Greensboro. I met her through a friend at Duke. After her sophomore year, she planned on attending Duke because they have a better Business program. Kate went to a school close to home to save money during her first two years of college."

"What happened between you two?" the doctor asks.

"We talked a lot and texted when we first met. We had a lot in common because we were both originally from New England. We saw each other a few times, and I used the excuse that I needed help studying to spend time with her. Plus, she liked the fact that I have a scholarship, a convertible, and played ball. She drove her parents' car, didn't have a scholarship, and had to work hard for extra money while living at home. I understood how hard she was trying to get ahead, and I liked that in her. But like I said, we only saw each other a few times since we were both busy all the time, and we did go to two different schools."

"So what happened?" Dawn asks before taking another sip of her coffee.

"The last weekend in June was the last time I saw her. We hung out that night, and when she went home, she disappeared. We took separate cars out to a party and met in Burlington. We drank for a while and mingled, then made our way downtown. Kate and I always had fun when we went out, but the distance was a problem. She decided we should just be good friends until she got to Duke.

That last night together was the night she died. I left her at two in the morning, and we drove separate cars home. I got home about a quarter till three. The next day, I didn't hear from her, and then the police questioned me two days after her death."

"What did they say?" she asks as she leans forward onto the brim of the table.

"I told them everything, and my story checked out. A few things saved me, like the university using security cameras in the parking lots, and I arrived at the dorms alone. The other thing was when she got gas for her car. She paid for it inside the store with the cashier. She used her bankcard and signed the receipt. The attendant at the gas station said the girl was alone. That was about two thirty in the morning in Greensboro. Nothing from the videotapes turned up any foul play."

"Why were you not a suspect?" she asks.

"Here at Duke, you have to use your University card to get into the dorms. I used my card at two forty-five a.m., which proved I was about forty miles away when she disappeared. The police have her car with her blood in it. They have no body, no leads, and no reason why anyone would kill such a nice girl so brutally."

"Brutally?" Dawn asks.

"Yes. The knife that killed her went through her into the seat. She was stabbed repeatedly, or an artery was severed because there was a lot of blood left in the car."

"Did the police take you in?" she asks.

"No, but I gave them free reign of my car, dorm, and whatever else they wanted. I had nothing to hide, and my car stayed in the lot all night. My roommate said I was home and never left until the next day."

"What did she look like?" Dawn asks curiously.

"Pretty. She was a very pretty girl. Petite, with brunette hair and dark skin," I say as I think back to the physical features of the late Kate Rush. "She was five four with shoulder-length glossy brown hair, nice smile, and puppy dog brown eyes. She was a nice girl, but not as pretty as you," I say as I reach for my orange juice and wink at Dawn.

"You're not funny," Dawn says as she sips her coffee.

"I wasn't trying to be," I say as I take another sip of orange juice. "I hear coffee stunts your growth also. Maybe you should drink more OJ and you'll grow tall like me."

"Ouch!" she says. "Aren't you a charmer? Please stop. No more compliments."

I just smile slightly and shake my head before continuing with my story.

"That's all I could tell you about her."

"So Kate is only the first girl, and the police never found the body. What about the other murders?" she asks as we both get right back into the game of unsolved mysteries and murders.

The sunshine from the outside of Paradise is warm and glowing with radiance. The restaurant is across from a cow field filled with emptiness and a few palmetto bushes. The restaurant runs alongside some of these very little gray-colored two-room apartments grouped together with the name Desoto Motel out front. This part of Florida is almost like the land that time forgot. There are no big buildings here, no traffic, no sidewalks, and lots of sand and tiny lizards. I almost forget that places like this exist in the civilized world. Places like Arcadia are where people come to forget about big city life and kick back with country living. Grits and cornbread live here, farmers with tractors, people pick oranges in fields for a living, and almost everyone raise families along with their cattle. I look across the street to the field and wonder how many secrets are buried in that field or in this town.

"What about the second girl?" Dr. Franklin asks.

"The second girl was Jenny Schavio. She was a freak!" I say as I think back to Jenny. "When she was found dead in July, they questioned more people than just me. She was a partier. She was in her twenties and was a talker. She thought I was cute. Always told me how handsome I was. She was always drunk and did lots of drugs to forget about life as we know it. She always had a party to go to, always had to be the life of the party, and she always needed attention. From what I heard, more men went down on her than the Titanic. A real insecure basket case she was. She wasn't even in school. She just liked going to the parties at Duke," I say to Dawn while trying to keep our conversation just between us as I speak softly about the murders.

"What made her a freak or psycho?" Dawn asks as she looks at me through her gold-rimmed glasses.

"She always had some sob story about herself. Always wanted to get drunk and would talk to anyone who would listen. And she lied so much that her reality was an illusion. Not that it mattered to me. I was just one of many. E pluribus unum, if you know what I mean."

"You got yours, huh?" she says with some curiosity as to find out about my behaviors.

"I was just one in the crowd, I'm sure," I say with no regret. "I just happened to be at some of the frat parties that she went to for about two weeks. Total coincidence, and I was attracted to her. Then she started telling other girls we were boyfriend and girlfriend. Jen told people that we grew up together in Boston. Then one night, about three weeks ago, I didn't show up at a party my friends had at their apartment. She got really drunk and told some of my friends that she and I had a fight and broke up. My friends knew she was crazy, so they laughed it off and told her to go home. She ended up leaving the party totally drunk, and the next day she was dead," I say.

"Why did they call you?" Dawn asks as she takes another sip of her coffee.

"People heard her story of us breaking up, and the police questioned me. I had a computer project due in my economics class. I put it off and talked with other people about it, and finally my economics partner and I tackled it on Saturday. I had to do it in the computer lab, so again I used my University card to get in the building, and I logged on with my ID to use the computer. My partner and I both had some problems with the terminology. So at about nine p.m., we checked out some books from the library to help. I went back to the computer lab at ten p.m. and was there until almost three a.m. After that, I went to Denny's because we hang out there on the weekends. I stayed there with some friends until four, paid for dinner with my debit card, and then went home. I used my card again to get into my building a little after four a.m., and my roommate said I was there when he got up at seven a.m. There is no record of anyone leaving the building before seven a.m. I was with people all day and all night. Plus there are cameras in the computer lab and the library. Total rock-solid alibi," I say to her. "My car never moved, and I was on campus with friends all day."

"How did she die?" Dawn asks from the other side of the table.

"The papers said it was a drug overdose. I don't think that was the truth since she was drunk when she left the party. That night, someone took her keys away from her because she wasn't sober enough to drive. Then the next morning, she was found in an apartment parking lot. Who does drugs in a parking lot and leave a dead girl behind and then not even try to hide her?" I say as I shake my head ever so slightly.

"Do you feel remorse for her?" Dawn asks.

"I don't know. At the time this happened, I was distancing myself from her. I'm disgusted by the horror of the situation. I can't believe this happened to her, but a drug overdose didn't surprise anyone."

"What did she look like?" Dr. Franklin asks.

"She was tall, thin, and pretty with blond hair. She looked anorexic at times, but all in all she was pretty and a really sweet girl," I reply.

"Tall and thin? How tall? How thin?" Dawn asks.

"Tall like five ten. Thin as 135 pounds. Nice ass but flat chest, with straight blonde hair that stopped at her shoulders. Is that good enough?" I ask.

"What were you thinking then about the murders?"

"I thought that the first time was a random act of violence. A dead girl is a part of life. A sad but true fact of life. The second girl died and I thought, what a coincidence. Two girls I knew were dead just one month apart from each other. A scary fact that just proves you must live life to the fullest every day. I know it is such a cliché, but it's a true one. Luckily, I was cleared from both deaths, and I never heard from the police after that," I say to her.

"Until Monday," she says with consequence. "This past Monday? This is girl number three, and just this week?"

"Yeah. Heather Collinsworth," I reply to Dawn with remorse. I feel guilty because her death leads directly to me.

Heather's murder is a reoccurring nightmare—one that lives vividly in my mind. Everything going on around Dawn and I seems to disappear in the comfort of the empty Paradise restaurant. I sit up and need to speak clearly and softly to Dawn because I don't want anyone else to hear about the horror. In this murder case, all fingers are pointing at me as I look at my glass and reflect on the most recent murder. Heather Collinsworth is the real connection between the murder and me. I look at Dawn and begin my sad story.

"I went to open gym at the University of North Carolina in Chapel Hill one night at the end of July. I wanted to see how some of the North Carolina players play. Jeff, my roommate, and I went there to spy basically. Coach knew nothing of the incident, but he knew we were leaving Durham to go play ball somewhere for a night," I say to her.

"How did you meet Heather?" she asks with full interest as she looks at me.

"Jeff and I played a few games at UNC and then decided to sit out a few games. No one knew who Jeff was because he's a transfer, and no one really knows me since I'm red-shirted. We sat in the stands a while until some of the UNC players took over the court. I sat next to Heather, and we talked for about an hour or so. When some other UNC players showed up, Jeff and I jumped on the team against them. Our team won that game and the next. Other players found out we were from Duke and talked a lot of trash to us. We wore out our welcome quick. Jeff and I decided to get out of there," I say to her.

"Is that how you and Heather started off?" Dawn asks.

"Since Heather went to UNC, she took Jeff and me around campus, and we just hit it off immediately. I told her about Duke and who Jeff and I were. She joked about conspiring with the enemy. We had a great time and decided to go out the next night. Heather and I texted a lot and hung out a few times. That was two weekends ago. Then last Monday, the police came and got me in my dorm room. The police questioned the hell out of me in front of Coach and the Dean. They told me Heather was dead and I was to blame. I pleaded my case that I was innocent, and I don't think anyone believed me," I say to her sadly as I relive the police interrogation vividly in my head.

"So what happened?" she asks.

"I had an alibi. I didn't see Heather on Saturday or Sunday because the fall term started on Monday. People said they saw her with me that night, and she lived in an apartment alone with no security cameras. The police showed me pictures of her mutilated body. Someone had beheaded her. She was found wearing only a Duke basketball jersey with my number on it," I say to Dawn with wide eyes. "Her head is still missing."

"No way!" she says in astonishment.

"Yep, still missing," I say.

"What was your alibi?" she asks as we sit inside the diner.

"I got an oil change Sunday, and they wrote down the mileage of the car. I didn't have the distance in mileage to go to Chapel Hill, never mind make it back. After I got my oil changed, I came right home. I didn't use my car again all day. I spent the day with friends, making copies of tests and notes from last semester's classes that I'm taking this semester. I was in the library for hours from six p.m. until ten p.m. Then we went to Denny's and were there until after midnight. After that, I went home with my roommate and slept while he talked to his girlfriend in Atlanta. He hung up at two a.m., and the police came to the school at six a.m. The crime couldn't have been committed between the time Jeff went to bed and the time the police came knocking on my door. Heather was last seen that afternoon, and she was found dead in her room when her friends came over that night. Heather was dead only about an hour before they found her," I added. "And no DNA was found in the room. Nothing, not even a strand of hair. The room was evidently cleaned thoroughly by the killer. Plus, there was no blood in the room. None in the tub, no blood anywhere."

"How did the murderer decapitate someone and leave no blood behind?"

"The way it was explained to me was that they were in the shower, and the killer probably choked her. Then used a syringe and tube to drain her blood out of her body. The killer took her blood and poured down the drain with a long tube. After that, Heather was decapitated, and her body was placed in her own bed. The killer kept the head as a souvenir."

"You're in very real danger, and again you had a rock-solid alibi," Dawn says as she takes her last sips of coffee.

"Her death opened everyone's eyes, including mine. I knew for sure by then that someone was out to kill me. Her death led directly to my door. Someone was trying to frame me for murder, and I know I'm next. The killer is going to come after me, and he made sure that I knew that. He is setting me up for the ultimate demise. My own!" I say to Dawn.

The restaurant is filled with the light of morning; it's almost 8:00 a.m. Dawn and I have been in the Paradise diner for two hours. I wave the waitress down and ask for our check. She drops it off and quickly goes to the cash register to attend to other patrons. I take forty dollars out of my wallet and leave it on the table with the check. I watch Dawn, and she looks up at me from her red bench seat.

"So what can I do now?" I ask her. "You're the doctor. Can you help me?"

"Only if you take me with you to Durham," Dr. Franklin tells me.

CHAPTER 9

WE WALK OUT of the air-conditioned Paradise restaurant and into the blinding sunshine and heavy humidity of Florida's new day. I haven't said a word to her because I really don't know what to say. I am still thinking about what she could possibly prove by going back to Durham with me. And what would I tell my friends? Where would she stay, and what would she do in Durham? She would need a University card to get in and out of the dorms or into any of the buildings at night. I would have to tell Coach that I suddenly have a bodyguard. People would know that I'm in some sort of trouble, and that would mean bad press for the school. In the midst of all my thoughts, I notice I'm in front of my Camaro, following Dawn to the passenger side door. I take out my keys, hit the unlock button on my key chain, and open the door for her.

"What are you thinking about?" she asks as she stands by my car door.

I just shake my head ever so slightly and say, "Nothing really."

I shut my car door after she sits inside the shiny black Camaro. As usual, my mind is traveling at a million miles an hour, foregoing the thoughts of how she could possibly help me without intimidating or interrogating everyone I know in North Carolina. I walk around to the driver's side door and get into my car. I might like her to come to Durham because she is the only person besides Jeff and I who knows what is going on. I wouldn't have to take care of her, but I am sure she would be in my way, and people would ask questions about her. Then if anyone linked the murders to me, my scholarship and basketball career would be ruined.

Thus far, the school has not had any bad publicity for the murders, and the press hasn't linked me publicly to the three girls. The cases are considered three separate incidents in three different cities within North Carolina. If people start asking questions, this could get out of hand. I would go straight to jail. The public would want to lynch me, and people would think I'm a serial killer. My life would be over in a flash. I am in enough trouble as it is! I can't handle my basketball career and my college life being over before it gets started.

"I don't know what bothers you about me coming to North Carolina," she says to me. "You seem deep in thought over the notion."

"I don't know either," I reply as I start my car. "I could use someone watching my back, but what if the news got out that my mother was murdered just days ago? In North Carolina, none of this has happened. I mean, no past life, no murdered mom and dad. Duke has worked very hard to avoid all the bad press," I say this as I pull out of our parking space and away from the diner. "They have already pulled a lot of strings to avoid some very bad press."

I am in such a daze; I don't even know where I am driving. I just head back to the county jail since Dawn's car is there.

"Don't worry. I have heavyweights working on my side, and all of our answers lie within you," she says. "Someone is following you around, and sooner or later, that someone is going to kill you. You need my help. Things will only get worse if you just sit back and wait for your problems to be solved," she says to me as I drive.

"I don't know what to do with you once I get to Durham. People won't believe you're my friend dropping in for a visit. You couldn't pass for my mom since you are short and blond," I say. "I am worried about what people will think. How will we handle all the questions? I have a reputation to protect as a scholarship athlete," I say to her.

"You're a legend in your own mind, aren't you?" she asks.

"I do well for myself," I say with a half smirk. "I still don't know what to say. I have to take you to the police station in Durham so they can check you out and let them know you're helping me. I'll have to tell the school about my mom being murdered and your involvement. Sooner or later, the press will tell an untrue story about the murders, and the community will want to kill me. Don't you think that's bad?" I ask with much concern.

"I'm here to help. I already called a lawyer in Durham to help with any bad press. We're both looking for the same things, remember? Answers! If you have nothing to hide, you won't mind me snooping around Duke for a few days."

"Can you get time off so quickly?" I ask as I drive back toward the prison.

"Arcadia is such a small town. I am sure no one will miss me if I leave for a few days. I'm due for a vacation, anyway," she replies.

I drive toward the Desoto County Jail with Dr. Franklin by my side. I wonder if this woman can really help me. I don't think she is much of a therapist, and I hardly have any faith in her counseling abilities at all. She is an emotional train wreck for a policewoman turned shrink. She doesn't trust me, and she doesn't look like much of a fighter. How would someone so little disarm a robber, never mind a serial killer? She would get her ass kicked. That's just my opinion though. She might surprise me and even solve this case.

"What's going to happen to my mom? Is there a funeral? I don't just want to go and leave loose ends lying around," I say to Dawn as we drive through the small and desolate shell of a cow town.

"Your mom was found days ago. Today is Sunday. Your mom's been dead since Tuesday night or Wednesday. She will be cremated since she has no family or surviving relatives. Your father and her are divorced, and your mom was an only child. Your grandparents passed away a long time ago, so I don't think anyone is going to claim the body. If your mom has any blood relatives that are alive, the ashes will be sent to them. The autopsy was done Friday, and police will keep her body until Tuesday. What will happen to the house is questionable, since her son is technically dead. An auditor will probably handle the estate and hopefully she had a will."

"Thanks for taking care of things for me," I say to her sarcastically as I turn off 17 and onto Cypress Street, the road the jail is on.

"What?" she asks as she glares at me from the passenger seat.

"I was hoping to see my mom again, that's all," I say disappointingly. "I lost my mother twice in the same lifetime, and even though I didn't know her, it's still sad every time I think about her being dead. I never said goodbye, and now I never will," I say.

"Turn here," she says and points to the road before the jail. "I'm here in the back behind the jail."

I turn down the street, and the only car behind the county jail is a Toyota Prius. The gray color is faded, and the driver's side window is down. The car looks dull next to my black Camaro. The four-door Toyota hybrid car doesn't seem like a car for a doctor.

"Your car?" I ask as I look at her awkwardly. "You care about the environment also?"

"Pull up next to it," she says as she undoes her seat belt and sits in the car seat quietly as I park the car and turn off the ignition.

"I plan to stay in North Carolina for a week or two," she says to me as she sits and looks down at her hands. "I can't promise anything. I'm going to find my daughter and find who is doing this. You look guilty as sin, but locking you up right now will do me no good. I need to know for sure whether my daughter is out there or not."

"Okay," I reply as I give her a crooked look and wink at her. "Guilty as sin, huh?"

"Yeah!" she says as she looks back as me. "But I still don't know who died in that fire. I don't know who your mother cremated. I still don't know where my daughter is, and I can't prove if you're Ray or Rodney Beacon. I also carry a gun and won't hesitate to shoot you if you try to harm me. I am going to Durham to look for answers. I am not going up there blind," she says to me with a harsh voice and a smirk.

"I understand. I really do," I say as I look into her eyes.

"I'm sure you have some things to do here in Arcadia before you go back to school. We can meet back here in a few hours. Let's say 10:00 a.m. I have to make some phone calls. After that, we can go hunt for a killer. Meet you back here at ten," she says.

"All righty then," I reply to her as the words *hunt for a killer* register in my mind.

She gets out of the car and walks to hers. She pops in and drives away. It won't be 10:00 a.m. for two more hours. I pull out of the parking space and drive toward my mom's house. Since I still have the key, I know what I have to do. And suddenly, in seconds, I am back in the driveway where I was before. My mom's house is not haunted by the memory of the fire anymore. I look at the house from inside my car and only see a house—just one empty house. The copies that I printed are still inside, and I need to use the phone anyway.

I step out of the car, and time stands still for me. I don't remember opening the door, but suddenly I'm in the house. I look around for a picture of my mom that I can take with me back to school. I don't have time to look for a nice picture. Any one will do. I will make my own changes to it with my scanner and computer. My college degree will be in advertising since the NBA is a dream far from coming true. My backup plan is computer graphics and Avid editing. When it comes to Macs, there's hardly anything I can't do. Therefore, any picture of my mother will do, and I can add myself in later or cut anyone out of it if necessary.

I walk to the back bedroom where the office is and retrieve the papers that I printed out yesterday. The answers to how my brother could still possibly be alive are all here in these headlines. I just haven't put the pieces together yet to figure it out.

I see the car accident involving the coroner. The caption explains how a doctor died with his entire family in the wreck. That explains why no autopsy was ever done on my brother. No coroner. Since the fire happened on Friday, going into the weekend, the state wouldn't have done an autopsy until Monday or until the city hired another doctor. That's the problem with small country towns—no sense of urgency. The mayor is also the judge and doubles as a mailman to save the town money. Just kidding.

The police would never have known whether it was a boy or a girl in the fire without an autopsy. The body was burned to the bone and then crushed by the collapsed ceiling. A coroner would have to have put the body pieces back together. Since there was none, the crime scene investigators here would have had done the job. Since the dentist office was vandalized and burglarized, that explains how the dental records could have been confused or never found. I watch a lot of *CSI* and police movies. I can put things together from the TV shows I watched. I could probably get away with murder from all the shows I've watched and things I remembered.

I come back into focus on the computer. The third page has a picture of Lee and me. The caption reads, "Raymond Beacon and Maria Lennon Disappear." In this newspaper, everybody dies if they are not found. There was a search for seven days headed by Dawn Lennon and her husband. Needless to say, we were never found. Imagine that. The other option is that Maria Lennon, Rodney Beacon, and Elvis Presley could all be alive and living in North Carolina, just like me.

Rrrring, rrrrring! My mother's office phone rings.

My mom has always been old-school, so it's no surprise she has a landline house phone. The first thing I look for is an answering machine or caller ID. I see neither, and the phone just keeps ringing. I lean over and shut the ringer off. I don't want to be disturbed right now. I can hear the phone in the bedroom still ringing. My mom probably kept the phone line for the fax machine. Again, she is old-school. She has a cell phone but always liked the home phone.

I get up and walk into my mom's bedroom to shut the ringer off. The entire time, the phone is still ringing, on its fifth ring, now sixth ring. Persistent person is what I am thinking. Then I notice the caller ID on the back of the cordless phone. I shut off the ringer and glance at the ID screen. I almost go into complete shock when I see the name flashing on the box. The name on the small screen is mine, Raymond Beacon. The number is my dorm phone, 919 555-7001. How can that be? Nobody at Duke has my mom's number, and I make all my calls with my cell phone. Jeff, my roommate, is in Atlanta, visiting his girlfriend. I know this for a fact. I dropped him off there on the way to Arcadia. Who could be calling here from my dorm room?

"Hello?" I say hesitantly as I pick up the phone. A dial tone is all I hear. The person has already hung up. Someone is playing a bad trick on me. But who? And why? More importantly, why now? I put the phone down and erase the phone number from the caller ID.

I shrug it off as I hang up and go back to the living room. I sit down on the couch, grab the remote, and click the TV on. I surf through the channels until I see CNN. I want to see what I missed over the last day or two. I like to keep up on current events and news, especially since I've been so much a part of the news and current events. I push the mute button on the remote and pull out my cell phone. I call Jeff in Atlanta to inform him I'm coming to get him with Dr. Dawn Franklin as my copilot.

Jeff Christian is my one true friend and roommate. We are both first year students at Duke and scholarship athletes. But unlike me, Jeff gets to play in basketball games this upcoming year. I got red-shirted and get to watch and learn for a year. Jeff already paid his rookie dues at Kennesaw State University in Atlanta. He played basketball there for two years and earned a reputation of being a good player. He was accepted to Duke years ago but wanted to stay near home for his first few years to save money. Plus, his girlfriend is in her second year at Georgia Tech, and being close to her made sense. Since Jeff transferred, he had to sit out one year, but it worked out for him. Coach accepted a transfer only because Jeff works so hard.

As for his relationship with Livia, Duke and Georgia Tech are Atlantic Coast Conference schools. They get to see each other every time the schools play each other. Plus, Durham is only about a five-hour very scenic drive away from Atlanta.

Jeff is a computer science major, and we both grew up in big cities. He's from the outskirts of Atlanta, and I'm from Boston. We met at basketball camp here at Duke last year. We hung out over the summer and ended up being roommates. Now we are best friends. We have a lot in common and usually sit in our room for hours, talking about everything. Unfortunately, I never told him that I was a runaway with a fake identity. He might not take that too well.

I dial the number, and the phone is picked up one the first ring.

"Hello?" I say.

"Hi, Ray. This is Livia. Jeff's told me all about you. When are you coming to get him?" a sweet voice asks.

"I'll be there later this evening. Can I speak to him?" I ask.

"Sure." Then I hear Jeff get on the phone.

"Hey, bud. How are you doing?" Jeff asks.

"Great! How about you?"

"Good," he says. "What did you find out on your journey?"

"Well, let me tell you. From the beginning."

I tell Jeff everything that happened this weekend from the deputies, to my mom and dad, up to Dawn joining us for a week or so. I gave him all the facts in a brief synopsis. He's all for Dr. Franklin helping me out since she works for the police. Jeff would hate to see me go to jail, especially since he doesn't have a car and I'm his only form of transportation.

After a thirty-minute conversation, I tell him I'll be in Atlanta about six tonight. Since Georgia Tech is right along Interstate 75, it won't be out of our way to pick him up. From Interstate 75, you would catch Interstate 85 right outside Atlanta and take the interstate all the way to Durham and Duke. All I have to do is stay alive until ten and then I pick up Dawn. From there, I just have to fight the eight hours of traffic to Atlanta, Georgia. Jeff can drive the rest of the way to Durham. All I have to do is not get myself killed before leaving Arcadia and I'll be fine.

Just be careful and don't get killed. That is today's goal.

CHAPTER 10

THE HOT FLORIDA sun is blistering down on the little tumbleweed town of Arcadia, Florida. The streets are still bare with people and traffic. With the heat and humidity, the world is silent, and not even birds are chirping in this small town. I decide to leave my mother's house for the last time ever. I step outside the house, lock the door, and literally throw away the key. I know I'll never return to Arcadia again. The little cinder block house that bakes under the Florida sun no longer belongs to my family. I walk backward from the house and take one last look at the haunting two-bedroom palace covered in bay windows. The September sun glitters on the peach-colored home, and there are no trees around the structure to shade the house from the elements. I feel like I am leaving the home of Alistair Crowley. There is a great omniscient feeling of exuberance as I turn and walk toward my glistening black convertible. Only one question reappears in my mind. Where do we go from here now that everyone is gone?

I shake the feelings of despair from my heart. My life in Arcadia is over, and I have no ties to this town anymore, or ever again. I don't ever plan on returning to the sand-infested, dissolute, one-road town, and I'm sure Dr. Franklin will fly back. I get into my car and back out of the driveway onto East Cypress Street. I push my foot down on the gas pedal and drive away from the house as I head toward the county jail to pick up Dr. Franklin.

When my dad and teachers told me that life was a journey, I never thought of that journey in the literal sense. As for now, my journey began in Boston, took me here, and now leads me through two more states to North Carolina. As I drive away from my never ever happy home, I can only wonder where else this journey will take me. I realize I have already been to Heaven and Hell. I must figure out what haunts me and do whatever it takes to keep sane while keeping my reputation and life intact.

Reality emerges as I drive past the little one-story houses that sit along the side of empty fields that make up this town. My Camaro pauses briefly for the stop sign at the end of the street. To the left is a grocery store and what everyone calls Uptown Arcadia. Uptown consists of one grocery store, a Walmart, and a two theater complexes across from a McDonald's in the unpopulated part of Arcadia. How sad! Nothing like Uptown Manhattan in New York or Uptown in Boston where worlds collide into a mixture of passion, amusement, history, and parties engulfed in different cultures with hundreds of people looking for a night on the town or fame in the daylight of the great city. All that in other cities and nothing here, in what we call Uptown Arcadia.

To my right, I see the two-car garage of a firehouse. Small and quaint, but it does the job, unless two houses are on fire at once. What would they do, flip a coin? Maybe they just pray for lots of rain, which would explain why so many people here believe in organized religion and have sprinklers. As I pull away from the stop sign and drive to the county jail, a sudden feeling of relief overwhelms me. I'm so glad I don't live here. Some people like this town, and I'm sure Arcadia is a cowboy's dream come true.

Durham, North Carolina, and Duke are my home. I'm a smart kid, and I can handle all this. Right now, it's an all-or-nothing game, playing chess with a murderer who is trying to make my permanent address a state penitentiary. That is not the way I want to be remembered. For me, the worst years of my life are behind me, and I am looking forward to the future. My future starts now and starts over again every day. I just have to ask the right questions and prove my innocence.

Within seconds, I pull into the Desoto County Jail, and Dawn is already waiting for me. She is sitting in her Prius, talking into a cell phone. She sees me pull into the space next to her, and she ends her call. She gets out of her car, and she looks stunning. Black high heels, of course, to match her black skirt that stops just short of her knees. Her black nylons give her legs more shape as she moves away from her car. Her white button-up blouse has no sleeves and is buttoned all the way up to her chin. A thin gold rope chain lays on the outside of her blouse with a gold cross charm hanging on it. Her blond hair flows around her face to her shoulders. Her blue eyes with her gold-rimmed reading glasses add extra emphasis to the beauty of her attractive facial features. She is much prettier than her daughter was. I just watch her for a moment and wonder what this police psychologist can do for me in Durham.

She opens her trunk and stands there for a moment. I am watching her as I realize I'm supposed to get out of my car and get her bags for her. I put the gearshift of my car into park and slowly arrive to her aid.

"It's about time! Where are your manners? Is chivalry dead where you are from?" she says to me as I approach her.

"No, ma'am. I was playing with the radio," I reply. "You look nice," I comment to her.

"Thank you," she says as she gestures toward her bags in the trunk.

Only two large Samsonite suitcases. Both are black, and thank God they have wheels on them because these things are heavy. I have to use all my strength to pull each of them out of the small trunk of the gray Toyota. I try to use one hand on each, and hopefully and I won't get a hernia.

"Only two?" I say jokingly as I strain to carry them both.

"There is a duffel bag in the car," she says as she opens the door of her car and pulls out a long red duffel bag.

I load everything into my car's spacious trunk. The great thing about a Chevy is it has a huge trunk. Her two suitcases, duffel bag, and my backpack of clothes all fit snugly into the Camaro's trunk. I then open the passenger door for Dawn, as a gentleman should, and we go on our way to Atlanta to pick up my roommate Jeff.

"Did you bring a jacket?" I ask as I get in. "It's September, and it gets cool in Durham at night. Gets down to fifty degrees."

"Really? This early in the year?" she asks surprisingly as she watches me.

"Yeah, Durham is in the northern part of the state, real close to Virginia," I say as I drive out of town toward Kings Highway. "But don't worry. I'll keep you warm," I say to her as I glance at her way with a smile.

"I am sure the Holiday Inn has heat. I have already made reservations, and I'll rent a car. So don't worry about me!" she says harshly as she stares at me for a moment, waiting for my comment.

"Calm down!" I say to her. "Don't forget, I'm a sarcastic kid that needs you a lot more than you need me. And if you didn't want me to think anything, why did you dress like a knockout?" I ask.

"I always dress professionally. Something you should learn!" she snaps back at me as an obvious strike at my attire of jeans, T-shirt, and white lowcut sneakers.

"Obviously, we are getting off on the wrong track again," I say. "Let's be nice since it is an eight-hour drive to Atlanta. Since it's going to be late, I'll skip the scenic route and take I-85 from Atlanta to Durham."

"What time should we get there?" she asks, sitting pretty all seat belted in.

"About midnight," I reply. "Maybe somewhere around eleven if we are lucky."

"You will have to drop me off at my hotel in Durham when we get in. I don't want to spend the night at Duke since I'll have to pick up the rental car and check in with the police department. You'll have to go with me to talk to the police. They need to know everything up front if they are going to help you."

"Yeah, all sounds good," I reply as I drive down Kings Highway toward I-75. "What did you tell your husband?" I ask.

"What?" she asks as she gives me a cocked look.

"How did he accept the fact you were going to North Carolina?" I ask again.

"I don't have a husband," she says to me.

"That's a nice ring on your finger, and Mr. Franklin?" I ask as I put on my sunglasses.

"There is no Mr. Franklin, like I told you yesterday. Franklin is my maiden name."

"Why do you keep a picture of a guy on your desk with kids if it's not your guy or your kids?"

"He's my dad, and the little kid is Maria! And why so many questions?"

"I was just making conversation. Don't get upset. It's a long drive," I reply.

"I'm not upset," she says to me.

"So what happened to your husband then?" I ask as we drive through Arcadia along the roads lined with old houses, wooden fence posts, barbed wire, and empty fields toward Interstate 75.

"Nothing. Once I graduated with my Master's Degree, I wanted to live life on my own. I got married right out of high school, became Mrs. Lennon, and went to an online college," she says as she sits in my passenger seat.

"What fun," I say as I look at her and smile as we head out of Arcadia. "Where did you get your Doctorate at?"

"I didn't. I just have my Master's degree," she replies from the passenger seat as we drive.

"How did you become Dr. Franklin?" I ask.

"I put my name on a plaque on the door and got one for my desk. I have a Master's degree in Psychology. I am the police psychiatrist. I just never got my doctorate," she says.

"So you're a fake doctor but a real psychiatrist?" I ask.

"Something like that," she says. "Before I got my college degree, I was pregnant with Maria. I quit going to school and just played happy pregnant housewife."

"How old were you?" I asked as I drove past the cow fields to Port Charlotte.

"Only nineteen. I didn't do anything while I raised Maria. Tom was a rancher. He earned good money. Therefore I didn't have to work. His parents bought us a house for a wedding present, and my parents had a nest egg for me. Our bills were nothing, and everything else was paid for," she says as she looks at the scenery around us as I drive.

"Perfect life," I reply as I glance at her beauty.

"Until I got pregnant again. Maria was only four and about to start preschool."

"I didn't know Maria had other siblings," I say as we sit in the comfort of the Camaro with only the sounds of the air-conditioning as our background noise.

"She didn't. I lost the child. I had complications because I was small. The child was born after seven months and weighed three pounds. They had to do a caesarian section, and that had complications. The child was stillborn."

"I'm sorry," I say softly as I turned on to the interstate and headed north toward Tampa.

I know by now that Dawn will do most of the talking on our trip through the wilderness of Florida. I turn on my phone and turn to my playlists. I hit shuffle on iTunes to the sounds of EDM and lower the volume to almost nothing. I want to hear the faint sounds of good music, but I don't want to be rude to Dawn. I want to hear Dawn's tale of youthfulness in Arcadia. This will give me insight into her life and even her. I know all I have to do is listen and be alert to the good parts. I take one long look at Dr. Franklin then kick back and enjoy the drive.

"I went back to school part time for eight years and became a substitute teacher. I received my degree in psychology. After I got my Bachelor's degree, I became a guidance counselor. Then I got my Master's and started working for the police. I was happy because I had a career. My husband, Tom, wanted us to have more children and have a big family. I couldn't see myself having another child because of what might happen. This put distance between us. Plus, Tom wanted me to be a housewife. A woman with a career intimidated him. My demanding career as a therapist put even more distance between us."

"Most men like independent women," I add. "And more income."

"Well, once I got my Master's Degree, everyone was happy for me. Everyone but not Tom. He wanted dinner done when he got home. He wanted a woman who cooked and cleaned. Then Maria disappeared, and our life went into a tailspin. That was when I decided I wanted to work for the police department. Everyone was behind me, except my own husband," she says to me as we drive through the warm air of Florida in September.

We get on Interstate 75, and we start heading north to Atlanta.

"Too bad," I say to her as I push the cruise control and idle the car at eighty-five miles an hour. "Are you going to arrest me for speeding?" I ask jokingly as I smile as I look at her through my sunglasses.

She just gives me a dirty look; she is trying to have a serious conversation with me.

"That was about eight years ago. I seriously pursued my Master's degree, and Tom went from being my best friend to being my worst enemy. Our relationship was just about over," she says. "The fighting was bad, and divorce was evident. We were growing apart, far apart, and now totally apart. We don't even speak anymore," she says as she looks down at her wedding ring and pauses briefly.

"That doesn't explain the diamond ring or the wedding band on your finger now, does it?" I ask as I look at her.

She looks down at her diamond ring and admires it on her hand for a moment, and then she looks ahead to the road, saying nothing.

"I took the ring off for years and just recently started wearing it again. The ring is mine, and it keeps the criminals from hitting on me constantly. That's the reason for the picture also."

"What ever happened to Mr. Lennon?" I ask.

"He moved to Texas for a while and became a ranch hand somewhere. He moved back for a few months, got his bills paid, sold the house, and moved right back to Texas. He was always a cowboy and loved the big plains and ranches."

"Have you heard from him?" I ask.

"Not for two years. Since the divorce. What about you? What ever happened to Mr. Beacon in Oviedo?" she asks.

"He is still around. He's a proud papa. I introduce him as my dad because of everything he has done for me. We both learned to trust each other. I gave him a son and a second chance. He gave me a home with love and someone to talk to. He never told me what to do, and I really respected him. I abided by the rules once I got settled in, and I worked hard to save money for college."

"You knew as a sophomore in high school you were going to college, which was three years away. Pretty determined."

"I knew I didn't want him to try to send me to college with what little money he had. As for my dad in Boston, I never told him that I was still alive. I liked being free of all obligations to what little family I had. I liked being on my own. Self-sufficient," I add with a smile.

"Did you tell him your mother found you in Oviedo?" she asks.

"Of course. She was happy that I was alive and well. She even gave me some money to pay for my college. She had a thousand-dollar savings bond that her and my dad bought when I was born. It's worth ten thousand dollars eighteen years later. She mailed them to me when she found out I was going to Duke. She's half the reason I have a brand-new car."

"Really?" Dawn asks as she looks at me with concern for my answer.

"I didn't know how I was going to pay for college, and I was very money conscious since I didn't want to ask Mr. Beacon for anything. I had about four grand when I moved in with him and got a job mowing lawns in the neighborhood and bussing tables at Chili's Bar and Grill on the weekends. That was when I was fifteen. I had money to spend during the school year, then all summer long I would work two full-time jobs, mowing lawns during the day and working at Chili's at night. I saved a few thousand over the years. I was a loner and a workaholic, so I had nothing to spend money on. Mr. Beacon was very proud of me for being money conscious. The next school year, I did the same thing, and the next summer before my senior year, I saved even more money. I had at least ten grand to go to college with."

"Plus, you have a full scholarship?" she asks.

"A full ride, depending on my grades, and I have to play basketball. I have other scholarships that gave me money for school also. Academic scholarships, some tuition assistance, and some financial aid just to have extra cash. Duke offering me a full basketball scholarship was better than winning the state championship," I say with a smile to Dawn.

"Good fortune just in time."

"If it wasn't for those savings bonds, I wouldn't have this car, so I do have to thank her."

"Did you get your aggressiveness and your personal drive from your father?"

"I guess. He was just like me. He worked hard and tried even harder than everyone around him. He was a great man."

"Hopefully, you won't end up like him," she adds.

"Well, you do have handcuffs!" I say with a big smile on my face.

"Funny," she adds as she raises her eyebrows in disregard to my statement. "What was high school like in Oviedo? Did you go to your prom? And what about the girl next door?" she asks.

I think back to my high school days and ponder about how I came out of my shell as an adolescent. The thoughts take me back only for a moment before I reply to Dawn's question.

I smile and know she is looking for some depth into my psyche.

"Were you popular? What did you do outside of basketball? Are you afraid to tell me anything about Raymond Douglas Beacon?"

"I went to both proms. I did the senior cruise and went to Grad Night at Disney World. I just didn't have any serious girlfriends in school. I just dated around and told girls up front that I wasn't looking for anything long-term. Life was fun, but I made sure to keep my defenses up."

Dawn and I talk endlessly for hours until we get near the Florida Georgia state line. We stop at the Burger King right outside Jennings, Florida. Since I am on a strict diet, I only get a strawberry milkshake. Dr. Franklin doesn't usually eat fast-food but makes an exception since we are in a hurry. We are only a few miles from Georgia and decide this is the perfect place to get gas and let the car cool down a minute. We stop at an all-in-one gas station with a Burger King attached. I get gas as Dawn goes inside to get the food to-go.

I decide to make a call to Jeff to tell him that we will definitely be there by seven since it's only two thirty in the afternoon now.

As I'm pumping gas, I see my phone has a few missed calls. One call is from Jeff, and I call him first.

"Hey, Jeff! It's Ray," I say.

"Ray!" Jeff says to me franticly. "Where are you?" he yells out. "They found Heather's head," he says in distress. "Security called me about a half hour ago. There was a break-in at our dorm. They found Heather's head in our dorm room," Jeff says distressingly.

"Jeff, calm down!" I say to him, trying to be calm.

"The police found Heather Collinsworth's head in our dorm room. Coach wants us back ASAP. Livia is freaking out. The school and police have been calling you for the last half hour. Everyone is wondering where you are!"

"I've already told everyone that I went home and we would be back tonight," I say into the phone.

"Coach wants you to call as soon as possible. The police want to get you get back in Durham now!" Jeff says in a frantic voice.

"Everything is all right, Jeff. I am on my way! I'll see you back in Durham."

CHAPTER 11

Dawn can tell instantly that something is wrong from the look on my face. I'm looking at her as I talk on my phone. I can see her worrying as my eyebrows jump with surprise from what Jeff is telling me. I'm basically freaking out but trying to look calm as I hide the anxiety from her. Dawn is walking toward me with a strawberry shake and her bag of food. I can tell she wants to confront me and to find out what's going on.

"What happened to Jeff?" she asks me with her wide puppy dog eyes as she hands me the milkshake.

"Nothing, except they found a head in our dorm room this morning," I tell her nonchalantly as I hang up the phone. "The police, Coach, and the Dean all want to talk to me tonight!" I say. "Jeff's girlfriend is driving him back to school now. We will go straight to Durham and meet up with Jeff at Duke."

"Are you serious? Someone found a head in your room?" she says in shock as her jaw drops and her eyes blister open. "Is it Heather's?"

"Yeah, I'm screwed!" I say as I finish pumping gas into the car. "I am in deep shit now," I say to her as she gives me a hug to comfort me.

The murders are without a doubt going to be linked straight to me, although I have a rock-solid alibi. Dawn is my witness that I spent all weekend in Arcadia. The word of a police officer should be good for something, especially since my life and scholarship hang in the balance.

"We have to go," I say as I put the gas nozzle back in the pump. "Everyone is going to want to talk to me tonight."

We leave Burger King and drive on to North Carolina. My mind is racing at about a million miles an hour. Now I know what a computer chip feels like. I don't worry about looking guilty. I am innocent of this misfortune, but the bad publicity will affect my scholarship and my status as a student at Duke. The last thing I want is to get kicked out of Duke. I have nothing to go back to and nowhere to go from there. I don't want to go to some community college, lose a semester of classes, and not be able to play basketball for a year just because I transferred.

"What are you thinking about?" Dawn says to me as we drive on at a hundred miles per hour.

"I don't want to be kicked out of school," I finally say in frustration. "Duke is my dream come true. I worked hard all my life just to get there. I didn't even bother checking out any other schools. I wanted to play basketball for Duke and win a championship ever since I was a little kid in grade school," I say as I keep looking forward into the night.

"Sweet dream," she says as she looks up at me from the passenger seat.

"It's my only dream right now, and I'm living it," I say to her. "At Oviedo High, we were among the state's elite three years in a row. We won the state championship. I was defensive player of the year in Florida. I'm on a great team, and if these murders turn sour on me, I'll get kicked out of school. School and basketball are all I have. Basketball and Duke, to someone like me, are everything. This, right now, is all I have," I say to Dawn, hoping she realizes the magnitude of my situation.

"It's not all you have," she replies as she sits facing me.

"Yes, it is!" I say sternly. "I have no family to go home to. Everyone in Boston thinks I am dead, so I can't go back there. I can't go back to Oviedo because everyone there knew when I left for Duke,

I wasn't ever going back. I have no real friends from high school and didn't care to keep in touch with any of my classmates. Basketball is a one-way ticket, and there is no going back. Sports and Duke are my life's work. I don't know or want to know anything else," I say to her as I sip on my milkshake.

"You could always go back to Oviedo," she says calmly from the passenger seat.

"I knew when I left Florida, I would never go back because of the circumstances I arrived under. I want to go back there as a somebody. I want to go back a success story on track with the life I once had."

My Camaro speeds past the Georgia state line right before dusk. My car glides down the highway at over ninety miles an hour. I can only wonder what awaits me at the university. I have fear in my heart as I look over and see my relief. The beautiful doctor from my past is here to defend my future. Thank God she's a cop. I know no one will believe I had nothing to do with this murder. Another rock-solid alibi that I know the Durham police will accept but not believe. In addition, I erased the caller ID that had my dorm phone number on it. I couldn't possibly be in both places at once, and neither could Jeff.

"Do you fear not accomplishing your goals in life? It is a common phobia," she asks as she keeps with her psychiatric self.

"What do you mean?" I ask as we drive onward toward Atlanta.

"Do you fear you won't become someone? A feeling that you won't accomplish your dreams, that you will grow up being a failure," she says nonchalantly as she lets go of my hand.

"Yeah. Don't we all? A fear of not being able to afford a car or a home. Not being able to make ends meet. A fear of not being able to provide for yourself or loved ones. I have a real fear of becoming a loser. That's why I've tried so hard to become someone. That's why I give everything my best shot. I want people to look up to me. I want people to ask me for help when they have questions. I want to be able to give them the answer. I don't ever want to be that guy flipping burgers at Mickey D's, walking to work while my girlfriend sits at home, screaming at me for not making enough money while complaining that she is pregnant, again!" I say in total exaggeration. "I would kill myself because I would consider myself a failure," I say aggressively as we pierce through the night in my black Chevy.

"Flipping burgers is an honest living. Thousands of people do that for a living."

"It is an honest living. It's just not a life I want to lead. I don't want to look back and say I'm a failure, a bum. I want to have kids, live in the suburbs, have one wife that loves me, and we take vacations to Europe and the Caribbean. I will work hard to have a good life, and I deserve it," I reply with a smile as I glance over at her.

"What would you do if you got paralyzed?" she asks.

"What? Why would you even say something like that?" I reply.

"It's an honest question. What would you do if you couldn't play basketball?"

I take a minute to ponder the thought. What would I do?

"I'd become a teacher, coach, or writer. Maybe travel around the world giving motivational speeches. In the words of Jimmy V., 'Don't give up, don't ever give up!' Tragedy wouldn't get me down. I only worry about things I can control. Losing my manhood, that would send me into a depression," I say with a sarcastic smile to Dawn.

"Losing your manhood?" she says, puzzled.

"Yeah, not being able to be a man. I'm half Italian and proud. I have high goals for myself, and only I can make my dreams come true. No girl will bring me down. No job would elude me, and I will lead a fruitful life," I say to her, still focusing on the road.

"What about these murders? What happens if you go to jail?" she asks.

"That's what worries me. All this bullshit will ruin my reputation. I've been lucky so far. If I didn't go to Arcadia this past weekend, how could I have proved I didn't kill that girl or didn't put her head in my room? My reputation as a student as well as a law-abiding citizen is at stake. If there is even a hint that I am guilty, I am sure Duke will expel me from the school, and North Carolina will expel me from the university system," I say as I shake my head slightly. "I won't be able to play basketball for Duke. My dreams would fall short then," I say as I glance at her and wait for a reply.

Dawn can easily see how much these events are stressing me out. The Camaro is on cruise control at ninety miles an hour. It's now after 7:00 p.m. and close to total darkness at night. The asphalt of Interstate 75 holds my car on its way to our destination of far. The towns slowly fade behind us as we glide through them, racing toward Durham. The night blankets us, and I didn't even notice the sky turn from gold to red to only black. Towns like Tifton, Cordele, and Macon disappear in the distance. Once I arrive in Atlanta, I take Interstate 85 north past Greenville, South Carolina, to Durham. Dawn is now asleep. It's almost 10:00 p.m., and we are still going strong. I need to get to Durham as fast as possible. I won't have to stop for gas again until I get past Charlotte, North Carolina.

I've haven't looked at a speed limit sign since Macon, Georgia. I know another shortcut that would save me some time. I take State Highway 49 once I get outside Charlotte. From there, I take the road that takes me right outside Burlington, North Carolina. I'm less than a half hour from the school. I got here a little after midnight.

I see the Duke sign illuminating the main entrance to the university. I live on Towerview Road and have a sweeping view of the Duke Chapel. Duke is a private school, and the cathedral is the centerpiece of the large university's two-sided campus. Mr. Duke stands tall in the center of the campus, in front of the huge Duke Chapel, to welcome all visitors. I drive down Duke University Blvd and head toward Wallace Wade Stadium and Cameron Indoor Stadium. I live across from the sports complexes in the Crowell Quads. I pull onto our road and drive the hundred feet to the dorm. I pull into the visitor's lot right in front and ponder about parking here. I realize this is no time to look for a parking space; therefore, I drive onto the grass and pull right up to the Crowell building doors.

Duke is a beautiful university with the greenest lawns, beautiful trees, a forest to the west of the campus, and old English stone buildings that surround the campus. Old statues and the Chapel brighten the Duke University appeal. The organs inside the Chapel and the stained-glass windows of the church are spectacular. The flowers of April turn Duke into a garden of colors and delight while the autumn leaves turn the campus golden. This is the Harvard of North

Carolina in every way. The courtyards, seasons, scenery, old stone buildings covered in ivory, and the education are compared to that of any Ivy League school. Duke is beautiful, far more beautiful than any woman I've seen, and beautiful because the traditions and the faithful followers keep the campus extravagant in every way. I love it here, and now Dawn gets to experience life at the university for a little while.

"Wake up, Dawn," I say to her as I shake her gently.

The car's interior light comes on when I open the door, and Dawn is shaken from her sleep.

"What time is it?" she asks in her groggy state.

"Well after midnight. Wake up. Come on," I say to her.

The resident assistant is up and waiting for us along with a security guard. Our RA is Keith, and the security guard is our friend Jack. Jeff, my roommate, is waiting up with them in Keith's room. My car is right next to the door entrance. I didn't want Dawn to walk far this late at night. Plus those suitcases she packed are hell on wheels all by themselves.

"Sorry about your mother," Keith says to me as he walks out the dorm entrance and into the cool night to help me with the bags. "You're sleeping in my room tonight."

"I had to put a lock on your door so no one will touch anything," Jack says to me as he holds the dorm doors open.

Jeff is standing in the doorway, just waiting for us.

"What's up, bro?" Jeff says as we bump fists, our male bonding ritual. "We are being evicted out of our room until the cops check it out more thoroughly."

"Yeah, Jack told me. I have Dawn, the policewoman, with me. I guess the couch will do," I reply.

"I got Livia here too. We took Keith's other bedroom," Jeff says as he grabs my other bag.

"Great! A sixsome," I say with a sarcastic and tired voice.

"Right!" Jeff says as he raises his eyebrows and cocks his head to one side.

"Livia needs to be back in Atlanta tomorrow, so she'll be gone in the morning," Jeff adds.

"I need to make sure everyone reports to the Dean tomorrow at eight a.m. sharp. Make sure you set your alarm," Jack says to us. "And I wouldn't park there on the grass."

"He'll move it," Keith says as he stands by Jeff outside our room in the quad.

"I'll call Coach and let him know you made it back," Jack says as he goes back to his kiosk. "Good luck, guys."

Keith and Jeff take the suitcases into the dorm room and leave them inside the doorway of Keith's room. Dawn is only half awake with the passenger door wide open. I grab the duffel bags and backpack out of the trunk and toss them toward the door.

"Come on, Dawn," I say into her ear as I slowly reach my hand around her and my other hand under her knees. She wraps her arms around me and hangs on as I carry her. She sets her head against my shoulder as I carry her into Keith's room and set her on the couch. I rush back outside to park the car in the student parking lot and then run back to the dorm. Again, Jeff is waiting for me, holding the door open. Dawn is safely asleep on the couch in the living room, and Keith covers her with a blanket. Livia is sleeping in the other bedroom and awaits Jeff. Since Keith is the Resident Assistant, he lives alone so he can have privacy when he needs to talk to students about their problems. The other great thing is that you always have a spare bedroom to crash in if you lose your room keys. The quad only has two floors and four very large lofts on each floor. Only sixteen people live in the quad, and ours only has the team and Keith. Fifteen students in all, two to a room. It's nice for now.

The three of us go into the hallway to talk so we don't disturb the girls. Keith brings out three Pepsis as we sit on the cold linoleum floor of the empty white hallway of concrete and soft white light bulbs.

"What the Hell is going on, Ray?" Keith asks as he opens his Pepsi and sits on the floor across from me. "Jeff told me that they found your mom dead, and this morning I find a head in a book bag in your doorway. How crazy is that?" he asks as he shakes his head.

"Crazy. Let me tell you. I think someone from Arcadia is responsible for all this," I say as I sip my soda.

"Why?" Keith asks as he gets comfortable on the cold floor besides me.

"Well, I'm sure Jeff filled you in," I say to Keith. "Someone is trying to ruin my life. I have no clue who or why, but someone is out there watching me. And now, I found out all these crazy things in Arcadia. I don't know what to do. That's why I brought her here with me. She can watch my back and find some answers," I say to the two of them as we sit in the hallway.

"What about this lady?" Keith asks. "Her ex-husband could be out for vengeance since his daughter disappeared and they blame you. He could be framing you. You know how some guys have trouble moving on," Keith says.

"All possibilities are open," I say as I sit on the cold floor during the dead of night. "It could be anyone from my past. Only people from Arcadia and Boston know everything about me, and I don't know anyone who would kill someone to ruin my life," I say.

Keith shakes his head ever so slightly in disbelief.

"And now someone has been in our room, violated our sanctuary, and walked right out of here after putting a head in our doorway," I add.

"It was freaky," Keith adds. "I knew you guys were gone, but your door was open. As I was passing by, I saw the backpack by the door inside the room. I figured I'd just throw it in your room and shut the door."

As Keith is talking, I'm hanging on every word. His facial expressions become more contorted as he talks about the backpack and its belongings. He is fighting to tell the story as he remembers his fear of what he has found.

"The backpack was really light, and nothing inside the pack moved. I was curious, so I unzipped it and hair came out. I thought that was odd until I saw a woman's face!" Keith blurts out! "It was so freaky!"

"Damn! I'm sorry, man!" I tell Keith.

"All the University cards have to be changed now," Keith says. "This place was crawling with cops, asking everyone questions. It was crazy up in here for a few hours."

"School security already took our cards, and they will confiscate all the others tomorrow. Everyone in the dorm will be scrutinized," Jeff says.

"I can't believe someone put a head in your room!" Keith says across from me.

Keith has his door open so he can hear his cell phone just in case anyone calls. He sits right next to the open entrance of his door. Keith is a good-looking guy, about twenty-four, and a graduate student here at Duke. He has all the answers and knows where everything is on campus. If you need a problem solved, he can help. That is why Jeff and I feel comfortable talking to him about my situation. Keith is one of the good guys. A true friend is what Keith is.

"Well, the good thing is, we both get to skip practice tomorrow. I am sure the police will be here, school security, and the school's President. They all want to know what is going on," Jeff says.

"Yeah, so do I. So do I," I say as I drink my Pepsi.

Jeff gets up, and we bump fists as he walks by. The love of his life is waiting for him in the spare room. Keith is also tired since it's late. Keith finishes off his soda and then bumps fists with me as he heads in the dorm room to retire for the night. Again, I sit alone, all alone, in the cold hallway.

CHAPTER 12

It's EARLY TUESDAY morning, and the university campus is business as usual. The great towering steeple, which dominates all the surrounding buildings, watches over the students as they go to their morning classes. The lifelike bronze statue of James Duke stands firm, ten feet off the ground, welcoming all to the university. Administrators and teachers hustle to their offices and classrooms in the early morning light. The courtyards are lifeless this early with only a squirrel or two running through the grass. I do my 6:00 a.m. workout and then break into my dorm room to get my books, along with other belongings to get me through the day. When I return to Keith's room, Jeff is walking Livia out to say goodbye. It's about 7:00 a.m. now, and the stone-cold evergreen campus is sparsely populated with students but fully aglow by the morning sun. I take my shower, change, and then call Coach and the Dean. The day is bright with adventure and the onslaught of questions that await us. We will meet with police at 8:00 a.m. in the administration building.

"Wake up, beautiful," I whisper into the sleeping maiden's ear. "Come on. Wake up," I say as I nudge her gently with my hand.

"I need my things from our room," Jeff says as he enters the living room.

"I already picked the lock," I say to Jeff as I stand in the doorway.

"What?" he says as he shakes his head.

"I need my stuff too. How are we supposed to go to class with no books or without our computers?" I ask Jeff.

Dawn takes her time getting ready, and since Jeff needs his books, he enters our dorm room despite the consequences that might arise from being locked out of our room the night before. It is our room, remember? Our prints are already there.

It's now just about 8:00 a.m. while Jeff, Dawn, and I are ready to face the committee that awaits us with their questions of why or how could this be happening.

"Half the police in North Carolina are going to be waiting for us," Jeff says as the three of us approach the administration building.

"I know," I reply as I think about the answers to the questions they could ask.

"I dreamed of this meeting, and let me tell you, it didn't end happily," Jeff tells me.

"I've already thought about this all night. I'm innocent, and I really have no clue why this is happening to me. That's my story, and it's the truth. There is nothing else we can do," I say to Jeff and Dawn as we walk.

"We're going to meet in that building. Just follow us," Jeff says to Dawn as we walk in the sunlight of a brisk new day among the mighty oak and lively elm trees here in North Carolina.

Dr. Franklin just nods as she is still worn out from the exhausting weekend she just endured. She is wearing jeans for once with her black high heels, a long-sleeve white button-up shirt, and a black blazer. Jeff and I are wearing khakis and long-sleeved dress shirts. I figure blue jeans and a Duke T-shirt would not be appropriate when facing dire consequences.

"I can't believe they found a head in our room," Jeff says as we climb the stairs into the huge and lustrous administration building in the center of campus.

"Jeff, you're nervous? We didn't do anything wrong, remember?" I say. "It's me they want, so don't worry about anything. And like I said, I'm innocent and didn't do any of this."

I notice that two uniformed police officers are waiting by the entrance. They open the doors and let the three of us pass without any attention.

"Business as usual," Dawn says as she points to the officers.

"We're screwed!" Jeff says as he acknowledges the officers opening the door for us.

"What does that mean?" I ask.

"Do you always have armed security opening doors for students?" she asks.

"Not until today," Jeff adds as he shakes his head, realizing the trouble we are in.

"Don't freak out, Jeff. It is all right," I add.

"I'm past freaking out," Jeff says as we enter the building. "I am now officially scared!"

The inside of the Administration Building starts with an enormous open area with several doorways and hallways off to the sides. The interior of the building is tremendous as we walk into the second floor and take the elevator downstairs. The grandeur of the momentous foyer was built to impress since the Administration Building is usually the first building students and parents go to when visiting the university.

A group of four officers are standing in the grand lobby waiting for us. Two are uniformed police officers, and the other two are detectives in suits with their side arms showing. All the men stop talking when we approach them.

"Hi. Looking for us?" I ask as the three of us approach the four men.

"You must be Ray?" the oldest of the four officers asks. "I'm Captain Adams. I will be taking over in this investigation," Captain Adams says as he shakes my hand.

Captain Adams is a Durham police officer of about forty-five years old in full blue uniform with gold stars covering the sleeves. Little gray patches on his sideburns mixed in with his short black hair distinguish the officer. He is probably an ex-football player by the size of his build and the force he shakes my hand with. He's excessively strong for forty or even fifty years old.

"Hello, sir," I say as I shake his hand.

We exchange introductions, and I introduce him to Jeff and Dawn. No need to tell him about Dawn being a fellow officer until we get inside the office. The other officers introduce themselves as Officer Steve Freedman, Duke University Policeman, and the other two are Detective Barry Tusson and Detective Peter Webber, Durham Homicide agents wearing suits and holding black all-weather trench coats.

Steve, Barry, and Peter are the officers who questioned me about the other three dead girls. I have never been taken downtown to talk to these guys before; they have always come to me and questioned me in front of my coach or school counselor. The two homicide agents are very intimidating. Steve, our university policeman, is a tall and trim guy with the short military haircut, and he's about thirty. He never tried to intimidate me and usually asks the least amount of questions. Detective Tusson and Webber are the complete opposite. They are physically superior beings with an intimidating presence and deep voices. These guys have no necks and square jaws, definite military background and total football player mentality with degrees from Yale and Princeton in Criminal Justice with minors in police brutality. The last time I talked with Detectives Tusson and Webber, they assured me I was guilty, and they threatened to break me. All conversations with these two ended with "I hope you're not lying, kid. We will kill you personally if we find out you're lying."

The four officers together look like an opposing football team's worst nightmare. These men are all taller than I am, and I'm six feet two inches tall. The three detectives from Durham just look men-acing, all weighing between two hundred thirty and two hundred fifty pounds. The justice system sends in the heavyweights to scare us probably. Either way, this is no joke. Officer Freedman seems the weakest, but these other guys could give Covey a run for his money in a fistfight. Not only do these two detectives look mean, but they mean business.

"Follow us," Captain Adams says as he waves us on.

The men walk down one of the long corridors as Jeff, Dawn, and I follow close behind. There is a door at the end of the corridor that leads to a room with a long black luster finish table that seats ten people. The one side of the room contains a huge window about ten feet long that lets us see everything that's eventful on the green outside. The cathedral ceiling is beautiful, and the twenty-foot ceiling only adds to the grandeur of the room. Since we are on the second floor, the view is spectacular and unobstructed by any trees. There is a sofa at each end of the room placed parallel with the wall. There is also a small counter with a coffee machine and cups on it. A water cooler is next to the counter.

Johnny, our assistant coach of basketball, and Frank Dawkins, Director of Athletics, are standing next to the couch drinking coffee and awaiting our arrival. President Altman is already seated at the table and ready to go.

"Have a seat, boys, and let me explain to you your rights," Captain Adams says to us as we are walking toward the table. "You will have to wait outside, Dr. Franklin," Captain Adams says to Dawn.

Dawn immediately made her presence known and replied to the captain.

"I am council for the boys," Dawn says quickly as she takes out a police badge and a lawyer's card. "I am board certified by the state of Florida in criminal law and serve as defense council and supporting witness to Ray's defense of innocence. The boys will waive the reading of their rights. They do understand the seriousness of the matter at hand and know anything said here can be used against them," she says with authority as she looks around at all the officers. "Any questions, gentlemen?"

Dawn stands and looks at all the officers with a stern look as if time stood still.

"No questions?" she says to the men as she looks around the table. "Then let's begin."

As Dawn takes her seat at the opposite head of the table, every person in the room pauses for a second. They are definitely puzzled by the little woman with the big mouth. Time resumes to full speed as the ten of us settle into our seats at the huge rectangular table.

"I'm the school's President, gentlemen," President Altman says to us.

Altman is a guy that looks like Santa Clause in a big black Italian suit. He has a trim white beard, round belly, and wears gold-rimmed glasses.

"There has been a very serious crime committed here," Altman continues. "Along with trespassing, breaking, and entering into a secure dormitory, there has been the murder of a UNC student. A head was found in that dormitory yesterday, and two young men have their futures hanging in the balance. Can you tell us what happened here, gentlemen?" President Altman says to Jeff and me.

Jeff and I look at each other as we sit among the alliance of achievers that want to figure out what is going on. I begin the story.

"Jeff and I don't know what to make of this. The attacks are targeted toward me, not Jeff. Three women I know have died recently, and my mother was found dead this past week in Arcadia," I say to everyone as I fidget with my fingers.

"Dr. Franklin, since your father is the Chief of Police in Arcadia, has anyone there uncovered anything? Any ideas, suggestions, or leads you may have for us?" Detective Barry Tusson asks her as he flips his notebook open.

"No leads as of yet. That's why I have been sent here to Durham. To better serve the police and uncover leads involving these crimes," she says, addressing the table.

"You are here just as council, Dr. Franklin. Am I correct in assuming that?" Detective Tusson asks.

"Arcadia police are under the assumption that the crimes committed in Durham now are related to crimes committed in Arcadia four years ago. We think they are by one killer, the same person. That means I am here to help the boys," she says sternly as she stares at the officers.

Both detectives are unfazed by her comments, and deep down we all know that North Carolina police are dictators when it comes to crimes committed here.

"What about you?" Webber asks me. "Any way you can help us?"

"Nothing solid. I can only say that none of the people in Oviedo knew of my mother in Arcadia. For the last three years, I lived with a legal guardian. No one in Oviedo ever knew of my mother or twin brother, and no one from North Carolina ever knew of them either," I reply as I sit nervously at the table.

"Where were you Saturday through yesterday?" Webber asks me.

"I went to Arcadia as a last-minute trip," I reply. "I actually spent Sunday in Desoto County Correctional, and I drove home from Arcadia with Dawn yesterday."

We are all sitting at the long table in the white room with a huge window overlooking the campus.

"What about you, Jeff?" Tusson asks Jeff.

Jeff looks up reluctantly. I can only imagine what's going through his mind.

"I went to Atlanta to go home and spend time with my girl-friend," Jeff replies.

"I didn't even know I was going to Arcadia until I was dropping Jeff off in Atlanta. We already talked earlier in the week about me taking him to Atlanta to see his girlfriend," I tell the officers.

"Are you sure these attacks are just aimed at you and not Jeff?" Coach Johnny asks.

"Yes, I'm positive. The girls are all people I've known since coming to school here. Now my mother has been murdered, and a head was placed in my dorm room just this week. Without a doubt, these attacks are aimed at me," I say as I look up at everyone.

"What about someone from Boston?" Detective Webber adds as he, too, jots down items on his iPad.

"I think someone from Arcadia is more likely, even though I haven't considered anyone from Boston. I haven't been to Boston in over four years," I say as I talk nervously. "I have some theories. There is the twin brother theory, the ex-husband theory, and the ex-girlfriend gone psycho theory. I was never in danger until I had my picture in the paper for winning the championship in Florida. I enrolled at Duke after that, and that was when people started dropping dead on me. All the murders have been committed since coming to Durham."

"We'll check out the people from Boston now living in North Carolina. I'll also look at the teams Oviedo played. See if anyone took the loss too hard and see if anyone has any connections to Durham," Webber adds.

"What about video surveillance cameras in or around the dorms?" Dawn asks.

"We have video camera footage of the dorm," Altman says. "But we don't have anyone suspicious coming in or out of your dorm," he adds.

"The burglar went in through a window and bypassed the alarm system. It happened at night since the daytime surveillance shows the window with no one going in or out. At night it's harder to see because it's dark and because of the bushes," Freedman adds to the conversation.

"How was the head found?" Dawn asks.

"Keith, your RA, saw your door was open but knew both of you were gone. He found a backpack inside the door. Once he opened the bag, he saw there was a head inside. He called the Duke authorities right away and left the bag in the doorway," Freedman says.

"The school wants to avoid any bad publicity about this case," President Altman says to everyone. "We do have strict security measures here, and all dormitories are locked all day and all night. We are now bringing in dogs to do the walks during the day and at night with our patrolman. Dogs will sniff out anyone hiding in bushes. The campus has escorts, and officers will patrol the campus twenty-four seven. This is an isolated incident," Altman says. "No one has ever been murdered on Duke's campus, and we would like to keep things that way."

"No one outside of this room besides Keith, the resident assistant, knows about the head in the boy's room as of yet. The police have not reported the incident. This needs to stay inside this room," Captain Adams says. "We are doing our best to keep this isolated, and it needs to stay as highly confidential information."

"Livia, my girlfriend, knows," Jeff says to the table. "She drove me home last night."

"We talked to her this morning," Webber says. "Jeff told us she was here last night, and we stopped her this morning. We made it specifically clear that this was information not to be shared with anyone."

"Also, the future reputations of these students as athletes will be tarnished if the school is implicated in these horrific crimes. The press knows of the three separate incidences. The press hasn't linked any of these situations together since they happened over a span ranging from June until now, all in different cities. We would like to maximize the safety of every individual on campus as well as capture this madman as quickly as possible," Coach Johnny adds.

"Captain Adams assures us he will work on this case around the clock, and Officer Freedman is also at your disposal, gentlemen," President Altman adds. "Campus Security will check all the buildings regularly and keep an extra eye on the boys to ensure their safety. Safety measures have been increased with fraternity patrols and more lighting at night along buildings. Along with Dr. Franklin, we will always have five officers working on this case around the clock," Altman says. "This school doesn't need its reputation tarnished at all."

"You boys do understand you are suspects?" Detective Tusson says.

"The boys understand and are willing to take polygraph tests to show they have nothing to hide," Dawn fires back.

"Good, because your scholarships depend on those tests," Coach Dawkins adds.

"Tell us in depth about your theories, son," Captain Adams asks.

I feel like everyone in the world is watching me. I have the floor now, and I don't want to get scared and mess anything up. I begin to speak slowly and calmly.

"Well, I had a twin brother. He supposedly died in a fire four years ago. Now I found out that no one in Arcadia did an autopsy. So we don't know if it was my twin brother that died in the fire or a girl that supposedly ran away from home that died in the fire. The girl, which is Dr. Franklin's daughter, has been missing since the fire, and she was dating my twin brother."

"You've got to be kidding me?" Detective Webber asks.

"No, he isn't!" Dawn adds.

"How small of a town is Arcadia that no autopsy was ever done? No coroner in a nearby town could have done it?" Detective Tusson asks.

"It's a long story of misjudgment and lack of guidance among the town's part. The body can't be recovered either because it was cremated. No evidence can be exhumed regarding the case in Arcadia. Not even dental records," Dawn says to the officers.

The detectives keep jotting down notes in their tablets. I am sure Jeff is thinking about misrepresentation right about now since Dawn's father is the Chief of Police in Arcadia. And when did we ever discuss polygraph tests? I must have missed that conversation. What else has she left out?

"What's your other theory?" Captain Adams asks.

"Ms. Franklin's husband could be doing this out of revenge because he thinks I am responsible for the death of his little girl," I say from my chair at the corner of the table as I lean forward and fold my hands on the table.

"Why would he think that?" Webber asks as he looks up at me.

"Well, a diary was found. Maria Lennon's diary. Her last entry in the diary was 'I made love to Ray Beacon, and this will change everything.' Only Maria was dating Rodney, my brother, not me. I pretended to be my twin brother just to sleep with her. That night, my brother never came home, and the next day was the fire—the fire that killed someone—and I thought it was my twin brother until this weekend," I say as I look down at the table.

I can already tell that the group of officers are disgusted with my theories. They sound weak enough to me, never mind how they sound to the officers.

"You deceived a girl that knew you? You fooled her, right? So why would we think you're not trying to fool us?" Webber asks me as he and Tusson are glaring at me simultaneously.

"That explains the ex-husband and psycho girlfriend theory also. She could be doing this to me also. Scorned at such a young age, never recovering. She was never found either after that night. It's just a theory," I add as I look down at the table.

I notice Dawn never looks anyone in the eyes as I am talking. I can tell she is disgusted with my theories and me as well. She is my next theory, even though I keep that one to myself—the psycho little woman with a vengeance to avenge her daughter's disappearance and horrible marriage theory. That one is the most concrete of all my theories, also known as the Psycho Doctor Theory.

"It could also be a fan. A scorned player from your past that lost his job or scholarship because of you," Captain Adams says to the group.

"No one in Oviedo or here at Durham knew about my mother. So I don't know if it would be a fan, unless that fan was from Arcadia, and I never played basketball when I lived in Arcadia," I add.

"So far, these crimes are isolated and focused only on Ray. I don't want this to turn into another Gainesville killer scenario like at the University of Florida in 1990. Enrollment will drop, and about five thousand parents will pull their children out of school here at Duke. I don't want that. This is a prestigious university, and I don't want anything close to the Gainesville incident!" President Altman says to all of us.

"The Gainesville killer theory could be another one to consider," Detective Webber adds. "A random act of violence by a psychopath. The only body parts of Kate Rush that were found were her hands. Kate's hands were surgically removed, not hacked off or torn off. They were precisely cut and removed with the greatest of surgical care. Since there is a medical hospital here at Duke and a mental facility, we are considering students of both practices and doctors as suspects as well. It could be a scorned lover of Kate's. We won't leave any stone unturned," Captain Adams says to Jeff, Dawn, and me.

"Today we are cross-checking all the student and employee records with our computer to see what we can come up with. I'll be on the case twenty-four hours a day, and you can call me if you need anything," Officer Freedman says to us.

"We searched your room yesterday and found no signs of forced entry. We questioned all the students that came back yesterday before the head was found," Captain Adams says to us.

"I can't believe there was a severed head in our room," Jeff adds.

"The door was open, and the head was in the doorway. The head was in plain sight," Officer Freedman says.

"We were in the room this morning. We didn't notice anything taken," Jeff added.

"How did you two get into the room?" Detective Webber asks sharply.

"We had a security lock on the knob, so it would be impossible to get in through the door. An alarm is on all the first story windows, and no alarm went off. So how did you get in the room?" Officer Freedman asks as he pulls himself forward toward the table and glares at Jeff and me.

"I used Cheez Whiz and a screwdriver," I say calmly to the officers as I look down at the table.

"What?" Captain Adams says out loud and in disbelief.

"I woke up, walked to the door, saw the lock, examined it, went back to the room, and remembered the Cheez Whiz in the refrigerator. I got an idea. I saw the keyhole at the bottom of the lock, filled it with Cheez Whiz, walked out to my car, and grabbed a screwdriver. Then I walked back to the room. By then the Cheez Whiz was hard and dry inside the lock. I then used the screwdriver and manipulated the head into the keyhole. The hardened Cheez Whiz and the force of the screwdriver broke the tumblers inside the lock. I forced the screwdriver into the hole, turned it, and the lock popped open. I then took the cover off the knob and walked into my room. The lock is still on the door and locked, but it can now be opened with a screwdriver," I say.

I look over at Jeff and Dawn, and both of them have their heads down and are looking at the table. I know Jeff wants to die and Dawn is in total disgust with me. The President of Duke University and my coach are in awe while the police don't know what to think.

"Obviously, no alarm went off, so there is half the burglar problem right there."

"You will pay for that lock, young man!" Freedman shouts out.

"Calm down. He will pay for the lock," Dawn says as she puts up her hand to warn the officers to be quiet and calm down.

"So you're a master locksmith and your accomplice is Cheez Whiz. You prove to be very resourceful in a jam. Are you always this clever?" Tusson asks as he glares at me.

"I heard about that from a friend, and I have a great memory. I saw the lock, I saw the Cheez Whiz, and I remember someone telling me about using Cheez Whiz to pop a lock," I say. "This is the same reason my grades are so good. This is how I got accepted to Duke. I remember vast amounts of knowledge that I can recall at any time—passages from books, lines from notes, regurgitate answers for tests. I'm not a criminal. Things just come to me. I tried the Cheez Whiz on the lock and it worked," I say innocently from my corner of the table. "A bigger problem would be that the alarm did not go off," I add.

"The alarm didn't go off," Dawn adds as everyone looks around the room in disbelief. "Why didn't an alarm go off if he broke into the room?" Dawns asks the officers.

"We'll look into it," Officer Freedman adds.

"You still need to come downtown with us and take a lie detector test. You and Jeff!" Webber says sternly.

"Don't worry about your answers, boys. I will be there since I am their counsel," Dawn says.

"Remember, these tests might not stand up in court, but your scholarships depend on the results," Coach Johnny adds. "The school's reputation is at stake here."

"Your future as students," President Altman adds with a sinister smile.

"We will change the lock on your door and find out why the alarm didn't go off," Officer Freedman adds.

"And I'll keep an eye out for a twin, an ex-husband, and a little girl named Maria," Captain Adams says as all of us get up together.

Nobody laughs, and Dawn shakes her head ever so slightly in disgust.

"Good luck, boys!" Johnny says as he shakes my hand and then Jeff's.

President Altman wishes us luck also and proceeds with the same gestures.

Jeff, Dawn, and I leave the room with our entourage of police and security behind us. The detectives drive an LTD that is out in front of the building and awaiting us.

"Since we aren't under arrest, I prefer to drive my own car," I say to the detectives.

"We will drive you to your car, and you will follow us to the Durham station. Then we will proceed with the test. Captain Adams will follow behind you. Understood?" Tusson demands.

"Fine with us," Jeff says.

Funny thing is, Jeff answers and I am the one driving. I think since he is the older one, he likes letting people think he's in charge. It's like I am the little brother with all the toys and he watches over me. Thank God he's not a control freak.

We ride in the LTD and are at my car in seconds. The three of us hop into my car. Dawn is next to me, and Jeff rides in the back seat as we follow the two detectives off campus and toward the police station in downtown Durham.

"Why didn't you tell me that your dad is the Chief of Police in Arcadia? I think that is an important factor in the situation I'm in," I say to Dawn.

"I didn't want my dad's help on this. He has influence in the town and throughout the police department. My father is the reason I was able to help you in North Carolina. My dad is how I get time off to help you. My father is very concerned and is using his connection to check things out for me. A very powerful shadow is looking out for us right now and keeping you out of jail. This is my project, and I'm here to find my key, remember?" she says sharply.

"This isn't some little project!" I explain in an outrage as I bounce my hands off the steering wheel. "This is my life! This isn't a game!" I yell out. "I have full trust in you, and I haven't held back anything. You know as much as I do about this. Is there anything else I should know about you or your family?" I ask in a loud voice.

"No!" she fires back at me angrily.

"Where is your ex-husband? From the picture I saw, he looks like me. He could be doing this to me. How come we can't get in touch with him?" I shout out.

"If you're not married, why do you wear an engagement ring and a wedding band?" Jeff asks Dawn from the back seat.

"Shut up, Jeff!" she fires back at Jeff.

"Whoa," Jeff says loudly as he sits back in the seat.

"Are you sure you're here to help?" I ask.

"If you don't want my help, drop me off," she says as she looks straight ahead at the road.

"Full disclosure between client and attorney, remember?" I say as I drive.

"You're not a client. You're a punk kid getting screwed for being such a jerk your whole life. I can't figure out why anyone would want to do this to such a great kid like you," Dawn says sarcastically.

She says these words in a rage; she is sulking now in my passenger seat.

"Don't get mad at me, Doctor. I'm just saying that your dad being Chief of Police is an important factor in my situation. Don't you think?" I ask sternly.

"No! And how do you think you walked out of that jail? Who do you think let you leave Arcadia, never doubting your innocence? My father and me! I'm keeping you in my custody. I understand you have a dream that you want to come true. If I am keeping anything from you, it's my prerogative. You don't need to know every detail about my life. You're not helping me. I'm not the one in trouble. I'm not the one facing jail time, and I'm not the one being set up for murder. If you don't want my help, drop me off! Got it?" she barks out in a pitiful rage.

"So why do you wear the engagement ring and the wedding ring if you're not married?" Jeff asks again.

"Shut up, Jeff!" Dawn shouts out again loudly.

"What are you being rude to me for?" Jeff asks.

"You told me you did everything on your own. It seems like you live in a fairy tale. Your husband pays all the bills, Dad gives you a job, your kid runs away, and you don't take your wedding ring off. You probably never left Arcadia until now. I'm having a problem trusting you. How hard did you have to work, knowing everything is given to you?" I say to Dawn, questioning her integrity.

These are questions I have to ask. Before this, she explains a situation in which I could relate. She was a person who did things on her own. She was someone who lived up to the expectations and accomplished her dreams. All that is a lie now. She gave me some sob story just to relate to me and keep us on the same level. She lied to me. Dawn says nothing as all this is unfolding before her. She just sits in the passenger seat, fuming with anger. Any minute she will either explode or cry.

"You're a counselor. You have to understand where I'm coming from. Surprises are scaring the hell out of me. I don't want to end up in jail in Arcadia just because your father is Chief of Police. That scares the hell out of me too!" I yell out.

Dawn still says nothing. The little woman is not much of a lawyer if she is intimidated by this conversation. Now I am wondering if she is even a psychologist or just some woman with a law degree that is given a job by her father just to keep her out of the way. For a woman in such a powerful and influential position, working with such dangerous criminals, she really makes me wonder if she earns her keep. That would explain why she isn't a very good criminal psychologist. Daddy gave her the job with the county just to keep her busy.

"I am here to help, remember?" she says so softly and sadly.

I can tell that she is about to cry. I look in the rearview mirror and see the somber look on Jeff's face as well. The car is silent, and nobody says a word as we roll through the city of Durham behind the detectives. I feel somewhat guilty about my attitude and the way I am treating Dawn. I'm sorry, but I still feel like I should tell her that she isn't a good counselor.

"I'm sorry," I say in a low voice to Dawn and then reach over to touch her hand ever so gently just to get her attention.

Dawn looks over at me and doesn't smile. She looks down again at her ring and then taps her hand on mine as I hold onto the gear shifter, as if saying thanks without words. She is truly upset with me, and it is difficult for us to relate to since we are on different sides of the tracks. It's a two-against-one situation, and I can't read her mind to reveal what she is thinking. All I know is that she is upset with me. I said I was sorry. Now it is her turn to communicate back.

"Put it on BPM, Ray, and put the top down," Jeff says from the back seat.

I reach for the radio and hit the Satellite button. I have Sirius Radio and Channel 52 in BPM. The bass hits the woofers, and the fast-paced beat flies out the speakers as the rave music is put on low. Dawn gives me a dirty look as she puts her hand on her head to readjust her hair. I just smirk back because I thought me hitting her on the head is funny. Childish humor or immaturity, call it what you want. I'm only eighteen and a freshman in college. What am I supposed to act like? A mature adult? That's what your thirties are for.

"Keep the top up. I don't want to mess up my hair," Dawn says.

"I hope we pass the lie detector test," Jeff says. "I hope our scholarships don't really depend on how they perceive us. If they kick me out of school, I'll kill you myself!" Jeff says somewhat seriously.

"Don't worry. Just tell the truth," Dawn adds to break her silence.

Just tell the truth is all I keep thinking. The lie detector test is your future, Ray. Your future depends on those tests. Wow! How much pressure could possibly be on me at this time? My scholarship is in jeopardy. My future as a student in the state of North Carolina's University system is at risk.

All I want to be is somebody, I keep thinking. Don't be scared. Just tell the truth. The lie detector test holds my future. Just tell the truth. Oh yeah, what is there to be afraid of? Right! If I fail this test, I will lose my scholarship and get kicked out of Duke, that's all.

The car in front of us pulls into a big parking lot. It's the Durham Police Station. We are here. My future depends on this.

"We are here," Jeff says.

Our destiny begins now!

CHAPTER 13

WE ARE AT the white courthouse with the adjacent Police Headquarters of Durham, in the middle of downtown. Durham is a nice little town that focuses around the university. Unlike cities in Florida, Durham enjoys all four seasons. Right now, the leaves of the huge trees are just starting to turn from their vivid green to an autumn brown and red. In October, the gold and auburn leaves will fall to the ground as I walk under the foliage for the first time since I've left my home in Boston. For now, I enjoy the view of the city scenery for only a second as I park the car and get rushed into the courthouse.

Captain Adams doesn't follow us into the police station; he must have work of his own to do. Therefore, the three of us follow Tusson and Webber down the corridor of white linoleum flooring to an office off to the side. Our footsteps echo off the white concrete walls, and the tones are heightened by my own fear as if walking through a valley of sound. I can see through the glass door at the wood table and omniscient vibrating soothsayer. The polygraph machine sits on the table, waiting to claim its next victim. I can only think, *What if I fail?* even though I am innocent. My heart is racing, and my mind is almost blank as I think about what I could say to ease my nerves. I am tense all over, and anxiety runs rampant through my body, making me fidget all over. We are in the domain of Detective Tusson and

Detective Webber. Jeff and I are playing by their rules, and whatever they say goes. The rules can change at any time. On their playing field of justice and criminal defense, we do things their way.

The five of us sit down at the table. I sit at the head of the table, Dawn sits next to Jeff, and I'm next to her, with Webber and Tusson opposite them. I'm the first in line to test the glistening machine of virtue and self. Webber and Tusson perform the ritual of transforming the dormant metal box into a lie-detecting wizard.

"Take your shirt off and hold out your arms," Webber asks me as I sit at the table.

He rubs alcohol swabs on my arms to make the connection between the machine and I more viable. He then sticks the white round electrode on the veins in my upper arms. The ritual continues until I have several electrodes connected to me. He places two on my forehead, two on my chest, one on each arm, and three on my back. One electrode lies on the base of the back of my neck. I guess they weren't taking any chances.

"The machine works by detecting electromagnetic impulses that cause stress within the body reacting against your nervous system and blood flow. Your body follows a natural order of impulses, which the brain regulates. When you lie, your brain knows it's a lie, and you are fighting the natural order. This machine is your brain's way of telling us, 'I didn't remember things that way,'" Webber says to me with that same stern look you give a child just before disciplining them.

"If you tell us you didn't kill those girls and you did kill them and the machine doesn't detect it, then you're the worst kind of criminal. Sheer madness since your brain doesn't know that you're a killer and you subconsciously believe that the lies you tell are the truth. Your morals are no longer controlling any judgments, and there is no natural order in your brain or your way of thinking," Tusson says these things and smiles at me from his position at the left side of the table.

"Then we must kill you because you are nothing but scum and you don't know the difference between right and wrong," Webber adds, sitting right next to me, giving me his natural expression of meanness.

"Knock it off!" Dawn says as she glares at the two muscle-bound detectives as they verbally work me over.

I sit in the room at center stage and await the first question, feeling the magnitude of the decision-making machine.

"Is your name Raymond Douglas Beacon?" Webber asks calmly and clearly as he stares at the graphing paper as it flows with lines through the glittering machine.

"Yes. Raymond Douglas Beacon," I answer.

The machines needles race back and forth on the paper grid for a second, and everyone then stares at me. I didn't expect that to be the reaction I would get. It doesn't take a rocket scientist to tell that the machine is telling them I am lying. The two detectives just look at me, unfazed by the waving needles, and then ask me another question.

"Is your eye color brown?" Tusson asks.

"Brown, yes," I answer as the tension inside my heart builds with anticipation.

The machine switches gears again, and the needles go into a lightning strike of side-to-side motions. My eyes are brown, and I am Ray Beacon. What the Hell is going on? That is the only wave of knowledge in my mind. The detectives are unfazed by the machine's reaction. Dawn and Jeff are in shock; they are looking at me with wide eyes and confusion. I'd be in shock if they were even breathing, which they aren't. I look at Webber and Tusson, and they are unfazed by the machine's reaction.

"We are going to give you a question to test the validity of the machine," Webber says to me.

"Great!" I say as I exhale. "Because I am getting really nervous!" I exclaim as I begin to perspire with nervousness and despair.

"Don't be nervous," Dawn says as she rubs my hand with her fingers.

"We are going to ask you what color the wall is twice. Say white the first time, black the second time," Tusson demands in his over-bearing demeanor.

Webber adjusts the machine, and I can feel my electrodes tingle my skin as the blood in my veins pulse faster with energy.

"Are the walls white?" Webber asks.

I feel an immense burst of heat explode inside my body. I feel the sweat transforming on my brow, protruding through my pores. I feel sick all of a sudden; the pressure of existence is shooting through my brain. I'm full of fear, primal fear, and inescapable fear. I become full of anxiety as I begin to speak.

"The walls are white, yes," I say apprehensively.

I watch the five little needles squander back and forth across the roll of graphing paper. Both detectives look at each other and then look back at me. I look at Dawn and Jeff as if to say, "What?" The tension in the room is running high, and that was only the first question.

"Are the walls black?" Webber asks again.

"The walls are black, yes," I say in a fidgety voice.

The ink-filled needles react the same way from within the machine. The needles act as if running for cover or detecting an earthquake. They scribble back and forth across the graphing paper, leaving another blemish in the array of straight lines. The two results are both the same. The walls are white though. The machine says I lied both times. No wonder these machines are not permitted in court. They're unreliable. And if I wasn't nervous before, I sure am now. I break out into a full sweat as I watch big guilty signs race before my eyes on those swift needles.

"Check the resistors," Tusson says to Webber.

Webber then firmly presses on each little round white electrode to make sure it is firmly secure and in the right places.

"All connections good," Webber says as he looks back at his partner.

"Again, are the walls white?" Webber asks.

"White, yes," I reply.

Again, the little needles go haywire and ruin their path of straight lines.

"I am a little nervous. Can Jeff go first and then me? This will give me time to calm down," I say this as I'm taking the electrodes off my arm and head.

The two detectives have no choice but to agree since we are going nowhere with this approach. Jeff and I change places, and the big boys go through the same ritual of attaching electrodes to Jeff as they did with me. They ask the same sample questions, and the machine acts according to Jeff's answers. The line goes straight when he tells the truth and waves back and forth when he lies. Jeff is calm with nothing to hide since the machine works; they go right into the questioning. Dawn and I sit silently next to each other, watching the progress. The gentlemen decide to videotape the session.

"Did you place Heather Collinsworth's head in your dorm room?" Webber asks.

"No," Jeff says calmly and securely as he takes a breath to relax.

"Did you kill Heather Collinsworth?" Detective Webber asks Jeff.

"No," Jeff replies, and the machine is unfazed by his answer.

"Do you know who did?" Webber asks.

"No." And the same straight lines persist.

"Have you ever murdered anyone?"

"No." The lines remain smooth and straight.

"Do you know anyone that ever murdered anyone?"

"No," Jeff says calmly from his chair, totally relaxed.

"Do you trust your roommate?" Webber asks.

"Half the time. We are involved in a strange situation," he replies as he glances over at Dawn and me.

"Has he done anything eccentric or extravagant that would let you believe he is a criminal or responsible for any criminal activities?" Webber asks Jeff.

"No." Again the needles remain straight and unfazed by his answers.

"Do you trust Dr, Franklin?" Tusson asks.

"No," Jeff doesn't hesitate to say. "Like I said, we are in a strange situation, and I just met her last night. I don't even know her."

"Are you hiding any evidence from the police?" Webber asks.

"No." The same straight lines, unchanging.

The two detectives look at each other and exchange the same blank expressions as if trying to communicate through telepathy.

"Change places, guys," Webber suggests as he points from Jeff to me.

Again, I sit in the hot seat. All wires are hooked up and all systems go. Same nervousness runs through my tense body. I'm so nervous that the lines on the machine are going to look as if the machine were detecting a ten on a Richter scale. My blood is pumping vigorously through my veins, and a stream of sweat is running down my brow. All I want to do is get the first question right.

"Is your name Raymond Douglas Beacon?" Webber asks.

"Yes," I reply nervously as I look at Dr. Franklin.

Again, an array of lines shoot back and forth as if the machine is freaking out from an LSD flashback. I can't even get the color of the walls right. I'm panicking now. I'm thinking that I'm going to jail for sure. I have nothing to hide though. I just want to scream out, "Why is this happening to me?"

"Look, guys," I say in protection of my own life. "I'm nervous. I endured a long trip yesterday and only had a few hours of sleep in the last three days. Plus, I found out my mom and dad are both dead. Now there is a head in my room. I'm missing classes and way behind in school. I need some time to get a grip on things before I do this again," I say as I take the electrodes off my head and then rest of my body.

"If you have nothing to hide, this shouldn't be a problem," Webber adds.

"You would think. I'll be back on Thursday. We could do it then or this weekend," I tell the men as I shake the magnetic pulses off my skin.

"You're not under arrest, but you're a suspect. We will be watching you. Any other incidents and we're sticking you in jail no matter what. Alibi or no alibi," Tusson says forcefully as he stands up and tries to intimidate me by pointing while talking to me.

"And this doesn't look good for you, not passing your test. Be here Thursday at five, and that is your last chance. After that, no more scholarship, no more basketball, no more Raymond Beacon," Webber says as he stands next to Tusson.

"Got it," I say in frustration as I put my hands up and look at Dawn for comfort.

"Give me your cell phone number so we can keep in touch. Carry your cell phone at all times," Webber says as he hands me his business card.

Dawn grabs me and leads me out the door as the three of us walk to the car.

"It doesn't look good that you didn't pass their test," Dawn says as we walk down the courthouse hallway.

"Nope, it doesn't," Jeff adds as he walks with his head down, brainstorming along the way to the car.

"I'm nervous. I got the walls wrong, too, and my eye color. I have nothing to hide," I say as I walk alongside the two. "I'm going through a lot right now. If I'm guilty, they would have me in jail right now. We have other things to do right now. I need to check you into a hotel," I add as I'm freaking out on the inside.

"I have reservations for the room and a car. I'm staying at the Holiday Inn, and they have a Hertz rental office nearby," Dawn says to us.

We are out of the courthouse in seconds and at my car. I need to drop Jeff off at the school so he can go to class and take notes for me. We hop into the car and roll. I drop Jeff off at the university first. Then I grab Dawn's bags and take her to the Holiday Inn about a mile from the school. This specific hotel is a grand one, with a large heated inside pool, Jacuzzi, complimentary breakfast. When we go upstairs to drop off the bags in Dawn's room, I see the beautiful and enormous bed. Nice, huge, comfortable bed.

"Look at this big bed," I say as I drop the suitcases by the closet and lay on the big bed.

As I stretch out on the bed, I grab the nearest pillow. That is when Dawn decides to lay down the law for me, and now we play by the rules.

"First of all, you will never spend the night," she says confidently as she stands in front of the bed with her hands on her hips.

"Really, you don't find me attractive?" I ask as she looks down on me.

She's standing in front of the bed and looking at me strangely. A stern look is on her face. She's mad that I would even think of such a thing.

"I'm not about to start having sex with kids. I don't find you attractive in any way, especially since you killed my daughter. Or did you forget about that? And you won't be living out any mother-daughter fantasies. That is a fact. Now get up and let's go," Dawn says to me. "You're a bastard for even thinking that! You know that?" she adds as a poisonous dart punctures my heart.

Maybe I've offended her. I almost feel bad. She must think I have a conscience or something. I don't think she realizes that an eighteen-year-old boy has a very positive, above-average sex drive. That and the fact that I'm immature could explain a lot about why I'm so conceited.

I apologize immediately, and off we go to rent a car. Dawn plans on renting a Ford Mustang for the week. The morning flies by, and the drive to the rental counter is awkward since Dawn is upset with me. She tells me just to drop her off and she'll be fine. If she needs anything, she'll call.

I pull up at Hertz and plead again for forgiveness.

"I have to get back so Jeff and I can go workout. I would love to take you out to dinner this evening. I know a nice place that I haven't been to yet. I would be honored to take you," I say as I look at her and smile.

"I accept and thank you. You might be a gentleman yet. You haven't been a male pig since we left the hotel," she adds with a smile.

"I'm on my best behavior," I reply.

She gets out and is on her own for the rest of the day. The rest of my day is full of catching up. I have to go see two of my professors because of the classes I missed. Since I'm a scholarship athlete, teachers get upset when you miss class. Being an athlete highlights you as an underachiever if you start missing classes for any reason. Teachers think you're trying to take advantage of the school that supports you. Since it is the beginning of the semester, it really doesn't look good that I'm missing class already. I'll let them think whatever they want for right now. I'm sure when my picture is on TV for being murdered, they will understand.

As for my classes on Tuesdays and Thursdays, I have class from 8:00 a.m. to 11:30 a.m. (College Algebra and American History for an hour and a half each). Then I work out after lunch, which is about 1:00 p.m. Workouts include two hours of strength training, no weights, just dips, crunches, pull-ups, push-ups, more crunches, exercise bike, and some kickboxing. After my workout, I do lots of stretching and end my adventure with a steam bath or swim. As for my Monday, Wednesday, and Friday classes, they are Introductory Spanish, Macroeconomics, and American Government. All my classes are over with by noon so I can work out and have practice in the early mornings and all afternoon. Basketball practice with actual coaches doesn't start until the first week of October. Schools can't coach players or have organized practices with their players until October 1. That way, every school will have the same time to develop their players without interfering with their education. Also, this rule states that coaches are not able to work with players over the summer and gain an advantage when the season starts. Therefore, every team starts practice at the same time to make the playing field even for all coaches, players, and universities.

By the time Jeff and I go to the gym, it is almost three. We work out for two hours to let out all our frustrations.

"What did you think about this morning?" I ask as I spot Jeff while he's bench-pressing 225 pounds.

"What is there to say?" Jeff replies as he pulls the weights down to his chest and pushes them back up again.

"I'm just wondering," I say.

Jeff rests the bar back in the resting position as the weights clang against each other. Jeff stays on the bench for a moment, long enough to catch his breath, then rolls off for my turn at the helm. Jeff is stronger than me by far as we both take off the five-pound and twenty-five-pound round plates that are on each side. We each put a twenty-pound plate accompanied by the forty-five already on there. Now it's my turn. Jeff goes up ten pounds each time, 215lbs-225lbs-235lbs. We do reps of ten, six, and four, and the last four are always a bitch, but the burn in my muscles feels good. Since it is early afternoon, few students are in the weight room. We are the only people working on the benches but still talk in a low voice so no one else thinks we are crazy.

"I think it really sucks that both your parents are dead," he says as I start my reps.

"We weren't a close family," I reply.

"I know," he says. "But I couldn't imagine my life without the support of my parents. They did so much for me. Livia's parents also. I have a huge support group to help me, and you're doing all this alone. It's got to be tough."

"Yep," I say as I complete my reps

Jeff and I switch places, and he continues his reps on the weight bench.

"Now go!" I say as we start Jeff's second set of reps.

We do our full workout and mostly talk about what to do next. What will happen to me now? How will this affect my scholarship? What is Dawn really doing here? Neither of us really trust her, but what can we do? What do I need to do to find out everything about her and any ulterior motives she has for being here at Duke? Our workout ends, and I keep thinking about how close Jeff's life is to mine. The only thing he hasn't done is run away from home. Or is he doing that now? With so much going on, I don't know who to trust. Especially since he does have access to my stuff since he is my roommate and teammate. It wouldn't be hard for anyone on the team to take a practice jersey. All these thoughts and nowhere they can go. What to do, what to do?

Since I want to be a total gentleman at dinner tonight and not act like a pig, Jeff and I get two super value meals from the sub shop. I don't want to eat like a barbarian at dinner, so I picked up a light snack. I want to make sure I eat slowly and make sure she finishes her meal before I finish mine.

Right now, it's past 5:00 p.m., and I'm back in my car heading toward the dorms. I already talked to both of my teachers. They were both very concerned with my absence since missing class means missing games. I explain my situation and got the days' notes and recover homework. I feel bad about missing class, but it was a situation out of my control, and everything is under control now. I also talked with Coach and told him that everything was fine, unless something else happened. I assured him of my innocence and gave him Dawn's room number and my cell phone number. I can be tracked down anywhere in the world now.

Once we get home, Jeff gives me a sports coat that matches my khaki pants. I threw on a dark-blue button shirt, brown boat shoes, and then jump into my black Camaro to whisk Dawn off into the twilight of Durham to have dinner at the Chateau Restaurant. What a beautiful night to have dinner with an attractive older woman that hopefully won't be dead in a week.

The Holiday Inn is only a mile or so away, and I arrive just after 6:30 p.m. I knock on door number 713. I wait for only a moment with a big smile before I hear a little giggle on the other side of the metal door. Then the door opens.

"Ray, hello. Come in," Officer Steve Freedman says to me with a glass of wine in his hand.

Yes, to my surprise, Officer Freedman is in Dawn's room. My date for the evening, Dawn, is keeping company with Steve Freedman. I look at Dawn as she is sitting on her bed, giggling as she takes another sip of her wine. I shake off the sudden impulse of twilight zone reality and enter the hotel room with some caution.

"Ray. We were just talking about you," Dawn says to me as I grab a chair and sit down by the bed. "You look nice," Dawn adds with a smile.

"Thank you," I say and smile back.

Steve sits down on the bed right next to Dawn and gives her a glowing smile that makes me sick to my stomach. Then Officer Freedman looks at me, wine in hand, smiling, sitting next to my date. Only one word comes to mind: *Bastard*.

"I've been working on your case," Freedman says to me. "I'll tell you what I've found over dinner. Come on. We can go to the Chateau," Freedman adds.

I must have a look of shock on my face. I'm stunned by his words. *We* are going to dinner. Great! Just great! All dressed up, and a third wheel to boot. All my dates have ended in ruin since I've been at Duke. Why should this one be any different? I feel betrayed, but I never said our dinner was really exclusive.

"Okay, let's go!" I say.

CHAPTER 14

SO HERE I am again, in front of Dr. Franklin, feeling very distant by no fault of my own. Again, someone is ruining my future, and this someone is Steve, I'm a Duke University Police Officer Wannabe, Freedman. At least this time I know who the obstacle is and I can answer the question of why. And I'm sure these two have been working on more than just my case. Not that their private lives are any of my business, but I was looking forward to spending a beautiful evening with an attractive older woman. Just the two of us, not the three of us.

"Come on, Ray," Steve says as he gets up from the bed. Dawn finishes her wine and bounces after him.

"I guess," I say in disgust under my breath.

I get up from the chair and follow the two of them out of the hotel room. I really cannot believe the three of us are going out to dinner. I should have called first and then canceled. I have no plan B either. I should have realized long ago that you should always have a plan B. Always be proactive instead of reactive. Those are words to live by.

"Steve found out some good news for you," Dawn says as she walks out of the hotel room, down the hallway, and toward the elevator.

The elevator is already awaiting us; Steve holds the door open for her as I lag behind. Dawn is in her jeans and white button shirt, while cowboy police officer wannabe Steve is in his best faded Wrangler jeans, a plaid shirt, and brown cowboy boots. I feel really overdressed for dinner now. I should have had a plan B.

"What have you found out?" I ask as the three of us ride the elevator down to the lobby.

"None of your theories have checked out," Steve says to me as we stand in the elevator.

"Really?" I add disappointingly. "How so?"

"I found Mr. Lennon in Amarillo, Texas, as a heavy machinery operator. He's been there for months, without any leaves of absence or time off. I also dug into those dental records and confirmed that it was your brother that died in the fire. We took the dental records your brother had from Boston. Your brother had no cavities and perfect teeth. No braces, no real overbite, no dental problems," Steve tells me as we descend into the lobby. "The teeth were an exact match with those on file at the coroner's office with the State of Florida."

"Lots of people have perfect teeth at thirteen," I add as I lean against the elevator wall. "I'm sure no dental mold was ever put together in Arcadia, and the jaw they found was broken into pieces since the roof fell in on the body," I explain. "Did your daughter have perfect teeth?" I ask as I look to Dawn as she stands next to Steve in the elevator.

"She never had a cavity. I know that, and she never needed braces. I guess she had perfect teeth," Dawn says as she huddles next to Freedman.

"I'm so glad you did all that significant and painstaking research on my behalf," I say to Steve. "What about Maria Lennon? What ever happened to her?" I ask as the doors open and release us into the lobby.

"I already went through this with Dawn earlier. We found some bone-chilling discoveries. Seventeen unclaimed bodies of teenage women were found in Florida in the last four years. Some of the bodies match Maria's description. We are matching photographs with computer composites. We will know for sure in a week," Steve says.

I look at Dawn as she gets a comforting hug of disbelief from Officer Freedman as she walks next to him out into the lobby.

"Steve and I have been talking all day. He's on top of this investigation and is Duke's number one officer," Dawn says.

"I'm always the one at Duke that breaks the case," he says.

"CSI Steve," I reply.

I open the hotel lobby entrance door for them and notice they are holding hands now. They pass by me and walk out to the curb hand in hand. I shake my head ever so slightly in disgust as I follow slowly, lagging behind in total disappointment. I can't always get the girl.

"You know?" I ask. "I really don't feel like talking shop all night. I'm not really that hungry either," I say to the two newly appointed lovebirds as I stand in front of the hotel entrance at the curb as they walk ahead of me. "Why don't you two go on without me? I'm sure it would be the best for all of us. I need to get some sleep and finish all my homework anyway. I've had such a bad week. I really need a break from all this," I say as I stand on the curb with my hands in my pockets.

"Are you sure? Dinner was your idea," Dawn asks as she stands with Steve Freedman just a few feet in front of me.

"Yeah, I'm sure," I say with a smile and total confidence as I stand alone in front of the hotel.

Steve shrugs his shoulders and leads Dawn away as if to say oh well.

"I'll talk to you later then," she adds as she walks across the parkway with Officer Freedman, hand in hand.

That's my night. No kisses, not even a goodbye. Just a talk to you later. My life sucks. What an ironic way to start an extravagant night! All is well though. No need to spend money on a girl who doesn't respect me or appreciate me. I would rather play basketball at the park with the boys for free anyway. I haven't picked up a basketball in days. Now is the perfect time. It will be getting dark soon, which is when the really good players come out and play. People who play basketball at playgrounds are very nocturnal; the better you are, the later you show up to play. Mainly because you play knowing you're going to take over the basketball court for the rest of the night. You know you will win; therefore, you plan on playing all night. That is when basketball games become majestic, and the shadows come alive with fury and presence. Playing basketball at night in North Carolina with the Duke boys is full of animosity and pure adrenaline.

I immediately walk to my car and drive back to the school. I'm back at the dorms in a few seconds. Keith Hastings, our resident assistant, has his door open and is studying with David Hodges and Bill Sharman. Keith is surprised to see me back so soon. Since Keith is an ex-ACC basketball player from Florida State, and David is the state of North Carolina's golden boy, they are always up for a good game of b-ball. Bill Sharman is the team's elder and jerk. He acts like a snob, and I really dislike him. Bill starts for the team now and won a championship at Duke years ago against St. Louis in a double overtime championship game when he was a freshman. He doesn't let anyone forget it either. He made the game-winning shot in double overtime. He forgets to tell everyone that was the only shot he made all game, but yes, it was the game winner. Now he is a senior at Duke and acts like an asshole to everyone, especially freshmen like me.

The story on Keith is he already graduated two years ago and is back striving for a Master's Degree in Business Administration. Keith is as smart as any Harvard student or any set of encyclopedias. He already has about three years of real-world experience as a supervisor and manager with a computer company. Keith is twenty-five, and the only reason he came back to school was to kick back for the next two years before he has to become an adult in the real world. He told me he was the youngest person at Honeywell as a team leader. Keith has it all. He is good with numbers, computers, and people. He is good-looking, tall, blond hair with blue eyes, and in great physical shape. He was the youngest and brightest manager at Honeywell and had a $65,000 a year job right out of college. Every other manager at Honeywell was in their thirties, had a wife, kids, divorce, second wife, mortgage, and second mortgage payments, car payments, and minivan coming out of their $80,000 a year salary. The sad part, all day long other department managers would complain to Keith about how bad the good life is and how everyone wishes they were Keith's age once again. Complaining about what they should have done was the way these has-beens could live life over again. Keith said, "Forget all that!" He was too young to be a counselor for broke assholes. He put in his two weeks' notice at Honeywell and enrolled at Duke to get an MBA. Since Keith was already sports oriented and graduated from Florida State as summa cum laude, Duke asked him to be the resident assistant of a sports-oriented dorm. Keith gladly accepted.

I like him since he is a Florida boy. Keith grew up in Fort Myers, Florida, idolizing his hometown heroes of Chris Sale, Mike Greenwell, and Deion Sanders. I admire Keith; he is smart and can actually tell me how to do things right, especially since he's been there. I like following in the footsteps of people who have been there before I have. They can tell me what to do to get it right. My dad taught me that you might not like the people on the ladder in front of you, but they are there for a reason. They did something that earned them the position they hold. Look up to these people. Find out what they did right so you can get there too. As for Keith, he did everything right thus far. His awards from Florida State hang on his wall, along with his college degree, honors tassels, and certificates from Honeywell. Keith listens first and talks sensibly to you with straight talk.

When I first got to Duke, I gave everyone an attitude because I thought the other students would be against me. Kind of like being hazed as a high school freshman, especially by seniors like Bill Sharman. Keith talked with me about the attitude I had and told me that college isn't like that. Maturity is how people judge me when they meet me, and no one won awards at Duke for being an asshole. College is fun with an education to boot; make the best of it. Most kids are not as privileged as Duke students are. I guess that is as straight as he could give it to me. Since then, we have been cool and good friends.

As for David Hodges, he is the rich kid of the team. Played ball all his life and came to Duke because of the pressure his parents put on him to win a national championship. David's parents give him everything—car, money, toys, a new computer, and games. Must be nice to have money and loving parents. I wouldn't know. Dave is

Italian looking, about six feet tall, and one of the best pure point guards you will ever meet. Bill Sharman and Dave make the perfect backcourt. Let's hope David doesn't turn into another dickhead like Bill though. The one thing about David is he always wants to play ball, and classes seem to get in the way of that. David might be an NBA player someday since he is good enough to start as a freshman here at Duke. That's a great accomplishment since he is a six-foot-tall white boy, and we contend for a championship every year. I'm sure David will be okay since his heroes are Jayson Tatum and Kyrie Irving. Those are big shoes to fill, but all those Duke graduates are great mentors to have.

"Back so soon?" Keith asks as I stand paused at his open door.

"Came back to get you two guys and play some ball at Gilcrest Park. See if you can hang with the freshman!" I yell out as I pause at his door and hang onto it as I make my presence known. "Especially you!" I take a look deep into Bill Sharman eyes.

"You're on!" David yells back in an excited voice.

"That wasn't hard at all," I say to myself as I spring into my dorm room and surprise the hell out of Jeff.

"Ha! Ha! Ha! Ha!" I scream at Jeff as I bust into the room.

I watch his eyes almost pop out of his head as his heartbeat pumps all his blood out of his heart in absolute terror.

"What are you doing back so soon?" he says out in aspiration as he sits at his desk talking to Livia on the phone.

I know I scared him with me bursting into the room like that. I bet he thought I was the killer.

"I came to get you so we can play some real ball at Gilcrest. Come on," I say as I sit on my bed and get my battle gear on. I change quickly from my khakis and button shirt to my thick gray T-shirt. I throw on my long blue shorts, put on two pairs of crew socks, and lace up my brand-new Nikes, all white with a clear swoosh symbol outlined in dark blue. Now I'm a Blue Devil—a demon of the basketball world at large, ready to devour my opponents like helpless prey. I'm transformed by the moment and the pressures of competition.

"Ready to go?" Keith says as he pops into the room with David.

"No Bill Sharman?" I ask. "Are we not good enough for him?" I ask as I change.

"No Bill," David adds. "He has to study for an exam."

Jeff is still on the phone and is trying to end the conversation without telling his faraway girlfriend that he'd rather play ball with the boys than talk to her on the phone. She is in Atlanta studying at Georgia Tech to be a chemical engineer. He would go to school there, but Jeff is an awesome basketball player with a great work ethic. Duke, not Georgia Tech, is the school to go to if you want to win a national championship for basketball in the Division I.

"You two are playing also?" he asks with his hand over the receiver so his girlfriend can't hear him talk to us. "Count me in," Jeff says and quickly ends the conversation with his long-distance love.

Jeff changes quickly into his Nikes and faded warm-ups. The four of us dart playfully out of the dorm like four bats out of Hell with our basketballs in hand, sweatbands around our wrist and small towels to keep us and the ball dry. We have a lot of fun playing basketball, but the key is not to get hurt. Never give 100 percent playing street ball; you might break an ankle or a finger. The point of street ball is to have fun and look good while winning. Therefore, we take lots of outside shots and attempt great passes that look difficult to everyone else except for you. Also, don't let the person covering you score a point, and never, ever, ever drive down the middle of the lane. If you drive down the lane and get tripped or sprain an ankle, you're done. Those are the rules when we play street ball.

"I can't believe I finally get to play with the Golden Boy!" I say as all of us cross the parking lot to my car while pointing to David.

"I'm gonna beat you down, freshman!" David yells back as he slams the ball down on the pavement of the parking lot.

"So what happened to your big date?" Jeff asks.

"Nothing at all. She has Officer Freedman there. Went out to dinner with him," I reply and try to shake that memory out of my mind.

"Ooh!" they all howl in unison like wolves as if Dr. Franklin and Steve burned me.

"You better hope I'm on your team because I'm going to treat you bad," I say.

"I'm gonna leave you hanging, just like Dawn did!" Jeff yells out as he palms his basketball and starts walking the funky chicken walk.

Dave and Keith make a low sounding "Oh" as we head out the door and down the hall. Once outside the dorms, the four of us jump into my Camaro. I feel superior, exceptional, and exuberant, ready to explode with energy. This is a time for friends and frolicking. I'm looking forward to playing ball with these guys so I can prove myself in the basketball arena of life and show them how great of a basketball player I really am. Since Jeff and David are starters on the team, I can show them I can play. I can show them that I deserved to win a state championship in Florida. Since Keith is my mentor, his opinion means a lot to me. The only reason I'm not playing now is because Duke has so many seniors on the team, which is why Duke redshirted me. Duke didn't want to lose me to another school, and I didn't want to play anywhere else. I'll make sure at least two of them are on the opposite team so I can use them like mops and wipe the court with them. I feel like I have something to prove to them and myself. I can win at a new level. In my mind, *It's on!* I can flip the switch. "It's on!"

The four of us drive through the night, telling stories about ourselves hitting game-winning shots with no time left on the clock. We tell stories of crowds going wild and twelve players on a court holding the championship trophy with one hand and a piece of the net in the other hand. As children and champions, we all dream big, knowing that someday all our hard work will pay off into a real-life situation known as an NCAA championship ring. We all came to Duke University to win a ring and get the best education we could.

Keith's dreams of basketball championships are over, but he plays along with us and laughs as well. I only hope that my dreams get a chance to come true and the phantom of my past releases the chokehold that he or she has on my future. For right now, we are young, wild, and free, having fun and making our dreams into a reality with no pressure of the real world as we walk these crowded streets of the campus that protects us. I look at Keith and know we can't be kids forever, and one day we will grow up and transform into adults of the real world away from Duke University. No more Denny's at midnight and playing basketball until two in the morning during the week under the majestic moon with friends. We will go from having dorm rooms, roommates, and scholarships to mortgages, wives, and babies. That is if we are lucky and strong. I know I'm strong. Let us see how lucky I am.

It's late in the evening, and the sky is already black. We approach Gilcrest Park and the bright racks of Mercury lights, which shine on the four full-length courts, light the sky ablaze. The park is in the middle of downtown and right off the main road. About four high schools hang out here, and some really good community college players come here all the time. These courts are where high school players see what the next level is like and community college players come to prove themselves. You very rarely see any Duke players here, but here we are. Time to play, and all four courts are running five on five. Tall and skinny high school kids are dunking the ball on their smaller opposition, draining threes and hitting high fives as they dominate the courts. We came to get on. We came to the right place. This is the life.

This park is a magical place in which no NBA jerseys are worn, no players with professional logos blistered on their shirts or shorts. All the kids here wear their own jerseys with their names on the back. The number they wear is their own claim to fame, to show everyone else that they have made it at their own level of gifted determination. They are proud of their school basketball team and their own feats of skill. They are here to show people that you once saw them play here before they made it big and your kids will be wearing their jersey with their number on the back one day.

"You're running with the big dogs now," Jeff says to me as we pull into the park. "It's time to play!"

The four of us park close to the courts and hop out of the car. We are just another group of players to these guys. Just like them, we came to play.

"Lock it up!" Jeff exclaims as we get out of the car.

There have been several cars stolen from the colleges in the last week, so I'm not taking any chances on getting my car jacked.

Beep, beep! I hear the alarm set as we walk down the long sidewalk that leads to the courts. Benches and picnic tables surround the concrete slabs for people to watch the youthful stars shine. The four of us put our orange spheres on an empty picnic table and start to stretch out in the deep, thick green grass. The courts are all in a row, side by side. The younger kids are playing at the far court, and the older guys play at the court nearest the water fountain and us. These guys, in the near court, are all college boys that play ball all day long, probably all night long. This particular game is really one-sided. A group of fresh guys are beating the probable longtime champions of the hard court. Everyone playing on the near court has a jersey with his name on it. No sellouts are here tonight, only Durham's All-Stars.

I feel good as I wear my high school jersey with number 44 on it. This number is with me always as it's tattooed on my chest in a basketball with my name engraved on it also. I have my friends by my side, and this is the first time in weeks I'm relaxed and having fun. Playing basketball is fun, and it lets me blow off steam.

A skinny black kid about six feet two inches tall walks up to the four of us as we stretch out before our first game.

"Can I jump in with you guys?" the young kid asks.

"Sure," Jeff says without hesitation.

As you know, Jeff is our leader, group chairman, and now speaker of the house.

"I'm Ricky," the young kid says.

We introduce ourselves and welcome Ricky to the tough and always challenging court of Gilcrest Park's A level.

"Ricky, you do know this is the big boy's court, right?" I ask as I stretch out across from where Ricky is standing.

Ricky sits on the picnic table and just smiles as he spins the ball on his middle finger. I take it as he knows what he's getting himself into.

"How old are you?" Keith asks as he gets up from the grass. The rest of us follow suit and get ready to play as we surround Ricky.

"Sixteen, but I can dunk. I won't make you old guys look bad," he says as he smirks at us.

"He's got jokes," Jeff says as he's the second oldest behind Keith.

We all join Ricky at the picnic table and wait for the preceding game to end.

"What's the deal with these guys now?" I ask as I am the last one to sit down on the picnic table with everyone else.

"I have downs, and we have the next game. These guys that are winning aren't any good. Just fresh muscle. If we beat them, the team losing will have the next set of downs. If we beat them, I'll be impressed. They are good old boys, live and dream hoops, all probably college boys that use their basketballs as pillows. They are probably good enough to play for Duke or North Carolina," he adds as he sits with us at the picnic table.

"We'll find out, Ricky," Jeff adds as he walks onto the court.

The present game suddenly ends, and the losers all get in line at the water fountain. The five of us take the court and make few warm-up shots. As for me, I take off the down the ninety-four-foot stretch of concrete and dunk the ball hard instead of taking any warm-up shots.

"Hey!" Keith calls to me from across the court. "No attitude! We are here to have fun. Don't get caught up in the game. Don't be so serious. You have nothing to prove here. It's just a playground. Nothing more," he says to me in a half angry voice from the other side of the court.

He's right. It's just a game. All of us are here to play and have fun. And the other five guys, well, basketball is a way of life for them, and they walk on the court as defending champions. Let's get ready to rumble. They get the ball first, and we play defense. We roll as the night watches us. It's on!

Right from the first inbound pass, the game is intense. It's really on! The defending champs pass the ball around and drive the lane every chance they get. We play man-on-man defense, and everyone on the court except for David is over six feet tall. We all match up evenly. Their team is four black guys and one really young white kid. We are four white guys with one really young black kid.

148

They score on their first possession, and so do we. David brings the ball up; he and Ricky play guards. I'm a small forward while Keith and Jeff are the big guys up front. We run the ball up the court fast and pass three or four times before scoring our first easy basket.

On their next possession, David steals the ball, passes to me, and I dish it to Ricky, who in turn drives the lane past everyone and lays it in. I realize then that this team isn't able to hang with our strength and speed. We pull away with a five-to-one lead, with each of us scoring a point. The other team doesn't really know who to cover or double-team. We stick with man-to-man coverage against their zone defense. David's man is a little taller and stronger than him, and he muscles in for the next couple of points for the opposing team. Dave doesn't let that get him down. David dishes the rock to me for two straight outside shots. Keith sets two perfect picks each time for easy buckets off the glass. The score goes from three and seven to five and nine with Jeff scoring our next two points. The game grows fierce, and with these guys losing, they decide to pick up their game. They do more passing, and we are double-teaming anyone inside the lane. Fouls run rampant, and the progress of the game is slowing down and becoming more physical.

Then the big moment. I'm defending my one-on-one opponent at the top of the key when I reach out and I steal the ball away from him. There is nothing in between me and the goal but opportunity. I look back and see that Ricky is the only player following me, and he is running full speed, keeping up with me.

"It's all you," I say to Ricky as I slow up and throw the ball easily off the side of the backboard.

Ricky jumps three feet into the air and grabs the basketball with both hands before slamming the ball down off the back iron of the rim. He misses an easy dunk. The ball bounces off the rim back to the free throw line. I grab it, dribble it once, and slam it down hard on the other defenders as they come closer to me.

I trot back down the court with a feeling of accomplishment since none of these guys have ever seen me dunk in a game until now. David, Keith, and Jeff all bump fists with me as if to tell me I did good.

Before I know it, the game is over, and we win. The losers of the last game come onto the court now. Five black guys all about twenty, all ready to play ball and win. Only we can stop the aggression once again.

"That last game was easy compared to what these guys are going to put us through," Ricky says as we get drinks from the community water fountain.

"I see you have gotten pretty good in such a short time," this one guy about twenty feet from me says to the five of us as we stand by the water fountain glued against the black night sky.

We all look puzzled because we didn't know who he is talking to.

"Who, me?" Ricky says as he points to himself.

The guy standing in front of us is a thin guy in his early twenties with not much tone. The guy has a military haircut and is dressed like the "white man can't jump" player. His shorts and shirt don't match, and he has the really wide red-colored laces in his new white sneakers. I figure if he is trying to pick a fight, he would be no match for any of us, or even Ricky.

"No. Number 44," he says as he walks across the court over to me.

I'm number 44. I don't know what this guy is talking about.

"Me?" I say as I point to myself. "Where have you seen me play?"

"Last weekend, in Chapel Hill. You couldn't hit a shot. Now you are dunking the ball and hitting fadeaway jumpers. You didn't miss out there," he says as he approaches me.

Now he is inches away and holding out his hand to shake mine.

"I was in Florida this past weekend, and I played ball my entire life. I play basketball for Duke with these guys," I say as I shake his hand in disbelief.

"Really, because I play ball at Chapel Hill, and I've seen you play, number 44. That is how I recognized you. Number 44," he says from among the darkness of the night.

This guy is tall, skinny, and crazy. David, Keith, and Jeff all know that I was in Florida this past week and that I never go to

Chapel Hill to play ball. What the hell is going on? Then, suddenly, I see the light.

"If it wasn't you, it is a guy that looks exactly like you. Exactly like you. Could be your twin brother," he says.

David, Keith, and Jeff are all blind with shock and in total disbelief at what this man is saying to us. He uses the words *my twin brother*.

"Do you know his name?" I ask as I step away from the fountain.

"I'm not really sure, but I think his name is Ray," the stranger says.

CHAPTER 15

"Yeah, Ray," the stranger says to me.

"That's my name," I say as I stand in shock under the black night sky in front of this mysterious person as my friends stare at us both.

Jeff, David, and Keith freeze with trauma and awe as the man reveals the name of my mysterious twin. The night feels thick with anticipation as we fall into the lush realism of what one arcane man can present to us, especially me. This man is a witness to our fears. The night keeps everyone fearful and fearless all at once as we creep into the unknown depths of truth and nonsense with this stranger. Everything is getting preposterous and out of hand.

"I'm Ray. I think I'm the only number 44 on campus," I finally say to break the silence.

Once again, I'm in the Twilight Zone. Everything around me is caving in. What else could happen to me in this harsh realm of Duke realism?

"Really," the unknown man says. "That's odd. You both have the same name?" he says awkwardly.

Now all I can keep thinking about is that my twin brother is here in North Carolina. The strange events of my past are now here in the present. An eternity of being someone else has finally caught up with me. My twin brother is out to conquer the Holy Grail with me as his cup, and he is here in North Carolina learning to play basketball. Holy shit! Worse, he's trying to become Raymond Douglas Beacon. He looks like me, thinks like me, and knows the people and the past that I know. Now he has my number and probably my mannerisms. The same drive, energy, and determination that made me who I am lives within him as well. Athletic ability is the only thing that separates us. I can't believe he is here, after me with a vengeance to become me, as I once became him. For me, it is now on. The game of cat and mouse is now for real. The scenario of death is as real as life itself. The twin brother theory is now true and all I can think about standing here under the black sky.

"Are you all right there?" the stranger says to me.

I look around and see that Keith, David, and Jeff are all stunned by the news just as I am. The four of us solidify apart from the night air with amazement. Life is no longer on hold, and every breath seems to be my last before the acceleration of my mind catches up with the reality of my soul.

"You said Chapel Hill was where you saw him?" Jeff asks as the four of us are crowded around this unknown man by the water fountain.

We are left hanging on the knowledge of this unknown person's words like an evil presence waiting to devour the innocent. I don't reveal anything about my situation just in case this is a setup. This could all be a hoax to entrap me—another trap I could get caught in. I play along because I don't want to scare him off either; therefore, I'm whimsical in presence and fearful on the inside.

"Not the park. The University. I saw him there Saturday and Sunday morning when no one else was out there. He plays by himself early in the mornings at the outdoor courts. You two look alike," he says to me.

We stand there for a second, and my mind is racing. I'm thinking about so much. I have so many questions I want to ask, but I don't want to interrogate this guy and seem like a freak unknowing about myself, doubting my own confidence.

"Do you know where he lives?" I ask as the four of us stand among him.

"No, I've only seen him once before," the stranger says as he looks at us in a strange way. "Is there something wrong here?"

"No, nothing whatsoever," Jeff says to him.

"Thanks, man," I say. "What's your name?"

"James Clark," he replies

"Do you go to school around here?" Jeff asks.

"No, but I work at Big Mart down the road. I play ball here all the time. My girl goes to UNC," James replies.

"Thanks, man," I say again, and then James walks away to play on another court.

"Hey, Ricky!" I say to our teammate who is at the water fountain about six feet away from us. "Have you ever seen that guy around here?" I ask as I point to James.

My friends, who are just as curious as I am about my twin brother and the one man that has seen him, surround me.

"Maybe," Ricky fires back with some curiosity then takes another drink of water.

"He saw your twin?" Jeff asks. "This is unreal, which means your twin came here to North Carolina. Why?" Jeff asks as everyone stares at me.

"Exactly! Why?" I ask.

"You have enough problems, Ray," Keith says. "Go straight to the police with this. Let them go interrogate that guy and watch the park. You should stay far away from this. Right now, you are the thirteenth man on a twelve-man team. You already have a few strikes with the school. You don't need this shit. Don't get sucked in. You'll get blown away."

"What is going on? You have a twin brother?" David asks.

I told you before that David isn't the brightest of light bulbs.

"We have to go, Ricky," I say as he walks up to us from the water fountain. Everyone follows suit and wishes Ricky well in his basketball adventures. "Sorry, but we can't stay. Something very important came up," I say as we run off.

The four of us grab our orange globes and white towels and head for my car parked in front of the basketball courts.

"I can't believe you were right. Your brother is alive!" Jeff says as the night surrounds us, and we walk the long sidewalk path to my Camaro.

Everything is silent! What is my next move now that I know Rod is alive? What can I do now? Rodney is a psychopath that looks like me, has endured four years of hiding in torment, and has killed at least five people in the last three months. Rodney is a killer at large. He is watching me from afar and waiting, waiting to get even for what I've done to him. Once he feels vindicated or destroys my life, then he will be happy.

"Your brother is at Chapel Hill, our rival. How ironic," Keith says.

"We need to go down there Saturday and Sunday with the cops and clear your name of all this bullshit that's been happening," Jeff says to me demandingly.

"If we find your brother or someone who knows him, you're free and clear," Keith adds as we cross the parking lot toward my car.

I notice that David isn't saying anything. Either he is holding back, or he hasn't caught on to the story of a twin brother killer looking for me. I don't know if these guys believe it either. It was, after all, my idea to come to Gilcrest Park in the first place. To them, this could all be part of an evil plan of mine to throw them off my scent. Misdirection and confusion is always a magician's best friend.

"We are not going anywhere!" I reply. "This guy is a horror story. He decapitated Heather, drugged and killed Jen, and cut Kate's hands off. He also killed my mom less than a week ago, and I know he is after me. We are going to the police. We are not going near Chapel Hill this weekend!" I say as everyone walks up to my car. "He could be watching us now. He's been in our dorm room and placed a head in my room. This guy is crazy! And he's no brother of mine!" I say as I get into the driver's seat and start my car.

I drop the top of the Camaro as two guys climb into the back seat and Jeff gets in on the passenger side.

"It's about time you tell us what really happened to you way back when," David says from the back seat of my Camaro. "The quick, to-the-point, condensed version of the truth. If we are going to stand by you, we need to know!" David says demandingly from the small back seat of my car.

"This affects more than you now. You're endangering Jeff's life and ours," Keith says from behind me.

"Yeah, bro. Tell us the truth. I have a future and a girlfriend to worry about. I need to know the truth," Jeff says to me from the passenger seat.

A Burger King is about a hundred yards ahead of us on the main road. I'm not really hungry, but the parking lot would serve as good a place as any to tell the bewildering story of two brothers; a freshman-year divorce; isolation; a very abusive mother; a pretty girl named Lee; a fire; the long road to Durham, North Carolina; my dead parents; and now the three dead girls.

I drive the Camaro to the drive-through speaker box. Since three of us are athletes, we are not supposed to eat any fast food. Diet and exercise are the keys to keeping in shape. I'm supposed to drink lots of water, take vitamins, workout, and not eat chocolate. No fried food or sugary sweets, and no eating anything after 9:00 p.m. Jeff and I already ate once tonight—foot-long grilled chicken sandwiches and Gatorades from Subway. According to Coach, players go to hell for cheating on their strict diets and definitely don't reach tournaments for being so undisciplined during the regular season. But what the hell. You only live once.

"Can I take your order?" the little metal box of dots says to us.

"Four strawberry shakes and four orders of large fries. Thank you." I then pull ahead to pay for the order with a twenty then pull into a fully lit parking space.

Every one of us grabs an order of fries and a strawberry shake as we sit in the parking space with the engine off and the radio on low. All the windows in the car are down. We are all comfortable in the car for now.

"So what happened?" Jeff asks, munching on his fries.

"A little over four years ago, my parents got divorced, and I was sent to live with my mom in Arcadia, Florida. I went from having the time of my life in Boston to living in a godforsaken little hillbilly town of sand, dirt roads, cows, and rednecks called Arcadia. I hated it. My dad had a new mistress and kinda wanted it to be him and her. My mom needed the child support to make ends meet, so she sued for custody. My dad's mistress told him that the kids should be with their mom. Therefore he let us go and willingly paid the child support."

As the four of us relax, the soothing night makes a calm atmosphere for our conversation. The four of us suck down our strawberry shakes and eat forbidden fries by the handfuls. I seem to attack my food by the handful of fries and more than enjoy the fries bit by bit. The others seem to do the same and inhale the food also. The night is calm, the mood is soothing, and the hot salted fries hit the spot. The four of us are sitting in the car, hanging out like teenagers with no place to go.

"What happened to your dad?" Keith asks as he gobbles his fries.

"After he rejected me, we lost touch, and this past week, I found out that he was murdered by his second wife," I say to my friends as we eat. "My dad was dead to Rodney and me long before he actually died. He literally didn't want anything to do with us once his new girlfriend, Betty, moved in."

"How horrible!" Keith adds as he munches on the delights of Burger King.

"Not really. He thought Rodney and I were dead a long time ago," I say as I sip my drink.

"Why?" Jeff asks from beside me in the passenger seat.

"Well, my brother died in a fire, and I ran away. I told my dad I wanted to come back home, and he said no. Therefore, I didn't go to Boston because I knew my father wanted nothing to do with me. Betty was his new wife, and they led a new life away from all the little things that reminded him of his past," I say as I eat.

"How does your brother fit in if he's dead?" David asks from the back seat.

"Rodney and I were never close, but we really grew apart in Arcadia. Mom didn't watch us or take care of us, so we were pretty much on our own. My mom was abusive—physically, mentally, and verbally. She ignored us, and she wouldn't come home on the weekends. We were alone from Friday night to Monday morning. After she didn't come for the third weekend in a row, I started going out on all-nighters, getting into trouble. Rodney always stayed home on the weekend, and I saw our family drifting apart. Rod had school and no friends while I had sports and a few bad apples as friends. Everyone was always picking on Rod and making fun of him. After a while, I did too. I joined the crowd instead of fighting them. Soon Rodney and I weren't even friends. We really grew apart when he fell in love with Maria."

"Dr. Franklin's daughter?" Jeff asks as he devours his french fries.

"Yeah. Only one day, I skipped class to play basketball. I went to Rod's locker, grabbed his shirt, and lo and behold, here comes Maria," I say from the driver's seat of my Camaro.

"Here comes trouble," Keith adds from the back seat.

"She sees me in Rod's shirt at his locker and assumes I'm him. I played along," I say and then take a sip of my shake to wash down the fries.

"What next?" Jeff asks.

"I end up talking her into skipping school. I told her I loved her and we should make love together, right then and there. We left school. Went to my house and did it."

I hear David and Jeff cough on their drinks as the story I tell them has taken them by surprise. Keith sits up in the backseat, and now all three guys are hanging on my every word, paying attention to the details of the story.

"Did you sleep with her?" David asks with avid curiosity.

"I laid her right down on my brother's bed and made her my first. She thought I was Rodney the entire time. I was her first," I say with a big smile as I look at my friends.

"No way!" David adds from behind me as he shakes his head in disbelief.

"She told me she was glad that I would be her first and it would be love. Those where her exact words," I say from my driver's seat under the black night sky.

"You slept with your brother's girlfriend before he did? You're a dog!" Keith says to me. "What were you thinking?" he asks in shock.

"Why did you do that?" David asks.

"Remind me never to bring Livia over for the weekend," Jeff adds.

"I was so jealous of what he had. I was the one who had everything in Boston, but now in Arcadia, my life was horrible. And I was jealous."

I'm sitting sideways in my seat now, and I'm facing everyone. Keith and David are sitting forward, focusing on me. Jeff is sitting sideways in the passenger seat, hearing the words flow as I tell the story. We look like four little kids telling ghost stories around a campfire, only we are four devils and this is no folktale. The curiosity of the story has all three boys at full attention as we sit in the black convertible, under the parking lot lights, surrounded by the cool night air. We sit among ourselves, quietly eating our french fries and drinking the strawberry shakes.

"Anyway, it gets worse," I say. "While I was having sex with her, I look up, and there is an eyeball looking at us. One single eyeball, looking through the crack in the doorway, at us. One single eyeball just watching, and I knew it was Rodney. Maria was moaning with ecstasy. I'm really going at it with her on my brother's bed. She's biting her lip and hanging on to me. I'm kissing her passionately. And all along one single eyeball is just watching. One eyeball focused on me, watching, doing nothing but watching."

"No way," David says and again shakes his head slightly because he can't believe this is a true story about two brothers.

"This is bullshit," Keith says with a huge smile on his face.

"No bull, guys," I say and continue. "At first it scared me, then I looked again and there it was, one single eyeball peering at us making love. I knew it was my brother, and I gave him my biggest smile as I had sex with his girlfriend. I looked down at her and then again at the door, and the door is closed. The eyeball is gone. Maria never saw a thing. She had her eyes shut the entire time."

"You're lying!" David says aloud as he leans back in his seat.

"No way!" Jeff says to me. "Pure bullshit!"

"He's right. You're lying!" David adds from the back seat.

"No lie! Every word true," I say as I grin at them. "When I got done with Maria, I opened the bedroom door. I was as scared as I had ever been. I was expecting Rodney to be there with a butcher knife or something. There was nothing there. No one. No one was on the other side of the door. I looked throughout the house and Rodney was gone, nowhere to be found. He never came home that night either. My mom didn't even care. The next day, Rodney and Maria didn't come to school. The next thing I know, my house is on fire early that morning. The firemen found a body. A body burnt to the bone and smashed to pieces. The firemen had to take the body out in pieces. I thought it was my brother, but I know the body they found was Maria's. Rodney killed Maria, he set the fire, and burned the house down to hide any evidence of foul play. That weekend, my mother would have what was left of the remains cremated, and I ran away from home. I haven't seen anyone in my family since that day. That was my freshman year in Arcadia," I say to my curious friends.

"You ran away?" Keith asks.

"Yep," I replied. "I emptied the bank accounts and roamed Florida for that spring and summer. Then Mr. Beacon took me in, claiming he was my legal guardian. My ex-girlfriend's mom worked for the school board in Massachusetts. She forged my transcripts and sent them to Oviedo for me. Everything was legit. It looked like I was never even in Arcadia. I started school in August like everyone else. I got a new social security number. I literally erased my past, and four years later, I won a state championship, got a scholarship to Duke, moved to North Carolina, and got framed for murder."

"How does your brother fit in to all this?" Jeff asks from my passenger seat.

"I took all the money and ran away. Meaning, he could never get even with me for taking what little he had. He killed Maria, no doubt in my mind. Once the press pictured Oviedo winning the state championship in Florida, he found me. The murders have happened since I've been at Duke. He followed me here, and he wants to destroy my life. Just like I did to him in Arcadia. End of story. He wants what I have, just like I took what he had. All he had," I say from my driver's seat.

"Great, you're screwed!" Jeff says. "And I have to tell you, Ray, I'm scared," Jeff says calmly as we all sit and think of the situation at hand.

"You're in a tough spot and because of that, we are now in a bad situation," Keith adds as he finishes his fries and drink.

"Any one of us could be next, Ray. Do you realize the seriousness of this? And you're just now telling us the truth about your past," David adds.

"Go buy a gun," Jeff says to me calmly from the passenger seat.

"I guess since your brother is a psychopathic murder runaway chasing you from Florida to North Carolina, we can assume all of our lives are in danger," David adds from the back seat.

"He brutally killed five people and put a head in our room. Yes, my life is in danger!" I say to David and the rest of the boys. "Not your lives since he has only killed women up until now."

"Why do you think he didn't just kill you right way. Not to sound gory or anything, but why?" Keith asks as the light from the lamppost surrounds us.

I am the first person to finish my fries and drink.

"Well, my guess would be I'm an athlete and I'm stronger than him," I say. "Plus, he knows what I did to him. He would want me to know it was him. He would have to plan this just right, or he's actually thinking about taking over my life since he is already dead."

"Well, I'm now glad the school has beefed things up and security is all over this," Jeff adds

"Yeah, me too. But he is me, and he could be anywhere," I say as I crush the shake cup in my hands and look at the big Burger King trashcan by the entrance. The other boys finish their food about the same time as me. The trash can is about twenty-five feet behind me. I crumple my french fry pouch, put it into the smashed cup for weight, and throw up a three-point shot from out of my convertible toward the trash can.

"It's going to be tough," I say as the cup misses the trash can ever so slightly.

"You missed!" David laughs aloud as my rock bounces off the rim of the garbage can and into the bushes.

David and Jeff also throw up shots of their own as my cup lays lifeless in the shrubs.

"Swish!" David yells as his cup goes through the cylinder.

"Three!" Jeff yells out as his cup joins David's inside the trash can. "Need some practice, freshman. It will come in time." Then everyone laughs.

I turn on my engine and shift the gears of my Camaro into reverse. I drive the car slowly out of the parking space.

"What's your next move?" Jeff asks as we drive toward the university.

"Talk to Dawn and Freedman. As of right now, my life is in danger. I'll talk to Coach K tomorrow morning," I say as I drive onward.

I drive the car at top speed to the Quad to drop off the three boys. I tell the three of them to stay tight and not disappear since I'm sure Dawn and Freedman will want to talk to them tonight. I'm sure Coach will want to know what is going on tomorrow, especially since I've failed the lie detector test.

"Well, back to the beginning," I say out loud for only myself to hear as I take my car to go see Dawn.

That is another dilemma. What will await me there?

CHAPTER 16

NOBODY EVER WANTS to think of themselves as nonexistent, but when a psycho twin killer with a vengeance is on the loose waiting to kill you, one tends to think of his well-being. Staying alive is the key to life. That and accomplishment. Being loved, wanted, and needed also ranks up there on my top ten list of life's little things, but staying alive is definitely number one on the list. Thus far, I am alive, haven't really accomplished anything outside of high school, and the police are watching me. Two out of three isn't really that bad since I'm only eighteen.

I drive by the Holiday Inn, only to see that Freedman's pickup truck isn't there, but neither is Dawn's rental car. I pull into the hotel and check to see if Dawn is here to tell her what I've found. I park in the valet and walk to the front counter.

"Can you check Dawn Franklin's room, 713?" I ask the attendant.

He rings the room and waits for an answer. I don't want her to think I'm bothersome; therefore, I'll be sure to announce my arrival.

"No answer, sir. Should I leave a message in her box?" the clerk asks.

"No thanks," I say and then leave without disgust or anger. But where can she be?

I walk back out to my car and head for the Chateau to see if they are there. The drive is peaceful. I still have the top down, and since my hair is so short, I don't worry about how I look. I really don't worry too much about my appearance anyway. My closet is full of T-shirts and sweatshirts. I wear jeans all the time and have muscle shirts during the summer months. Besides that, I have about two pairs of khakis, two pairs of black pants, four button-up shirts that I never wear, and a pair of dark-brown boat shoes that I've only worn once, and that is today. Nice clothes come with clout, and since I don't have any need to impress anyone outside Coach K at this point in my life, I feel no need for clout.

"No one at the Chateau," I say out loud as I drive past the extravagant restaurant with huge front windows and even bigger prices on the other side of those elegant bay windows.

I see no signs of the rusty pickup truck or red Mustang and don't see Dawn or Officer Freedman inside. I pick up my iPhone and call the hotel to see if she got there after I left.

"No, sir. She isn't in yet," the front desk clerk says to me over the phone. "Would you like to leave a message?" the young attendant asks.

"Yeah. Write this down," I tell the clerk. "Rod is back. Call me ASAP, Ray. Thanks," I reply and then I hang up.

What is my next move? I need a strategy until I get some help. The best offense is a good defense. I need to defend myself; therefore, I need a gun. That's right, a gun. For protection reasons only, and I need to learn how to use it quickly. Since I'm not up-to-date on my covert operations or underworld crime, how do I get a gun overnight? I would have to wait ten days if I buy one over the counter at a store. The store would need to run a criminal background check on me. This would alert Tusson and Webber. Plus, I need to tell someone that Rod is alive and out there, ready to devour my life like a hungry wolf on a cold dark night. No one will believe me. I can see it now, your brother, who has been dead for four years, is trying to kill you or frame you for murder. Oh, by the way, he's learning to play basketball to become you. A guy you never met before has seen him and will vouch for you. Okay! That will sound ludicrous, even though it is the truth. It seems a little bizarre even to me.

I pull the car over into an empty shopping center parking lot and think about my options. The last thing I want to do is look stupid or even more guilty than I do now. Captain Adams is the closest police officer to me since I am in downtown Durham. To the police station I go. I drive back to the crisp, pristine big white building in which the polygraph test called me a liar earlier today. I pull into the back and go inside looking for Captain Adams.

I walk the halls of the Durham Police Station and can hear the echoes of my own footsteps bounce off the linoleum floors and solid white walls. I walk down the main hallway and toward the front desk, which is as good a place as any to find the answers I'm looking for. I reach the end of the hallway, and I'm at the front desk. There is a huge oak desk that looks like a fireplace mantel with big glass windows behind it. An eighteen-year-old cadet in training—an actual pimply faced, short-haired ROTC youngster—is behind the desk, looking straight at me.

"Can I help you?" he says to me with wide eyes and enthusiasm.

I'm looking at this little kid. He couldn't be more than eighteen, couldn't catch a moth in a closet if he had to, and he is running the front desk of a major metropolitan police station.

"Are you in charge?" I ask as I put my hands on the desk and look around for someone that could possibly help me.

Maybe someone older than me, preferably with a badge and a gun, is around here somewhere. I'm afraid to tell this little kid anything because I'll confuse him or scare the crap out of him.

"Yes," he says to me as he outstretches his hand. "I'm Cadet Ward Russell."

I look at this skinny kid and finally realize why there is so much crime in the world. People like Cadet Ward Russell are left in charge to guard the world as the captains of police and police chiefs sleep. I'm in serious life-threatening danger, and Cadet Russell is the future of law enforcement. Days like this just make me wonder about the future of the world as I shake his hand in a gesture of good faith.

"I need to find out if Captain Adams is on duty or the next time he works," I ask the cadet nicely.

The cadet immediately checks the in/out logs and hunts down Captain Adams's name.

"He's not here. It's almost third shift, and he usually works first shift, which starts at 6:00 a.m. He will be here in the morning. Can I help you in any way?"

I fold my arms on the desk mantle and lean up against the hardwood frame. I'm pondering whether I really want this little kid's help or not, or am I wasting my time talking to him? I'm here anyway. I might as well ask.

"I'm involved in a matter of mistaken identity that Captain Adams is handling for me. He told me that if anything comes up that I should contact him immediately."

"What have you found out?" the young cadet asks me from behind his desk.

"A kid tonight from UNC mistook me for someone that he sees regularly at the basketball courts at Chapel Hill. I needed someone to check it out for me. This matter could really uncomplicate my life a whole lot," I say to Ward Russell with much disdain.

"Really," he says with enthusiasm.

I reach for a piece of blank scrap paper resting on the desk. I write down my name and phone number on the blank paper. I write in big letters "Attention Captain Adams" at the top and then write the date and time in the right-hand corner.

"The guy impersonating me has been using my name and plays basketball at Gilcrest Park on the weekend mornings," I tell Cadet Russell. "Early mornings about seven or eight."

I write "Gilcrest Park, early morning, James Clark/Big Mart" underneath my name and number. "Here is the name of the guy that can confirm the story for you. I'll try to get in touch with Captain Adams tomorrow. Can you make sure he gets this message? It's really important," I tell him. "Detectives of Homicide Tusson and Webber are also involved with the case. Could you please inform them?" I ask as I hand Cadet Russell the piece of paper.

"Sure. I'll make sure this matter gets the proper attention, sir."
And then Cadet Russell salutes me as if I am an officer.

"Do you run this place by yourself?" I had to ask, reassuringly.

"Yes, sir," Ward Russell says.

"What would have happened if this was an emergency?" I ask,
trying not to patronize the young officer in training.

"I would call 911, sir," he says confidently to me with a smile.

"Makes enough sense," I say out loud as I shrug my shoulders
in disbelief.

Off I go, back to my car. My sneakers scuff the rock-hard floor
and echo off the silent surroundings of the emptiness within the
police station. I go out the back door and jump down the stairs into
the parking lot that contains my Camaro. If I'm lucky, Rod will be
waiting for me at my car, then I could beat the shit out of him, drag
him into the police station, and put him behind bars myself. I realize
that when your life is in danger, you become paranoid and fearless all
at the same time. Paranoid that you don't trust anything at face value,
and fearless because you can face down anything and survive.

I look at my car plainly as it sits underneath a blanket of stars
in the parking lot as I slowly approach it. I look first in the back seat
to make sure no one is there, and then I walk around my car to make
sure nothing is wrong with it.

"Everything looks fine," I say as I get into my Camaro and drive
to the nearest grocery store.

I want to call my dad in Oviedo from a payphone so I can keep
my phone free just in case someone needs to get in touch with me.
Plus, I don't want anyone to hear my conversation just in case my
phone is tapped. I go to the convenience store on the corner to get a
prepaid phone card. I want to ask for some help from the one adult
I truly trust. Maybe he could give me some insight on the situation.
I don't think my dad's phone in Oviedo is tapped yet since Tusson
and Webber have to use out state agencies to tap his phone. That
could take a day or two. It has been about a week since I last called
Mr. Beacon, whom I call Dad. He is my father now. He raised me
willingly for three years, and he never asked for anything in return.
We had some really good times. He would always watch me play ball,

came to all my games, watched me win a state championship, and I thanked him for always being there for me in an interview. When he saw the tape played on the news, he cried and hugged me. That day we were as close as any father and son could ever be. I knew early on in my high school career that he would always be there for me. He loves me like his own son, and when I call him, I tell him of all the great times and tell him how well I'm doing. Today would be a different kind of phone call—one he needs to hear but not necessarily wants to hear.

I already told him about the deaths of Kate and Jen. I said their deaths were pure coincidence and not related to me. I haven't told him about Heather Collinsworth or my parents. I never even told him about Maria Lennon, even though he knows about my brother's death and the circumstances that surrounded my departure from Arcadia. I guess I did leave some things out to protect my own innocence when I talked with him. I was immature then, and I definitely learned from my mistakes. Now I must confess everything to him.

I get to the pay phone by the police station and dial the 1-800 number on the back of the phone card and then enter the gazillion digit pin number as well. This is probably the last phone booth in North Carolina, but luckily, it's right by the police station. I wait for the little computer voice to stop talking and dial the 407 area code and number. It's only 9:30 p.m., so I don't think my dad is asleep. After the second ring, he answers his cell phone with a friendly "Hello?"

"Hey, Dad. It's me, Ray. How's everything in Oviedo?" I say into the receiver.

"Great!" he says in an excited voice.

I can tell that he is surprised to hear from me. Since Mr. Beacon is now alone back home, I try to call about once or twice a week.

"School is going well, but there has been some trouble," I say then pause briefly. "My mom is dead," I say to him while covered by the night air and neon signs of the corner store across from the police station. "And I found out that my father is dead also."

"Oh no, what happened?" he asks with much concern.

"That's not the bad news. It gets worse."

Just then, I hear his voice reply, "What?"

"Another girl was found dead," I add. "Now all the cops think I'm guilty of murder. Remember way back when I told you my brother died in a fire? Well, it looks like he lived. He burned up someone else in the fire, and now he is here, after me. People have seen this guy around Durham that looks like me. I'm in real trouble," I say from the pay phone, standing in the cool night air of September.

"What can I do to help?" he asks with sympathy.

"I need one of your handguns. Something that is easy to use and will stop someone even if I graze them. I'm really scared, and things are getting crazy," I say.

"Tell me exactly what happened from the beginning. Don't leave anything out. If I'm going to believe in you, you have to tell me everything that is going on," he says.

I have no doubt that he believes in my innocence. I tell him everything from the story about Heather to the head in my dorm room, from Dawn and Maria Franklin to her chief of police father, Officer Steve Freedman, Captain Adams, and the homicide boys who presume I'm guilty, and finally about the kid at the park. We talk for a while, going back and forth with questions and scenarios of how and why, as well as where this person that haunts me could hide while watching me from afar. My dad thinks and tells me that Dawn is trouble and the only people I should trust are Jeff and Captain Adams.

"Well, I'll send you two guns and bullets with an extra clip," my dad says. "Be very careful with it. I'll send you a nine-millimeter with hollow point bullets. Keep it with you at all times and go to a gun shop and ask them how to use it. Guns are dangerous, and carelessness kills people. Make sure you don't get pulled over with it either. Don't be speeding or running red lights in that car of yours. And for God's sake, just be careful," he says to me in a worried voice.

Mr. Beacon grew up with guns as a kid in Florida. Since he always wanted me to be safe around guns, he took me shooting all the time. I can handle a gun safely, and I was really good shooting at targets at the range. About half the time, I could hit a bullseye from about forty feet away.

"I will be very careful, and I have many people checking up on me. If you could look into Dawn for me and into Arcadia, see what else has been left out of this mess. A fresh set of eyes might uncover something new for me," I say.

"I will, and I'm sorry about your mother and father. You should get the gun the day after tomorrow. Call me by the end of the week and tell me if anything new comes up."

"I will," I say.

We say goodbye. and that's when I realize it's almost 11:00 p.m. We have been on the phone for almost ninety minutes. I realize Dawn still hasn't called me back. I guess that she is having such a good time with Freedman, she probably forgot what she came up here for. What a bitch. I guess I can't blame her. If I was stuck in a small town all my life, I would go hog wild in a big city too.

I hang up the phone, get in my car, and head back to the dorms. That is when reality sets in. I run the university card through the slot to release the electric door lock. My card doesn't work since I haven't got a new one just yet. I notice that my dorm door is open, and all the lights are on. I bang on the door furiously until someone answers. Keith and Jeff both pop their heads into the corridor from Keith's room. My roommate is still up, which is surprising. Keith lets me in, and I bump his fist as if to say thanks. I walk down the corridor past our room, following him down the hallway. Keith's door is open, and his room has Jeff hanging out with him with all the lights remaining on. I think nothing of this as I walk into the room.

"Hey, what's up?" I say to Jeff as I walk into my room as Keith sits on my bed.

"Nothing much," he says as he slightly shakes his head while sitting at his desk.

Jeff is on the phone with his back toward the wall. We do our bonding ritual as he continues to talk to his girlfriend in Atlanta.

"I have to go now. He's here," Jeff says into the receiver of the phone.

I'm putting my basketball in the closet when an eerie feeling overcomes me; there is something definitely wrong here. The other shoe is about to drop, and it is going to drop on me.

"So what's up?" I ask as I sit on the dorm room bed next to Keith as Jeff ends the call on his cell phone.

Jeff sits up in his chair and folds his hands together with his elbows on his knees. Keith sits up in the same position. With the both of them looking at me, right at me, with a disappointing look on their face, I knew something was up. I sit and await the news.

"Ray, I don't want you to think that anyone is coming down on you," Jeff says to me very calmly as he stares at the floor. "But you are in some trouble. All this twin brother murder stuff is scaring the hell out of me. If someone is going to kill you, they will probably kill me to get to you," Jeff says calmly as he looks at me.

"And?" I say as I lean up against my wall with my feet stretching out against the width of my bed as I wait for his answer.

"I worked hard to get into Duke. I already went through enough when I transferred here. My girlfriend is a state away. My major is hard enough, and this is the first time I've been away from everything and everyone I know. I have all sorts of pressure on me. Basketball, school, relationships, my future, and now all this! I don't want to worry about my life also. I don't want anything that you have done in your past to jeopardize my future," Jeff speaks cautiously and truthfully as he looks to me.

"Maybe it would be best if you moved out of the dorms and into a room by yourself," Keith adds. "Things are getting pretty crazy. No need for things to get out of hand."

A sadness fills my heart. I almost want to cry, but I'm a big guy and hold the emotions back. I can handle all this. I've been through so much worse than this. I see the point of my friends, and they are right. No need to put their lives in danger. It just sucks since right now I really need my friends to stand by me, and they are afraid too. A bad position to be in, that's all. This just comes at a bad time for me.

"I understand," I say without hesitation. "I really do understand," I say as I look down at the floor, hiding the frustration within my body and fighting back the tears in my eyes.

"Once all this blows over, you can move back in, but in the meantime, Livia is scared, I'm scared, my parents are freaking out, and everyone you know is putting their life on the line hanging with you. For God's sake, there was a head in our room just this past weekend," Jeff says as he runs his fingers through his short black hair.

"Guys, I understand," I say loudly as I stand up. "I know all this is bullshit, but I have to handle it. I can't help what is happening. Okay! But I understand. No need to point out the obvious. I really do understand!" I say in frustration with my arms flaring out as I get up from the bed.

Keith's dorm room is quiet now. I know I have upset everyone, although I'm not trying to make anyone feel guilty for not being there for me. There are problems in my life that I need to deal with alone.

"Jeff is not leaving my room since someone has already got into your room once," Keith adds. "We're all in danger if you stay in the dorms. Anyone on the team could be next, and this guy looks just like you. Who knows what this person has already done or what plans he has already made to infiltrate you and destroy your life. I'm sure this psycho isn't taking things day by day. He has a plan," Keith says as he sits on the bed.

"Guys, I know, and I understand," I say calmly and disappointingly. "I'm getting a Pepsi. I need something," I say as I walk out of the room.

I walk out the door and pull a dollar bill from my wallet. The funny thing is, we are in an athletic dorm in which we are supposed to be on strict diets of healthy foods and drink only water or Gatorade, but there is a Pepsi machine in every hallway. Some things don't make any sense. I'm just glad the Pepsi machine is here.

"Hey, you have to consider what Jeff has already gone through just to get here," Keith says as he walks out of the room behind me and follows me to the machine. "You can't blame him for backing out on you. He hardly knows you."

"I know!" I say sadly as the dollar bill slides into the drink machine. I punch the oversized Pepsi button and a huge *kathunk* sounds as the plastic bottle hits the shoot. I take the Pepsi and leave the quarters in the coin catcher.

"Want one?" I ask as I slither to the floor and take a seat across from the Pepsi machine on the cold linoleum floor against the white concrete wall.

I pull another dollar out of my wallet and hand it to my buddy. He feeds the dollar into the machine and hits the button. *Kathunk* sounds again. Keith grabs the Pepsi from the slot. Then he sits next to me on the cold midnight floor. Everything is quiet for a second as we fill our souls with the intoxicating soda. The floor acts as our barstools, and the hallway is our dimly lit drinking hole.

"I forgot what it was like to drink sodas and stay up late," Keith adds. "When I played at FSU, basketball was my life. Four years of protein shakes, every carbohydrate imaginable, Gatorade, two liters of water a day, and workouts that stung. I loved it—all the hype, being the Atlantic Coast Conference champs. I loved it all," Keith adds with a smile on his face.

"Wait a minute. Florida State hasn't been ACC champs in my lifetime!" I added sharply right before I take a huge gulp of my soda.

"I know," he replies. "But it was always our goal," he says with a smile as he sips his soda. "I know what it's like to have things not work out the way you plan. We never won the ACC title while I was there, and we always lost in the first round or second of tournament. We went to the big dance four years in a row, barely squeaking in all the time, and always went home losers," he says as he fantasizes about his years at Florida State.

"Sixty-four other teams went home losers, too, every year," I say to him as I watch the sweat on my soda run down the side of the bottle.

"Yeah, I know," Keith says as we sit in the lonely hallway.

"There can only be one," I reply.

"I said after my first year, I would work harder to improve my game. I will work on my shot, workout more, become stronger, run faster, dribble more, and work as hard as possible to be the best player on the team. I will be the team leader as a sophomore, I would say. I will be a starter and show the world I'm the best there is," Keith says.

"Here's to being the best there possibly is," I say as I hold my Pepsi in the air and we toast.

"To being the best," he says as we clash plastic Pepsi bottles together in the dimly lit hallway and take a big sip of our sodas. "Once school started, I was aggressive. Hitting Js from downtown. I could drive the lane, dish the rock, thread the needle, and slam dunk without taking any steps. Straight up slam dunk, an 'in your face' player. That was what I was. All the noise, all the hype was true," he says excitedly as he thinks about the game he once played and loved.

"I never heard of you. How come?" I say to my newly anointed drinking buddy.

"I got back to school in September and was stronger, faster, and could dribble like a veteran point guard. I started playing everyone one-on-one and beating them. By the time practice started in October, I had it in my head that I was the best player on the team. I had an attitude like no other, and I drilled players for being lazy at practice. Then I started to lose control of my dribble. I was picked and robbed by better defensive players. Got stuffed on dunks and even missed dunks while trying to show off. I would drive the lane totally out of control and lose the ball. Always trying to make impossible passes and losing was everyone else's fault but mine. I went from a starter to being benched. FSU went nineteen wins and eleven loses my sophomore year, no thanks to me," he says unenthusiastically as his memories take him back to the days of playing basketball in Tallahassee for Florida State University.

"Not good," I say as I sit and listen to his story. "Nineteen and eleven."

"Good enough to squeak into the Big Dance come March, right behind Duke and North Carolina."

"How did you do?" I ask with much concern for my friend.

"Big exit, first round by Valparaiso. I vented on my team, calling them quitters and made enemies. I was only a sophomore and realized I was the one who let my team down. I played ball for me, not for the team. I was angry all the time. I called it a hunger for winning. My coach and other players called it an attitude. I did everything all wrong. I had blinders on, and my skills started to slip away. Just because I loved basketball and did things my own way doesn't mean my way was the right way. All those people that tried to help

GEMINI

me, I thought they were against me for trying to change me. I didn't see the light because my own agenda blinded me."

"Moral of the story?" I ask as we sit in the dimly lit and cold hallway at midnight.

"We are here to help you. You need to look at things with an open mind, not just from your point of view. If you want to do what is best for the team, you have to listen to all your teammates and the coaches. You moving out is in everyone's best interest, and it doesn't mean anyone is against you," he says as he looks straight at me as if to say okay with his eyes.

"Here's to doing what's right," I say as I hold my Pepsi in the air for a toast.

"I'm your friend, Ray," he says to me. "We are both from the same neighborhood. Arcadia is right down the road from Fort Myers. Both of us lived in Small Town, Florida, and all we had in school was our love for basketball. I wouldn't steer a friend wrong," he says. "I know how much you want this, but it's for the best."

We finish off our drinks. That is where we left off. Right there in the dim hallway by the light of the Pepsi machine sometime late at night among the cold night air of North Carolina.

"At FSU, what number were you?" I ask as I stare into the abyss of life.

"Number 44," Keith replies. "Number 44."

Number 44 is my number, and he's from Fort Myers, Florida. Right down the road from Arcadia.

CHAPTER 17

WEDNESDAY MORNING IS business as usual in the grand scheme of things at Duke. Jeff and I are wake up at 5:30 a.m. to a little buzzing phone alarm. Jeff and I are in the habit of waking up early and running five miles every day. Since our dorm is still under lockdown, we both spend the night at Keith's.

"It's five thirty. Wake up!" Jeff says to me as a morning ritual.

Jeff clicks on all the lights in the dorm room and heads for the bathroom.

"I'm up," I say as I get up out of bed.

I walk over to the dresser turn off my alarm since Keith is still asleep is the other room. I get up, walk to the kitchen, look through the cabinets, and grab a Pop-Tart. Since Keith only has a microwave and a refrigerator, he doesn't keep much food around. We have Pop-Tarts, cold cereal, multigrain bars, cereal bars, a loaf of wheat bread, cans of tuna, milk, bottled water, Gatorade, and of course, Ramen noodles. I always try to eat in the cafeteria for lunch and most dinners during the week. Weekends are for pizza, pretzels, mixed drinks, and parties. For right now it's a Pop-Tart and a bottle of water. I find the remote to the TV and click over to CNN. CNN is our wake-up program just because sometimes the news is interesting and we don't really have to watch it, just listen to it. Plus, SportsCenter doesn't come on until 6:00 a.m.

I can't believe today is only Wednesday. To think all the killings and tragedies have taken place in just over a week. Last Monday is when Heather Collinsworth was found dead. My mother and her boyfriend died on Wednesday and were found Friday. I drove Jeff to Atlanta Saturday, got to Arcadia Sunday night, and spent Sunday in jail. I got back to Durham Monday night and found a head in our room over the weekend. Besides that, I lost all my friends, mail ordered a gun, lost an older woman to Officer Freedman, and failed a lie detector test. I found out my mom and real dad are dead, and his killer's child inherited everything that should have been mine. And to think, it's only 5:30 a.m. on Wednesday.

No need to dwell on the dreadful past. With the dawn comes a new day. My new day starts off with running, then intermediate Spanish, macroeconomics, and American government. I have a break after Spanish for an hour, then back-to-back classes before another workout at noon.

"Let the day begin, freshman," Jeff calls out as he enters the room.

He must be eating coffee beans in the bathroom because he is too damn perky in the mornings. I hate morning people! I really hate perky people at five thirty in the morning. I also hate five thirty mornings, but someone has to do it. Might as well be me.

"It's the beginning of a beautiful day. Carpe diem!" Jeff yells to me as I slowly get up from sitting on my bed. I'm still half asleep.

All I keep thinking is that he is way too perky in the mornings. Then finally, I throw on my shorts, socks, shirt, sweatshirt, and running shoes. I'm finally ready to go. Slowly but surely, we take off out of the dorms and run toward the track, which is a mile away. The track is one-fourth of a mile long; we take twelve laps around the track and then start the mile jog back to our dorm room. We head out about 5:40 a.m. for our five-mile run and always get back before 6:15 a.m. Before the light of another day, Jeff and I take our first steps on our five-mile run. We usually don't talk while we run. We quickly hit stride here as we pass the Cameron Indoor Stadium, the Wallace

Wade Football Stadium, and the Aquatic Center heading toward the soccer field. I think it's better just to run and focus on your pace. It's still nighttime, and we jog into the darkness along the old brick buildings standing tall in the moonlight, past the old elm trees along the dimly lit path past the school's sports complexes. Our breaths and footsteps are the only sounds as we breathe slowly and deeply during our run. Our morning jog is almost religious, like the campus that engulfs us. The neo-Gothic chapel that looks down on us adds energy to our young souls as well as determination and strength to our minds. Only the illuminating moon follows us as we run from our own shadows. We pass the stadium buildings like many athletes before us and like the many more to come. This isn't something that we have to do; it's something we must do. It's tradition here to work hard, make good grades, and follow the triumphant achievements that will accompany us throughout our lives. As the minutes go by, time neither follows us nor holds us back from our destination. We run for ourselves and chase the memories of our glorious past

We approach the track, fenced in and surrounded by stands for the fans to watch our accomplishments. Today, as in every day we jog, the stands are empty, soundless, and cold, lying dormant until the weekend or until signs of life approach during the daytime. We take our steps, one after another, million after million, the running, like our minds, never stop, and the conditioning never ends. Just like the day is followed by the night and the night followed by another day, our cycle never ends. Our training and conditioning to be the best never ends either. As a person, I will never give up, and as a team, we will never fail or let each other down, as long as we work together. That is the Duke philosophy, which is Duke's tradition, which is our way.

Our laps around the majestic soccer field are over within what seems like a minute, and our stride takes us back past the stadiums and Aquatic Center to the path that leads us home. Today, we get all the way back to our dorm before Jeff says a word to me. I am the first to reach the door, and Jeff enters behind me.

"You give any thought to last night?" he says to me as we end our trip at the dormitory doors that lead to our room.

"Yeah," I say as I catch my breath and lean against the wall of our concrete home. "I'll tell Coach K today that I plan on moving out of the dorm. I don't have a problem with living someplace else until this all blows over. Since I've been redshirted, I don't think he will really mind either. All the coaches already know what is going on, so I don't think they will disagree." I open the door and enter into the hallway.

Jeff enters and leads the way to our room. We are both tired and sweaty even though running will boost our energy in the large scheme of life and longevity.

"I plan on moving upstairs. Someplace off the first floor where I'm not so accessible to burglars and murderers," Jeff says as he heads for the shower, almost exhausted from our run.

I sit at my desk and eat the other half of my previous Pop-Tart. I have to go tell Coach that my life is in danger and I must move out of the dorms, with his permission of course. You don't want to tell the man that pays your bills what to do. The last thing the school wants is bad publicity. I don't think this will cause any problems since I'm a low-profile and redshirted freshman.

Keith is still asleep, and I take a quick shower. I review all my homework and go over my class agenda for each class. I make sure I'm more than fully prepared for each one. I split with Jeff and go to 8:00 a.m. Spanish. Spanish is a sleep-through class since I took four years of Spanish in high school. Plus, I have a photographic memory; it's easy for me to remember definitions and spellings of all the words. I didn't want to CLEP out of the class since I could use the easy A toward my GPA. Plus, I get to look at my beautiful Hispanic teacher all day, Ms. Rosé. She is a petite woman of about thirty with long black hair, a pretty face, dark skin, and a beautiful smile. I like waking up to her three days a week even if it is Spanish at 8:00 a.m.

At 9:00 a.m., I take an hour break between classes before going to my hundred-student-filled economics lecture with Dr. Death. The teacher's real name is Dr. David Davis, a professor with a doctorate degree, tenure, and white hair. He is known for making his class really difficult, as if we are all going to be economists, and he fails 20 percent of the students that don't drop the class every semester. Since

I understand the books' terminology and obscure language, I'll do well. I have no problems keeping up with all the homework, schoolwork, workbooks, and projects. I have no problems with the class.

Then finally, at 10:00 a.m. I'm in my government class of over one hundred and fifty students taught by Mr. Cumo. Mr. Cumo is a misplaced New Yorker who just graduated with a teaching degree. As for me, of course, I sit right up front in the first row, last seat. What a good student I am, right?

As for my last class of the day, it's College Algebra. I wasn't going to be an Engineer, so I took the easy way out and avoided Pre-Cal and Calculus. I took both classes in high school but wanted College Algebra as my math credit. Since I have to keep focused on school and grades as well as basketball, I don't really have any classes to waste. I wanted to start with an easy schedule. No other basketball players are in any of my classes, and I don't want to get to close with any of the beautiful girls because they might end up dead. Even though there is one young girl that is in two of my classes, Carrie Russell. She is the forbidden fruit of Duke since she is dating Bill Sharman. Only she doesn't know she is dating him. She just wants to be friends with him, but he puts a lot of pressure on her since he is big man on campus. As for her, she sits right next to me in algebra and right behind me in Spanish.

Carrie's the type of girl who always wears long-sleeve button-up shirts and tight blue jeans. She has long curly brownish-blond hair—not frizzy, just curly. She looks good, not too tall, not to thin, an average build, and has very pretty facial features. I didn't pay attention to her long enough to notice what color her eyes are, but I'm sure they're a pretty color. I would talk to her, but then Bill would make my life even more miserable! I'm sure Bill could get away with hazing a lowly freshman like me with no problems. Here at school, Bill is King of the Crap, and I'm bottom of the pile.

My life is really complicated right now, and no one is calling me back to let me know what is going on. I have to see Coach first, then call the two detectives and reschedule my lie detector test, then off to see Captain Adams about the leads, and then Dawn. Dawn is another story. She goes off with Freedman, never calls me, and leaves me hanging. She is supposed to be working with me and keeping an eye on me. She is here to help me find the killer. She's no damn help. All she came up here for was to get some attention—the kind of attention only a man can give, if you know what I mean.

"Hey, talk to Coach yet?" Jeff asks as we meet in front of the gym at noon after our classes end.

"Nope, I have to blow off our workout because I need to get everything done before three," I say to Jeff as we bump fists. "I'm off, man. Wish me luck."

I head to Coach K's office in the Sports Complex at Cameron Indoor Stadium and no one is there. Lunch, maybe? I leave messages at the secretary's office for Coach K and Coach Johnny to call me on my cell phone. Captain Adams is sure to be in his office; I jump in my car and head straight to downtown Durham.

"Captain Adams, please," I ask the front desk clerk.

She picks up her phone and pages him. In seconds the tall, muscular, balding Captain Adams is approaching the front desk and smiling at me.

"Got time for a friend?" I ask as I shake his hand.

Captain Adams is in full uniform and looks dignified. This man may be forty, but he has a death grip for a handshake as he shakes my hand.

"I always have time to help the needy," he replies and then points the way to his office.

I follow Adams and take my seat in front of his huge desk.

Captain Adams has many trophies, pictures, marksmanship awards, and certificates, as well as his college degree hanging on the huge wall behind his desk. Captain James Montgomery Adams is a very accomplished man. He was born and raised right here in North Carolina. He started his career in the Air Force as a pilot, and he got an engineering degree while serving his country in the 1990s. He was given accolades for his services during the Gulf War, and then after twenty years of military life, he retired. He returned to North Carolina after the service and took legal studies classes to better his understanding of our laws to work with people on a higher level. Captain James Montgomery Adams now sits in his chair with a smile on his face. He did things his way and is very proud of the accomplishments that followed him. On his desk is a picture of his wife and two daughters in a frame facing sideways. There are many pictures of his family and friends on the walls around him also. I know this man has seen everything and doesn't care about bullshit. I feel I can trust him with my life. I can only hope he trusts me.

"Did Cadet Russell tell you about the kid at the park?" I ask as I sit in front of him.

"Yes, he did. A little puzzling, though. A kid you never met before said he played basketball with you at Chapel Hill?" he asks me curiously.

"Never seen him before in my life. He said I couldn't hit a shot a week ago. Says there is someone that plays ball at UNC that looks just like me," I say as I look him right in the eyes.

I hope he doesn't think I'm lying. This does look like a lame college fraternity prank, without the three dead girls and dead mother thrown in of course.

"It's hard to believe, a look-a-like killer running loose in parks playing basketball. And why?" he asks.

"My brother hated me. He was supposed to have died one day while I was at school. The house fire, I'm sure you read the report," I ask him as he stares down at me.

"I did," he replies. "The abusive mom, two twin brothers, a fire, the missing little girl, I know the whole story." He nods to me. "I think there are a lot of holes in it. A lot of holes," Adams adds.

"The whole story is true," I say in my defense. "How do you explain all those people seeing me on the night of the murder when I was right here?" I'm pleading my case and shaking my head. "How can you explain my mom's death? The missing girl? It's my brother!" I say excitedly.

"Calm down, son. I didn't say I did or didn't believe you. I just have to be careful. I don't want to shoot you thinking it's your brother, the killer. Right!"

I just look at Captain Adams as I comprehend the situation.

"Things like this get complicated now," he says. "I can't put out an APB on him because my officers will bring you in. We have to find him or whoever and nail this shut. You're the bait. You see?" he asks calmly. "I have Tusson and Webber working on the case with my men. Also, Cadet Russell's in the buddy program. He works with an officer as an assistant. They will both go down and talk to the fella who saw your brother, and then they will go down to the park to see what they can find. Until we find this mystery man, you need to stay with Dr. Franklin or Officer Freedman and keep out of the way of our investigation," Captain Adams tells me as he nods to me to make sure I receive his message crystal clear.

"I got it. Also, I'm moving out of the dorms and into the Holiday Inn until this all blows over. The Holiday Inn has security cameras so you guys can keep track of me and anyone else that goes into the hotel. Plus, Dawn is already there for the next week. She can keep a close eye on me," I say as I get up from the chair.

"Well then," he says as he gets up from his chair and outstretches his hand. "I have other business to take care of. Good luck and keep us posted."

"I will." I shake his hand and leave him to his business.

Off I go again. Tusson and Webber haven't called me; therefore, they can't be in dire need of that lie detector test. As for right now, I guess I'll go past Dawn's hotel again and see if she ever came home last night.

I drive to the Holiday Inn and park my Camaro upfront. I notice that Dawn's rented Mustang GT isn't upfront. That's when I get curious and walk around to the side of the building to see the back. Dawn's car is parked behind the hotel. Since Freedman is at work, she must be in. I walk to the front desk and wait for the clerk. He arrives shortly with his glued-on smile and greets me.

"I need to check in for a week," I say as I hand him my credit card and driver's license. "Do you have anything on the seventh floor?"

"I'll check," he replies as he punches digits into the computer terminal.

"Also, is Dawn Franklin in?" I ask.

He checks while I'm filling out my room information.

"She's never left, Mr. Beacon. Should I ring her?"

"No, I'll go up," I say to the clerk.

"Your room is 707, right down from Dr. Franklin. Enjoy, sir," he says as he hands me my credit card and license, as well as my door key.

I go right up to the seventh floor, and my phone starts to ring as I approach Dawn's door.

"Hello," I say.

"Where are you at?" Dawn's little voice speaks out through the receiver.

"Knocking on your door."

Knock. Knock. Knock. I rap on her door and it opens instantly.

The door opens, and I walk into Dawn's room. I notice she is wearing a white button shirt with no sleeves and a short blue-jean skirt. I know it's none of my business, but it is killing me not to say anything to her about Freedman. I walk in and see clothes on the floor by her bed. Her bed is in disarray also. Her suitcase is open on the far side of the room, clothes lying on top both sides of the open suitcase.

"Rough night," I say to her as I stand before her bed and look around at the mess in her room.

I'm thinking the doctor is just as easy as her daughter was to sleep with—first date type of girl. But again, it's none of my business. I take a few steps aside from the mess and sit down on the chair across from the bed. Dawn walks around the room, picking up pieces of the mess, and throws her clothes and shoes on top of her open suitcase that sits in the midst of clutter that now overwhelms the room.

"I just talked with the police and found out that someone else has seen your brother," she says to me.

She walks over to the bed and sits across from me.

"Yeah, at the park at UNC," I add. "Pretty strange, huh?"

"You're moving out too?" she asks as she sits across from me.

"Yeah, it's better for my friends," I say as I look down disappointingly. "We did find a head in my room, and just about everyone I know is dead," I say calmly from the chair as I look at Dawn. "Probably best that I move out now."

"What have you done so far?" she asks as she runs her finger through her hair and briefly scratches her head as she looks around her room.

"Nothing much. I've checked in here. I'll move my clothes and books in tonight. I'm over one and down the hallway. I left a note for Coach, telling him what's up, and went to Captain Adams to tell him about the sighting," I say to her.

"What did he have to say?" she asks from her bed as she just looks at me.

"Keep up my regular routine, stay away from UNC, and stick by you or in my room at night. Keep accounted for and out of trouble. The police will send two people down to the park to check things out. For right now, it's just classes and homework, workouts and waiting," I say as I shrug my shoulders.

"Did anyone check out this guy that saw Rodney?"

"Not yet. What about you? What have you found out?"

"Lots of things," she replies. "I talked with Coach and Johnny, and they like you. Johnny said he recruited you, and Coach thinks you're a good kid, but they don't really know you. Other players on the team don't really know you either. David Hodges, Keith, and Jeff are your only friends, while this guy Billy Sharman seems to hate you already. Sharman called you a good-for-nothing prick with no respect for others. And for some reason, I couldn't interview any women. Seems they're all dead."

"They are all dead. Is that the only reason?" I ask in disgust with her sarcasm.

"Lots of mixed opinions from your peers. And you do know Detective Tusson and Detective Webber want to prosecute you? They don't trust you at all," she tells me as she sits on the bed.

"And then there's you," I say.

"I'll keep my opinion of you to myself," she says with a devastating smirk.

"This must make you very happy, knowing that my life is falling apart just like yours once did?" I ask with a smile on my face to insult her sarcastic tone.

"I'm not here to watch you suffer. I'm here to find my daughter. I have no control over your past or your new set of friends," she says to me.

"I guess I have a lot of work to do when it comes to making friends," I say to her.

"You better get started then. I'm exhausted and need to get some sleep," she says to me.

"It's noon!" I say to her as the words slip out.

"I had a late night and an early morning working on your case!" she fires back. "I'm tired. Get out so I can get some sleep!" she says to me in an agitated voice from her perch at the end of the bed.

"Hey, no offense." I put my hands up in defeat. "I'm going," I say as I get up from the chair. "I just want to make sure you're keeping an eye on things. This whole thing didn't seem real until this last week. Someone is stalking me, killing my friends, and looking for me. I just want to make sure you're not off gallivanting with cops while I'm dying in a ditch somewhere."

"Off gallivanting with cops while you're dying somewhere!" she yells as she gets up from the bed as her jaw drops from the words I say. "Just in case you didn't know, this has been real for me for four years," she says as she stomps her foot down. "You're the reason my little girl is gone, my husband left, and my life is in shambles," she says to me as she gives me a dirty look and crosses her eyebrows.

I can tell now that she's really upset.

"I'm here for me, to find the truth!" she yells out to me. "To me, you're still the same little shit that took my daughter and then ran from the responsibility of your own life! What I do, I do for me. Now get out!" she yells as she opens the door for me to get out.

I walk outside into the hallway, unfazed by her irrational outbursts.

"Why did you come here anyway?" I say. "You could have been a bitch and a slut in Arcadia!" I say harshly.

I watch her face contort as she gives me a mean and shocking look. She slams the door with a thud. A mighty thud at that. Probably shook the entire building. She's mad now. Oh well, I will let her sleep it off.

CHAPTER 18

I GO TO my room and the first thing I do is call my dad in Oviedo. I relax in the room and call while sitting in my lazy-boy chair.

"Hey, Dad, what's up?"

"I haven't found out much," he says. "But I traced Dawn's family tree for you through police records. Nothing interesting."

"Really, nothing?" I ask.

"Dawn has only a sister for a sibling, but her dad is in a long line of officers from Arcadia. Dr. Franklin has no sons, and her mother died years ago when she gave birth to her younger sister."

"That would explain why Dawn only had a picture of her and her father on her desk. Nothing of her mother or sister."

"Her sister is divorced and has a little girl that is two years younger than you."

"Really, what's her name?" I ask only out of curiosity for Dawn.

"Olivia. Named after Dawn's mother."

"Where is she now?" I ask.

"Who? The daughter or Dawn's sister?"

"Both?" I reply.

"It didn't say. I stumbled across this information through the Desoto County historical society that could trace people back to Ponce De Leon and Hernando Desoto. Dr. Franklin is not related to either of them, but her dad has lived in Florida his entire life. Her grandfather was the sheriff in Arcadia, and his father was a judge there. Both served full tours in the army—World War II and Korea— and then retired. They are a very accomplished military family that lives in Arcadia to raise cattle. They have been there since before the 1900s."

"Pretty tight family?"

"A family owned business, that's pretty tight. Dawn works the Desoto County office as an attorney, and her dad is Chief of Police. He retired from the military with full honors and worked in Arcadia for many years."

"Great!" I say in disgust.

"Be on your best behavior. She's packing heat from all sides. Military family, family owned successful business, and works for the police. I bet they give a lot of campaign money to the higher-ups," he says.

"I'll be on my best behavior," I say, and then we basically end our conversation.

Dr. Franklin has all her bases covered, and everything can be dumped on me without a moment's notice. Great, that's all I need. In an instant, I could have federal, military, and local authorities coming down on me. Needless to say, I didn't talk to Dawn for the rest of the day.

I really like my hotel room. This place is equipped with a kitchen area, which includes a two-burner stove, cabinets, microwave, and coffee machine. There's a breakfast bar and a doorway separate the kitchen and the living room. I have furniture now, a La-Z-Boy chair, coffee table, and sofa. I also have a forty-two-inch flat-panel TV in the living room, equipped with cable, an X-box, and Netflix.

This palace is better than my college dorm room any day. The rest of the living room includes a small hallway with a closet on one side and bathroom on the other. Down the short hallway is the bedroom, which includes another cable-linked TV, dresser, nightstand, bed, work desk, and a walk-in closet. Like I said, this place is better than my dorm room, and it's all mine for about $600 a week.

I look around the hotel room and realize I have a new car, nice new temporary place, and lots of credit, which is pretty good for a freshman in college. Once Dawn leaves this hotel to go home to Arcadia, I will look for an apartment of my own to move into. No need to deplete my bank account or max out my credit card over this situation. I still need to think about my future, you know.

I go back to the dorms at Duke and wonder what will happen with my future at the university in jeopardy. I ponder my fate as I go to pick up Jeff so we can hang out. We both avoid the elephant in the room and make plans to go back to the hotel. Once at the hotel, Jeff and I hang out at the pool that stretches along the back of the building. Tonight, we will have dinner in the Holiday Room. The Holiday Room is the very fastidious restaurant inside the hotel that is decorated with chandeliers, crystal vases, and freshly cut white, red, and yellow roses. Jeff and I enjoy every minute of the good life while it lasts. We are on our way to dinner now.

Jeff and I enter the restaurant and are seated right away by a beautiful hostess with long blond hair. She smiles at us, and we are mesmerized by her beauty. As instructed, we follow her to our table. Jeff and I are dressed down in jeans and polo shirts. I notice we are the only kids in the restaurant as well. Our table is a square with freshly cut flowers as the centerpiece and a freshly starched white tablecloth.

"This place looks expensive," Jeff says as he looks at all the beautiful waitresses in black-tie attire and white starched aprons.

A busboy comes by, drops off fresh rolls, fills our water glasses, and asks what else we would like to drink.

Meagan, our beautiful waitress, is right there to answer questions about the menu. She is very pleasant as she describes the specials. Jeff and I are intrigued by the beauty of our tall, thin, redhaired waitress with green eyes and a perfect smile. We tell her we both need a moment to decide.

"Damn, we should have eaten here sooner," I say to Jeff.

"You're still buying, right?" Jeff asks as we sit across from each other at a table in the middle of the restaurant.

"Of course I'm buying. I'd like to keep the only friend I have left. Everyone else is afraid of me," I say as I unwind at the dining table.

"You always did like to impress," Jeff says as he gazes at the decor of the room. "Nice car, good grades, and you can ball!" he says with a smile.

"Enjoy the good life while I'm still alive," I say with a humorous smile.

"Don't talk like that!" he says to me sharply. "Even if you're joking around, that isn't funny," he says with crossed eyes and a stern voice.

"I know," I reply with disappointment as I look over the exquisite menu.

"So what's up with you and Dawn?" he asks as he fumbles through the extravagant selections on the enormous menu.

"You know the story. I haven't worked things out with her just yet."

"Not good," Jeff replies as he reads the menu.

"What's Liv's last name?" I ask right out of the blue.

"Where did that come from?" Jeff asks.

"I'm just wondering," I say with a smile.

"Nues," he replies as he starts to laugh.

"As in, eye-witness news?" I ask as I laugh. "During sex did you ever say, 'This just in'?" I ask with tears in my eyes from laughing so hard.

I don't know why that's so funny either, but Jeff and I are both at the table laughing, looking like the kids we are. Immaturity is so much fun.

"Dumbass!" Jeff says in a low voice as he throws his napkin at me.

After a minute, we regain our composure and calm down just in time to act like adults for our waitress. Since we have no clue what half the entrees on the menu are, we both order Chicken a la King and Caesar salads. I figure you can never go wrong with chicken.

"Oh, yeah. I also got a gun," I say to him nonchalantly as we wait for our salads.

"What?" He gasps as he almost chokes on his drink.

"My dad sent it to me. I should get it tomorrow," I say as I lean toward Jeff so no one else can hear our conversation. "I feel like I really need to protect myself just in case anything serious happens," I say to him quietly.

"You're gonna shoot someone by accident. Then you'll really be in trouble. I can see it now. Student killed in accidental shooting. You're no redneck. You know nothing about guns. I think it's a bad idea for you to have a gun," he whispers from the other side of the table as he leans forward where only I can hear him.

"It will be okay. I shot guns in Florida for years. My dad taught me everything about guns, and I plan on going to a shooting range. There I can learn how to take it apart, clean it, and fire it. If the gun jams or something, I need to know what to do. I'm not going into this blind. I plan on doing this to help myself, not hurt myself," I say. "Go to the gun range with me, fire a few shots, and then tell me what you think," I say as the salads arrive at our table.

Our waitress looms around and refills our water and sodas, and as soon as we finish our salads, our meal arrives. The chicken ala king is a large portion of chicken, an entire rotisserie chicken to be exact. Just enough for a huge appetite like mine.

"Grace and Cheers," Jeff says right before we devour our meals.

We compliment the food with just about every bite as we eat. We actually eat our meals as if we are civilized human beings instead of starving college basketball players being stalked by my identical twin murderer. The food is breathtaking, as the portions of chicken are hot, juicy, and tender. The chicken almost melts in my mouth with each bite. With a meal this good, I'm actually savoring each bite and enjoying the taste of the food. As I eat, I feel like a grown-up instead of the kid genius and great basketball player that I am. The meal is awesome, the atmosphere is great, and this is the first time I've felt relaxed in months. I guess staying at the Holiday Inn really can change your life.

"What do you feel like doing after dinner?" Jeff asks as he finishes off the last morsel on his plate.

"I have to study and get all my homework done, but what did you have in mind?" I ask as I throw my napkin on my plate to signify the defeat of dinner.

"Rent some movies from Redbox and watch them here. Relax a little before studying. And since I've been here in a real palace, my dorm room seems insignificant and boring."

"Sure, take my car, go get some movies, and you can crash on my couch if you want," I say.

Meagan comes by the table and asks us questions about our meal and if we enjoyed the chicken. We assure her that we enjoyed every bite and ask for the check. I pay the check and Jeff leaves the tip. That's the teamwork we have!

"Hey, look who it is," Jeff says and nods to someone behind me as we get up from the table.

I turn and look behind me. It is Dr. Franklin and Steve the policeman. I guess they have every right to be here. I'm just not mature enough to handle seeing them together, that's all. So this is what jealously can do to a man—make him insecure. Plus, Steve is married. I guess since he is a cop, he can use the excuse of all-night surveillance to get away from his wife. He could use the excuse; it's a big case, and he can't tell her anything about it for his wife's own protection. Then spend the evening with another woman. Policemen get to have all the fun.

Since Jeff and I are on our way out, we have to walk by them as they wait for a table. I'll try to be nice.

"Well, well," I say as I approach the two.

"Hello, Ray, Jeff," Freedman says with a smile as he shakes our hands. "Surprised to see you two here. What do you recommend?"

Jeff puts one hand over my mouth so I can't say anything else. Then with his other hand on my shoulder, he gives me a shove toward the door.

"Try the chicken," Jeff says to them and keeps walking, leading me out the door with him.

"Okay," Steve says as he watches Jeff drag me out of the restaurant with his hand over my mouth and his other arm around my neck.

"Ray is sorry about this morning also," Jeff says as he pulls me away from them.

Dawn says nothing to me, not even a hello. That's gratitude for you.

"I didn't want you to make an ass out of yourself," Jeff says as he keeps his hand over my mouth until we are out of the restaurant. "I saw that look on your face and knew this wasn't going to be a good situation for any of us."

"You're right," I say as Jeff releases me.

"You having a one-night stand with her isn't going to make you happy or change the course of your life. You make yourself happy by working hard," Jeff says as we go from the restaurant to the lobby of the hotel.

"Really?" I ask Jeff sarcastically as I listen to his wisdom.

"It's not how many women you have or how many you love. It's the memories you have with the ones you did love and what you learned from each one of them. Women will teach you and you will learn, my young friend," he explains to me.

"Learn what, Jedi Master of Love?" I ask as I stand in the lobby, laughing at Jeff.

"That there is no perfect woman," Jeff replies. "You just have to pick one with the least number of flaws," he says as we walk into the grand foyer of the hotel.

"Please share more of your Duke wisdom with me, please, oh, King of Blue Devils," I say jokingly as we stop in the lobby of the hotel and I bow toward him gracefully.

Jeff puts his arm over my shoulder and tells his philosophy as we walk.

"Women are like diamonds. They all look good and are perfect in their own little ways. But if you pick this large, beautiful, brilliant diamond that shines for miles for everyone to see, everyone will want that diamond, and someone just might take it from you. You need to pick a diamond that will suit your needs. Not too big, not too small, just the right brightness, clarity, and most important, the right cut and style. Something tailored just for you."

"Princess Liv taught you all this? What kind of diamond is she?" I ask as we stand in the middle of the foyer.

"You will never know." He laughs as he pushes me away from him.

"What kind of diamond am I?" I ask as we walk to the elevator.

"You're still coal!" he says and starts laughing aloud.

"Really? Black coal?" I say as I laugh out loud as well.

"You need to be polished off before you ever become a diamond." Jeff puts extra emphasis on the word *ever*. "You're a diamond in the rough. Matter of fact, your still in the mine. You haven't even been found yet," Jeff says as we both laugh passionately at his joke.

We both laugh like little kids as we have our fun in the hotel lobby. I'm sure people are looking at us strangely since we are in the middle of the lobby with Jeff pointing at me, calling me a diamond in the rough.

"Go get the movies," I say as I throw Jeff my car keys and go upstairs.

The thing I like about Jeff is that he is honest and mature for his age. He seems to do things that make me and his other friends look up to him. He has a serious girlfriend and doesn't play head games with her or us. Even though she is so far away, he does not cheat on his girlfriend either. He works hard, studies hard, and really knows where he wants to go in life. You have to be very smart to get accepted to Duke. It's a prestigious college with a history of standards of most Ivy League schools. With that in mind, most students here are rich, high school valedictorians and know they will be taken care of. Duke is the best university in North Carolina with an awesome basketball team.

Jeff doesn't get caught up in the preppie college life of fraternities, jocks, and rich kids. He doesn't act like a snob and doesn't treat me different because I'm a lowly freshman with a working-class background. Jeff has taught me so much about being an adult in such a short time, and we always have a good time when we are together. Out of all my friends, I hope his dreams come true first. He's one of the good guys.

Jeff comes back from Redbox with action-packed movies, karate fights, shootouts, and lots of explosions. Unfortunately, I have lots of homework to catch up on, so I left Jeff, with his Pepsi and potato chips, on the couch, watching his rentals. I sit at the table across from the bed and do my homework while facing the TV. I usually don't watch TV or movies, just sports, Sports Center, and news. When I was in high school, I did watch C.S.I. all the time, but that was it.

I finish up the Spanish exercise and listen to the Spanish audio on my laptop to complete the workbook. In two hours, I'm done with Spanish. By then, I can hear Jeff saying how awesome the movie is, and he tells me all about the killer ending, acting out the scene and dodging explosions as he tells me the finale of the action-packed movie.

"Okay, this is what happened," Jeff says as he gets ready to act out the scene. "A cop busts a high-profile, rich as hell drug dealer. The drug kingpin goes back with his men and beats up the cop. The druggies brutally beat him, mess the cop up, but leave him alive. The cop then disappears, stitches himself up, and heals. The drug runners and kingpin then go to the cop's house to kill his family. The cop, who is a badass, one-man army, is waiting for them. The bad guys storm the house, the cop kills them one by one, choking them, stabbing them. He even broke one guy's neck. The cop sent another through the second-story window and killed another druggie with a flying saw blade into the guys' skull. This cop is one bad mo-fo," Jeff tells me, and I just watch.

Jeff is jumping around my bedroom as he acts out the action scenes. I'm just looking on from the desk and trying not to laugh at him.

"Then, finally, the only two people alive are the cop and the kingpin drug dealer. The house is on fire and the wife and little girl are stuck in the trunk of the bad guy's Cadillac. The cop is above the bad guy in the loft over the garage. The cop only has one bullet left. The drug dealer opens fire into the loft from below with his Uzi machine gun. The cop endures the pain of being shot several times. He never screams or anything, just keeps quiet. Then you hear a loud click. The bad guy is out of bullets. The cop hears this, then jumps through the window of the loft, does a flip, lands on the driveway, and fires his last bullet into the drug dealer's head," Jeff says to me as he aims his fingers at me as if it were a handgun and does a flip onto the bed.

Jeff is jumping and diving from my bed to the floor to show me exactly what happens in the movie. As Jeff lies on the floor, he makes a shooting sound and finally takes a break from all the gymnastics. I just sit and watch from my desk, holding in the laughter.

"The cop shoots the drug dealer right between the eyes, killing him. The cop saves his family and is the hero again. Probably a true story," Jeff adds as he lies exhausted on the floor.

"Yeah, hurray!" I yell and then I clap for Jeff's heroics.

"The bad guys always make one vital mistake," Jeff says as his stands before me out of breath from his action sequence.

"What is that?" I ask as I applaud Jeff's dynamic acting skills.

"They always make the mistake of leaving their enemy alive after they kick his ass. And that is always the same guy that goes on to come back and kill you. Always kill your enemy. Don't you know anything, Rookie?" he says as he throws his hands in the air to suggest defeat as if he is disgusted with me.

What a ham he is! Good for me, there is another movie he can watch since he rented two of them. I still have homework to do. Back to my homework. Tomorrow is Algebra and American History. I usually do all my algebra homework in the hour break between classes. College Algebra is easy since I was taking calculus as a senior in high school. This is another A on my report card. As for my American History class, it is full of reading. I keep up with all the reading, workbooks, and projects. With history, you learn the same things every year but forget most of it. I didn't remember it was General Meade that defeated Robert E. Lee at Gettysburg, not Ulysses S. Grant. See, I learn something new every day. The other thing about history is that it is boring. Within minutes of reviewing the lesson, I'm asleep.

I have a dream that is wild with imagery. Sigmund Freud is my guide with his book of dreams on the long road into my psyche. My dream is vivid with savage colors. I dream of an awkward long-feathered bird. A silver crane or ibis with bright red spots for eyes, leaving a trail of glittering silver as it flies through a jet-black sky. The bird's feathers are long and wide with a glowing silver color. The bird is a huge glowing silver zeppelin against the black sky. In my dream, Jeff and I are on our daily run through the Duke University campus toward the track. The day is early, and the sky is black with a light blue rim. The majestic bird flies toward us, leaving its magical silver trail. The sky slowly turns from black to blue as we run onward, watching the ibis. Then the bird darts down from the heavens toward us. With amazing speed, the silver object is coming toward Jeff and me. We stop with fear and wide eyes as the bird just misses our heads. The large majestic creature crashes full speed into the cold cement walkway. The bird is now a crippled silver blur in agonizing pain. The wings of the huge bird are broken, feathers sprayed across a twenty-foot radius. The silver ibis wails with pain as Jeff and I run toward it. The bird looks so sad with tears running from the red dots it has for eyes. The excruciating pain is noticeable with his bright red eyes pulsing with fear and agony. The scheme of my dream is in chaos. Vivid colors blur the scenery as all I can focus on is Jeff and the silver bird. The bird has two broken wings, and all the beautiful silver color is fading from the bird's feathers. I feel like I am in Van Munich's painting *The Scream*. Jeff and I slowly approach the gimp bird, and then amazingly the bird speaks out to us.

"Kill me. Kill me!" the enormous glittering bird yells out in agonizing pain as it lays twisted on the pearl white concrete. "Kill me! Kill me!" he yells again and then screams in pain with tears flowing from its red eyes.

"We must help it," Jeff says as we both look at the bird dumbfounded.

I walk over to the twisted bird as he screams out, "Kill me!"

Without excuse or passion, I stomp on the bird's head. The bird screams with pain as a dying man would if being beaten. The silver image in my dream flutters, and I keep stomping on its head, trying to kill it. The bird yelps in dying pain, an agonizing high-pitched scream of dying pain. The glitter fades away, and I keep stomping on the bird's head until the bird lays flat against the concrete. The bird is dead as the bird's color is fading from silver to a dull gray. All the vivid colors of deep blue sky, forest green grass, and pearl white concrete are fading to gray, a dull blurring gray. The bird is dead, and the only movement is from twitches of deteriorating nerves as I stand above the fading mystical creature.

"I can't believe you!" Jeff yells out as he pushes me away from the bird.

Jeff begins to cry as he cuddles the dead bird in his arms as if it were his own child. As he cries, I can only think, *The bird wanted to die. I killed it. I did nothing wrong.*

That is when Jeff wakes me up. Only the memory of the dead bird and Jeff's glare remain in my mind.

Jeff wakes me up well after midnight. His second movie is already over, and he needs a blanket and pillows so he can crash comfortably on my couch. I neglect to tell him about my dream. Maybe tomorrow, if there is a tomorrow.

CHAPTER 19

THURSDAY AND FRIDAY came and went without interruption or incident. I spend little time thinking about the case and try to focus on school, basketball, and working out. I'm watching out for my killer and Dawn; either could be forcing my demise. Right now, I'm practicing my fundamentals twice a day with David, Jeff, Keith, and today Bill Sharman is tagging along. Bill Sharman is Mr. Know-it-all at Duke University. Bill and David make the perfect backcourt at Duke. They both control the pace of offense and defense on the court. David is good and will learn more because he's only a sophomore. For Bill, this is his senior year, and there is no hope for him to do better next year. Bill's either going pro or going nowhere after this season.

This is what happened to Bill. He had trouble adjusting to the next level, going from high school star to lowly college freshman that no one knew. After sitting on the bench, he went into a depression after half a freshman season with the Blue Devils. He tried hard in games but was still making turnovers and only scored minimal points coming off the bench. He didn't do too well on defense either. He had a tough time against stronger players and couldn't keep up with the smaller, faster, more agile guards. Bill thought of himself as a liability. College ball was everything to him, and if he didn't play ball, he didn't want to go to school. That is the kind of pressure one has to endure as a college player at Duke. The pressure of ACC competition! Just because you made the team doesn't mean you play. You earn your playing time here, especially since most ACC games are televised to half the nation. That is why only the best players get to play the most minutes at Duke.

Duke, when Bill was a freshman, was a great team. Despite the one flaw of Billy's untimeliness, Duke and the Blue Devils went all the way to the finals against St. Louis. It was an intense playoff game. The final took the game into double overtime. The score was high; all the players were shooting threes, the crowd was going wild, and it was a seesaw game going back and forth, back and forth. Our small forward and shooting guard unfortunately fouled out of the game with only two minutes left on the clock. Coach is calling on his two backup guards to go the distance. That's when Coach put Bill Sharman in as a last resort. Bill was now in the game until the end. There were no other guards left to replace him that could handle the ball. There were two minutes left in double overtime, and someone was going home a loser.

The guard spot is very difficult in basketball; one has to be able to dribble the ball up and down the court without being picked. The point guard in basketball sets up all the plays and has to be one of the best defensive players on the court. The guard has to be able to pass the ball and be able to stop the other team from scoring against your team. Bill was in for the final two minutes of double overtime. This moment would determine his life, and it did.

With seventeen seconds and counting down on the game clock, Bill Sharman drops a pass inside the lane. Immediately the ball is passed right back to Bill. Time is flying by, and Bill is wide open at the top of the key. He throws up a three-point shot, and everyone holds their breaths as this would be Duke's final chance after being down by a point. Bill's shot goes in; he hits a three-pointer. Duke is up by two points, and the crowd is going wild. There is seventeen seconds left in the game. The Cameron crazies are going wild, jumping up and down, stomping their feet and cheering wildly.

St. Louis has no time-outs. They inbound the ball and fly down the court and set up against Duke's defense. With five seconds left on the clock, the St. Louis guard throws up a three and misses. There is a scramble for the ball. Bill Sharman ends up with the ball and runs down the court, scoring on a layup. The Blue Devils fans go crazy and storm the court. Duke wins the NCAA championship. Bill Sharman is a hero, no more depression.

That was three years ago. Bill is a starter now and scores about twenty points a game. He handles the rock and plays defense like no one else I've seen. What a turnaround. He thinks he's the next NBA superstar, but Bill is a bad role model. He tells younger players, "You shouldn't have missed that shot. Work harder. You're not giving it your all. Be more like me." He is always yelling out that kind of stuff. I'm glad he will already be gone by the time I'm playing full time. Since the girl he likes, Carrie, is in two of my classes, I see him more than I want to. He tries to push books out of my hands or tell jokes at my expense. All in all, I think he's a dick head.

As for present day, Jeff, Keith, David, Bill, and I have the gymnasium to ourselves. The five of us play basketball games like Freeze, Left, Three, and Bank. Bank is where you have to bank every shot off the backboard or it doesn't count. Freeze is when no one dribbles the ball. If the ball is passed to you, you stop and either pass or shoot. No taking steps or dribbling, but layups count. It's a fast-paced game where you need to know where your teammate is at all times. It's stop and shoot from one end of the court to the other. The game Left is when you have to dribble and shoot with only your left hand. If you're left-handed, you can only use your right hand going from one end of the court to the other. And finally, Three is when one person takes a three-point shot and the others rebound, race to the other end of the floor, and take a three-point shot while the others rebound. Three is the funniest because of the fighting under the boards. Believe it or not, David and I usually get the most rebounds, and we are the best three-point shooters out of the five of us. Keith is the worst rebounder and three-point shooter, but we let him play with us anyway.

Our game is all in fun, but as we know, the competition between old and new players grows. Jeff plays his best always because he wants everyone to know he takes playing ball seriously. That way we know what to expect from him. As for me, I like to have fun when playing court games, and my games begin with Bill.

"Asshole," I hear Bill whisper under his breath as I push his arm away from a rebound that I claim as my own.

He gives me the look of demonic position as I trot down the court and shoot my three-point shot.

"Swish!" I say as I score to lead the playful pack of ballers.

Bill and I have been going back and forth, plaguing each other little by little to show how much the other player can take without losing control. Billy and I play mind games, but since he is much more of a seasoned professional than I, I can tell my fouls bother him more and more with each passing second.

Since Keith has the least amount of points, he takes the ball up. Jeff guards him well. Bill, David, and I wait outside the three-second lane to either cut him off or pounce on his rebound. Keith drives hard down the right side of the court and does his best Michael Jordan vs. the Cleveland Cavaliers impression. Keith runs left to the three-point line, stops dead, and throws up a shot from the top of the key. The rebound is wide right to the side Bill and I are on. I tip the ball over Bill while he waits for me to come back down to earth. Suddenly, I lose the rebound and fall into Bill, taking him down hard on the parquet floor.

"Get off me!" Bill yells as he pushes me aside. "What's that?" Bill screams as he jumps up off the court and stands above me, fuming with anger.

"It was an accident?" I say as I pick myself up off the same floor. "You were covering me too close. How was I supposed to land?" I say in my defense.

None of the other guys step between us as they knew the hard foul was unintentional. No need to get upset over the incident. The three guys stand with their hands on their knees as we are all tired and close to exhausted. The ball is at my feet, and I pick it up with no convictions.

"Bill, it was an accident. Let's finish the game so we can go home," Jeff says.

We all stand in a close circle as to continue the game.

"Give me the ball!" Billy yells to me as he is just a few feet from me and beside the others.

I bounce the ball to him and wait to see what he does.

"You have been fouling me all game, Jackass!" And as he goes to scoop the ball up with his palm, he throws the orange globe right at my face with one swift gesture.

I luckily catch the ball with both hands as I am shocked Billy tried to hit me with the ball. Now I'm alert with adrenaline and pissed with anger. Two things I don't need right now. I only see red as I react.

Pow! I throw the ball right back at Bill, and the sphere hits him right in the center of his face. I see that his nose is bloody, and I can tell I stung him.

"Asshole!" he yells out after the ball bounces his head back.

With one mighty blow, he punches me, and I fall backward onto the ground inside the gym.

"No! Bill!" Keith yells as he grabs onto the future of Duke basketball.

David and Jeff react by getting between Bill and me, making sure I don't return the aggression. I jump right back up before anyone can help me. My buddies stand in my way but I'm over it. I'm just standing there in the gym, catching my breath.

"Just let it go!" Jeff says to me as I keep looking at Bill as he is being led to the locker room by Keith away from Jeff, David, and me.

"What the fuck was that for?" Dave yells at me. "He's a starter and you're a damn redshirt, freshman. Damn! You really know how to make enemies," Dave adds as he starts to walk to the water fountain. "He's your teammate. You're killing us!" he yells.

I stand in the gym with only Jeff by my side while Dave is collecting his things. We are all tired and catching our breaths when I state my case.

"I was going for a rebound and he wanted to fight over that?" I ask. "You saw him throw the ball at me first, Dave!" I yell out calmly to him in my defense.

Dave doesn't even look back; he just shot me the bird from over his shoulder.

I walk around to cool down and get my belongings since we are calling it a day.

"Ray! You're in enough trouble as it is. Do you think you can make some friends?" Jeff shouts at me as we walk to the wall to calm ourselves down from our workout.

"I don't know what that was about!" I say as Keith, Jeff, and I grab our towels and drink water from the silver fountain mounted inside the wall of the gymnasium.

"You were pushing him all game, Ray," David says from the side of the court. "You better watch it. Bill can cause a lot more trouble for you at Duke than any crazy person on the loose can. He's already on the team, remember? If he goes to Coach, who do you think Coach will believe?" David says as he waits his turn at the fountain.

"You need to let it go," Jeff says to me as he drenches his head with the cold water of the fountain. "Two wrongs don't make a right, and if you act like him, who's the jerk? You two look more like two peas in a pod."

"What's up with you guys anyway? He seems to dislike you more than the average freshman," David adds. "He's my friend, Ray. You better cool down. He's got nothing to prove. Only you do!"

"I know. I'll apologize," I reply as I cool down from our hours of ball playing.

I just lean up against the wall and wonder why everything is such a competition with Bill and why he bothers me so much. Dave takes a long drink from the fountain after Jeff, and we wait in silence as the gymnasium calms us.

David, Jeff, Keith, and I are all exhausted after a long workout. We all wait and take turns drinking from the water fountain. Bill walked out of the gym in a hurry, leaving his towel and drink bottle there.

"He told me you're all over his girl too," David adds.

"That's bull!" I reply. "I sit next to some girl in class and he's up my ass over it. I don't even talk to the girl. You know what happened to the last three girls I dated. Why would I want any more attention? He's crazy."

"Just let it go," Keith adds as we get ready to leave the gym.

"It's already gone," I say as we gather our things and call it a day.

"Maybe he'll steal your car," Dave says and smiles.

"Don't even go there!" I say to Dave as he knows how much my Camaro means to me. Plus, it's Jeff's only form of transportation.

I drop the guys off at the dorm and head to the room. When I get to the hotel, I see a huge care package at the front desk for me. I take it upstairs and open the assortment of chips, cookies, some clothes, sports magazines, and more Duke paraphernalia. Inside the big box was a much smaller box made of wood. Inside that box are the two guns and two clips with bullets. Dad sent me a .9 millimeter Beretta handgun with a clip that holds thirteen bullets. He also sent me a three-shot .22 caliber Derringer that fits in an ankle holster or side pocket. The Derringer doesn't have a trigger safety because it would be too small for me to get my finger into. Therefore, I have to be very careful with each of them. Tomorrow, I plan on going to the gun range with Jeff to learn how to use and clean them. When it comes to guns, we both are clueless, very clueless!

For now, I shower, change clothes, and go back to the university to get the boys to do our strength workout.

As for Dawn, I've spent the last two nights at the hotel and haven't seen her. Her Mustang has been parked there, but no Dawn. She's another mystery, but I do have to tell her I have the two guns now. So far, only Dad and Jeff know I have them. I want to learn how to use them first just in case Dawn wants to quiz me on my knowledge of magnums. I want her to know I'm responsible with guns, not acting like a gun-toting kid with a new toy to show off.

After an exhausting workout with the boys, Jeff and I head back to the hotel.

Jeff and I walk into the Holiday Inn as if we own the place. I head to the front desk with Jeff in tow.

"Any messages for Ray Beacon?" I ask as I lean on the counter.

"Nope," the clerk replies after checking my mailbox.

"What about Dawn Franklin? Any messages?"

"One," he replies.

"Going to check out the park in the morning. See you around nine a.m. for breakfast. Friedman."

I show the note to Jeff and just shake my head.

"Don't worry about it, buddy. There are lots of younger fish in the sea, and you can't love them all."

We laugh as I hand the note back to the clerk. I nod to Jeff to follow me as we head straight for the pool for a relaxing swim.

Since it is Friday night, we avoid the local parties to stay out of trouble and just rent movies and drink beer in the safety of our seclusion. We then call it a night at about 1:00 a.m. Everything is going great while Jeff and I plan to go for our 5:30 a.m. run. We will get back around 6:00 a.m. Then we change and meet Keith downstairs for breakfast. Since organized practice hasn't started yet, we plan on going to Charlotte Saturday night for a concert. We plan to go see *The Young Anglo's* play at the Hard Rock Cafe and party all night downtown, then come home Sunday night. I'll be wearing jeans and my favorite Duke sweatshirt. I plan on being comfortable, relaxed, and ready to enjoy my day.

We start Saturday early and get all our running around done. Now we go downstairs to meet Keith for breakfast.

Keith is already at a table waiting for us.

"Look at this," I say as I read the front page of the paper at the breakfast table. "Students blamed for stolen cars."

I read the excerpt that tells about ten cars in two months being stolen from homes around campus. All vehicles are SUVs, Hondas, and Nissans. Cars that you can easily disable the GPS and alarm system. BMWs, Lexis, Audis, and Mercedes-Benzes have much more complicated computer systems with tracking. I have On-Star with my Chevy, so my Camaro is safe. Our lives are perfect with satisfaction until my cell phone rings while we are eating breakfast.

"Hello. Ray speaking," I say in my illustrious mood.

"Hey, Ray. It's Dawn. Where are you?" she asks in a concerned voice.

"I'm at the Holiday Inn eating breakfast with Jeff and Keith. Why?" I ask.

"I can't talk right now. Webber and Tusson are on their way to get you. Stay there until they get there. Don't go anywhere, okay?" she says to me and then hangs up.

The concern in her voice is startling. Something is definitely wrong.

"What's up?" Jeff asks as he eats as much breakfast as he can.

"That was Dawn. She told me to stay put. The two detectives are coming to get me. Something bad must have happened," I say as I wonder what happened.

"We'll just have to take the Honda to Charlotte, that's all," Keith says as he eats the complimentary breakfast provided by the hotel.

I sit and enjoy the hot breakfast rolls, bacon, biscuits and gravy, fruit, milk, hot scrambled eggs, and orange juice. My mind is racing again, trying to consider what could have happened between last night and early this morning. It's only 7:00 a.m., and she seemed really worried. Plus, neither Officer Freedman nor Dawn are coming to get me. I wonder if something happened to them involving the case.

Within ten minutes, Detective Webber and Detective Tusson are in the Holiday Inn looking for me. Webber goes to the front desk, and Tusson comes into the dining hall looking for me. I raise my hand to get his attention and he comes right over.

"Get up!" he demands fiercely as he stares me down in his black suit and Ray-Ban sunglasses. Then he kicks my chair to motivate me. "I said get up!" he shouts again then whips out his cuffs.

"What's up?" I say quickly as he grabs one of my wrists and pushes me onto the table and forcefully arrests me right in front of everyone inside the hotel.

"We can do this my way or the hard way. I'm giving you the chance to avoid any unwanted attention."

"Go on without me, guys. I might be a while," I say as Tusson swings me around and literally pushes me out of the hotel and puts me into the back of his squad car while reading me my rights as we walk to the car.

Both Keith and Jeff just look on in shock and say nothing as the situation unfolds.

Tusson disappears back into the hotel after he leaves me in the car. That big gorilla that calls himself a cop just manhandled me, arrested me, threw me into the car, and then left me. I wait for about twenty minutes, locked up in the back of this car with no clue what's going on.

Finally, after twenty minutes, Tusson and Webber return. They don't get into the car immediately. They wait until other police officers arrive, talk with them, and finally Tusson gets into the car. To jail I go, leaving Webber behind.

"What's up with this?" I yell out to Tusson through the bullet-proof safety glass.

"You'll know soon enough," he says without looking back. "Sit back and enjoy the ride. You surely know where you're going."

"To the World Series? Or to the basketball game? It is a home game, you know?"

He says nothing, just drives on with his Ray-Bans shielding his eyes from the sun. In minutes I'm at the Durham Police Station. Again, Tusson manhandles me, drags me inside the station through a side door, and throws me into a closed room with a bulletproof window. The room is empty except for four chairs against the wall. I struggle to get up from the cold floor since I'm still in cuffs. I sit down and bring my hands from behind my back to in front of me. The cuffs are cutting off my circulation. I try to sit and wait as patiently as possible. It is useless to try to get out of this secure holding room. I figure I might as well see if the door is locked.

"Locked. What have I done now?" I say out loud to no one as I shake my head and wait to be included into the loop of knowledge of what is going on.

Within minutes, I see Dawn and Detective Tusson walking by the window with Captain Adams. They don't stop, and only Dawn looks over to notice me. Then she is gone before I can say anything to her. I wait about ten more minutes and see Jeff and Detective Webber walk by. Jeff looks over to notice me and is gone before I can say anything. Other people walk by the window, and nobody pays any attention to little old me. From what I can tell, I'm at the back of the police station along a main hallway, close to the back exit. Either way, I'm stuck with no place to go. I wait about an hour and a half before Jeff comes by to see me.

"What's going on, Jeff?" I say as Jeff enters into my confinement.

"Things aren't looking good," he says as he enters the room and takes a seat. "They quizzed me for about twenty minutes about where I was this morning and last night. How long were we together today? Who saw us last night and this morning? They took the videotapes of the hotel. They are looking for something. They also asked me if I knew our dorm room was bugged," Jeff says to me with much concern.

"Bugged?" I ask surprisingly to Jeff who sits across from me.

"As in telephones with microphones," he says as he sits in front of me on the other chair. "Tusson and Webber asked all the questions. Dawn, Adams, and Freedman all teamed up against me. Asked me all sorts of stuff about you," he says in a voice that worries me.

Jeff knows the trouble I'm in, and from his expression the trouble just went from bad to worse. Jeff rests his chin on his hands and just looks at me as I play with my handcuffs. I can't even imagine what has happened now.

"I don't know what to tell you. Any clue what they are looking for?" I ask.

"Nope, but something went down last night. Something bad," he says. "Every time they would ask me some questions, they would go outside the room and talk, then come back inside and ask me more questions. Again and again. I don't know what they're looking for, and I didn't tell them anything," Jeff says as he looks at me with a fearful look on his face.

"I can only imagine," I say as I sit up and place my head in my hands. "The good news is, everyone working on the case is alive, and so are we. Our friends are alive, so what could have happened?" I ask out loud.

Jeff and I talk for about ten minutes before I notice my assistant coach, Johnny, from Duke walking by the window with a police escort. This only leaves Jeff and I to wonder if someone on the team has died, or if I'm getting kicked off the team. What happened last night, or what did they find last night that would warrant all this concern? My mind runs with questions, and only negative answers appear. I wonder if they found the guns I have in my room.

"Go talk to Dr. Franklin and Johnny. See what's up?" I ask Jeff as I sit in the room, still handcuffed and waiting for answers.

Jeff jumps up and grabs the doorknob. It's locked and only opens from the outside. Now Jeff and I are prisoners together. We both sit in the room, alone.

"Did you tell them about the guns?" I ask Jeff as he sits down again.

"No. I forgot all about the guns, so it can't be that."

"I still can't believe the room was bugged," I say. "It would explain things. It would explain how someone knew I was in Arcadia. It would explain the connection between the girls and me. All our calls were recorded. Someone out there has their finger on the pulse, and since we haven't been in the dorm at all lately, something had to give."

Jeff and I sit in the room for about ten minutes before a crew of police walk in. Tusson, Webber, Adams, Freedman, and Dawn all file in one by one. Jeff jumps up from his seat and stands by the door to make sure he can get out if need be. I hold my hands in the air with the cuffs still around them.

"Please uncuff me!" I say as soon as Tusson walks into the room.

Neither Tusson nor Webber respond to my plea. They both lean up against the big window, side by side. Captain Adams sits down in front of me with Dawn by his side. Freedman stands by the door near Jeff, and Johnny is nowhere to be seen.

"Did anyone hear me?" I say as I hold the cuffs in the air.

"Shut up!" Adams says in a voice loud enough for everyone to hear. Then he reaches into his pocket, pulls out keys, and uncuffs me.

"Were you with Bill Sharman yesterday?" Captain Adams asks as we both take our seats in the middle of the room.

"Yes, we played ball together yesterday afternoon," I reply.

"Did you two fight at all?" Captain Adams asks.

"Nothing serious. It's competition about basketball and being a freshman. Like I said, nothing serious."

"Well, last night someone broke into his room. He was jumped, and someone attempted to throw him out of his second-story window. The perpetrator disappeared without a trace, and Bill will swear in court that it was you."

The look of shock on my face must have said enough as my eyes widened and jaw dropped when he told me the news.

"It wasn't!" I say in my defense. "I was at the hotel all night. Check the security tapes. Ask my friends."

"We did ask. You guys were drinking. They all fell asleep around one. You could have easily snuck out. Your alibi is shaky at best. Bill Sharman is scared, and things are getting worse," Captains Adams says to me. "Your coach is scared too. What's going on?"

I am in alarm because of the tone of Adams's voice.

"You know as much as me," I reply. "Plus. there are video cameras in the hallways of the hotel. There are video cameras in the parking lot too. My car and I didn't leave the hotel."

"Here's what happened this morning," Adams begins as he takes the seat in front of me. "Cadet Russell and Officer Freedman went to investigate the Chapel Hill Park at about six this morning. Someone found them. Cadet Russell is in ICU," Captain Adams says to me half-heartedly in a low but angry voice.

"Russell was almost burned to death!" Freedman yells as he approaches me from his spot against the wall. "The killer came up from behind us, hit me with an iron club, probably beat Russell unconscious before lighting him ablaze. When I came to, Russell's back and legs were on fire. I open fired on the person, but he got away. And he took my truck! Now my truck and your mystery man are all gone. He was waiting for us," Freedman says as he rubs his head. "He was waiting to ambush us at six this morning. What is going on?"

"Hey, detectives, what part of six people murdered did you underestimate about this guy? This person is a ruthless killer!" I say in my defense as I look up at Freedman. "Again, ruthless killer."

"Your dorm room phone was bugged," Adams says. "We found this out when we searched through your room. We found a low-key bug in the living room and bedrooms. Someone isn't playing around. The bugs are short-range transmitters. Someone close by is listening. This doesn't look good for you," Adams says to me as he stares into my eyes.

I can't do much, but I'm aware of what's going on and realize this is serious. Dawn doesn't make eye contact with me the entire time Adams is talking to me. I realize this isn't the bad news. The other shoe is about to drop, and I sit waiting.

"We checked you out this morning," Adams says again. "We have the hotel tapes. We know of the wake-up call that you answered, the five-mile run, and we know you were at breakfast this morning at seven. But we need answers. An officer has been attacked, and a cadet is almost dead. Russell is brutally burned from head to toe because of you," Adams says to me in a stern voice. "Now just about everyone linked to you is dead."

"Hey, hey. Hold on. Not because of me. Because of some crazy that you guys can't catch. I haven't done anything," I say as I let my mind come up with an answer.

"What is going on?" Freedman asks.

"It could be a police officer is behind this. Dawn especially. She knew you were going to check out the park today? Not me," I say from my seat.

"Bullshit," she says as she stands up.

"You're an ass!" Freedman shouts out.

The room erupts into a mosh pit. I'm the first to strike a blow in my defense.

"She knew Freedman and Russell were going down there!" I yell out as I jump up from my chair and point at Dawn. "We saw the note at the hotel desk yesterday. She knew about Jeff also!" I yell out. "It isn't me!"

"You are a punk, kid!" Freedman yells out as he approaches me, pointing at me.

"She's done nothing to help me. She bugged my phone, her and him!" I yell out as I point at Freedman as I stand before him.

"This is bullshit! You're jealous of him!" Dawn yells out.

"Shut up! Sit down!" Captain Adams yells out as he stands between Freedman and me.

"She hasn't been around. She's done nothing, absolutely nothing for Ray!" Jeff yells into the crowd of already yelling people.

"Shut up and sit down!" Captain Adams yells once again.

"She had access to the dorms, she killed my parents, probably kidnapped her own daughter for money, and is setting me up. And why didn't the killer burn Freedman? Why just Russell? They knew where I was, always! Where was she this morning? Question her and him!" I yell out as I point to the two of them.

The room is crazy with five people in each other's faces yelling with Captain Adams in the middle of it all. Jeff stands aside while Detective Tusson and Detective Webber get close to the crowd to enforce police aggression.

"I'm not going down for this!" I yell out while Captain Adams tries to separate me from the crowd of police officers.

"I can't believe you! You bastard!" Dawn yells out again among all the confusion. "You're such a bastard!" she yells in frustration.

"You're a punk!" Freedman yells as he reaches across Adams and grabs me by my shirt to pull me toward him.

That's all it takes for me to explode into a violent rage of anger and stupidity. I jump up and push Officer Freedman. I push him hard, almost knocking him to the ground. Jeff jumps right in and bear hugs Freedman from behind. Both fall to the ground, and Freedman cuts his lip open as his face bounces off the cement floor.

"You bastard! Let go of me!" the officer yells from the floor to Jeff.

Tusson pulls Jeff off Freedman effortlessly. Everyone is yelling at me, and Freedman slowly gets up as Captain Adams's voice fills the room.

The entire incident only takes a few seconds. The accusations, the yelling, the push, and the separation all happen in a flash, and then it's over. I'm against one wall with Webber in front of me. Freedman is against the other wall with Dawn yelling at him and me at the same time. Tusson is shielding Jeff, just in case another relapse happens. Captain Adams once again gains control of the room.

"What the Hell is going on here?" Captain Adams yells out in a rage of his own.

"I'll take you on anytime," Detective Tusson says to me as he laughs at my struggle with Officer Freedman.

"Stop that!" Captain Adams yells out from the middle of the room. "Just in case you didn't know, it's illegal to hit a police officer!"

"You two! Go wait outside!" Adams yells to Dawn and Freedman.

Dawn, without saying a word, walks outside. Freedman looks right at me as he wipes the blood from his mouth with his shirt cuff. He looks right at me and speaks firmly.

"You little shit. This isn't over," he says calmly as he points to me.

"Anytime!" I say from behind Webber, looking Freedman right in the eyes and meaning every word I say. "It's on!" I yell out to the dumb bastard as I'm shielded by Webber.

Captain Adams turns and points at me. That is when Webber nods to the Captain and in one quick motion, he punches me right in my stomach. The pain. More sharp pain. I'm out of breath and dizzy all at once. Webber punches me right in the stomach again. I'm on the floor now. The pain is causing me to gasp for air. I wasn't expecting either punch. I'm on my knees gasping for air. The shock and the pain. I'm speechless for about five long seconds as I try to recover. I try to breathe in the air after Webber rocks my world.

"Listen up, you little shit!" yells Captain Adams as he picks me up by my hair and leads me like a rag doll into the chair.

He still has a hold of me with both hands as he starts yelling in my face.

"I have to go tell a good friend his son is in ICU. Now I want answers!" he yells right into my face.

"Investigate Dawn. It's her," I squeak out in pain. "Why just try to kill Russell when Freedman says he was knocked out cold? It doesn't make sense," I say slowly as I recover from his powerful stomach punch with much anticipation. "My life has been a living nightmare since I met her," I say from my chair with much subdued fear of police brutality.

"Give me a reason to believe you!" Adams says as he hangs on to my hair with one hand as he is just inches from my face. "You've been lying! And James at Big Mart is a fake. Keith and your roommate said they saw him, but you probably set them up. It was your idea to play basketball at the park that night!"

I jump up out of the chair, furious. "It's them!" I yell out. "They are lying!"

Captain Adams grabs me as I stand up and he yells, "Now tell me the truth! Just like you knew they would be at the park today!" He bangs my head into the concrete wall.

"Only because Dawn stood me up. All this is her fault!" I yell out.

"You told me to check out the park. Now one of my cadets is almost dead. Sharman will talk to the press, and the papers will have a field day with this. What am I supposed to tell everyone?" he says as he still has a firm grasp of my hair and has me pinned against the wall.

"I don't know!" I say as the pain thrashes my skull.

"This is all going to be tomorrow's headlines!" he yells into my face. "You have half a day to save your ass!" he says as he reluctantly lets me go. "Now where should we start?"

"Look into Dawn's past and investigate Steve Covey also," I say as I lean against the wall. "Covey works at the jail in Arcadia. It is hard to believe Dawn didn't know my phone was tapped. She has access to the dorms since she is a cop. She knew about my mom. She could have easily had someone kill her. And you said she searched my room. I have two guns in my hotel room. Both registered to my dad. A Beretta and a Derringer. It's hard to believe they can find listening devices hidden in my dorm room, which are hidden, but didn't find those guns. If either one of them took the guns out of my hotel, that's armed burglary, which is a felony. Search them! They took the guns and plan on killing me with them and I don't know why. It's those two, not me!" I reply to Captain Adams in fear for my own safety.

"He does have two guns which he got just yesterday," Jeff says on my behalf. "I've seen them. They are in the top drawer of the dresser in the hotel. If they are gone, Dawn and Freedman took them. They were there this morning. I was looking at them. Stealing guns is a felony, even for police officers," Jeff says. "Armed burglary is a jailable offense, even for a police officer," Jeff says from his spot by the door.

Detective Tusson and Detective Webber, without a word being said to them, go outside and talk with the other two officers. Captain Adams starts to pace back and forth in front of me for a while before taking a seat himself.

"I can't give you answers I don't have," I say to Captain Adams as I get comfortable in my seat. "I'm sorry more people died, but I had nothing to do with their deaths. I didn't make any calls last night, and I stayed at the hotel all morning. It wasn't me," I say to him innocently from my chair. "It isn't me doing this. I wouldn't hurt anyone," I ensure him.

"Ray, Bill Sharman said it was you. He will testify in court. You will be kicked off the team and out of school. You will be jailed for a minimum of assault, maybe even attempted murder. Either way, you're out of Duke. If you want to turn this around, I need your help. You need to give me something."

"At breakfast today, I read that a lot of cars have been stolen from the area the park is in. If someone is out there, he is the one stealing the cars, making his living."

Jeff takes a seat next to Adams. Tusson and Webber escort Dawn and Freedman away from the window, and I sit and wonder, if this is my twin brother, what would I be doing to become me or become invisible until the time is right?

"All the cars are being taken within three miles of the school. Ten in the last two months. That's a record, and now Freedman's truck. This killer now has a police truck, shotgun, and a scanner. He took the truck with no problems. Gone before Freedman could get up," Captain Adams says.

"He is stealing the cars for cash," I reply. "A killer wouldn't have a job if he is trying to be invisible. Sleeps in the daytime. Lives along a bus route. If he drives a car, he might get stopped. Also, gas stations have video cameras. He doesn't want to be seen, so he doesn't ever get gas or food from gas stations. He's bussing himself in, and then stealing the cars as he walks around at night. He gets on at a busy bus stop to go unnoticed. That's my opinion. He's out there, and now he knows we are looking for him. He'll never go to the park again. He won't steal anymore cars either. He'll start hunting for me. That's how he got to Bill. He already knows how to get in and out of the dorms. He's close, and he knows it," I say to Captain Adams from my chair. "He's very close, and he has to work fast. He came to Duke last night to kill me."

"I'll check out your theories. I'll give you the benefit of a doubt. Get my best computer tech on it. I'll get a warrant and check Dawn and Freedman for anything and everything. Your stupid theory is the only other theory we have, and that theory is about as far-fetched as they come," he says as he tries to calm down, standing before me. "If I even think you're in on it, I'll burn you up myself. You hear me!" He growls mere inches in front of me in the almost empty room. "Other than that, we need answers before all this hits the news this afternoon. If not, you will be in jail this evening, front page news tomorrow!"

"I hear you loud and clear, sir," I say.

"Don't move. I'll be right back," Captain Adams says to us as he lets himself out.

This is one crazy situation. I sit on my little chair in pain as Jeff blocks the door from closing. Jeff doesn't want to be stuck here anymore, and this isn't his situation anyway. He is a good friend, and I would like him to stay that way.

"What do you think?" I ask Jeff in disarray from my chair.

"I think you're going to be off the team," Jeff says directly to me.

"Why?" I say in total alarm.

"Bill Sharman. He's scared of you. After yesterday's game, he talked to Coach, and then last night he was beat up by someone. Now you just pushed a Duke University police officer. I'm pretty sure they will consider you a liability to the school and team. Plus, the fact of stolen guns and listening devices in the dorms. This is all way too much for me to handle. Too many people look guilty, and now there is a dirty-cop theory. Dawn might be doing this to make up for the loss of her daughter. This is all crazy. If you were me, what would you think?" Jeff asks as he stands alone by the door keeping it open.

I have to tell him the honest truth. Jeff is my best friend, and I want him to be safe. I would hate for him to get caught in the middle of all this because of me.

"Why don't you go and see Liv this weekend? Get your head right before this gets any bigger than it already is. Someone is after me. So honestly, go home for the weekend and hopefully this will all be over when you come back," I say to him from my chair as I nod to him.

"Hang in there, man," he says to me as he puts out his fist.

We bump fists, then Jeff leaves the room. This time the door is unlocked. In time, Jeff, like all the others, is gone, and I am once again alone.

I don't think it's my twin at all that's after me. I think it's my past.

I still have the cuffs and accidentally lock them around my left wrist like jewelry, thinking, *Why me?*

CHAPTER 20

I'VE BEEN IN this room alone for such a long time now. I pick a spot along the wall, sit down, and steal a short nap. The noise of the surrounding area wakes me up after an hour or so. When I look up, people are in the doorway. I look at my watch, and it is just after ten. I've been here for three hours already, and I still don't understand what is going on. That's when I notice the big older gentleman from the picture in Captain Adams's office walking by. An entourage of police officers follow him. Carrie Russell from my classes follows right behind him with a circle of police escorting the two as they walk. They both walk slowly by and look stricken by grief. Instantly, I put the connection together. Carrie and Cadet Ward Russell are brother and sister. The good friend of Captain Adams, in the picture, that is their father. I'm in deep shit now, never mind skipping my Spanish and Algebra class for the rest of the year. As the grief-stricken pass by, I can only sit and watch while sadness overcomes me.

It's 10:30 a.m., and the door is still locked. I'm wide awake after my nap, and I'm still stuck like a rat in a cage. I walk over to the door and lean against the window ledge. I can see Officer Freedman walking toward the exit with an officer escorting him out. He is glaring at me. That's when I raise my middle finger at him and put it against the window with a thud so he could clearly understand my meaning. He sees me and starts yelling into the window while he is being escorted out of the building. I didn't hear a word he said, nor did I care.

Minutes later, I see Dawn in her blue jeans and white button shirt, taking a seat opposite me at the end of the hallway. Captain Adams is by her side with Mr. Russell and Carrie. Since I feel guilty enough about what happened to Ward Russell, I step away from the window so no one can point me out to the Russells. The guilt beguiles me; I feel the physical pain of losing a loved one once again. I clearly visit the memories of my family in my mind. Sorrow settles in, and I feel regret once again because of the loss of my parents. I'm sure the Russells are a much closer family than mine was, and I'm hoping Ward will be okay. I feel their pain as if it is my own, since I did meet Ward Russell. Now he's in the hospital, burned up. I feel partly responsible for his anguish. I'm guilty that his tortured future, once again, is the fault of my past. How many more people have to die of innocence because of the actions I underwent four long years ago? How long of a sentence must I pay for deserting my horrible family? How many of life's lessons must I endure at only eighteen years old?

I sit and ponder my being here on earth while the rest of the world ignores me. That's when I hear the door open. I look up and see Captain Adams opening the door. Then I see Covey passing him by. By the look of sheer amazement on my face, Adams sees concern, turns, and looks at the huge man walking past the glass window behind him.

"That's Covey," I say in amazement as I point to him. "What is he doing here? That is the guy I told you to investigate," I say as I quickly walk to the window. "How did he get here from Florida so fast?"

"He must be taking Dawn back to Arcadia," Adams says. "We found your guns also," he says as he enters the room.

"Where?" I ask as I head for the door and Captain Adams.

"Don't worry about where. Just be glad I have them," he says.

I walk out of my little glass prison and wait for Adams to lead me in any direction. I see Covey and Dawn standing together at the end of the hallway, about thirty feet from me. Covey is a huge man. He looks bigger in the daylight than I can remember. He towers over Dawn by almost two feet and weighs well over three hundred pounds.

The mysterious phenomenon that confronts me is if the incident with Cadet Russell happened between six and seven this morning. How did Covey get here so fast from Florida? It's only 11:00 a.m. right now. It took me almost twelve hours to drive from Arcadia to Durham, and I drove at ninety miles per hour all the way here. He is here less than four hours after the incident. Maybe an hour or so after Dawn calls on him. Even flights from Ft. Myers to here take five hours because you would have to fly to Atlanta, Georgia, then Raleigh, North Carolina. The drive from Arcadia to the airport takes at least an hour, if not more. It's another thirty minutes from the airport in Raleigh to here.

My only thought is that Covey's been here the whole time. Something definitely isn't right. Now I realize she is a dirty cop. She had something to do with all this. What a fine mess she has caused. I now look at the two of them in disgust while my mind races with questions and self-confessed answers. They both look at me as I glare at the two of them standing together. I see only the word *guilty* as I see the two of them together.

Adams points me in another direction, and I follow him to his office and sit in the chair in front of his desk. Captain Adams takes his seat behind his desk. Webber and Tusson come into the office quietly and stand behind me. I notice there are at least eight pictures of Captain Adams with the Russell family scattered around the room. I'm sure it wasn't easy to tell his longtime friend that his son might die. This is a crime that needs to be solved by immediate action. I'm pretty sure we are going to be in a full court press until the culprit is caught and set ablaze.

Captain Adams hands me the key to my cuffs. I take them off and ask.

"Where are my guns?" I say before Captain Adams can begin to speak.

"I have them right here for safekeeping." Captain Adams taps on his desk drawer.

"Armed burglary. Lots of bad press," I say in my defense.

"Shut up and let him talk," Tusson demands from behind me.

"The detectives have found two bus routes that travel from the park to downtown and around the school," Adams begins. "One of those routes is the busiest passenger route in the city. The other is along a route that travels between the school, town, and into the surrounding suburbs. There is a supposed chop shop for cars along each route. If someone is becoming invisible like you say, we think they are hiding in those mountains. They're not far from the park, and there are caves up there that we have found runaways and transients hiding in before," Adams says to me calmly, slowly, and sadly.

"And what about me?" I say as Tusson and Webber tower behind me.

"I want you to go with the detectives and find out if our computer techs are right. They say he's there. We need to find out what happened," Adams says. "I can't cover for you anymore. Today is your last chance, and then we unleash the press on the story. I have no choice."

"You're coming with us," Webber says as he stands behind me.

"I have to go," Adams says as he gets up. "I have some explaining to do to some friends." Then he walks away, leaving me there with Tusson and Webber.

I sit at the desk not knowing what to do. The detectives stand behind me.

"Take a minute to think about your future. If you have anything to tell us, now is the time. The press is hours away, and you have no way out," Webber says.

"We'll be outside," Tusson adds.

I don't know what to do. If the press find out about the murders and my involvement surrounding them, I'm going to jail. Tusson and Webber, the two hit men from the justice department, are my only hope, and they are waiting outside for me. I get up and walk around the desk. I open the drawer, and there are my two guns. I reach down for them and pull them out of the drawer. I press the release of the

Beretta and the clip slides out effortlessly. I see the clip is full of bullets, and the Derringer is still loaded also. I slip the guns under my sweatshirt and into my belt, then off I go to meet my destiny.

Off I go, out of the office. I see the two detectives waiting for me at the end of the hallway. I say nothing as I follow the two muscular detectives to a large four-door dark-brown Chevy Impala. There are no police lights on the outside the car, only a single dash light, rear panel police lights in the back window, and square strobe lights in the grill of the car. I've been in this car enough lately and now know it well. Tusson opens the back door for me to file into peacefully. Then we are off to the hills behind the University of North Carolina that outline the city of Chapel Hill to find a killer, to flush him out. This journey will lead me to find many things; one of them will be myself. I'm scared, really scared.

The drive to Chapel Hill is about twenty minutes, and we drive a while without speaking. Only the voices over the police scanner break the thick tension inside the car. I feel like I'm going to be executed as I sit silently in the back of a police car. Tusson and Webber don't even talk to each other during the drive. I now think of them as robots; they both show no emotion or expression while they drive onward toward Chapel Hill. If that is the way homicide work is best completed, so be it. I just hope I don't disappear into those hills along with them. These guys could be the killers, and no one would ever doubt their word that I just disappeared. I just went from scared to terrified as I think about what possibly could happen to me in those hills. I am now terrified as I sit quietly inside the dark-brown Impala.

I realize that after the first ten minutes, I can't take the silence anymore. I have to say something. You figure I'm only a kid, but to me, not talking inside a car is torture. I can't take it anymore; therefore, I speak up.

"What is up with you two guys? Got families or kids or anything?" I ask.

"Why do you ask?" Webber asks me.

"Because the silence is killing me. I can't handle just listening to the scanner all the way there. That is cruel and unusual punishment," I say from behind the safety glass.

Webber doesn't even turn around to acknowledge me. Tusson just keeps driving.

"Hey, thanks for the small talk," I say sarcastically.

We drive for about five more minutes, and finally a conversation occurs.

"I have a wife and four-year-old son," Tusson says.

Finally, conversation. Thank God.

"Really? Is your wife pretty?" I ask.

"Very. College cheerleader, thin, blonde, loves to work out and doesn't mind that I'm a homicide detective," Tusson says as he drives.

"Been married long?" I ask from by back seat prison.

"Ten years. We met in college at Alabama. I was a football player, and she was the best-looking woman I've ever seen. Love at first sight. We married right after graduating college together, and we waited a few years before starting a family."

"What is his name?"

"Michael Tide Tusson," he says with a smile.

"You named your child Tide? As in the Crimson Tide? After your college mascot?" I ask from the back seat in dismay.

"Yeah, we both agreed it would be perfect," he says to me.

"If you say so," I say as I ponder the name Tide. "What about you, Webber? What's your story?"

There is no reply from Webber. Not even a smirk. He ignores me.

"Webber is a two-time divorcee with three kids, all girls," Tusson says.

"Too bad. I'd hate to have girls, never mind the child support, headaches, jealousy, and alimony payments that go along with it," I say. I change the conversation quickly as I think of the dream from the night before. "Maybe you two could help me out with something." I lean forward toward the police glass. "I'm assuming your intelligence is far greater than mine, so stop me if this gets too technical for you two," I say as I get their attention. "I had a dream the other night that a huge silver bird that could talk crash landed in front of Jeff and me."

"A talking bird," Tusson replies as he drives on through the ever-green scenery of North Carolina. "What did it say?" he asks.

"Well, nothing until it crashed. Once the bird realized it couldn't fly anymore, it kept shouting, 'Kill me, kill me,'" I say to the two as I lean forward toward the glass partition that separates them from myself.

"What happened?" Tusson asks me as he drives.

"Jeff wanted to save it, but it was badly hurt and dying. Its wings were broken. It was all dilapidated and kept saying kill me. Over and over, kill me, kill me."

"What did you do?" Tusson asks as he drives onward, never looking back.

"I stomped on its head and killed it," I say. "That's what it wanted."

"What did Jeff do?" Tusson asks, and Webber does not partake in our conversation.

"He almost killed me for killing the bird. He tried caring for it, but it was too late. Then he cried and cursed me for killing the bird. That's when I woke up. What do you think it all meant?" I ask as I lean forward and wait for their answer.

That is when Webber turns around to look at me and gives his opinion.

"Seems like you're always taking the easy way out. Not too open-minded to other people's opinion. You didn't know it was a dream, and yet you killed a talking bird that could have been worth thousands of dollars, probably a million dollars," Webber says.

"That pretty much sums it up, kid. You took the easy way out," Tusson says.

I just sit back in my seat and absorb what they say to me. Am I really like that? Always looking for an easy way out? Am I closed-minded? Do I listen to other people's opinion before assuming my own opinion? I don't really know.

"Seek to understand before trying to be understood," Tusson adds.

"Take the diplomatic approach into every situation," Webber says to me.

"The other thing," Tusson adds sharply. "You're still our main suspect. If you step out of line, this case will end with my bullet in your brain."

"These conversations are pleasant since we mostly deal with ignorance, but we will not hesitate to kill you if either of us feels threatened by you or if you try to run from us," Webber says to me.

"Okay!" I say as I kick back and keep quiet.

I realize that these guys are all business. Then, finally, as I ponder their sayings, we arrive at the park in Chapel Hill. To one side of us is a mountain; to the other side, off in the distance, is the large campus of the University of North Carolina. We are between them both at this park. The three of us get out of the Impala to investigate the crime scene in the middle of the afternoon. That is when Webber narrates the story of Officer Freedman and Cadet Russell to me.

The accident scene is marked with police tape and wooden horse barricades. We look at the scene but don't get too close to give away our presence. The marked-off area isn't guarded by police or security guards. We stray away from the Impala at the scene and ponder exactly what happened.

"Over there is where they found Russell's body," Webber says as he points to a police line to our left, along the trees just a few yards from our parking space.

"Freedman's truck was taken from this spot. The suspect came out from the trees behind us. Hit Freedman over the head with a pipe. Freedman says when he hit the ground, he heard Russell screaming in pain. Freedman got up and drew his gun. The perpetrator hit Freedman a second time across the head with an object, something like a metal pipe. The gun went off and supposedly hit nothing. When Ward went down, he was doused with gasoline then ignited on fire. Once Ward was engulfed in flames, that is when the perp clubbed Freedman repeatedly. Freedman was dazed, and that was when the perp took off with his truck, leaving Cadet Russell to be burned alive," Tusson says in a matter of seconds.

"That's when the officer helped Russell by putting the flames out with his jacket. Russell was burned, but it could have been a lot worse," Webber adds.

There is a burn spot in the green grass of the park's manicured lawn. Around the burn spot is Russell Ward's body. We are alone here, and we can only guess the turning of events. Only God really knows what happened here in the early morning hours.

"Those are the hills we need to search behind us. There are several caves up there. We all go in together. We all come out together. Got it?" Webber says.

I decide to take a stand and tell the two detectives what I really think.

"You know we are wasting our time going into those hills. Freedman and Dawn are more than likely behind all this. They even stole the guns out of my room," I say as I stand before the two.

They both glance at me for a second, unfazed by my comments.

"Everything actually points to you," Webber adds.

"Sharman says it was you also," Tusson says to me. "And you know why we are such good detectives. We leave no stone unturned."

"No lead uncovered," Webber echoes. "Nobody is totally innocent!"

"I got it," I say.

"Then let's get up those hills," Tusson says as he checks the safety on his magnum.

Webber pulls out the rounds into the shotgun and loads them one by one. He then pumps the shotgun to load the chamber. I'm ready. I am only guessing that he will be ready when the time comes. The three of us are off, out of the park across the street and up into the foothills of North Carolina. I put the Derringer in my pocket, and my Beretta is securely tucked into the back of my jeans. I feel more anxious now than I ever have before in my life. I've never gone looking for a killer before. I don't really know what to expect. It's the middle of September, and I'm in the mountains looking for my dead twin brother. How ridiculous is this? The killer is out there, and here I have two guns and two Neanderthal cops looking with me for Rodney Beacon, my look-alike. I'm going to explore caves until nightfall, looking for a mystery. I'm fearful because what happens if I find my brother? Can I kill him? Will I kill him? Who will I really find? What justice needs to be served here, and how can that justice prevail? What am I getting myself into? *I must be crazy* is all that is going through my head as I cross the street and approach the huge hills across from the park. Freedman never said he saw my brother. He said he was hit from behind. How could he see the killer's face? Then he was knocked out. What could he have seen? Freedman's story doesn't make any sense. This trip seems pointless when I know that Dawn is behind this whole misguided adventure.

We cross the street and I figure we are all in this together. It's too late to turn back now. So we climb the hill. We approach the first of a series of small caves about two hundred feet up the side of the hill. The cave is camouflaged by a young tree that can be easily moved to reveal the narrow opening. Webber and I go in as Tusson stands guard by the concealed entrance.

"Jackpot," I say as I shine my military-size wide track flashlight on a makeshift bed made of straw and old newspapers.

The dirt ground is covered with old boxes as if it were a floor with the boxes in place of floor tile. There are no furniture or radios. Webber and I flash our lights around the small cave and look for anything that would give us a lead as to whom occupies the rock tomb.

"Over here," I say as I shine my light on some garbage near the corner. There are several small candles in the corner and open cans that lay there empty. I find an empty Tupperware tray and an ashtray, which are also empty.

"Does your brother smoke?" Webber asks.

"I don't know. He didn't then, but it's empty," I say. "If he plays ball, there would be a basketball, sneakers, and other clothes. He wouldn't be a bum. He would be neat and clean, just like me. This isn't where my brother lives," I say as I shine the light around a little more before leaving the cave.

"What did you boys find?" Tusson asks as Webber and I come out of the cave. Tusson stands in his black suit and sunglasses as if he were the enforcer for the mafia. Tusson looks like a thug guarding drugs or counterfeit money. He is mean looking with no expression on his face. He is built like a gorilla and carries a big gun, which I'm sure he is capable of using and killing me with.

"We found nothing," Webber says as he comes out behind me.

"If I were a killer and in hiding," I add, "I wouldn't want people to see me, so I would pick a cave on the other side of the mountain away from the road. Or a cave close to a back road so I could steal stuff then just drop it off without any hassles." I look around at the huge and wide mountainside that roars up from the two-lane highway below. "Either way, I would be behind the mountain, incognito," I say as I raise my eyebrows to the officers as if to suggest my knowledge of hiding.

"Well then, that is where we will go," Webber says as we track along the trail to the other side of the mountain. "Let us go to the top of the mountain, look around, and work our way down. No use climbing up into caves when we can take the trail to the top and then investigate our surroundings," Webber says as he follows behind Tusson and me.

These guys aren't as dumb as they look. If we start at the top, we can see everything and everyone below us. Then we can go lurking toward anything suspicious. We might not be able to see many of the caves from below, but we should be able to see all the nooks and crannies of the mountain when we are on top of it looking down.

We reach the flat top of the huge rock in minutes. We are high above the winding street below and have a full aerial view of the park from our plateau that's two hundred and fifty feet high. There is a steep dirt road that leads to the top of the mountain that is covered with brush and trees. The flat top of the large rock is only about thirty feet wide and twenty feet long. Along the two sides is a jagged drop of over two hundred feet to the street below. One side is covered with dirt trails and ledges, and then there is the small path behind us camouflaged with wild brush. I am the last one to the top of the monstrous hill and stop to check out the view. Webber and Tusson check out the dirt path that leads below.

"This path must lead to the bottom of the hill," Webber say as he approaches another dirt trail that stops at the top of the flat.

"This is no wild brush," Tusson says loudly. "These are chopped-down trees. Come look at this!" he yells to his partner as he waves us to come closer.

I look at the two and notice what they are talking about. The four large trees have been put in the way of the small dirt path that leads down the back of the mountain. Four trees have been chopped down and are now covering the path entirely.

"These trees aren't that old," Webber shouts as he investigates the stump of the chopped-down trees.

"How do you know?" I say as I walk closer toward the dirt path where they are investigating.

"These trees are not dead yet. I can't pull any splinters from the base. It's still hard as a rock. The color of the chopped area is still tan colored, not black like the rest of the tree. This is about a week or so old," Webber says.

"The path is disguised, incognito as you may call it. This might mean we found someone who wants to keep people out. Doesn't want to be disturbed and strong enough to chop down four trees. Four large trees at that," Tusson says as he walks through the brush and back toward me.

"Then there should be a cave with an ax somewhere up here. Let's find that person, and hopefully that will lead us to your brother," Webber adds.

"Let's make it easy. Look for footprints along the edges. It gets wet up here, and the footprints in the mud should lead us to our destination," Tusson says as the three of us stand on the flat surface at the top of the mountain.

Sure enough, within minutes after we start looking for footprints, I see dried mud footprints leading across the flat stone surface to a rock ledge and then down the side of the mountain.

"I found something," I say as I kneel next to the fossil of a footprint traced in mud. "It's a Nike sneaker print," I say to the officers.

The others hustle around me and investigate the footprint.

"Either that's a rich transient that likes expensive sneakers or one well-planned runaway," Webber says.

"Let's go down and see," Tusson says. "I'll go down first."

Below the footprint is a tree rooted into a small rock ledge. It's about an eight-foot drop from the flat we are on to the ledge below. We can't really see if anything, like a cave, is beyond the ledge because

230

of the angle we are at. The ledge then leads around the mountain to a flat that leads to the wilderness. The ledge is narrow and small enough only for one person at a time. If any of us fall, it's about a one-hundred-foot drop through a crevasse to the bottom of the mountain. The flat that leads to the wilderness is about twenty feet away from the mountain. If we fall, there is nothing to catch us, and no one will see us either. It will be a merciless death onto the jagged rocks below.

Tusson slowly lowers himself down to the ledge.

"Sure enough, there is a cave here. Throw me down a flashlight!" he yells to us.

Since Webber and I investigated the first cave, he and I take the only two flashlights we have. Webber throws Tusson his flashlight, and Tusson looks through the tree's foliage and into the camouflaged entrance of the cave.

"I think I have found something!" he yells. "You two get down here!" He then enters the cave alone with his flashlight and his gun both pointing forward.

I'm the next one down the limber tree and onto the small ledge. I slide down and hit the ledge with enormous force; I lose my balance and start to fall backward down into the abyss. I grab on to the tree and pull it with me. Webber lands on the ledge behind me and pulls the tree back toward the ledge. He reaches his hand out and grabs me. Then he pulls me up with all his might. I am speechless as I do a back bend over the ledge and amid the crevasse. Webber takes a hold of my arm and, with all his might, pulls me back safely to the ledge.

"Holy shit!" I yell out. "That was close." I gasp for breath as my heart races.

"Look," Webber says as he knocks on the wood doorframe of the cave. "This is a doorframe. This wood is solid. Someone built this entrance, squared it off, and made the ledge smaller by covering it with dirt. This person really doesn't want to be seen or found," Webber adds as he examines the wood.

I notice that there is a deer skin cover over the small doorway entrance. The skin is thick enough to keep any wind out and dark enough to keep all the daylight out as well. I maneuver around

Webber and shine my flashlight onto the door. I kneel down with Webber beside me and move the deer skin aside to see in the cave.

"Tusson! Tusson?" I yell again as I shine the light into the cave.

Nothing. I am puzzled because there is no reply.

Webber reaches for his police radio/walkie-talkie, depresses the speaker button, and calls for his partner.

"What's going on in there, partner?" Webber says into the police radio.

We both hear nothing from the speaker, but we hear immediate noises from inside the cave. Someone is moaning and moaning loudly. My eyes grow wide with anticipation. Webber darts into the small two-foot by two-foot opening leading into the cave.

Then the cave entrance explodes into disarray.

Dirt everywhere! I'm blinded. I hear a man screaming. I'm blind and can feel myself sliding down the mountain. I'm covered with dirt.

"Tusson! Tusson?" I hear Webber screaming.

Bang! A thunderous shot rings out from inside the cave. *Bang*. Another gunshot blast immediately follows.

"Tusson! Tusson?" I hear Webber still screaming as I land on the ledge.

I'm hanging on to the tree with one hand. I'm flat on my back against the rock and facing the sky above. I'm no longer sliding or falling, but I still have dirt all over me. I shake my head to regain my balance and wipe the dirt out of my eyes.

"Webber! What the Hell is going on?" I yell out in a blind rage of confusion.

The cave entrance just exploded into pieces. It went from hard dirt and rock into a huge opening. The dirt and rock are in a pile of rubble on the ground around us. I look around, and the ledge is now wider and bigger. I slide on to the ledge where my entire body lies on. The cliff's edge is no longer the small ledge but an enormous ledge concealed to look small to keep out visitors.

Bam! With a thud of a freight train, a body lands right on top of me, almost crushing me. I'm half blind, delirious, and now in enormous pain.

"Raaawwwww!" I scream as I throw the body off me and roll to safety.

I can only think it's a dead Tusson or an ax-whittled Webber.

"What is happening?" I scream out in pain, still in dismay by the situation at hand.

Cha-chic! That is the only sound I hear. That is when I realize that the cha-chic sound is the sound of a shotgun reloading just inches from my skull. All I can think about is, *What have I gotten myself into? And why me?*

CHAPTER 21

I HEAR THE thundering sound of someone loading a shotgun chamber echo in my ear.

"Get up!" I hear the words command me.

I shake my head to get my bearings, and I'm up in a flash. I'm thinking that this is all a setup and Tusson and Webber brought me here to kill me. They would surely get away with it.

"You okay?" The question is directed toward me as I'm being shaken off by Detective Webber.

After a second, I can see clearly. The cave opening is now six feet tall, and the cave is about eight feet wide. The fuselage of the cave outstretches ten feet into the mountain, forming a ledge. The slender rock ledge is actually a clearing now where all three of us can walk about safely. Webber and Tusson have their guns drawn, and there is a man curled up into a ball, barely lying on the edge of the embankment.

"Okay, so you're not going to kill me," I whisper under my breath.

"You bastard!" Tusson yells at the ailing degenerate from inside the cave as he quivers on the ledge.

"This guy's a bum," Webber says as he kneels down and grabs the derelict by his nappy, dirty hair. "This guy couldn't have built all this."

That's when I notice that Tusson has an ax lodged in his back.

"What's happening?" I yell as I run around Tusson and look at the ax stuck in his back.

The ax handle just sits perfectly in place with the blade lodged in Tusson's body.

"This is for almost killing us!" Webber yells and then starts punching the vagrant in the back four very hard times.

The man, soiled from head to toe, is in obvious pain. He jerks in pain and opens his mouth to scream after every punch, but nothing comes out. He screams in silence and agony. He is so weak after the struggle with these two homicide agents that he doesn't even have enough strength to scream. I step away from the man and attend Tusson as the man only lies on his side, holding on to the tree for dear life with tears running rapidly from his eyes because of the tortuous pain of Webber's fist. The grueling and excruciating pain of infliction that an officer dishes out to defend himself. I see the ax is in Tusson's back and can only think this guy should be glad these officers don't kill him by beating him to death.

"Cuff him," Webber says as he turns and throws the cuffs to me.

I go back around Tusson to handcuff the bum. I put his arms around the tree and cuff his wrists together tightly so he can't go anywhere. That way he's tied to the tree as we look around the cave. The dweller that lies in pain on the ledge is a very thin man, about forty, ragged looking with dirty black pants, and a dirty black-and-brown plaid shirt. He is very thin with matted black hair and a beard, wearing old boots with holes in the soles. He lies on the ground, distraught by the environment, time, and now by us.

"What happened?" Webber asks Tusson as Tusson holds himself up against the rock wall of the mountain.

"I crawled down the entranceway. When I came out into the darkness, I saw the inside of the cave. I started to stand up, and that was when that tramp hit me with an ax. I pulled out my gun, and then he jumped on top of me. That's when the gun went off again. I flipped him over me, got up, punched him, and then threw him into the wall. The wall gave out. He went right through it, and here we are," Tusson says as Webber examines the weapon.

"Good thing for you you're wearing a bulletproof vest. The ax is stuck right in the vest. Did the blade pierce your skin at all?" Webber asks as he examines the blade closely.

Tusson is standing up with his hands grabbing onto the cave wall. He doesn't show any pain at all, but his body knows he is injured. He is shaken up by the surprise attack from the unknown man. I'm done cuffing the prisoner and go aid the two detectives.

"Hang in there, Buddy," I say as I am at a loss for words.

Tusson just stands there with his face staring into the mountain, and he lets his partner doctor him.

"Let's take your suit off," Webber says to his ax-widdled friend.

He slowly pulls the ripped jacket over the wooden handle and off Tusson. He then pulls the ripped and bloody shirt off his partner the same way as well.

"We're not going to be able to take your vest off. This might hurt, but we are going to pull the ax out," Webber says as he grabs ahold of the ax.

"Pull," Tusson says. "Go!"

Webber pulls on the handle as the ax comes out and the vest comes off. The cut is about two inches long, but we can't see how deep the ax went into Tusson's back. It looks bad and is bleeding steadily. The wound is deep, and his back muscles tore when the silver blade penetrated into his skin. Tusson is going to need stitches, and he will be sore for a few days. No major damage to his body, and thank God the blade didn't hit Tusson's spine or neck.

"It's not that bad, big guy," Webber says.

I grab Tusson's shirt from the ground and press against the slice to stop the blood flow or at least congeal the wound.

"Fuckin' loser!" Webber yells as he takes a step over to the derelict man lying on the ledge handcuffed to the tree. "Ax this!" he yells.

Webber summons all his might into one fierce kick. *Bam*. A thunderous right foot struck into the caveman's kidney. The pain must be excruciating. The force of the blow sends the victim over the edge of the cliff. He dangles and sobs uncontrollably as he hangs almost lifelessly from the tree's base. The only thing saving him from a mountain high death is the handcuffs as he dangles over the deep crevasse. I don't feel bad for the guy. He almost killed Tusson. He deserves the punishment. Do the crime, pay the fine. Every action has consequences. Webber, as the punisher, is the consequence to the derelict's actions.

"Don't kill him!" I shout out. "We still need to question him."

"Yeah, there is no way this scumbag built this place and camouflaged it so well. This is a predator's cave. Someone who knew what they were doing. It cost money to do something like this and lots of strength. This social outcast is a weakling," Tusson says as he towers over the crying man.

Webber walks into the cave and shines his light on all the goodies that loom behind for us to discover.

"Look at this," Webber says. "It's silverware, shelves, books, a radio, and an antenna leading outside."

I'm still pressing the shirt against Tusson's wound as we turn and face the cave converted into living quarters. The cave isn't looking like a cave once the doorframe that hides the entrance is exposed. The cave has a floor covered with cardboard and a futon bed with a wood frame that takes up the left side of the cave. The blankets are almost brand-new and aren't dirty at all. Right across from the bed is a small table, a deep firepit for cooking, and two small shelves with magazines and candles. A battery-powered radio and a wind-up alarm clock sit on top of the small shelves. Under the bottom two shelves each are cardboard boxes filled with dry goods and napkins. The room is organized, and there is a chest in the middle of the room that probably serves as a dining table.

Webber, Tusson, and I briefly examine the room, and I know that it takes a lot of effort for a person to create a place like this. I can't tell if this is where a killer lives or some rich teenager runaway. Either way, we are about to find out.

Webber flips open the chest.

"Bingo," he says. "Deodorant can, clothes, bars of soap, and razors. A stainless-steel Zippo lighter. This dirty bastard definitely doesn't live here," Webber says as he shines his light at the contents of the chest. "The guy that lives here is clean and organized unlike this ugly loser!"

"The room is clean. Maybe we can get some prints," I say as I hold the shirt to Tusson's wound. The detective stands there and tries to ignore the pain in his back as his partner investigates more thoroughly.

"Now we have a Zippo. Something we can definitely check for prints," Webber says as he pulls a plastic bag out of his pocket and puts the lighter in.

"Do me a favor," Tusson asks. "Hit me with the lighter and deodorant can. It will stop the bleeding. Then we can go on."

My eyes must have popped out of my head. I was in shock. I think Tusson is crazy. He wants Webber to turn the Arrid Extra Dry can into a flamethrower to cauterize the wound. The look of shock on my face must have said it all. My jaw instantly dropped four inches, and my eyes were wide open as if to say, "You're crazy." The pain of a flamethrower burning his skin to make the gash stop bleeding isn't something that sits well in my stomach.

"Hold him, Ray. This will only take a second. Then it will be over. Just takes a second, so hold him tight. Brace yourself, partner," Webber says.

Webber didn't even think twice about Tusson's request. Webber is going to charbroil his partner. Webber holds the lighter with the plastic ziplock bag. He flicks the lighter with his thumb, and a big blue flame appears. He then sprays the aerosol over the flame. The can starts shooting flames instantly. Webber then grabs Tusson by his shoulder and puts the flames right to his back over the cut.

Tusson screams with pain as he thrusts himself forward, almost knocking me down.

"Hold him," Webber says to me as I brace Tusson.

I can see the pain on his face and the agony in his eyes as the heat and flames try to stop the bleeding of the ax round. Tusson jumps as Webber and I hold him. I have my eyes shut by now. I can't look, never mind being the one executing the act of cauterizing a wound with a deodorant can and a Zippo. After only two or three seconds, the act is done. Webber puts out the makeshift blowtorch as the wound stops bleeding.

"All done, buddy," Webber shouts as Tusson falls to his knees in pain.

I can smell burning flesh. It's awful. I hold onto Tusson, but his weight drags me down with him. I feel his pain and smell the grief of his skin. There is no more adrenaline flowing through him to keep his spirits up and going strong. The high of fighting is gone, and his pain is almost unbearable. He is no longer the big strong Mafia gorilla that I make him out to be. He's now Detective Barry Tusson, wounded and in pain, needing a doctor and is probably thinking of his wife and four-year-old son right about now.

I realize, at my young age of eighteen, that there is more to life than I will ever know. Life isn't about being right all the time. There is more to life than clothes and cars, women and parties. It's not about bragging rights and who has the bigger cock or most money. It's about honor and being happy. These guys are risking their lives because of me. They are not taking any shortcuts and never take the easy way out. They already know the consequences are death if they fail at their job, and still they get up every day, fighting through the street trash, scum, and drug dealers to make one life better. They investigate homicides and do their jobs well, without fear, and come back for more, day after day after day without reward or retribution. All in the name of helping people, people like me, even if it kills them.

"Ever wish you could go back and make a different career choice?" I say to Tusson almost under my breath.

He kneels with his head on his knees. His back arched, and his arm around his stomach. All his muscles are tight from the enduring pain.

"I wouldn't give this up for the world," Tusson says as he looks up at me.

He has a smile on his face as if he wants to laugh because of the irony.

"Me either," I say to him with a smile.

Webber walks over to the contemptuous degenerate and, with a mighty swoop and a subdued groan, he lifts the man to safety by his shirt collar. The bum is wearing old and worn pants with no pockets, and the knees are ripped. He wears boots with no socks and has a dark undershirt with a thick plaid shirt over it. He doesn't shave since his beard is matted, and his face looks more worn by misery and despair than that of old age.

"I just wanted food," the dirty man says as he endures the pain and recent punishment dished out by the detective.

Webber then drops the man hard on the rock ledge. The man still whimpers from the pain he endured over the last few minutes. This man already knows he is in for more punishment because he starts to cry before Webber touches him. He lies on the rock ledge whimpering, waiting for the mighty blows of Detective Webber.

"Why did you try to kill my partner then, scumbag?" Webber yells into the man's face as he pulls his head off the ground.

Webber, in his black suit and shiny shoes, is yelling just inches from the vagrant's face, and the man, in turn, is crying like a newborn baby.

"I don't know," the weak and intimidated man says in a whimper of tears.

"What do you mean, you don't know!" Webber yells into the man's face with a snarl of great big Kodiak bear.

Webber then grabs the man by his dirty hair and bangs the man's face into the dirt a few times. The man's face hits the ground hard and starts to bleed immediately. Webber then steps back and kicks the guy in the stomach again. The man is helpless. He is still handcuffed to the tree base and screams aloud in pain with tears flowing like wild rapids from his eyes. The man begs and cries for his life as Webber towers over him like a vampire looking for blood.

"P-p-p-pleeeease. No more," the helpless man cries as he puts his hands together and begs for his life before us. "No more, please," the dirty man cries as he lays there, bleeding on the rock ledge.

He makes no effort to get up and doesn't even have enough strength to pick his face off the ground. As he cries, the dust and tears make his face dirtier. The blood sticks to the dirt on his face and runs into his mangled beard. This man has no more will to live, no more energy to exert, and only wants to be left alone to die. He sobs uncontrollably as he begs for Webber to stop abusing him. He begs and he cries to no avail. The dirty helpless bum begs and cries for Webber to stop, only making the detective more destructive and outraged.

"You almost killed my partner! You put an ax in his back, and you don't know why! You don't know why!" Webber yells and then kicks the man in the stomach again.

The man wails in pain now, louder than ever. Half the sounds that leave his mouth disappear into silent gasps of air that I'm sure only dogs could hear. I can feel the pain as I look on. I'm still kneeling with Tusson, almost holding him up. I can't stand to look at the brutality anymore. Webber and Tusson, I'm sure, are used to beating down criminals. They feel no pain or guilt and see no mercy in sight for the weak they abuse.

The derelict falls over the cliff again from the mighty blow. He dangles with the handcuffs as the only thing keeping him from sure death, even though the detectives might beat him into oblivion. I know he wishes that Webber would just kill him. His pain is that of a hundred broken bones and of a thousand shattered dreams. He is starving, humiliated, and constantly being abused by Detective Webber. No one ever has ever felt such physical pain before such as when the vagrant screams. The pain is so bad, no sound comes out of his mouth. A silent scream of agony. His facial expression and tears are loud enough for me to hear. Even though he tried to kill Tusson, I feel remorse for him. I feel his suffering and look away from his pain.

I realize that everyone has two sides. Webber and Tusson, big and strong, family men and dedicated to the law with the anger of a hurricane hiding inside them. I remember them saying no one is totally innocent. Not even myself. Not even the two detectives. I see this as Webber picks up the man again with one hand and drags him onto the surface of the ledge by his dingy collar. The man still screams in pain as he is dragged onto the surface again. Webber then picks up the can of Arrid Extra Dry and lighter. He flicks the Zippo open, and the same bright blue flame appears. Webber again makes the deodorant can into a blowtorch and aims the shooting flames at the dirty desolate man.

"Tell me what I want to know!" Webber screams at him.

"I'll…I'll tell you, any…any…thing," he cries out to Webber in obvious pain.

"Who lives here? Who lives here?" Webber yells into the dying man's face with the flames blowing out of control into the air just inches from the sad man's face.

"He…he…he does," the dirty man sobs out with fear and pain in his stutter.

He said he does? I think to myself as I wonder who he is.

He said, "He does!" The fear overcomes my body.

CHAPTER 22

IT'S THE BEGINNING of the afternoon. It's cool in these mountains even though the sun is shining on us. The old dirty man says, "He does."

I look to see what this man is looking toward. I see no one inside the cave, and no one else around us on the ledge. We are alone out here in the North Carolina sun, but for how long?

"Who? Him?" Webber asks the derelict man as he points at me.

Webber still has the mini flamethrower in his huge hands as he terrorizes the degenerate of a man.

"No, no!" the man screams in fear as he tries unsuccessfully to avoid the scorching flames. "He does!" The old man screams and points as he cowers from the burning flames.

As I turn to look on top of the mountain, time elapses in slow motion. I look up toward the mountaintop and as I do, I see an arrow slowly pass down from the plateau toward Webber. I can't react. I can't point. I can't yell. I can only watch as the arrow passes in still frames past Tusson. I don't see anything except the arrow heading straight for Webber.

The arrow penetrates right through Webber's upper body and outstretches into the spray can that he holds in his left hand. Webber's body jerks upright as the arrow passes through the skin of his back, then out through his abdomen, and gliding into the deodorant can effortlessly. The can explodes into flames that consume Webber's face and body. There are no screams of pain from Webber, not any cries for help. In one quick second, Webber becomes consumed, covered with hot red burning flames. Webber turns his head to face his assailant as he transforms from a detective with a flamethrower into a detective absorbed in the flames of agony.

"Webber!" I scream with amazing fear.

Detective Peter Webber falls stiffly over the edge of the cliff without any screams of pain, covered in flames, then down into oblivion. All this happens in one breath, in one second, then Webber and the burning flames that engulf him are gone. Gone over the edge of the cliff over two hundred feet to the street below.

"Webber!" I yell again from the mountainside as I am consumed with fear.

My heart stops, and I watch as Webber's fiery body disappear over the rock falls. The derelict is screaming with fear, and I roll away from Tusson for my own safety. I draw my gun as I roll alongside the cave. I see an image that has his sight locked on the bent-over Tusson. I have my sights aimed at the killer above. Tusson draws his magnum, and we both open fire on the assailant. We are firing on the killer as he lets go of yet another arrow, aimed at Tusson.

The bright sunlight blinds us from a full view of the crouching monster bearing down on us as we are in the midst of our own demise. The narrow tree is the stranger's only cover, and I have a clear shot right into the midsection of our hunter. Tusson and I both fire off four shots each toward our killer. The crouching figure has already let his fierce arrow fly. I can see the outline of the predator from above as he stands in the sunlight. He is thrown back and then disappears from our sight. I think my bullets hit the hidden person in the chest. I saw the body of our assailant jerk back right after the person let the second arrow go. I really can't tell if we hit the criminal since I haven't fired a gun in months and the sun was behind the person blinding us.

Life resumes at full speed once again as I look over at Tusson and our predator has struck another blow. The vicious arrow went right through the detective's torso between his ribs. He has the arrow sticking out through both ends of his body. The arrow tip is a small narrow razor tip for killing dear. The sharp tip went right through Tusson, and the razor tip is showing out of his back, dripping with blood. A stream of red blood is flowing out of the officer's body as the wound before once did. I'm in shock that the arrow passed right through the body of Barry Tusson as he is alive.

I'm filled with fear, but I slide right over to aid him. Tusson is along the rock wall holding his back with one hand and hanging on to the feathers of the arrow with the other. I hear the petrified calls of the cuffed man as he is still screaming hysterically with fear and pain. He is suffering physical and mental trauma after being tortured with all the agony of the last ten minutes.

"This is going to hurt," I say as Tusson lies on his side in even more pain than ever.

The arrow is sticky and soaking wet with Tusson's blood. I take over the situation immediately by helping the wounded Tusson while looking over my shoulder for the killer. I grab the feathered end of the arrow with both hands and break the feathered end off to shorten the size of the arrow.

"I need you to stay down, sir. Your heart needs to be below the wound to slow the bleeding," I say as I desperately try to comfort Detective Tusson.

I can see the pain in his face as he clinches his teeth. His eyes are tight as he is fighting the pain. He is bleeding steadily from both entrance and exit wounds, and I'm his only help. I try desperately to help by putting his shirt over both wounds and pressing on them as hard as I can. I can feel the wooden arrow protruding from both ends of his body. I'm very scared as I press harder, trying to help as well as look over my shoulder to prevent myself from becoming a human shish kebab.

"I'm all right," he says finally as he grinds his teeth to endure the pain. "I'll call for backup. You go see what happened to him. Be careful!" He then grabs his cell phone and calls in the situation. "Two officers down. One man armed and dangerous. Need help immediately." He calls in our position to the local authorities.

I'm scared now, really scared. I'm shaking with fear as I have the blood of my friend on my hands. I hear Tusson behind me in obvious pain, and I can still hear the bum screaming hysterically. I need to be the savior. It's not like a basketball game; it's not "give me the ball and I'll save you" like it was in Boston or high school. It's "be very careful or be dead." My heart is pounding as I wipe the blood off my hands on to my jeans. I get up and walk with my gun drawn as I go up and around the mountain to the top. I walk cautiously through the wilderness and then up through the brush to the top of the mountain into the clearing. I slowly lurk to the top of the mountain with my gun drawn before me. I see nothing as the entire flat comes into sight. Nothing. There is nothing up here. I follow the edges around one side of the mountain and see no one going down or coming up the mountain. I have my gun drawn leading my way. I have an eye on everything all at once. I go to the far side and see nothing again. No blood, no mess, no dead body or wounded person.

"Great!" I say aloud in disappointment as I see no one.

Then, in the middle of the flat, in the short brown grass, lays a large black object. I look around, being very paranoid. I move to the object twenty feet in front of me and notice it is a black bulletproof vest lying in the middle of the flat mountaintop. I am reaching for it now. I see the black Kevlar vest with four bullet holes enlarged in the front of it. The murderer who killed Webber is still on the loose and unfazed by our bullets. We are still being hunted instead of hunting down a killer. I stand up to show Tusson the vest and tell him our killer got away.

Bang! I hear from below me. One very loud gunshot is heard. I hit the deck in fear. My heart is pounding. Is someone firing at me? I hear no cries of pain from Tusson. No screaming or yelling, just one single shot that rings out among the mountains and echoes back toward me. What should I do? My heart is pounding. My mind is racing. What should I do?

"I need to be the hero," I say to myself as I lie low in the grass, full of fear and adrenaline all at once.

This killer already knows I'm here. This demon has seen me, and I've seen the killer. It is time to hunt or be hunted. I won't run. I must help my friends. I must win this game of cat and mouse to save my own life as well as the lives of others around me. I must prove my innocence.

"Tusson?" I yell as I slowly crawl to the edge with my gun drawn.

I realize I should put on the Kevlar vest. I'm scared enough as it is. My heart is pounding, and I can hear the disturbing silence. There is no reply, no screaming man, only silence! I lurk back from the edge and take off my Duke sweatshirt, put the vest on, secure it in place as fast as I can, and place my sweatshirt on back over the vest.

"Tusson?" I yell again as I pop up, looking over the edge to my friend.

All I see is sadness. Detective Barry Tusson lays motionless, laying up against the rocks with his gun drawn and another arrow through his muscular framed mass of a body. The arrow runs across his body. The arrow enters under his left arm and exits out of his right side. I have my gun drawn and the bulletproof vest on. I must be alert and careful. The killer knows the mountain. That person could be behind or below me, anywhere and everywhere all at once. I am alert and paranoid at once as well. My hand shakes as the gun directs my sight. Any sudden moves and my target is history. The heavy gun is ready to kill again, and I'm ready to capture the murderer. I'm still scared, but I will not run as I move forward to the mountain's edge. I will fight for what I believe in. I'm fighting to live my life and bring the senseless killing of innocent people to an end. I'm fighting to be free once again; therefore, I move onward toward the edge and look to see who lurks beneath me. To see if my destiny awaits me.

"Tusson!" I yell as I look at the derelict still lying, cowering at the edge of the ledge, in extreme fear. He isn't even looking up. The vagrant's face is buried in the dirt, and he isn't making a sound. He is just lying outstretched, shaking in fear.

I slowly take another step, and I'm at the edge of the cliff, looking down below to the ledge and the cave. I see only Tusson and the derelict, nothing else.

Swoop! An arrow flies out from the cave below me, and then a scream of pain.

The vagrant is speared. An arrow runs through his body from behind his shoulder and again comes out his chest. That is a very sharp arrow and one strong bow to have enough force to pass through a person's body. The vagrant's body bounces with pain and agony, then I can tell instantly he is dead. The shot is dead on, and all his targets are now down. All except for me. This is my chance. The killer has to reload. The killer is in the cave below me, shooting his arrows at the two helpless men. I take one step forward and jump into the air toward the ledge below. I turn toward the cave as I descend through the air. I jump down to the ledge below, and my gun is aimed into the cave. While still in midair, I start to fire my gun into the cave opening.

Bang! Bang! Bang! Bang! Bang!

I fire several shots into the cave before I hit the ground and roll to my knees in a crouching position as if I were an actual detective. The Beretta keeps sixteen bullets in the clips plus the one in the chamber. I can't see my target, but I'm armed and ready to go. I've already fired nine shots. Eight left. My vision is clear, and I am kneeling on the ledge with my gun drawn toward the cave. I wait to see anyone or anything. The flashes from the shots of the gun light up the cave like a strobe light. The bullets fly into the cave filled with emptiness. I am focusing and drawing on the cave. I still see nothing. My heart beats the fastest it's ever been, heavy and loud like ancient drums. I wait to see my monster, but again nothing. Only daylight and darkness—nothing among all the somethings we have yet to find.

Bang! Bang! Bang!

Still nothing as I fire my bullets into what little furniture remains in the cave. My gun is now is almost empty. I only have a few more shots. The adrenaline is pumping through my veins, and my mind is racing at a million miles a minute. *Where* is the only word that comes to mind over and over and over again as I lay on the ledge in front of the cave.

I know time is precious and roll toward Tusson to check him.

"Tusson? Tusson?" I say as I go straight toward him.

I pull his gun from his hand and push on him to see if he opens his eyes. I've never had to check to see if someone was alive or dead before, so I really don't know what to do.

"Tusson! Tusson!" I yell again as I shake him with both hands.

He blinks as he grimaces in pain. He shuts his eyes and keeps them shut for a few seconds before opening them again.

"I'll get help," I say to him as I hang onto him.

"Go after him," Detective Tusson says in almost a whisper as he is bleeding intensely while he sits up against the rock of the mountains edge. "I call this in," he says.

He only stares straight ahead and doesn't move as he slowly and softly speaks.

"You need help now!" I say, trembling with fear. "I'm not going to leave you." I watch the blood cover the rocks he leans up against.

"You were right," he says as he whispers again. "Through the cave."

Only a whisper as he closes his eyes.

"You were right. Through the cave."

What?

CHAPTER 23

I'M NOT SURE exactly what the detective means, but instantly three names come to mind—Dr. Franklin, Covey, and Freedman. I am right? What does Tusson mean? How am I right? The detective is dying right in front of me. I know he is weak, but I must find the killer. I have to help Tusson. What is the right thing to do? How am I right? Time is essential, and I'm wasting it looking for explanations with my wide eyes and mind full of anticipation. I must find what he sees. The killer? The answer? I must be right. It's all through the cave. It's on right now.

I look into Tusson's eyes and see him fading off into a deep sleep.

I dial 911 from my phone and call the police in a frantic manner. I ramble as I describe my situation as quickly as possible. Tusson and Webber are down, we need paramedics, and police here now. I pull out Tusson's phone and text Captain Adams. "Nine-one-one. Man down! Trace the call!"

The police have already been called. I can do nothing else to save him. I'm a scared kid, not a doctor. I can only capture his assailant and make that person pay for this hideous crime. I want to make this person feel the same pain that Tusson and Webber feel.

"I'll be back for you. Don't worry. I'll be right back," I say to Tusson as I take the clip .9 mm bullets from the belt.

There is still one clip in the gun and a bullet in the chamber of Tusson's gun. He can still use it if necessary. I put his full magazine cartridge into my gun then take the half-empty clip and put it in my back pocket. I am armed for a fight now. I have about twenty bullets, a bulletproof vest, and a small .22 Derringer. Plus I'm wearing my lucky Duke University sweatshirt. I'm ready to go. I remember all the *CSI* episodes and think, *Remain calm, breathe, and let your gun lead the way.*

"Hang in there," I say as I look into the cave and quickly make my way toward it.

I take a few steps into the cave and see a small slit of an entrance that leads out behind the cave into another cave. There was wood and dirt covering the entrance, camouflaging it, just like the cave entrance. I race to the second doorway in the cave and peek my head in with my gun leading the way. I'm the only one that can save myself here. Webber is dead, Tusson is dying, and if I don't find any answers, I'll be to blame. I am shaking with fear but enter the tunnel behind the cave, looking for my own way out. I look for my own answers and the solution to the mysterious killer. I must find the courage to surge on. I'm already dead in the eyes of my family and guilty in the eyes of the law. This is my only chance of avenging a powerful new life from beyond the circumstances before me.

"Nothing," I say as I enter the tunnel.

I see nothing except for a long tunnel leading down the mountain. It is a winding tunnel—a very large, long, and dark tunnel. The walls are at least five feet apart, and the tunnel is about eight feet high. Someone can easily make their way through the tunnel only being distracted by the darkness. Once out of the sight of the cave entrance, there is nothing except darkness. If the cave ended after the first turn, you would never know until you hit the wall in front of you. It's that dark inside the tunnel.

I pull out my phone and turn on the flashlight. Into the dark tunnel with my light and still I see nothing. The killer is getting away. I must be fast. Even if this is a trap, I still have two guns and a phone-light. I must move fast. I trot down the tunnel with the light from my phone leading the way. The ground is all dirt, and the tunnel is cold with only a small amount of light bouncing off the black walls as I make my way through the darkness.

I hear nothing except for my own thunderous heartbeat. I see nothing except darkness as I'm descending down toward the bottom of the mountain. I start jogging quickly to make up ground on the killer. My gun still aims forward with the safety off. All I think about is the infatuated life I once led, and now all my dreams are shattered. I flash through the good and bad times that made me the person I am today. I have no images of my future, and I am wondering if the history of my life will end here.

I know I'm going the right way through the tunnel because the entrance ended at the cave above. I see no light shining into the tunnel to show an exit. I have come down about one hundred feet by now, and I press onward, descending into the pit of hell following hopefully the unknown killer. I'm scared even more because I haven't come across the bow of the killer. That means the killer has it and is waiting for me. He knows how to use the bow and is an accurate shot. I could turn any corner, and there in the midst of darkness could be my arrow of destiny. That one arrow could end my life, but still I surge onward through the darkness to find my killer.

My gun and phone lead the way, and I'm an accurate shot. I've already shot my unseen killer dead-on. Now the monster has no bulletproof vest and is being hunted instead of hunting me. I run faster and follow my beam of light as I descend through the tunnel. I still see nothing except for the dirt floor and dark walls of the cave. I can only hear my heart beating and the sound of my own footsteps. I'm scared, really scared, but I press on to avenge the death of my friends and avenge my own life. If this case doesn't end here, my life will end. The case and killings must end now, end here today, before my life is over. I'm responsible for all this. It started four years ago, and I'll finish it here now. First, I must find the killer. I must find a way out. I must find the answer.

I hear something.

Smash.

"Awweee!" I scream as I fire my gun into the darkness.

I hit the rock-solid wall with an enormous thunder. "Awweee!" I scream in a rage of pain and fear.

Someone has jumped out from a hidden entrance and grabbed me. This person caught me from the side. I am being thrashed against the rock wall and smashed into it at full speed. The force of the collision against the wall knocks the wind out of me. My head collides with the rock tunnel. I can instantly feel the enormous pain thrusting from my head throughout my body. The person still has me. I've dropped my phone, and the light is gone. I've dropped my gun. The killer still has his arms around me as we hit the ground. The killer is holding me with a bear hug grip around my body, squeezing the life out of me. I'm spinning, then we both fall. I hit the ground hard. I'm facedown in the dark cave with this person on top of me. My body bounces off the ground with a huge thud that crushes my body and soul. The pain all comes at once—the collision, my body being propelled against the wall, my head bouncing off the rock ground, the pain of being crushed as I hit the ground with this heavy beast on top of me, and the surprise of an attack catch me all at once as I scream in agony.

I scream in pain after I hit the ground and realize the agony from within.

In an instant, I'm being held down.

"I don't want to die!" I scream out.

I only hear my own fears echo in the dark cave. I've dropped my gun. I have no defense. I've dropped my phone. I can't see. I'm going to die.

"Oh, God, help me!" I scream all in one breath.

The Derringer. I instantly reach for my pocket and pull out my gun.

Bang! Bang! I close my eyes to shield them from the blinding gunpowder flashes of my own bullets.

I open fire with both shots into the killer at close range. The entire incident all happens in seconds. It's over, and I'm lying on the ground, breathing hard with gun in my hand. The blasts are so loud that my ears are echoing and ringing all at once. I have my eyes closed, and I see nothing but flashes of lightning from the gun underneath my eyelids. I can feel the blood pouring on me from my assailant. Then, suddenly, an overwhelming wave of blood covers me a sea of emotions consumes me as the person dies next to me.

"Ugh!" I groan as I roll the heavy body off me.

I can feel all the blood from the murderer all over me. I can't see anything, but I feel overwhelmed.

I scamper against the wall of the tunnel. I'm hiding in the darkness. My phone is facing down, and the light is hidden under the phone. The phone is only inches away from me, shining into the dirt away from my victim and myself. My heart his thumping, thumping, thumping as I gasp for a breath. I drop my empty Derringer to the rock-hard ground. I'm in shock. I'm in pain. I can't breathe. I'm covered in sticky, smelly, rancid blood. I can't move. I've just shot and killed someone, somebody. I'm afraid to look. I'm scared. I'm so scared that I feel my jaw and hands tremble. I still can't hear anything because my ears are ringing so loudly. I am being tormented from within. I am sick to my stomach, knowing what I have just done. My head is pounding with pain, and I feel the tears filling my eyes as I absorb the agony of what I had just done. I've just murdered someone.

"Catch your breath. Calm down. Nothing can hurt you now," I say out loud as I lean against the tunnel wall among the darkness and emptiness.

Then I pick up the phone but do not shine the light on the person. I can't see the consequences of my actions yet. I start to breathe deeply and slowly in the darkness of the cave. I'm covered in blood. I keep thinking nothing can hurt me now. My ears are still ringing from the gunshots. Who did I shoot? Did I really kill that person? Am I okay? The adrenaline still pumps through my body, forcing me to tremble. I'm in tears because of the fear. I'm so afraid, so afraid to look, but I have to. I must see what I've done. The tears are now rolling down my face. I still can't hear anything except the ringing in my ears as I shine the light on the body.

"Oh, man. What have I done?" I say in a whisper. I can barely hear myself.

The light shines on the person as I sit back against the stone wall. I slowly see the body. I can see that the dead person's feet are the closest to me. They are bouncing with the joy of a life ending. The kind of jitters one gets when they're choking or being electrocuted. The light shows the persons' dusty boots, and I watch the feet jerk from the nerves dying within the poor dead bastard's body. I slowly raise my light and see the jeans of a man covered in blood. The body is only lying only inches from me in the darkness. The body is face up, and I slowly raise my light to reveal the huge body of a man. I keep going slowly, raising my light to reveal the upper torso of a plaid shirt that is still moving and choking within the cave. I raise my light further with sickening grief. I see that the bullets of the gun went through his throat and chin, for there is nothing there under his jaw except for a gaping hole. This man is covered in blood, dark red, sticky, stinky blood. From point-blank range, I put a fist-sized hole in his neck with those .22 caliber bullets. I still raise the light slowly but still higher to reveal the horrific face with wide-open eyes. The man is dying and choking on his own blood. The man is paralyzed with the notions of death, and he is dying right before my eyes. There is nothing I can do to save him.

"Covey!" I say in amazement. "I've killed Covey!" I say aloud.

He's the killer. I can feel the overwhelming compassion of death consume me. I cry with betrayal knowing this is the man that killed Webber and Tusson. He would have killed me also. The thoughts of him killing my mother and the three other women that I've known race through my mind. The game of hunt or be hunted, kill or be killed, is over. I sob uncontrollably because I never wanted to hurt anyone. I think of all the people that have died senselessly—Maria Lennon, Heather Collinsworth, Jenny Schavio, Kate Rush, Detective Peter Webber, Detective Barry Tusson, my mother, and at the end of that line lying in ICU is Cadet Russell. All dead or hurt because of me. All because I was a rotten kid in high school. Covey is now added to the long list of dearly departed. All because of a sexual encounter with a policewoman's daughter. I can barely hear my own cries as my ears are still ringing with the sounds of gunshots. Just like everything else thus far, Covey's death leads me back to Dr. Franklin and Arcadia. The end of the line leads me back to the beginning—Arcadia.

"I never ever wanted to hurt anyone," I cry out loud as I drop the light and sob into my own hands.

I will never get Covey's blank stare out of my haunted dreams. The face of death will haunt me forever. Why me? Or even better, why now?

"Why me?" I cry to the heavens as I stay frozen in place from the horror of death and destruction around me. "Oh, God, why me?" I ask as I sit in the darkness of my own destruction, crying out loud in the darkness.

"Because you were destined, the golden child. You were always the good son, remember?" a stern voice says to me from the darkness of the cave. "And nice guys always finish last."

I can barely hear, but I hear the words softly and clearly. I wipe my eyes for a better view and shake my head to get my senses back. I'm startled in my own depression. I keep wiping the tears from my eyes and scramble to shine my light from the phone in the direction of the man's voice. The flashlight reveals the same Nike sneakers that I have, all white leather with a clear blue swoosh symbol. I raise the light higher to see Mr. Beacon's .9 mm handgun aimed right at me. I slowly raise the light higher, and my light reveals a body wearing blue jeans and a dark-blue Duke University sweatshirt. I shine the light on the face to reveal the truth, and then I see.

"How are you doing, Ray?" I say in amazement as I wipe the remaining tears from my eyes.

There he is, standing about five feet from me. The real Raymond Douglas Beacon, bearing down on me with my own gun. He's wearing my shoes, my same short black hair, the same muscular build that I have, and my Duke sweatshirt. He's come to take his life back.

That night with Maria was a long time ago. Ray, after sleeping with my girlfriend, never came home that night. I went to his class that morning to confront him, and Ray never showed up. Rodney was then marked absent from school, and I just sat in Ray's first period class, unaware of what was happening at my mom's house. When the fire started and Rodney wasn't in class, everyone assumed

I was dead and Ray was alive. As I sat across from the flames of my own house, I knew everything was going to change. I knew Colleen's mom in Massachusetts would help Ray with the transcripts. I also knew that together, Ray and I had lots of money, so I planned on taking all that money. All of it. I could easily get the passports from the house and bank, empty the accounts, and could become Ray. This was the main reason I knew I was going to fail the lie detector test. I couldn't get my name right because I'm Rodney. The tattoo on my chest of a basketball and the number forty-four was to remind me of the brother I once had.

"I've been bad!" he says to me loudly with a snarl as he aims the gun at me.

"That's not good," I say as I fight back the tears and sit in pain up against the hard rock wall.

I'm clearing the sadness from my thoughts and vision to see everything more clearly. I'm still in amazement and bewildered by all this—the ledge incident, then seeing Detective Webber bursting into flames, the shooting, watching the old man die, Detective Tusson getting shish kebabbed by arrows, and now after I just killed Covey, my brother, Ray, is alive. Which pretty much means I'm dead.

"I can't believe you became me, Rodney," my brother says as he keeps the gun on me. "Well, I'm back! And I want my life back," he says to me. "So it's time for you to go!" he says with my gun aimed at me as I shine my flashlight onto him.

"How did I get involved in this? And why? What did I ever do to deserve all this?" I say to Ray who bears down on me with his omnipotent presence and frightful demeanor.

"Good thing for me, you came along," he says with an evil smile as he kneels down before me. "The giant here had me. I barely broke free when you ran right into him at full speed. You knocked me down, and he grabbed you. Then you went ahead and killed him for me. I made it all the way to the end of the tunnel before I realized Dr. Franklin is there waiting with the police. I figure I would come back and we could get reacquainted," Ray says as he still has his gun aimed at me from among the dimness of the flashlight.

"Lucky me!" I say as I now see my twin brother clearly for the first time in years. I sit against the dark rock ledge in massive pain. "Why? Why now?" I ask as he towers over me.

"Why?" he says. "I can't believe you took my life. Took all the money. Told Dad you were me so when I went to him, he called me crazy and told me to go back to mom. I was mad. I was now broke. You were the smart one, but I would have never guessed this. Now that you took my life, I want to get even," he says as he points the gun at Covey's jittering body.

Bang! He pulls the trigger and shoots Covey in the head. Covey's body jumps once more and then settles down in a grave of calmness.

"As you were becoming Raymond Douglas Beacon and learning how to play basketball, I learned about death. I even hate killing with guns because there is no sport in it. No fun," he says in a sinister voice as he stands before Covey's lifeless body.

"Really?" I ask to my murderous and disillusioned twin brother. "And you learned all this because of me. I feel special now," I say as I feel the pain of my broken ribs shoot through my body.

"You should," he says as he aims the gun back at me. "All this was for you, and I will get away with murder. Again, since I'm the real Raymond Beacon," he says as he flashes me a huge smile. "You're an imposter."

He begins to chuckle as he takes the magazine of bullets out of the gun and then aims the gun at me.

Bang! He fires the bullet from the chamber into my leg.

"*Awweee!*" I scream as I grab my leg.

The pain. He shot me right above my knee. The large muscle is burning with the sensation of a bullet burrowing deeply into my already bruised skin. I lose my phone, and the light goes out as it hits the ground.

"Awwweee!" I violently yell into the darkness as the blood from my muscles leaves my leg.

It is only dark for a second before Ray ignites a red road flare to light the dark tunnel.

"No one can hear us, so scream all you want. The entrance is blocked by trees, and the road noise drowns out any other sounds," he says with confidence as his face glows with redness from the road flare. "I don't know how Covey found the entrance, but he did. Then I'm sure he told Dr. Franklin."

"You will never get away with this," I say as I hold my leg, trying to stop the bleeding, trying to ignore the pain of a gunshot wound.

"Why?" he asks. "We have already done so much. We changed our lives, murdered, and relived. You actually killed me, Rodney. You took all I had. You even sat in my classroom and became me back as a freshman. Then you left me and took all my money. Now after all these years, you're saying, 'Why now?'"

"Why now?" I ask.

"I've finally found you!" my brother yells. "I've been looking for you for years. Years, little brother!" he shouts. "Four fucking years!" he yells louder as he throws the empty gun at my head.

The bullet-empty magnum bounces off my face as I hold my leg. Again, the pain rips like lightning through the nerves in my body. The thriving, burning pain. I couldn't stop the gun from hitting me. I couldn't even move. The gun hits me and bounces to my near right after hitting me in the face.

"It's all finally coming together now! You asshole!" he yells as he is now just inches from me, towering over me.

"Why?" I ask again as tears once again fill my eyes.

"You fucked up! You bastard!" he says as he kicks me in the face.

I'm rocked by the kick. I'm dazed. I'm still in obvious pain, and I can hardly breathe and now can hardly see.

"Ugh." Again the pain consumes me, but I hold back the emotions of agony from within.

"This is all because of you!" he yells as he kicks me again in the side as I lay on the dirt ground of the tunnel, still bleeding from the gunshot wound in my leg.

The pain. I feel like the bum being tortured by Webber. This is what humiliation feels like—an overpowering pain, physical pain, and humiliation with vast doses of mental pain.

"Why me?" I gasp out in a lame breath.

As he calms down a little, I see him running his fingers through his hair as he takes a step away from me. I'm still gasping for air. I

259

know now that my ribs are definitely broken. I can hardly breathe. Each breath endures a sharp pain in each side of me. Lucky for me, I have the vest under my sweatshirt. If not, all my ribs would be broken. The pain is still overwhelming either way. The pain burns; the pain, it burns inside my head, my leg, my stomach, and my dying soul.

"Lee came over that morning to talk to you. She wanted to tell Rodney how horrible of a brother Ray was. How I tricked her into sleeping with me. I ended up killing little Lee. She was crying. I was yelling. She started yelling. I grabbed onto her to shut her up, and we fell. I snapped her neck right there in our bedroom," he says as he walks in front of the red light of the flare. "What was I to do?" he yells aloud into the tunnel as he flares his arms into the air. "I had just killed the love of your life! All because of you!" he yells and then kicks me in my side again.

"Oohhh!" I gasp with all my strength for air as an unrealistic agonizing pain consumes me.

I can hardly breathe. I'm suffocating. I'm in devastating physical pain. The pain. The dull, burning pain. The pain of suffocation. I'm hurting all over. The burning gunshot wound… I think my ribs are broken. Oh God, make the pain stop. Make the pain stop. Oh God! Make it stop! I'm in agony!

"Go ahead and cry, you bastard! I did!" he yells at me in anger. "I cried with Lee in my arms. She was dead, her neck broken. I lost my temper. I just wanted to shut her up. I snapped her precious neck. What was I to do?" he yells again to me as he towers above me, pointing his gun at my head.

I don't answer as I gasp out in a crying breath of pain as I hold my ribs.

"I grabbed her and put my hand over her mouth!" he yells. "She tried go get away. We fell, and I twisted her around. We both hit the ground, then suddenly she wasn't breathing. I was scared. I went outside and there, in the carport, was a can of gasoline. Mom filled the lawnmower up so I could cut the grass. I got an idea. I poured what was in the gas can on her dead body and then emptied the rest of the gas in the mower throughout the room. I got one of Mom's cigarettes and lit it. I placed the filter of the cigarette over the edge of the dresser. As the cigarette burned, it would fall onto the floor, igniting the entire room with Lee in it."

I look ahead of me and see the empty .9 mm to the right of me. My brother is ranting about the past, and I'm still in extreme pain. I can see clearly now that I've fought back the tears. I'm thinking at a mile a minute. What will my brother do to me next? How will he try to get out of this? How will he try to kill me?"

"So there I was, walking out of town with nothing. I had nothing!" he screams as he walks among the light of the glowing red flare. "Nothing! I kept thinking, how am I going to get out of this? They would have to identify me by dental records. I broke into the dentist and trashed the place. I switched the files and hung around the woods of Arcadia so I could go back and kill you. Only you disappeared. You vanished just like me. You never paid for your crime of betrayal. But don't worry. You will today," he says as he walks in the midst of red light and darkness.

I'm breathing very slowly as my pain is heightened. I can fight the pain only for now since I'm getting weaker, and the pain is unbearable. I'm calm now, and the suffering will not subside. I have to come up with a plan. I must bring Ray down by hitting him with all my might at his knees. Take him down, fight him on my level. I must be quick. I must fight the pain. I must be fearless.

"You will never get away with murder," I say as I gasp for air, still holding my leg, trying to stop the bleeding.

"I already have, my naive brother," he says calmly as he towers over me. "The blood all over your body is from Covey. The blood from Tusson is on you. The bow and arrow are Freedman's from when you took his truck from the park. And the best part is all these guns are yours. You've already killed Covey. Besides that, I've killed all your witnesses. After I kill you, I will kill Dawn and leave the unsuspecting Freedman holding the bag. I've already gotten away with murder," he says as he walks through the darkness and redness of the tunnel. "Then I'll go to Duke University, play basketball, and become a star!"

"It's that easy?" I ask in pain, still on the ground with Ray before me waving his gun around as he speaks.

"It is," he says. "I made my way to Boston by stealing just four short years ago. You took everything. I had nothing!" he yells as he paces back and forth. "I would go to rest stops and find single women and take their money and car. I knew you would go to Boston. Only you never did. Once I was there, dear old dad didn't want me. He said he would report me as a runaway. He wanted nothing to do with me. He gave me some money, so I lived on the docks and worked the ships. I lived in condemned buildings, spent weekends in libraries. Spent holidays working as an adult in my own hometown and almost froze in the bitter cold and snow. I was going crazy because of you, Rodney. I was a fourteen-year-old kid. A bum among my own peers in the city I loved! Do you know what that is like? Do you know what that is like?" he screams at me just inches from my ear as he grabs hold of me and throws me to the rock ground.

"No," I whimper out in a little wounded voice.

Ray is raving and ranting now like a madman. He is yelling as he speaks and kicking at the dirt under his feet. Then he kicks the dead body of Covey that lays among us.

"No! Of course you don't!" he yells. "I started killing! Learned to kill with knives, poison, arrows, and choked people with my own hands. Then, in February, right before Valentine's Day, right before I went totally mad and out of my mind, I see this basketball team from Florida, on ESPN, with an undefeated school record and two highly recruited prospects. The news was talking about the best two white kids in a state unknown for basketball. I look up at the TV, and there you are. My long-lost brother lives in Oviedo, Florida. In his senior year in high school. Raymond Beacon plans to go off to college at Duke and play college basketball. All his dreams all coming true. Only I'm Raymond Douglas Beacon. Not you!" Ray yells right into my ear. "All his dreams coming true! You bastard!"

"Sorry. I had no choice," I say in a whisper as I cower against the wall in severe pain.

"You're sorry!" he yells. "You're sorry!" he yells again as he kicks me in my side. "Of course you're sorry! You're gonna be real sorry when I kill your sorry ass!" he yells into my ear then kicks me again.

The pain is more humiliating now than excruciating. My mind is working on my defense. If he makes any wrong moves, I will have a chance to take him. I still have Tusson's backup clip in my back pocket. The empty gun is lying on the ground, and the flare sputters, for it will burn out within the next minute.

"Hear that, Rodney? The faint sound of a woman calling. It must be Dr. Franklin. Time to go, brother. Time for the real Raymond Beacon to take over," he says as he jerks my body away from the rock wall.

He sits me up and thrusts my head against the wall. He then punches me in the face as hard as he could a few times. I could do nothing to stop him. I've lost so much blood that I am now dizzy; the pain brings tears to my eyes almost instantly. My vision is cloudy from the pain, and I know I am dying.

"That's for fucking up my life." Then Ray takes my watch off my wrist then takes my wallet and car keys.

Good thing the extra clip is in my left back pocket.

"You bastard," I cry out in a weak voice filled with pain and despair as I sit against the wall.

"I'm pressed for time," he says as he slaps my face to wake me up. "You see this?" And he shows me a gun. "This is Freedman's gun. I went straight to his house with his keys. I took this gun, and I'm going to kill you with it. Then I'll kill Dawn too. Once your dead brother, I'll become me again. I'll take your money, then your car, and right after I blame Freedman and Dawn for everything, I'll get my life back," he says.

"You won't get away," I say as he is just inches from me.

"Yeah, right!" he says just inches from my face as he is crouching to look into my eyes.

My chance of escape is right now. My mind is racing with solutions. I'm in great shape and strong despite the bullet wounds. I make one last ditch effort to jump at Ray and bring him down to the ground and wrestle the gun away from him. I have the element of surprise as a dive toward his knees and bring him to the ground. I hear him hit the ground with a thud. We both roll on the ground and suddenly, I feel his shoe kick me right in the face.

"You bastard!" he says as he falls away from my grasp.

Then suddenly, he aims his handgun right at me.

Bang!

He shoots me in the chest. I stare in awe as the pain overwhelms me.

Bang!

Again, another shot to the chest. The red flare fades as everything before me dims into darkness. I can see nothing now as I pass out from the excruciating pain.

Bang!

I hear him fire one last shot from the gun before my senses fade into silence.

CHAPTER 24

THREE SHOTS RIGHT into my chest. I'm either passed out and dreaming or awake and hallucinating. The efforts of a bulletproof vest can stop or hold the bullet in the vest, but it can't stop the force of the bullet. You still feel all the pain and momentum of the bullet except the bullet never actually penetrates your skin. Therefore, here I am in massive pain after being shot a few more times.

I'm still in the cave, in total darkness. The pain is detrimental, and I don't know how long I've been in here in this cave. I have no sense of time or reality by now. I'm fading in and out of consciousness from the pain and blood loss from my leg. I can hear better now, but my head is hurting. I realize I must save myself; I can't wait around for help. I lean forward in my daze and feel for my gun. There it is, still to my right.

"*Awweee!*" The pain is consuming me, fighting my conscience with every move as I hunt through the cave for my gun.

I use all my strength to pull the clip out of my back pocket and load the .9 mm. I have to save myself. Ray has the element of surprise, but he made one mistake. He left me alive. Now I must expose him.

I can feel Covey's body in front of me. The sorrow of death bestilled in myself. I must get out of this dark tomb, as painful as it is. I take off my sweatshirt, very slowly, and tie it around my leg to slow the bleeding of my wound. I am weak enough as it is. I know I must stop the bleeding. I must get out of this tunnel. I would keep the vest except it has three types of bullets in it; the vest already served its purpose. I'm too weak to take it off.

How will I ever make it out of the tunnel? How will I save myself?

Then I hear voices coming toward me.

"Dr. Franklin, keep up. This way." I hear a voice then see a faint glimpse of light.

I make sure the safety is off. I pull back on the hammer with all my remaining strength and load a bullet into the chamber. I load the clip into the gun, and I put the gun behind my back and lean back against the wall, awaiting their arrival.

"This way, Dr. Franklin," I hear Ray's voice say again.

"I'm coming," I hear Dawn's sweet voice cry out. "I'm right behind you."

I can see a light in the darkness, and they both appear around the corner at the same time. They both shine their beams of light on me simultaneously. They are both in shock to see me alive. I can tell by the look on their faces as the light makes the cave glow. Dawn's wide eyes and open mouth tell a story of amazement with complete shock to see the two of us, Rodney and Raymond, together at last.

"You are alive, you bastard!" Ray says to me as he approaches me slowly.

I must look like a train wreck. I can't talk. I can barely breathe because of my broken ribs. I've been beaten severely, shot three times, and left for dead in a dark cave. It's been a really bad day. I'm too weak to talk, and by now I'm gasping for air with every breath. I must have broken my ribs when Covey slammed me against the wall, then he fell on top of me. I'm suffocating. I can't move, and I don't want to die. The blood loss is making me dizzy, and I can only look at the two and wonder what will happen next.

"Oh my God!" she cries out in amazement. "William!" she screams!

Instantly, I realize her situation. Two people closest to her are dead—William Covey and Maria Lennon. If Ray and Rodney are alive, her daughter is dead, and now William Michael Covey is bullet-ridden, right before her own eyes. Someone will have to pay for their deaths. Her revenge is bittersweet.

"My God!" she shrieks again as she sees Covey lying there with no neck and a bullet in his forehead.

Dawn then begins to cry uncontrollably as she falls to her knees beside Covey.

"See what you've done, you bastard!" Ray yells at me as he smirks, almost laughing at me. "You bastard, you killed him!" he yells out in amazement as he fights back the irony of the situation.

Dawn cries aloud in the dark cave as she kneels besides Covey's dead body. I have my light on the ground for I can hold it no longer. I am so weak and know this is my last stand. I have to do something.

"You bastard!" she shouts out, and the words echo in the tunnel. "You bastard!" Then she pulls her little silver-plated gun out of her holster and aims it toward me.

"No!" I whisper. "No!" I gasp out softly as I shake my head with my eyes widely focused on her gun.

I'm trying with all my might to speak, but I cannot. The pain in unbearable. The pain, the suffocating pain, the excruciating pain, overwhelming pain. I have tears running down my face uncontrollably. I can't say anything except for the word *no* as I shake my head ever so slightly, defeated by my own misery.

As she cries, she yells out, "Give me one reason not to kill you!" She walks toward me with her gun aimed right at my head.

"No" is what comes to my mind first.

"Give me one reason," Dr. Franklin says again as she puts her gun to my head.

"It was just sex," I say so softy under my breath with all my remaining energy.

Dawn is now inches from me with her gun to my forehead. She is ready to pull the trigger—the trigger of her new life. As my story ends, hers begins again. She will pull the trigger to end her own suffering as well as mine. For her, I'm her killer. I'm the nightmare lurking around her country fresh dreams. I'm the rain clouds on her beautiful day, and she can make all the suffering go away with a single flick of her finger on the trigger of the gun pointed at my forehead.

"Just sex," she says.

She processes the words I speak. I can only see her gun and not her face. I can't see her reaction.

"Remember?" I say ever so slightly in the darkness of the tunnel as Rodney's flashlight illuminates my face full of despair.

Smack! I hear right in front of me.

I close my eyes for a second and hear Dawn scream. She is now lying on the ground next to me in pain. The next thing I see is Ray kicking Dawn right in the chest and stomach, again and again. I can do nothing as he beats her. He then takes the gun out of her limp hand.

"You stupid bitch!" he yells as Dawn cowers on the ground in pain. "You should have killed him!" he yells as she cries in pain from the blows inflicted onto her.

"I'm your master now!" he yells into her face as her grabs her hair and yells into her face.

She can only whimper on the ground before me as he hits and kicks her again and again. I reach out and struggle to put my arm over Dawn to try to protect her from my destructive brother who now has two guns—Dr. Franklin's and Freedman's.

"Oh yeah?" he says as he sees me try to protect her.

Bang! Ray shoots me in my right arm.

I scream since the pain is excruciating! Everything is turning black once again. I can feel the fire burning in my arm and throughout my body.

Bang! Again, he shoots me. This time in my left arm.

"Aaaaahhhh!" I scream with tears running down my face.

The pain! The punishment of dying and being reborn. All the agony of a life gone wrong, all the pain of death, here now inside me.

The pain is like fire igniting my body and my burning dying soul. The pain, the pain, the pain. I now realize I'm dying. The pain is slowly killing me, and my life leaks out with every drop of blood that leaves my body. I'm falling faster and faster to God. I feel a presence calling me as I fade into darkness.

"Master. Master, you should have obeyed," I hear him calling out as he rants and raves into the darkness of the cave, firing his guns.

Dawn screams in horror as the sounds of bullets echo through the cave.

"What the hell are you going to do?" he yells to Dawn. "You should have killed him when you had the chance!" My brother yells out. "He who hesitates, dies! Haven't you ever heard that?" Ray yells as Dawn presses herself behind my wounded body.

Dawn hides her head behind my shoulder and tries to hide from the terrifying Ray in front of her.

I'm screaming on the inside as I watch my twin brother lower his guns toward us.

"Now you must die!" he says right into our faces.

There is no more adrenaline pumping through my veins. I can barely breathe. I feel like a puppet that can't scream, can't be heard from within, and from within my own tormented body as my soul tries to escape.

I see Ray raise his hands into the air and bring the gun down toward us.

My muscles tighten as I save one last breath in my agony.

"I'll see you in Hell!" I say under my breath, just loud enough for him to hear.

Then my eyes fall shut.

Bang! Bang! Bang! Bang! Bang! Bang! Bang! Bang!

These are the last sounds I hear.

Then the pain ends.

CHAPTER 25

It's been a year and a half since I last smelled the Carolina air or stepped onto the soil of the Duke University campus. This is the university I once loved with all my heart. It's Saturday, March 16, and I park my Camaro in the lot that I once visited every day. I see the Duke Tower from where I sit, and I remember the organs playing their sweet song. That was a long time ago, and for what feels like an eternity later, I return. I return to the school that I believe could have made my dreams come true. Instead, my nightmares found me, and my life fell apart on this very campus. I fell far short of the dreams I once had.

I step out of my car and place my first step onto the asphalt parking lot outside of the Cameron Indoor Stadium, just past the Quads where I used to live. I can see the Aquatic Center and remember running down the broken path in our early morning runs. I remember Duke as a place in which stars are launched high into the sky. Stars that shine as bright as any fire in the night sky. I was supposed to be the next star added to that long list of Blue Devil accomplishments, but I fell far short of shining greatness. Because of the incident, I was expelled from the university system of North Carolina. Needless to say, I was kicked out of Duke University and then the state.

"It's been a long time," I say as I look around at the scenery of brick buildings with lush spring greenery among which I once lived. "A very long time," I say as I close my car door and walk toward the arena.

I am parked at the far end of the parking lot as I used to do when I was in enrolled in school here. I like the long walk to the small arena. The walk lets me think a little before each game, and I enjoyed the walk through the beautiful flowers and thick green grass. My thoughts now focus on my life and myself. Thoughts of Dawn, Covey, and Ray are long gone, but the disappointment of a life that once was lives fresh in my mind as I begin my walk toward Cameron Indoor Stadium.

I haven't seen Dr. Franklin since the trial. She is the reason I'm alive. Everything was crazy once I got out of that tunnel. After the shots went off, I faded into a coma. The police found me and rushed me to the hospital. I had surgery, accompanied by two weeks of morphine dripping into my IV to help ease the pain of gunshot wounds. I was unconscious for four weeks total, bedridden for a week after that. Then came the long weeks of rehabilitation since the three bullets that forced their way into my body destroyed muscle tissue.

I spent the next eight weeks of rehabilitation at a prison hospital. Once I was out of the hospital, I spent the four weeks in a maximum-security prison undergoing monitoring and more rehabilitation. The North Carolina District Attorney charged me with six counts of first-degree murder. Yeah, six counts of murder. Since two police officers were killed; one prison guard; my twin, Ray; and three women. With all that said, the police needed a scapegoat. The patsy was me, Rodney Beacon.

The police had the body of my twin brother, Ray, riddled with bullet holes. When Dawn went to hide behind me, she found the gun behind my back and opened fire. All the bullets unloaded into Ray's chest before he dropped dead in the cave. Since Ray had my watch and wallet, many aspects of my innocence were doubted, and I stood trial for murder.

See, I knew that Colleen's mom ran the school board back in Massachusetts. If I was going to disappear, I still needed transcripts to go to school, or I would be sent back to my mom's. I knew Colleen would not help me, but she would help Ray. So I called Colleen, Ray's middle school love, and told her I was Ray. I got her mom involved and bang, transcripts. I had Ray's passport and got a Florida driver's license. Then I filed for a new social security card after that. I became Ray, and Rodney was dead in Arcadia instead of the other way around. The police were not really buying my crazy story of how I really became Ray in high school after he became me to sleep with Maria, which started this whole mess. Well, let's just say pretending to be Ray for years didn't help me any. My tattoo of a basketball and number forty-four on my chest was basically the only thing that saved me. That was really the only way we could be identified.

I got a really good lawyer for the trail. The best trial lawyer money could buy was Lisa Franchina. I spent everything and had to sell my car to pay for the lawyer fees and services. The trial went right to court as soon as I got out of the hospital. There was a three-week preliminary hearing while I was in police-guarded hospital and then a lengthy battle in court. The grand jury trial went on as planned. When I wasn't in court, I was being held tightly inside a maximum-security prison.

As for what happened, Dr. Dawn Franklin testified that she didn't know who she shot. She was traumatized by the entire experience. I know what Dawn was thinking during the trail; she wanted justice and wanted to see someone pay for the death of Covey and her daughter, as well as a ruined marriage. Killing Ray and ending everything there in the cave was not good enough for her. She wanted me to pay for starting this entire mess in the first place. Dr. Franklin's thoughts were this: I should have just stayed in Arcadia and lived the life of Rodney Beacon instead of running away.

Anyway, I watched Dawn's testimony, and her words were very disturbing to me. She was setting me up and filling the judge and prosecutor's mind with doubt as to my identity and motives as well as questioning my innocence. I guess she wasn't that bad of a doctor after all because she had all of us fooled. Dr. Franklin said I was such a handful. She called Covey the day before to come help keep an eye on me. That's why he was there.

"Oh well," I say as I walk through the parking lot and think about the trial.

Lisa Franchina was the best I could get. She did all she could. I could see her struggles. Captain Adams testified about the facts; I failed a lie detector test and was found with illegal firearms. On all accounts, things did not look good. My friends from school, like Dave Hodges, testified that he barely knew me. My coaches basically testified by saying I worked hard, but they barely knew me as well. My coaches and the other players did say I showed up with the tattoo, and I was the guy they recruited from Oviedo High School.

Doug Beacon, my new dad, came to my aid by telling the story of a great kid and honor student that wouldn't hurt a fly. He told a story about a kid giving an old man a second chance in life. He said I saved his life and gave all the people of Oviedo hope because we won the state basketball championship. Mr. Beacon explained my life was just like a basketball game, always having its ups and downs. This was just a down time, but I did nothing wrong, and Covey's death was accidental. The policemen on the mountaintop were doing their job to the end, and now my evil twin, Ray, was dead and gone.

Keith Hasting came to my rescue by testifying that I was the victim here. All this was no fault of my own. Who would have known all this would have happened? I was just a kid running away from my mom and the horrifying realization that my twin brother was dead after my parent's divorce. Keith said it wasn't my fault that Ray went psycho and we happened to be identical twins.

Then there was Jeff's testimony; he saved me the most with his speech. He said I was a great kid, hard worker, determined athlete, great student, and the best friend he ever had. I could never do anything bad on purpose. Jeff also hinted that Dawn was a slut, having sex with Freedman and Covey, so surely she had it in for me.

As for Steve Freedman's testimony, it was discarded from the court's preliminary hearing because he kept swearing and was mad that I beat him up. Plus, it was his crossbow and gun found in the cave. As soon as it became known that he might have had sex with Dawn, his wife divorced him. Freedman was then fired from the

University Police department and became very bitter toward me. Oh well, life goes on, and this isn't anything we haven't heard before.

As for Detective Barry Tusson and Detective Peter Webber, they both died on the mountaintop. Peter died of an arrow wound through the stomach and bled to death after he fell from the ledge. The doctors said he was alive as he burned. The fire didn't kill him, neither did the fall. Barry Tusson endured the pain, but two arrows went through his body, killing him before help could get there. Both courageous men will be missed. Tusson is missed greatly by his beautiful wife and loving child as well as me. Barry Tusson and Peter Webber died as heroes in the line of duty and will always be remembered as heroes. The police department gave each of them a policeman's burial fit for a king. That's what I heard. I was still in a coma when all this happened. I did visit each of their graves the day after I was released from prison. I placed roses on each of their graves. They did not die in vain, and both officers will live on in memory.

Now I walk through the long and empty parking lot at Duke University toward the buildings. I'm now officially back to being Rodney Beacon, coming for a visit. I'm about a hundred yards from the small arena. It's only 9:30 a.m., and Duke fans won't be celebrating for several hours. I came here today to see whatever happened to the Blue Devils and the team I was once a part of. It is sad to know that I'm not a part of any team anymore, and because of the gunshots I endured, I will never play college ball ever again.

Days like those, in which loss is such a great factor, change your life forever. My life has been changed forever so many times. From Boston to Arcadia, from Oviedo to Duke, from trials to the errors of our ways, I learned from my journey through life. I did learn from my mistakes.

As for my trial, it seems so far away now. The grand jury trial was not lengthy at all. After the preliminary hearing, I was only charged with one count of manslaughter. The jury found me guilty, and I was sentenced to confinement for another year on top of the time I already served. Lisa Franchina gave her best defense, but she couldn't disprove that it wasn't myself or my actions that led to the officers or anyone else's death. Either way, the jury found me guilty on one count of manslaughter. I served time for the death of William Covey. Even though his death was an accident, someone had to pay, and I admittedly confessed that I shot him by accident. When it was all said and done, I was sentenced to 366 days of prison time.

I was already in a jail hospitalized for three months that were counted toward my sentence and another two months I spent in jail during the trial. I was sent to an out-of-state prison because my dad pleaded with them not to keep me in North Carolina. He thought since two well-known policemen were killed, my life would be in danger. He was right, and I was sent to Jacksonville State Prison in Jacksonville, Florida. Two hundred ten days of Hell in the humidity that I hated. The time was a complement to the pain and frustration I endured throughout my life.

Once in Jacksonville, the rumor was I killed a prison guard and was tried for killing two other officers. The guards in Florida didn't take that too well, and I got beat up almost every day by guards. I would always fight back, making it worse when guards picked on me. I spent almost all my time in solitary confinement. One week at a time, I was in confinement. Out for a day, get into a fight, get beat up badly, and back into confinement I went. One week some guards came down to my solitary cell and asked if I wanted to fight them right then and there. The guards didn't want the hassle of letting me out and bringing me back. Therefore, they beat me up right then and there and threw my bruised body back into the same hole. It was pretty bad.

As for how I became a basketball star, it was luck. Ray and I always played ball together, but he played for the school and organized teams. I played for fun. Once I realized I could dunk as a high school freshman, I knew I had Ray's gifts. After all, he was me. Once I learned some moves and learned how to dribble around defenders, life got easier. I could dunk and started hitting threes. Crowds started cheering for me. That's when I got the tattoo and became Ray full time. Literally it was pretty easy learning how to play basketball since Ray showed me the game for years.

Basketball was not a part of my jail time. Life in jail was hard. I thank God for letting me out early. I got 122 days off my sentence and was let out early because the prisons were overcrowded. For every two days served in prison, you can get one day off your sentence. The warden ordered my release to make room for more dangerous criminals. I can only think, there is a God, and he felt sorry for me. I need to send the warden a Thank You card!

Where did all my money go, you ask? Well, my lawyer took care of all my personal affairs while I was in jail. I got the money from my mother's estate, her 401(k), and her life insurance policy. After taxes and paying off the house, I had some change in the bank. Then someone bought my mom's house. My attorney finalized the deal, took her percentage, and I got the rest. I also got some of my real dad's life insurance money. You have to be missing seven years to be dead, and I was only missing for four. Therefore, Betty's little girl only got half. Since Betty's daughter wasn't eighteen yet and I was a missing person, money was held aside for me. Since I was alive, I got half the life insurance. I wouldn't have to worry about money for a while.

Once out of jail and with some money, I got another black Camaro convertible and applied to colleges. All my applications but one was returned denied. The only school that accepted me was the University of Central Florida in Orlando, right near Oviedo. The school is right down the street from where I live, with Mr. Beacon, once again. As for now, I live at home in Oviedo, go to college at UCF, have friends, and even a steady girlfriend, Kelly.

Kelly is very beautiful and my rock. After a history like mine, she has taught me to learn from my past and look toward the future. Even with almost everyone in Oviedo knowing about the trial, murders, and jail time, Kelly loves me, and none of that matters to her. I know she's my one and only. I have many nightmares about the past six years of my life, and she is there next to me until they go away.

As for now, I walk the long parking lot and get closer to Cameron Stadium. I suddenly see two familiar faces in the distance. I cross the street to the arena greens and see Jeff and Keith sitting on the bus stop bench, waiting for me as when we hung out together at Duke. I see them and smile. They wait for my arrival. Keith and Jeff are still my best friends, and I'm filled with sadness knowing it has been a long time since we were last together as good friends.

"Hey, after all this, you two still don't have cars!" I yell out.

"Hey!" they both yell back in unison as they both get up from the bus stop bench to greet me.

"We've been waiting for you, Freshman!" Jeff yells out as he gets up and waits at the edge of the sidewalk for me to get across the campus street.

I run across the street toward Jeff and give him a big bear hug. Keith laughs at us and welcomes me back. I'm suddenly emotional and almost break into tears, as this is the first time I've seen them since the trial.

"I'm so glad to see you guys," I say as we stand there by the bus stop.

Suddenly, our ritual begins again as we all bump fists.

"We're glad to see you came to watch the tournament," Jeff says.

"Yeah, can you believe that we get to host March Madness here in North Carolina? The Sweet Sixteen game. Duke is favored to win the championship. First time in five years!" Keith yells out excitedly.

"I'm proud of you. I'm glad I can be here. Thanks for thinking of me," I say to Jeff as he shows me the ticket to get into the game.

Duke is in the NCAA tournament and hosting two games in Raleigh, North Carolina, later in the week. Once they win both games, they will go to the finals at the Mercedes-Benz Stadium in Atlanta. This is their chance to win another NCAA championship. I'm very proud of Jeff since he is one of the keys to the team's success, and I'm glad he wants me here to see him win. I'm glad to see that someone's Duke dreams have come true.

"It's been a long time since I've dreamed of Duke basketball. Thanks," I say as I take the ticket from his hand and Keith grabs hold of the other one.

"Livia and my mom will get the other two tickets. You know they will ask about the past. I hope that doesn't bother you?" Jeff asks.

"No, it doesn't," I say in the early light of Duke's fabulous university.

"Play any ball?" Keith asks.

"No," I say in sadness. "I tore too many muscles in my leg and arms when I got shot. I can hardly raise my right arm over my head anymore, but I don't worry about it much. I only worry about what I can do," I say to him and smile as we stand together as friends.

"Thinking positive! That's good," Keith says.

"Well, I hope you learned something from all that?" Jeff says and smiles.

"Like what?" I reply.

"One-night stands are no good for you," Jeff says with a smile.

We all laugh, and I realize I'm happy. I'm truly happy that I have another life to live. Just like basketball, we all have our ups and downs. Live for the ups while learning from the downs, and you will be just fine.

By the way, Duke won.

The End

ABOUT THE AUTHOR

PAUL KLARC WAS born and raised in Somerville, Massachusetts, a suburb of Boston. Living in the big city, he had dreams to play sports, write novels, travel the world, enjoy great movies, and read as many novels as possible. Paul moved from Boston to Florida and graduated college from the University of Central Florida in Orlando. Go Knights! There in Orlando, he worked for a production company and pursued his dream of becoming a writer while working on movies and learned video production. Since graduation, Paul has moved to Atlanta, Georgia, and became an award-winning restaurant manager in which he runs some very successful restaurants. Paul loves being a foodie. He has traveled to ten different countries over the years and keeps increasing his book collection. He is an avid lover of Boston sports teams, which have been doing well over the years. Paul's son, Grant, is also a foodie and goes to college in Sarasota, Florida, preparing to be a pastry chef.

CPSIA information can be obtained
at www.ICGtesting.com
Printed in the USA
LVHW091315150222
711199LV00003B/5/J